CRYSTAL SHADE
ANGENI

VOLUME 1

ISTVÁN SZABÓ, IFJ. & ORLANDA SZABO

CRYSTAL SHADE: ANGENI
VOLUME 1
by
Ist␣ván Szabó, Ifj. & Orlanda Szabo

Illustrations by István Szabó, Ifj.
Edited by Orlanda Szabo

First Edition

I'm a book, so young and fragile. Please take care of me!

ISBN 978-963-08-2688-4

Printed in the United States of America
First digital edition published on November 11, 2011, first paperback
edition published on January 15, 2012 and first hardcover edition
published on January 15, 2014 by István Szabó, Ifj.
Budapest, Hungary

www.crystalshadeangeni.com

To everyone who lives to dream and dreams to live.

1 – CRYSTAL NIGHTFALL

"Thousands of stars could tell thousands of stories," whispered the old man with a gentle smile. "I hope others also see the story of our beautiful star."

Decades creased the countenance of the weary old man. He propped himself at the balcony, the silky wind ruffling his grey hair. His aged eyes never tired of the stars that pierced the infinite night sky. But despite the enchanting skyscape, his soul, which desired endless peace, was restless. He had one final promise he had made ages ago still unfulfilled; to share the past with those living in the present. A long held secret, a story to tell. Sorrow embraced him, as he knew as the sun rose to greet a new day one unheard story would pass along with him to vanish for eternity. And the time was close.

His sigh as soft as the night breeze, the old man pulled his robe tighter around him before he wandered away from the balcony. Slippered feet chafed against the cold stone floor as he shuffled to the middle of the large hall. Images of fighting angels and demons in the agony of their long forgotten war adorned the eleven immense columns surrounding a strange chrono device.

Thousands of energy orbs formed the mass of a majestic miniature galaxy under the tip of the long tapered crystal shard. Each star, a shiny orb, in this chrono device shone its story, its own truth in sapphire, orange, red, green, and purple among countless colors without a known name. Clear and bright, the shard hovered untethered over the middle of this tiny world like some large mystical sundial. The little galaxy gracefully turned between the stalwart columns. So peaceful and magnificent, its true purpose was hidden behind its enchanting mask.

The shard's polished surface mirrored the tired face of the old man who watched the device with endless respect. His eyes focused on the shadow of the sundial, which slowly crept around the crystal shard. The shadow didn't come from the sun, which slept beyond the horizon as night stood silent sentry outside. It came from the shard itself. Even now, some of the orbs within the crystal's untouchable dark shadow slowly changed color.

The old man closed his eyes. He was still in the hall, but his mind was far away in a forgotten world.

Majestic golden and silver colored eagle shaped crafts appeared in the bright blue sky to fly in formation under the brilliance of the sapphire sun; its eternal glow reflected from their metal bodies and sectioned wings. The crafts dove into battle against hideous dark flying creatures. Like dozens of sleek predatory birds, they fought against the evil web-winged serpentine enemies. Hunted down one by one, the metal bird crafts were ripped to pieces and their wrecks left to explode in the hot white sands, where yet another battle raged.

Among the white dunes, brave winged warriors, evil demons, and humans in their shiny armour battled desperately with their crystal weapons to challenge death itself. The old man could still see the eyes of the fallen that knew they had no chance for survival, but were determined to die with courage for something in which they believed. Dignity filled their eyes, even in their last moments seeing the blade of death before it struck them down. But they never failed to bravely face their destiny.

This vision was banished by a bright flash, to be replaced by another. The old man stood in the middle of the crystal shard. Alone. Intense white light surrounded his body, young and healthy once more. An illusion of his blurred memory, he felt energy strings from the crystal tentatively run over his body and embraced him like a caring mother with her beloved child. He knew the energy strings would not harm him. His consciousness became one with the crystal. Alas, this was a long time ago, maybe in another life. Everything around him became a blur, and voices echoed in his mind as the crystal shard forced him to remember, to never forget.

A wise voice emerged with certainty. *No one comes back from there alive,* it declared.

That is my rightful place! shouted a distorted, chaotic voice. *How dare you, puppet!*

I'm sick of people dying because of you! This ends, not just for the next Crystal Shade! But forever! his own young voice echoed determined.

I will be with you. Always, whispered a kind female voice that flooded the old man with endless love, snapping him back to reality.

He sighed as he studied the crystal chrono device. One of the red orbs within the shard's shadow suddenly changed to azure. The shadow of the crystal was forced away from that area. The old man's fond smile returned.

"You never rest, old friend. You never rest," his soft voice addressed the crystal. "Our destiny ties us together. We will meet again. Soon."

The light flicker of soft footsteps was accompanied by a stifled chuckle behind one of the columns. The old man's head bowed slowly as he curiously approached the column, but his memories rushed to remind him again of the forgotten past.

In his mind, he was young again and stepped between the shadowed columns of a marvelous dark temple. Sapphire sun streamed in stripes through the stone balcony and window casements. The chuckling of a young woman, different than he heard moments ago, caught his attention. A dark silhouette of a woman passed between two columns. His eyes tried to follow it, but the friendly shadows hid her as she reached the pillar. Silence.

His brown eyes mirrored the slick rune-covered columns before they noticed the shadows of the woman at the corner of a pillar. He moved ahead in silence to catch her from behind. They had played this age-old game forever. But as he reached the woman's still, dark silhouette, it dissolved in his arms as he tried to hold her.

Outwitted again, the old man hung his head as he found himself again in reality, between the walls and columns of his little sanctuary. There was no hiding the loving smile that broke his heart anew. He did not want to remember. While most of his memories gave him happiness, some only caused pain. This was one of them.

The muffled chuckle of a child tickled his ears once again. It came from behind the closest column.

"I got you," the old man crowed as he looked behind the stone pillar. But no one was there.

"No! We got you!" a little girl shouted victoriously from behind him.

The old man raised his hands and slowly turned around, his loving smile stretched into a grin that only a grandfather could achieve. "I give up."

The little girl and boy who tricked him stood right in front of him, grinning in merry conquest.

"You may consider yourself the prisoner of the Knight of the Light," the young boy proclaimed, his wooden sword pointed at the old man's belly.

"Oh, I'm too old to be a prisoner, young knight," responded the old man.

The boy and the girl looked at each other, and then the girl stepped forward and crossed her arms.

"On behalf of Princess of the Celestials – just to make that clear, that's me..." She pointed at herself proudly, "You may redeem yourself, prisoner. For a prize." Then she could not stop impishly grinning up at the old man as he played along.

Amused, the old man shook his head and smiled. He recognized the girl's behavior, and her mischievous smile, too. The little one had learned, rather, inherited this behavior from someone who meant everything to the old man.

"And what would that prize be, little Princess?" he asked with a curious glance at the child.

"Tell us a story," the boy added with a grin not unlike his sister's.

"A story?"

"Yes. A story about brave knights and be-a-utiful princesses," the girl added in graceful majesty while she gestured slowly. This gesture was also so familiar to the old man.

"And war, where valiant heroes are born," the boy added.

"Can you tell a story about *her*?" the girl asked wistfully. The young boy nodded his agreement.

The old man sank deep into thought, and then nodded to the children.

"Come," he invited them to the other end of the room and his chair, where he watched the chrono device day by day. The children followed in excited silence. But suddenly everything blurred and tilted around the old man. He tottered, but at the very last moment, he sat in his chair. The voices came to haunt him again.

Not willing to believe. No explanation is possible, the woman's great disappointment echoed in his mind.

There is no mercy for weaklings! shouted a demented voice.

To reveal the truth, to understand what surrounds you, now, in the present, you must reveal the truth of the past, a wise male voice added.

When your journey ends, we will be together. Again, an angelic female tone whispered.

Slowly reality surrounded the old man as he heard the woman's voice. "Soon," he whispered. The children looked at him. He felt they were always a little afraid when he talked to the air.

"Are you alright?" asked the boy.

"My body is old and tired," the old man said. He sat himself comfortably in his chair. "But my soul is younger and healthier than ever."

Deep in thought, the old man smiled before he looked at the children.

"So, you'd like to hear a story about her?" he asked and the children nodded.

The old man let out a sigh tinged with fond memories. He never thought anyone would ask about the mysterious guardian angel that changed everything. Yet they did and they deserved to know who she really was.

The children sat down on the carpet at his feet and watched the old man's youthful anticipation. He gathered his thoughts and smiled fondly at the children.

"Then I will give you a story that both of you want. A story about an era where light and darkness clashed at mythical legendary places, where valiant heroes lived and fought, loved and died. But foremost it's about the life of a lonely angel, who has challenged even death itself, so others may live. It's the true story of the Crystal Shade; or as she called it in her beautiful, forgotten language, the Eecrys Denara."

"The Crystal Shade? What is that?" asked the girl.

"As she always said, the crystal; one of the most beauteous elements in the universe. And all galaxies, others, and our own are just like a crystal. Beautiful, perfect, shiny, and faultless, whose brilliance whispers peace and eternal harmony. But even crystals have a shadow. A dark shade that hides the mistakes dulls the cruelty and the void."

He looked at the crystal chrono device.

"The Crystal Shade is the story of beginnings and endings; the brilliance of life itself whose shadow is also able to make us all vanish if we live our lives blindly. Everything we do throughout our days, our history, we challenge its mighty power that determines what our future will be; as the present battle of the past conquest is always the key to determining the future. It can be everything we ever desired and it can be the greatest illusion of all. Whoever faced with it always needed to realize; nothing and no one was what they appeared to be within the Crystal Shade."

The old man paused as forgotten memories flooded him again for a blink of an eye.

I don't care about a world in a slow, purple prose fairy tale. I care only about the people, little one. Get to the point, his own young, impatient voice had declared.

You, human are so impatient, ignorant, and selfish. What is worse, you're so proud of it, a disappointed angelic voice responded. *You believe everything is just about people, yet you don't know anything about the world that surrounding you.*

"Everyone cares about people. But someone must care about the world itself," whispered the old man and smiled at the irony; he just realized the once resisting young man had become the one who tended to the world the most. He knew the story was far more than the woman's life. The young angel's story was also about the world itself.

He looked beyond the children at the chrono device once again, focused on a tiny orb that swam amidst the thousands of others around the crystal; truth shone within every star, every planet. While he didn't know the story and the truth of the rest, he knew the life of this little one, as this was the closest to his heart.

"Eecrys Aredia. A fragile, heavenly place so distant, yet so close, our known and also unknown world. Oh, you should've seen her home, that true paradise!" His old heart beat with excitement as he continued, "The old sapphire sun brought smiles, happiness and life, watching over and embracing every continent with her nurturing motherly light. The calm breeze whispered the ruling peace and equality, singing to everyone as it sighed among the leaves and branches of the rich lands. Crystal clean drops in rivers and vast oceans flowed peacefully, boundless and undisturbed just like life itself on our fragile home world. Nothing evil. No hate, grudge, wealth, poverty, misery, nor mastery. Just harmony. Oh, and the angelic vanguards of peace, our Guardians; the brave and noble Aserians have watched over, guarded and guided mankind for so long, since Eecrys Aredia existed." His smile was kind as he looked at the swimming little orb, which seemed so peaceful, but it's long history was always born in pain and suffering.

"But beneath the surface, Eecrys Aredia was a place of myth and buried secrets shadowed by the legend of the Crystal Shade. Many feared it would return one day to destroy the peace which ruled for so long, to erase everything the Aserians ever created. But no one knew how and why. Although no one ever turned against their fellow kind, and no human ever wielded a weapon, the Aserians were ready to fight for mankind if need be to keep their souls clean even in the darkest hours. Generation after generation the Guardians prepared and patiently waited for the dreaded Crystal Shade. But it never came."

The old man paused as the night delusively gazed at him from outside.

Please, let me tell her story, he wished. There was so much to tell and his time was so very short.

"How are Guardians born? How was she born?" asked the girl.

"Oh, she wasn't born as a Guardian. She was a human once." The old man smiled warmly. "Grace Sessa Aredia, 'the graceful bright guardian'; earning her name by being born when the sapphire sun, Sachylia was the brightest in the sky. A seemingly ordinary little girl who had dreams, the desire of knowledge that loved her family, sister, mom and dad. Just like you, little Princess," he put a kindly hand on her head. "But in the fragile shell, her sleeping soul was ancient and forever, destined to seek an answer for an eternal question and fight for the sake of all creation when the time comes."

Long forgotten voices, and images became vivid memories in his tired mind; voices he had never heard, but knew existed. Words thought by a fragile soul millennia ago, but only memories remained of them that he never experienced, but someone else did who had been born, lived, and fought in that forgotten era of the Crystal Shade.

"Dreams haunted her from her first breath that no one, not even the wisest of Aserians could decipher. Dreams that many times foretold her future became stranger and more mysterious as time passed. But they enlightened her path and slowly shepherded the mist aside to connect the beginning with the unavoidable end; as for her the end was just the beginning."

* * *

Strange. I have wings, beautiful white guardian wings like I always wanted. But I hate flying. I don't know why. Mother told me that Guardians are never afraid of anything. But I'm afraid of the height. I was never afraid of it before. Father and Mother always were proud of their little girls, because we're brave. Because I'm brave. I love to fly in our silver eagle among the clouds, high above the mountains and vast grassy fields. Father promised that he would teach us how to fly our silver birdie. But now, I'm not in our Anshara. And my beloved parents and Aurora are not with me. But why? We're always together. We help each other. That's what a family does. Father and Mother never left me alone. But now they're not here and I'm not a child. It is strange because I feel I am an adult.

My breath is so cold, but everything is so real. Am I still asleep? Am I dreaming all of this? I'm scared. I want to go home. And I will. But not now.

Now, I'm flying almost silent in the night. Somehow, I feel safe in this black diamond. It is embracing me. I'm drawn by the Sacred Crystal that lies on the dark horizon; its faultless brilliance is the beacon to us in the darkest night. It's calling us.

Us. I'm not alone. I feel someone is with me. But the dreaded deep dark calls me. The endless depth, I fear it. I don't want to think of it. I don't want to fall. I want to see who is with me. I feel safe with him. But my soul forces my eyes closed to not see the depth. Strange.

"Grace," a feminine voice wove its way into her mind.

I'm safe, but I hate flying.

"Grace Sessa Aredia," whispered a woman's voice into Grace's tiny ear. "Wake up. Get out of your bed. The sun is already glowing brighter blue than the aura of a Sapphire Guardian. Wake up, my darling."

"Is it morning already, mother?" Grace balked with closed eyes while she pulled her pillow over her sleepy face.

"And your breakfast is waiting for you," her mother's kindness continued. "What have you dreamt about this time, little one?" she asked.

Grace immediately pulled the pillow off her face and turned a hard look at her mother, who sat on the edge of her bed in a dark yellow saree, and watched her kindly.

"I'm not little. I'm already seven," Grace retorted resentfully.

"Oh, I know, my princess," smiled her mother while she stroked Grace's blond hair. "So?"

"My dreams are my fantasies, mother," said the defiant and secretive little girl. Her soul yearned to share her strange, vivid dream with her, but not now. Maybe later. Her mother smiled tenderly and shook her head in amusement.

In her blue saree, Grace looked around the large room. The sapphire sun, Sachylia had already left the horizon, its rays flowing into her room. The wooden bed on the other side of the room was empty.

"Is Aurora awake already?" she turned to her mother.

"She is not sleeping all the day away as you do sometimes."

"I just..." She paused for a thoughtful moment, "Had some work to do last night." Grace gestured and tried to seem mysterious and important, imitating her father. "After I worked so hard, I have every right to sleep as long as I can."

"You always learn the worst things from your father, young lady." Amused by her headstrong daughter, her mother shook her head.

"And I always have the right, Lady," Grace added as she crossed her arms and raised her nose with pretended defiance.

"Like this one." Her mother smiled warmly, but then she turned motherly serious. "You do know the Daharra come to snatch young ladies who do not sleep at night."

"The shadow mingan is just a legend of the adults, mother," Grace determined as her little heart dictated to her.

"Never forget, every legend has truth in its voice," responded her mother in an icy tone. "The Daharra always know when you're sleeping and when you're awake. It is always watching, unseen from the darkness. And when the Daharra sees you're not sleeping, its cold howling is a warning it's coming to get you."

Grace remembered the night when, under the protective cover of darkness of her blanket, she had worked to finish Aurora's gift. She really had heard the howling of a mingan. Maybe the Daharra have warned her it will come and snatch her. She already wondered why the shadow mingan spared her. Her eyes peeked at the small light crystal near the bed, which gave her the tiny light under the blanket to protect her from darkness.

"A crystal's brilliance mirrors its shadow; only sleep and sweet dreams can hide you from the shadow mingan, young lady," her mother continued almost silently as she also looked at the light crystal.

Grace held her breath as silence settled. Her consciousness waited for the help of her protective inner voice, which always whispered what to do, even in the most desperate moments, like this one. Except now, even the voice that always guarded and guided her remained quiet.

The little girl looked at her mother worried; her sleepless eyes begged for motherly protection. She feared the creature will come for her tonight and as every light has its own shadow, - shadow, which is the land of the dreaded Daharra -, no one will be able to protect her.

"Usually there is no hope for a sleepless soul," her mother just shook her head resignedly as she watched her daughter, then she took a soft sigh. "But I'm sure the Daharra has forgiven you, for now, because selfless, you were awake to make a gift to give happiness to your sister." She leaned closer to her daughter to whisper into her tiny ear. "But to earn its full forgiveness, you'll have to go sleep earlier tonight. You must promise."

"I promise," smiled Grace while hope mirrored in her eyes and embraced her mother. She felt her mother may be right and maybe, just maybe the creature wouldn't snatch her as the sun goes down. Her mother's seriousness was replaced by happiness and she gave relieved Grace's cheek a kiss that for a change watched her savior with endless love.

"Come, Princess. Maybe we'll wait for you before we go to the feast of Odess'iana. But if you do not hurry, Aurora is surely going to eat your breakfast too."

"I give my portion to her," Grace played her majestic princess role further. "She is my little Princess sister after all. What is mine is also hers."

"Well now, her majesty is a giver and merciful as always." Her mother bowed her head respectfully. "Princess Aurora is surely going to enjoy your gifts. Moonlight jam, Andrenian bread, apple cake, spicy frozen whipped cream with cocoa, and…"

"With the exception of this once, Lady Margey," Grace interrupted quickly while she shoved her blanket off, and sprang out of the bed.

"Is there Ambrosia too, mother?" excited, she asked.

"The freshest Ambrosia that you ever drank, your majesty," Lady Margey gestured kindly with her hands. "So, did you finish Aurora's gift last night?"

Proud of herself, Grace nodded while she picked up her blue cotton slippers from the floor beside the bed, and then she pulled her mother to a large closed oak chest at the far end of the room excitedly. "I hope she likes it," she whispered. With a slipper hanging from one small hand, she opened the chest.

"She surely will," confirmed Lady Margey while Grace carefully took out two small, intricately carved wooden winged dolls beside a large old children's book, Spirit Guardians Eriana and Iria.

With eyes that glistened like pearls, her mother looked at both dolls. Their bodies and faces exquisitely carved, they represented young female Aserians. The elder was wrapped in a sapphire silk saree, while the younger woman was similarly adorned in amber orange. Their hair was made of straw, but the young woman's hair was stained dark red. Their large fluffy angel wings were made of white cotton.

"You, you've made the Spirit Guardians!" Lady Margey exclaimed.

"Yes. But I changed some details," Grace hesitated just a little while she watched her mother. "Artist's freedom," she added proudly. "But I couldn't figure out how to make their mighty crystal blades," she continued with some guilt and disappointment. "I never saw one."

In her eyes, the dolls seemed incomplete and so empty without their mighty weapon; the weapon that was capable of maintaining eleven shapes as needed to protect the innocents from the evil that the legendary dreaded era, the Crystal Shade carried within.

"Very few have laid eyes on an Eecrys Suria. If they ever saw it at all," her mother encouraged her. "Maybe the crystal blades are just a tale, a legend of the Aserians."

Her mother smiled as Grace nodded and offered her master works. "The blue one is me, the great princess, Eriana, and Aurora as the youngest princess, Iria."

"They are beautiful. Aurora is surely going to like your gift. Even without the crystal blades," amazed, she turned the dolls in her hands.

"Thank you, mother," Grace said softly while she added this deep in her proud heart. "I really hope so."

Margey kissed Grace's cheek. "You're the best sister that anyone could have," and she meant it.

Grace nodded thanks and took the angel dolls back from her mother. She carefully laid them in the box right beside the book of their story. Then she stopped and watched them for a moment.

"Always remember. Their soul is the mirror of your soul, my little girl," whispered her mother into her tiny ear.

None of you will ever be alone. I promise, thought Grace while she studied the illusionary happiness in the eyes of the dolls, the same happiness within her own soul. *Here the Ice Born Soul can't hurt any of you.*

For a moment, she felt chilled by the name of the mysterious and legendary cursed being that she had always feared. It was the only one capable of destroying the soul of her invincible legends. But she never understood how and why. Her brave Spirit Guardians always defeated evil so easily; at least as she always imagined their story. But the Ice Born Soul was so different and untouchable.

As the top of the box hid the dolls and the little lock clicked, Grace knew she did this to keep her legends safe from the dreaded soulless soul; whatever it truly was.

"So, where is my breakfast?" Grace's brown eyes glimmered happily as she turned to her mother with a grin.

* * *

Sweet cold wind hit Grace's face as she stepped out into the large hanging garden. Calm tinkling of a wind crystal chime greeted her. Beautiful vines twisted around the tall columns and flowers that were her mother's pride, hung like bright colourful ribbons from the walls. The old green oaks and the multitude of other trees throughout their large land slowly dressed in brown, yellow and orange while they dropped their leaves. Luscious aroma of flowers and crops tickled her nose; flowers that hung along the walls already prepared for the long cold nights of the approaching snowy first season, Slumberous. The second trimester, Prosperous was long gone along with the colourful life outside the garden, but Grace didn't miss the warmest season at all as it was also the rainiest trimester; the time when her home world shared the life giving water with the plants. As she looked at the distant golden grass field as she did every morning, she missed the wild tasunkes who thundered there, the yellow apoideas, and other flying insects that dusted the flowers to create their delicious aya nectar. The field was so empty without them. Even without their presence, the entire valley of Seradelphia was still so beautiful.

Behind the field, the vinyards of the colourful vinifera grapes covered the whole side of the hill behind the glamorous sprawling house to show the last season of the three trimesters. Deciduous ruled. The harvest season, the time of great harvest feasts, and what was most important to her, it was the season of her birth.

The sapphire light shone right into her eyes and stroked her skin. Grace raised her hand to touch the untouchable distant sun, but she focused on her hand, which was surrounded by the gentle blue glow. An imaginary illusion of the little girl as if her being were embraced by a sapphire aura, the aura that embraced every living being invisible and unseen and told the nature of every single being to those, mostly celestial beings, who had the talent to feel and know everything by a gentle touch.

"Your new day welcomes you Eecrys Aredia," quoted her fairy tale heroine, Eriana; the brave Spirit Guardian whose words made her heroine a real guardian when she determined to save her home world from evil. "You'll shine in the light for eternity. Don't fear, I..." She stopped to smile as the illusion of light danced around her hand. For a moment, she felt endless power in herself like she would be a true Guardian of her home world, just as Eriana. "I will protect you. I promise."

The light started to blind her, but she watched her hand. Illusion of her mind, for a moment she felt she had the large white wings she always wanted. The cold breeze embraced those wings and ruffled them gently. The little girl swam in the sapphire daylight, in her sapphire aura that she always dreamt of. She had always wanted a loving, nurturing and protective nature, and one who lives by her heart and emotions and dedicated a share of her efforts to the greater good. She wanted her purpose to serve, help and love others, to have the inner knowledge and she desired wisdom; to be the same kind soul and have the aura that her beloved Eriana always had.

But the light slowly faded in front of her eyes as a large cloud crawled in front of the sapphire sun, Sachylia to break her illusion. There were no wings on her back. She was still just a little girl full of dreams. Now, she hoped she was living the life and making the right decisions so her nature and aura would develop into this beautiful sapphire for her adulthood.

The zephyr of Deciduous gently blew among the yellow leaves to caress her cheek while her mind slowly switched from her dream world to reality. While disappointed, she watched the cloud that ruined her game. Grace pulled her thick silk saree together to buffer the wind with her left hand and held her rolled up papyrus scroll pamphlet tightly in her right as she looked around.

"And I welcome you, my guardian," she whispered lovingly. "Wherever you are." But no response came. She heard only the small fountains that continuously poured water from the top of wall into the large leveled pools that lay in front of the garden. Blue petals fluttered around Grace were carried on a gust of wind while she looked around. She was alone in the garden, yet she felt her guardian, her conscience, her guarding and guiding inner voice watched over her at this very moment, invisible, unseen, just as she had since her birth. Grace waited, but this day was no different. Her guardian did not show herself.

Like every other day, she wanted to see the face of her guardian. And now as she had just finished a delicious breakfast, Grace knew she had a bit of a time before they departed for Odess'iana and the long awaited feast. The little girl sometimes went to great lengths to lure her guardian out, but the Aserian Guardian was always one step ahead and knew what tricks Grace was up to. The guardian always stopped her from doing something foolish; but had never shown herself directly.

As her mother and father taught her, the graceful noble winged Aserians never interfere in the lives of humans, unless they drifted into danger or there was no other recourse. Of course, they walked among the people, but in most cases, they hid their identity along with their wings, acting like humans to help their charges without their knowledge, sometimes as a best friend throughout the entire life of the one being guided. Although a guardian spirit on Eecrys Aredia protected all humans, be it an Aserian guardian spirit, spirit animal, or soul, few humans knew what their guardian looked like; her parents were no exception. Even so, they watched over, guided their charges, and rarely showed themselves in their original form.

Grace always guessed who watched over her parents. Maybe those two eagles, which always soared in the sky above their house, just as they did now. Maybe not, but as for her sister Aurora her guardian spirit was still not revealed to her for the first time. It was a bit strange, but not unusual. Grace knew that the first meeting between her sister and her guardian would be unavoidable. A guardian spirit always waited for the right moment. They had time. Their lives were bound together from Aurora's birth until her death. It was the way of life.

What Grace was the most curious about was when her own guardian would reveal herself again and in what form. She didn't know. Her eyes curiously looked around the garden as she did every morning in the hope that she might see her guardian again, at least for a moment. Only a light breeze blew the small leaves in the garden.

"Where are you?" she whispered, while her eyes looked for a sign that would betray her guardian; the echo of her Guardian's spirit and soul, the color that describes the nature that even her guardian can't deny. Grace knew only the Aserians were able to see the auras, the nature of others from their own realm. As a legend said, during the last Crystal Shade in the battles that raged millennias ago on Eecrys Aredia, the Aserians knew their allies and their enemies with a glance. Grace also knew the Aserians could use their aura to create items, and sometimes life from it as her guardian had made gifts for her many times. Regardless how her guardian mastered this skill, one thing had never changed, the color of her creation.

The color Grace looked for now was the echo of an adventurer's soul. A spirit with an inner urge to be creative, active and always enjoyed life to its fullest, loved the challenge and excitement of forming and shaping physical reality; an individual, independent and very capable of integrated physical and mental qualities. At least that's how the teaching described the nature of this aura color, but Grace didn't understand the half of it. Not yet. What she knew from the color; her guardian was a strong willed Aserian who loved a challenge. And maybe that's why the Aserian chose her as Grace's Guardian. Grace believed she at least, gave her guardian those challenges every day.

Her eyes watched the different colors of the garden; azure blue, jade green, topaz yellow, amethyst purple were only a very few of the countless color shades. But she looked for one in specific. As the colors gazed back at her, Grace wondered again how it was possible that there were no red, black, or darker colors in the aura spectrum, auras that only shadow darkness, or as the legends said, some hostile thorned flowers, buried forgotten crystals or dense, hot fire had. Of course, flowers and vegetables had these darker colors, like one of the four traditional maizes of Seriana, which was red. But as her parents taught her; the color of the skin doesn't represent any nature or aura. A material body doesn't represent the soul and the spirit that resides in it. The existence of these colors, but their lack in the aura spectrum gave Grace the faith to believe that these dark, evil auras once belonged to the souls of the mythical Shaina; the deadly demonic enemies of human and Aserian alike, that they had vanquished during the last Crystal Shade countless millennia ago.

"There you are," she whispered as her eyes lit upon an orange jasnaia flower, in full bloom. It stood out among the dozens of sapphire tziavi, - as she called the gracefully beautiful, but defiant thorny flowers, the Flowers of Gracius -, the ones she'd planted with her mother in her own little corner of the garden.

"You weren't here before, little flower," she talked to the full-grown flower, which slowly opened its broad orange petals to greet her on this beautiful day. Grace crouched and smelled the sweet flavor of the jasnaia flower that merged with the atmosphere of the third trimester of the cycles that she always loved.

As her hand touched the flower, a winged mid-aged woman flashed into her mind; a real Aserian she had seen, a blurry memory from when she was very young. Maybe one of the first memories of her life, the memory was so joyful and nurturing. She didn't know the winged woman's name and she couldn't remember her face but from that moment, Grace knew she was safe, and she will be guided and guarded for the rest of her life. A bright glowing orange aura surrounded the woman and blinded Grace in that blurry memory before her guardian vanished from her eyes.

"I hope you know the color always betrays you, my guardian. You can't deny your nature," she whispered victoriously. "You're here and watching over me as you always do. But where?" Grace asked as she looked around in the hope that her guardian would reveal herself, but she was alone. The sweet scent of the flower lingered.

"Please show yourself. I," she hesitated and looked at her scrolls in her hand, then at the large winged statue that stood without flowers or foliage in the middle of the garden. Her grandfather had sculpted the beautiful winged female Aserian Sentinel, Nara to honor her after she revealed herself and saved him to from falling into the nearby canyon. "I would make a beautiful drawing of you to show my respect. Just as Grandpa had shown his respect to Sentinel Nara," Grace continued with the most honest tone in her voice, while she stepped closer to the statue. Her hand gently stroked the lowered elegantly carved bony Sentinel wings, which had sharp feather tips, just like the real Aserian Sentinels have. "See? Beautiful statue, isn't it?" She waited again, but no response came.

"Why don't you ever show yourself?" she asked disappointed. "I know you can tell what I think, what I feel, what my deepest secret is from a touch. All Aserian can. You see what humans cannot; the true nature of the soul. Then why don't you trust me?" she paused for a moment. "Am I a bad soul? Did I scare you or hurt you when you revealed yourself once?"

In her devious little mind, she had hoped that her disappointed tone would breed guilt in her brave protector. Sometimes she felt that her guardian enjoyed playing this game with her and eagerly watched to see what devious ploy Grace would try next. Since Grace swore that one-day, she would trick her guardian into showing herself. However, it never happened and this day was no different.

"I would never tell anyone. You know that," she whispered with real honesty to give bravery to the unseen Guardian. "Please," she added with her kindest smile. She waited patiently, but the kind woman who gave her protection did not show herself.

"Maybe tomorrow. Maybe you will reveal yourself." Grace sighed as she looked at the orange Jasnaia, which became the new inhabitant among the Flowers of Gracius. She treasured the fragile flower in her heart. "But thank you for your gift," she added gratefully, almost silent.

You're welcome, my child, whispered a kind, motherly voice in her mind, the voice of her Guardian who always watched over her. Then the windy silence of Deciduous surrounded the proud, wildly smiling little girl.

* * *

The arven pencil swiftly and precisely stroked the papyrus paper. The dark lines slowly filled out the shape of the vision that Grace had seen in her dream. She felt this picture was going to be the perfect way to start a new scroll. This was the first scroll in her new papyrus pamphlet and the third scroll pamphlet of her life. Her father traded for it in the tenth province, Hijaz five sunrises ago, but she had just now gotten the chance to draw in it, but foremost the reason.

Her hand had worked fast like the hand of a true master; the lines slowly revealed the desired shape. She was only seven but she was already considered a professional sketch artist. No one knew where she learned this skill, not even her parents. Except for Grace, there was nothing special in this. She simply drew because she liked it. Her hand was led by her instincts and imagination. She never let herself make a single mistake in her drawings – mostly because she still remembered her father's advice when he gave Grace her first papyrus scroll; they're rare in their province. Her soul always reminded her hand of this. That's why her drawings became better and better; that was her little secret. Now, for the first time, she promised herself that she would try to make all of her drawings perfect, and to not rip any pages out as she had done before when she wasn't satisfied with the result.

These scroll pamphlets were her most valuable treasures, which let her tell stories, and moments when they were filled with her sketches. She got her first pamphlet scroll when she was four and contained her first attempts, mostly little stick figures. Her personal favourite was also in that pamphlet; the very first self-portrait where she imagined herself with wings. While her first sketches were not masterpieces, they represented the first steps in the world of art. The second pamphlet contained better drawings and sketches; most of them were of family, mother, father and sister. Her parents treasured both of her scrolls; her drawings that gave life to the stories and made the simple papyrus speak to everyone who looked at them.

She stopped for a moment and studied her drawing.

"The Crystal Shade. The beginning and the ending," she recalled the first line of the legend and the teachings that she learned over the cycles. In Eecrys Aredia, the Crystal Shade was the holiest, the most feared entity and belief for both human and Aserian; and foremost it was the greatest mystery of all. Ancient scrolls told many legends of the forgotten era, which brought joy and freedom, but also death and suffering to the people of Eecrys Aredia. Everyone feared that the era of the Crystal Shade would return one day and the Aserians prepared to bravely fight it. But it has never come.

The arven pencil in her hand had quickly stroked the paper further on the drawing of this legend; the legend which fascinated her. Grace believed her guardian; her conscience also helped her keep her faith regarding the Crystal Shade even if she'd never gotten a direct answer to any of her questions in this matter. Her guardian wanted her to learn everything by herself, to explore the unknown and enjoy a taste of individual victory before Grace made the final step to understand the great revelation... someday.

The lines slowly shaped the faultless crystal, the mother, and father of all on the paper. In the belief of the people, the Crystal Mother was the only one who could create and destroy. She watched over and cared for everyone. No one ever confirmed her existence, but also no one ever found proof to deny it. No one knew what the sacred Crystal Mother looked like, but everyone had a picture in his or her mind about it. And in her mind she looked like what she saw in her dream.

She softly stroked in the last lines to complete her drawing, then as she finished, she looked up to the sky; Sachylia curiously watched the little girl who sat in the small wooden pavilion, which floated on a small island in the middle of the large pool in the backyard of the garden. Two saplings grew on either side of a small bridge that connected the small island with the mainland. Grace still remembered the last Slumberous when she had planted the left tree while little Aurora planted the other with mother's help. Now she watched smiling as the young trees had lived through their very first Deciduous and dropped their first-born leaves one by one.

Her father built the island for his daughters, hoping that they would love the place. And her father was right. Grace spent most of Prosperous there when she had time to read and draw. It was so peaceful. And now her new masterpiece was born at this time, in this place.

The little girl looked at her sketch; her eyes stared at the Sacred Crystal. It enchanted her, pulled her deeper and deeper. That faultless shining crystal, the beacon in the darkness that called to her; a crystal so beautiful and perfect, she had never seen anything like that. And that music - the purest sound, the most beautiful tone to ever caress her ears. It tickled her ears, just like in the dream. To her ears, the music was so beautiful; it called her.

"What are you drawing, little angel?" a motherly kind voice drew her out of the trance. Grace looked to the left where her mother sat down beside her.

"Just what I saw in my dream," she studied the picture with a critical eye. "What I remember of it."

"May I see?" asked Margey. Grace showed her the drawing. Her mother studied it for a moment, and then smiled fondly. "It is beautiful," her voice tinged with awe. "Do you believe the creator is this beautiful?"

"I'm not just believing, I know it. I believe she is much more beautiful than my drawing," she said with a giggle, and then she turned a bit disappointed as she looked back at her drawing. "I can draw joyful and sad sketches. But the Crystal Mother seems both. She can't be happy and sad in the same time. Something is not right with my drawing, yet my soul whispers I have drawn the Crystal Mother as it should be."

"Light and darkness are opposites, a mirror of each other. Never forget that," whispered her mother. Grace nodded and then she faded into the daydream with great excitement in her eyes.

"Someday I'd like to know the real story. Someday I'd like to know everything about the Crystal Shade, mother."

"Why?"

"There are many tales in the world, but my heart whispers to me to know the true story of the Sacred Crystal, the real story of the Crystal Shade."

"Do you really want to know everything about the Crystal Shade?"

"If I had one wish, this would be mine. To know the truth," said Grace, determination in her young voice and turned away to pack up her papyrus and arven pencil. Her heart beat faster and faster, while her hand rolled up the papyrus pamphlet.

"You're the only one who truly wants to know instead of believe. Soon, you will know much more about me than everyone else," her mother said, but her voice was more mysterious than Grace had ever heard it before. Her instincts cried out to her that something was not right.

"I'm waiting for you, my child," the sad, calm, and loving voice continued behind her. Except it wasn't her mother's voice, nor was it her beloved, mysterious guardian. "Live and enjoy life. We'll meet soon," the crystal-clear chiming continued. Grace snapped her head around, but her mother was not there. No one was. The soft crystal chime music again teased her mind, but this one sounded like the cleanest flute. Something bright in the sky lowered toward her. Shocked, she looked up. Thick clouds split the daylight sky to reveal the tapestry of stars beyond, right above her.

The faultless Sacred Crystal watched her from above. The sapphire sun, Sachylia was gone. Now, Eecrys Aredia peacefully swam in the large carousel of distant stars, as one of them, around the Crystal Mother who watched over all of them, but mostly Grace with motherly love. The crystal's enchanting tone called the little girl without a word, its light became brighter and brighter, too bright.

Grace snapped out of the trance staring down at her finished drawing. She had not packed up the scrolls and pencil. Her hand still held her arven pencil, its point parked at the bottom right corner of the papyrus.

The little girl shook her head to clear her mind, while the false crystal chime stroked her ears. She felt that she had forgotten something that was in her mind few moments ago. She wanted to remember why she shook her head, what she forgot. It was gone. Her little heart calmed down, but she didn't remember why it beat so fast before.

"Your thoughts have strayed again, Gracie my dear," she whispered rigidly. She took a long last look at the drawing. The arven pencil quickly drew four tiny vertical lines on the bottom right corner; her art signature. She didn't know where this strange habit came from. She just signed all her sketches this way since her very first stick art.

Her hands slowly rolled the pamphlet with her arven pencil, while she looked at the wind chime to see why it sounded so different. But the chime was calm and silent, it didn't move.

Where is this restless and false crystal music coming from? she queried her mind while she looked around and searched for the source. She didn't find. The false crystal chime, silently and almost unnoticed played further in the back of her mind.

"Grace!" called her mother from the building as she stepped out through the broad entrance. The sun glanced on her small beautiful headdress and her elegant golden silk cloth. Just like everyone else who lived on Eecrys Aredia and visited the Great Feast of Odess'iana, she was dressed in her finest to represent his or her beloved province in this great event.

Her mother held a small, red headed girl in her arms that reminded Grace of her mother. Little Aurora looked around in her little hat as they stepped outside into the fresh air; her brilliant green eyes searched the garden for kimamas, which she had always loved. She loved to chase and play with them, but she saw not a single one today. Aurora's little pout immediately turned to a smile as she saw her big sister. "Gracie," Aurora called.

"There you are, little princess," said her mother excitedly as she noticed her. "Your father is waiting for us."

Grace hurried to them and gave Aurora a kiss. She was rewarded with a big hug.

"I missed you," Aurora's little voice chimed. Her sister adhered to her much more than to anyone else. She was her sister's best friend.

"I missed you too, little sister."

* * *

The large, majestic silver Anshara stood silently on its large metal claws at the edge of a huge grassy canyon, which was at the border of the valley of Seradelphia. The craft looked like a large peacefully sleeping brave eagle, its head bowed to stare at the ground with artificial, lifeless eyes. Its large silver wings were folded up and back in landed position and ran parallel to the shiny hull. The main and the tail wings were connected into three coarse circles to the hull itself. The segmented feather-like wing elements could slide along these circles to the intended position in flight very quickly. The tail feathers were bowed up a bit, which reminded Grace of Aurora's hair after she woke from a long sleep.

The graceful craft rested under the shadow of a tall beacon house. Grace noticed that his father already aimed the large mirror at the top toward the distant, usually stormy Syayina Mountains where shy Carenia Seli will rise to take Sachylia's place at night. The tower with the help of the crystal-light always was the safe beacon to guide flying craft home at night.

The polished silver hull of the Anshara reflected Sachylia's cold blue sunbeams right into Grace's eyes for a moment while along with her mother and Aurora, she slowly descended on the gentle grassy side of the valley. The Anshara was much more than five hundred cycles old, but its age wasn't visible at all. The craft was clean and shiny; her father cared for it greatly. As the legends said its wings and hull were forged by the eternally vigilant God, the man-of-all-work Dernaia Vira who wanted to give wings to the humans. Other legends also said these craft were eternal and the legacy of humanity's great abandoned and forgotten knowledge.

Many legends connected to these mythical craft. As Grace watched the Anshara from a distance, she wondered which legend was the truth. Are these craft really capable of reaching the stars as some said? Do the Aserians really respect, nay, fear the power of these craft? She didn't know. In her soul she felt the truth fell somewhere between all and none of them; it's a gift for mankind, a present from the oldest Aserian High-Guardians, Eve and Aaron who asked the most talented humans to build these craft to share the sense of flying with their protected ones. Or maybe not; whatever the truth was, mankind used these fast, graceful, and highly maneuverable craft to travel throughout the twelve provinces and reach even the farthest corners of Eecrys Aredia.

Eion, her father sat near the claws, resting in the lush green grass under the shade of the craft with closed eyes and whistling softly. Her mother grinned mischievously and put a finger to her lips to show Aurora and Grace to stay quiet. They rounded the craft in silence to catch Eion by surprise. As they approached, the young mother put little Aurora down and nodded to her children; it was time to catch their beloved prey.

Grace let Aurora get to Eion first. The youngest jumped at her father to initiate their play fight. As always their father let Aurora win and after a short fight, it was not surprising that Aurora emerged as the victor.

"I got you," Aurora grinned.

"Give me mercy, little princess," her father begged.

"I would never hurt you, father," Aurora threw her arms around his neck in a loving embrace.

"I know you would never hurt anyone," Eion stood up with his daughter.

"Some children are certainly making a lot of noise today," the motherly tone addressed the eternal child soul of her husband as she joined them along with Grace, who still held her papyrus and pencil in her hand. "I hope we didn't make you wait." The young woman smiled with a little twinge of conscience as she stepped closer to her husband.

"For you, I can wait forever, my love. You know that." He gave his beloved wife a great kiss, and then passed Aurora to her. Eion smiled at his children. "Are you ready to go?"

Margey and Grace nodded with smiles, but Aurora looked up at the large silver flying machine, right to the top with her big curious eyes.

"Are we going to fly with birdie?" her tiny voice asked with excitement building.

"Yes, sister. We're going to fly," Grace explained.

Grace grinned as Aurora quickly padded to the large metallic claw of the sleeping bird and stroked it lovingly. "Chosovi. Wake up. Wake up," she whispered and called the bird by the name she personally named the Anshara – in the dialect of the neighboring province of Seriana, instead of their native one. The silver hull of the craft gleamed in the sapphire sunlight and the name perfectly described the sleeping bird, but Grace knew her sister was calling the Anshara a *Blue Bird* for a different reason.

Throughout the twelve provinces of Eecrys Aredia, many aura-based technologies helped the people and the mechanical, mighty and ultimately beautiful flying craft; Ansharas, Kerecsens and Sanayras were one of them. They used the spirit will of the humans to fly. These majestic flying machines, fashioned to imitate predatory birds, revealed the true nature of the controlling spirit to any who saw them. And soon, her father's will, his aura would give life to Chosovi.

Aurora looked back at her father. "He will wake up soon," her determined voice insisted. "Hurry," she waved to her family. "We should get in before Chosovi flies away." The little one already hurried under the Anshara's belly and stood on the small circle shaped hull plate that connected to the belly of the craft above.

A small pedestal stood with a crystal ball embedded in the hull circle. Her father touched the small crystal ball that filled with azure light; his aura gave it the power to lift. The metal circle slowly lifted all four of them up into the craft.

The interior was large enough to house four persons. Strange shaped comfortable cushion-like seats crouched on the floor, one for the master who controlled the craft in front and another in the middle plus two behind them in a row. Two large half crystal domes were inset on either side of the large first cushion. They were the heart of the Anshara.

There were no windows on the craft, but they saw everything, the windswept grassy plain below, the clear azure sky and clouds high above, the valley of Seradelphia and the canyon all around. All the while, the safe strong body of Chosovi surrounded them. The entire hull was solid on the outside, yet the walls from the inside seemed transparent. The closed wings gleamed blurry silver and half transparent, as did the small tail wing behind them, which still pointed up toward the sky. The eyes of an eagle gave a great panoramic view to the master of the Anshara, who navigated the sky.

Eion sat down cross-legged on the first cushion while her mother sat on the last cushions with excited Aurora. Grace put her papyrus and pencil under the cushion before she sat down behind her father.

"Would you like to master the Anshara?" her father glanced back at Grace.

Grace measured the fragile controlling crystals; they called her. She wanted to touch them just once to see what cannot be seen otherwise; her aura. Every time her father gave her the opportunity, she resisted the great temptation. The greater part of her soul feared that the nature they would reveal would be something else never dreamt of.

Shy, she shook her head to say no.

"Then when you're ready," said her father kindly and he laid his hands on the crystal domes to each side of his cushion. They slowly filled with his aura; azure light started to spread out from the crystals into the transparent walls of the control chamber, and then throughout the entire craft from bow to stern, center to port and starboard. The aura energy that came from Eion extended his spirit will to the craft. The gently whirling blue light was the string that held the entire craft together and controlled it.

The aura reached the eagle's eyes through the very thin pipes that now glowed blue as the eyes filled with the power. Grace looked back to see Aurora's eyes gleam with happiness as the blue energy gave life to her beloved Chosovi.

As the aura wrapped within the walls the craft itself created an invisible gentle force of nature, Grace's fragile body felt a tingling feeling that pulled all of them lightly to the Anshara's floor. Her eyes followed the flow of the energy as it quickly spread its way into the walls through the rifts to the two large circles, and the small tail circle; the aura-cauldrons. They quickly filled with the life-giving aura concentrated there while the rest spider webbed into the wings. The blue energy quickly filled the missing gaps between the large closed wings and shaped small aura feathers on the wings. Her father's will reached all parts of the craft in seconds; his mind and will connected to the aura-cauldrons, the wings, and finally reached the legs and the great metal claws.

Now you'll look just like a proud eagle, Grace smiled. *Awake, my silver birdie! It's time to fly!* Her mind ordered the Anshara as if she was in control the craft.

The awakening of the bird took only a few moments. The outline of the transparent eagle head quickly looked up in front of her father while the large segmented wings, the coverts and the cross feathers slid upward one by one on the circles. A quiet crackling slid into Grace's sensitive ears as the large aura-cauldrons began to swoop down from their vertical position, while the folded-fan wings on them opened like a blooming flower. The tail also filled with the swirling aura, along with the tail feathers it slowly lowered to center position. The large main wings reached their final position as the ninth and last cross feather slid into position. The wings along with the aura feathers looked like large eagle wings with the blue glow flowing through them like blood in arteries. The left wing tilted forward while the right wing tilted backward through their cross axis. Then at the maximum point, they quickly flexed in reverse to their threshold and then quickly set back to their original horizontal position. From the corner of her eye Grace saw the tail turn left and right before it regained its horizontal position; as always, her eternal child father grinned as he tried his *wings*. He loved to fly.

Like her sister, Grace loved to watch take off, whether she was inside or outside. Their awakenings were amazing, also, as the craft majestically opened their large wings and came alive, stretching like their flesh and blood cousins after a long dream. And now the Anshara was awake.

"Fly Chosovi! Fly!" came Aurora's small cheering voice from behind. Grace smiled warmly.

"Let's fly, little Doli," Grace called the blue bird in the native Odess'ianan dialect. The wings suddenly elevated slightly. The Anshara screamed like a flesh and blood eagle as the aura swirled faster within the aura-cauldrons. The large silver eagle beat once with its large wings while it pushed itself away from the ground with claws and powerful metal legs. Chosovi quickly pulled up her metal claws on the second mighty beat of the wings as the will of Grace's father had ordered them.

Grace looked down as the ground slowly shoved out from under them. Their house on the grassy plain soon became so small as the Anshara climbed higher into its realm, the endless sky. The majestic wings beat a few more times while clouds slowly embraced them.

We're climbing higher and higher up into the sky. The wings beating as the clouds embrace us, then we break out of the top of the clouds to reach the sun, thought Grace. She imagined herself from the outside as they break out of the top of the clouds. In her mind she saw the shiny silver and azure craft, which looked to be a messenger from the Gods as it silently glided through the sapphire daylight. For a moment, she heard the false crystal chime music that echoed in her mind, like a silent whisper. It reminded her of the irrational fear she had felt in her strange dream.

It's so strange. I'm safe and I love flying.

30

The white clouds swirled around the Anshara before they split to reveal the great capital of the eleventh province, Odess'iana; the city of myth and forgotten knowledge.

Grace smiled. In the hands of her mother, grinning Aurora had already put her nose to the transparent wall to peek out. Her little sister had waited for this moment a long time and now she watched the endless tapestry of the great capital, silent and amazed. The green eyes mirrored the desire of the little girl; she wanted to touch, play and take care of the town like it was one of her huge sand castles that she lovingly built with her tiny shovel in the backyard of their home.

Grace wasn't surprised by her sister's amazement. Odess'iana was simply beautiful from the sky and in the clear daylight. The capital and its outskirts were much larger than her home, the great valley of Seradelphia, or even hundreds of small villages together. From the great height they clearly saw how the city was weaved through with beautiful, long, wriggling aqueduct systems. Like arteries, they carried the clear water from the nearby lakes and rivers into the dozens of baths, small pools, underground cisterns, fountains, enchanting imitation fishing lakes, and small oases throughout the capital. It also supplied water to the farms that surrounded the whole town.

Her father mastered the Anshara with due foresight as the craft majestically began to descend. They passed above the thick soaring segmented exterior walls that buffered the city from the worst sand storms and also protected lives and their achievements within. Mansions, libraries, schools, parks, lakes, and various other buildings curiously watched the Anshara from the ground as it passed above the widest middle segment of the town. In the distance, the smallest center district was visible. Only a few large buildings stood there, the palace of the rulers and the citadel of the Aserians.

A large eagle shadow looked back at Grace from the ground, it slowly flapped its large wings. The Anshara passed above the walls to the internal districts of Odess'iana, which housed the markets, other trade areas, tasunke stables, and the port for the flying craft; that's where they were headed.

The port where they landed with their Anshara and where Chosovi fell asleep was already full of these beautiful craft and their sisters. The graceful saker falcon shaped Kerecsens that were used by the people of the central provinces, - including the capital of Eecrys Aredia, Andrenia -,

31

were nestled at the port. With them were the colourful and majestic firebirds, Sanayras, usually used by the citizens of the large eastern provinces of Hijaz and Yaana.

"Sleep well, Chosovi," Aurora waved farewell to the sleeping bird from the arms of her mother. Grace smiled at the row of nestling craft with their wings folded like obedient chickens waiting for their supper.

After a short walk, Grace and her family entered the bustling outskirt marketplace full of traders. This was the very first day of the long awaited feast, and the city was already brimming with bustling humans and Aserians alike. Farmers, traders, fishermen, explorers, historians, musicians, artists, entrepreneurs, and simple wanderers crowded the squares and the streets. From neighbouring lands and distant continents they came to celebrate with friends and family, to trade, learn, or simply enjoy the feast and the performances.

The Great Deciduous Feast of Odess'iana was only one of the extraordinary events on Eecrys Aredia and the grandest in the eleventh province. The rulers of Odess'iana, noble and wise Thobadzistshin, and his beautiful wife, Hastseolti believed, like their citizens, that their work was the lifeblood of their prosperous community, their culture.

The family walked deeper and deeper through the thronged market. As Grace looked around, she knew the rulers had done everything they could to make the feast greater and more luxurious than the previous cycle. Their touch was visible. The whole city was dressed for the festivities. Beautiful flags of the twelve provinces waved proudly from the smallest house to the largest temple. Flowers covered arches, columns, and pillars. A pallet of colourful flora stretched from one to another and gave more life to the already beautiful city of Odess'iana. Large arabesque awnings stretched between many of the rooftops to give shelter from possible rain, as well as the midday sun.

Twelve great capitals, twelve great feasts. Each cycle's fest was as different as the twelve cities that hosted them and each of these festivals ran for thirty days. The previous fest was held in Odess'iana's sister city of Seriana, the capital of the seventh province. It was only dozens of leagues away from Odess'iana, far across the great White Sands desert.

The Long Town, as Grace and many others called Odess'iana, unlike Seriana that was built symmetrically, was longer than it was wide. And today, all eyes were focused on Odess'iana. On these festival days, it was the town of endless celebration and happiness that reminded people of the approaching cold season, when everyone took a well-deserved rest and prepared for the work of the next cycle.

32

As always, the opening ceremony and the real parades started just after the clear blazing white dawn of the first day. The daily closing performance was always different. There was one that Grace, her family, and many Odess'ianans waited all cycle to see, Azen and Vessa, the two talented Aserian hall singers from Andrenia. They always came to the feast to share their unique and beautiful performance in the renowned Long Hall of Odess'iana. But nightfall was far off and day was still ahead of Grace to discover the Feast.

"We'll meet you right here before twilight," said Eion as they arrived at the great fountain in the marketplace.

"As you wish, father," Grace nodded and quickly looked around to memorize the place.

"May I go with her?" asked Aurora hopefully.

"No, my dear. You're coming with us now," responded her mother. Aurora pouted and turned sad eyes to Eion.

"Sorry, Aurora," said her father kindly. Aurora crossed her arms, defiantly looked away, and turned her nose up. "But if you want, we can search for some Serianan tasunkes," her father added.

Glee sparkled in Aurora's eyes as she completely forgot about her defiance and Grace. "I love them, father. May I hug them?" Her father nodded with amusement. Aurora searched the area with wide eyes in hopes of spotting a tasunke. "Where are they? Let's find them."

She loved the animals, the graceful tasunkes with gleaming coats and flowing manes, especially those bred in Seriana.

"Go and explore the feast, little angel," said Margey with a kiss to Grace's forehead. "And remember. Your Guardian is always watching over you. If you lose your way, just ask her guidance."

Her parents knew that she was fully capable of taking her bearing anytime and never worried that she would get lost anywhere on Eecrys Aredia. She had the senses to find a place, home, or any person. Just like every other place throughout Eecyrs Aredia, Odess'iana was safe; no one needed to fear anyone or anything. The Aserians guided and protected them all as they had for thousands of cycles.

Grace enjoyed their full trust. Now she could hunt out everything that she was curious about and not only those things her parents wished her to see and learn. She had earned total freedom until dusk and Grace intended to use it.

Leaving the marketplace and her family behind her legs already carried her to the destination she had planned to visit a long time ago; the district where her great heroes, the Aserians live.

If the guardian doesn't come to Gracie, Gracie goes to the guardian, she thought happily as she strolled closer to her destination. Her heart beat faster and faster in her endless excitement, her eyes scanned the crowd to find one of her heroes. Then after a long search, her eyes opened wide. In the crowd, she noticed the first winged Aserian who slowly marched up the polished stone steps and into the large temple. In the Aserian culture, the shape of the wings represented the class they belong. From the large graceful, strong feathery white wings, Grace knew; he was an Aserian Guardian.

Cold air embraced Grace like a shy second shadow, the little girl followed the Aserian into the temple and moved from column to column. Excited, Grace curiously peeked out from behind the column and watched him from a distance. She hoped her eyes would find something to remind her of the almighty crystal blade – so her Spirit Guardian dolls wouldn't be empty anymore.

The footsteps of the Aserian echoed on the long marble corridor. His azure toga, like his large white feathery wings waved gently in the air as the sunlight highlighted them through the windows. A golden metallic piece hung on his belt. It looked as if two cavernous mingan skulls had grafted to the two ends of a long strange golden scroll holder. It was masterfully crafted and elegant. Grace glanced up in time to see sunbeams touched them. Other than that, which made Grace believed the Aserian were some sort of messenger; she hadn't seen anything that would look like a crystal, a blade, or the combination of the two.

Disappointed, she shook her head. Then the large beautiful angel statue, which looked down at her from close by, reminded her why she was really here. The Imagination of a daydreaming little child insisted that the statue pleasantly smiled at her, the gazing stone eyes bolstered her bravery.

I can do it, Grace reassured herself as she watched the majestic Aserian from behind the column. *Yes, I can do it.*

Grace took a soft sigh as she gathered all her bravery to face the legend; a real Aserian. The angel statue watched over her as the little girl stepped behind the Aserian and his new shadow followed him from a distance as they slowly arrived at a great hall doors. In Grace's eyes, the Aserian seemed so majestic and graceful even from this close.

Yes, I can do it. Her hand gently pulled his large white wing once from behind. The Aserian stopped and looked back with a kind smile; his deep-set brown eyes curiously looked down at her. Grace took a huge breath.

"Dear Aserian!" she started as she looked up at him. "I'm here to pledge allegiance to Eecrys Aredia and her people! I promise I will be faithful and true and for exchange I'd like to be an Aserian Guardian!" she declared proudly, then hesitated for a moment. "And I'd like to get wings this big!" she giggled while spreading her arms as wide as she could. "Please," the little girl added with a wide smile and awaited the answer.

Deep silence fell as her excited voice faded away. The Aserian watched the daydreaming girl kindly. His face turned sorrowful and he crouched down to her.

"I'm sorry by all my spirit and soul, brave little girl," he said after a short hesitation. "But I can't fulfill your dream," full of sorrow he put a hand on her shoulder. Shocked by the answer, Grace immediately took a step back.

"But, but why? Am I a bad soul? But I try to be a good girl. I pray a lot to the Sacred Mother. I was good with mommy, daddy, and sister. And I know many things about the Crystal Shade. I, I..."

"No, it's not like that," the Aserian started to explain with great sadness in his voice.

"But, but I would be the greatest and the kindest guardian of all. I promise. Please," she begged with eyes that filled with tears. Her dream, like a mirror was already shattered to pieces since the first words of the Aserian hit hear ears. "P-Please," her whisper begged to fix the broken dream so desperate. The Aserian Guardian wanted to say something, but Grace stepped back, turned, and ran away fast, out of the great hall.

She didn't see where she was running, she just ran and ran as if she wanted to run out of the world, to leave the cruel words of the Aserian behind, who crushed her greatest dream within a moment.

Only the tree's great shadow and the trickling of a tiny little fountain tried to hide the heart-broken little girl and her weeping.

"I would be a great guardian, the greatest and the kindest of all. I know."

* * *

"I greet that place where you and I, we are one," a woman's kind voice greeted her. Sad and crushed, Grace just sniffled as she looked up. The calm toned woman had round brown mauve eyes that were like two beautiful bronze coins. Her thick, wavy, black hair was worn in a style that reminded Grace of a pennant blowing in the wind, her deep-tanned skin glowed in the sunlight.

"What's wrong little girl?" a dignified man behind the woman asked with concern, while he put a large ceramic tasunke hair dye pot down on the cobblestones along with some white ribbon and silk.

"I dreamt that I'll be a graceful guardian one day, with wings, large white wings," she whispered and sniffed once again, while she wiped her tears. "But I never will be."

"There is a road in the hearts of all of us, hidden and seldom traveled, which leads to an unknown, secret place to choose what we desire," said the man as he sat down near her on the ground. "A guardian is a guardian in their soul. Never forget that."

"But I can't have wings," Grace whispered sadly. "And I won't ever see a crystal blade. I won't ever learn what it looks like. I never will learn what the Crystal Shade really is."

The man raised her chin; his almond-shaped brown eyes, which mirrored his intelligence looked deep into hers.

"If your soul wants to be a guardian, then you're already a guardian, even without a crystal blade," he said.

"But, but I want wings, beautiful wings," she whispered as she lowered her head.

"Only Aserians can have wings," said the man, then he looked at the woman, who smiled kindly and nodded. The man looked back at tearful Grace. "But maybe, just maybe you can be a winged guardian for today. If you want you can live the life of a guardian in disguise who is hiding her large white wings in the spirit realm."

"R-Really?" Grace's eyes sparked immediately in her excitement.

"Yes. But first, you must go through the secret magical ritual of eleven-eleven," confirmed the woman.

"Secret magic of eleven-eleven?" Grace whispered the magic words. "What is that?"

"Eleven is a mirror to our inner self. But some says it represents the Sacred Crystal Mother and her shade," answered the man. "Or the one who is watched over by her and her angels. Others say; it's a crack, a bridge linking light and darkness; a doorway in our past and future, good or bad decisions. And for many; it's just a myth, a legend of the Crystal Shade."

"It always remembers who you truly are and where you come from," stated the woman. "Whoever wears eleven, that one protects Odess'iana's bright future and her shaded forgotten mythical past with it."

"That's why there are two elevens at the gates of Odess'iana, right?" Grace asked curiously. "The magic numbers are protecting our province from the evil Shaina. The reason we haven't seen any in a long time."

"You're a very-very good observer little girl," nodded the woman with great respect.

"Everything is told by the numbers," whispered Grace enchanted, while her mind began to wonder what other numbers might hide, what secrets they can reveal about her beloved legend, the Crystal Shade.

"What is your name?" asked the man.

"Grace Sessa Aredia from the outskirts of Odess'iana, the valley of Seradelphia. And yours?"

The man and the woman looked at each other, and then smiled at Grace.

"We're just an ordinary man and woman, two strangers of Odess'iana who are dressing this beautiful capital in joyful colors," the woman said and smiled as she proudly looked at the large colourful freshly painted silk ribbons that covered the trees and dried in the sun.

"Are you ready for your commencement day, young one?" he asked. Grace nodded. "Then please step forward and show your respect to Sachylia," he called her with a regal tone. The woman crouched down, dipped her finger into the dye pot, while Grace looked into the sapphire sun. Her nose picked up the unmistakable aroma of the Odess'ianan ground blue corn dye, the same that Aurora used to use when she painted back home with their mother.

"Decisions never come from the body, they come from patience and control; one decision comes from your spirit and one from your soul," the female spoken in rhymes, while she gently drew two short lines diagonally from the top center on Grace's forehead with her dyed finger. Basking in the sapphire sunlight, Grace enjoyed the moment with a wide smile. "But never forget, young guardian; when you take a road, the other will fade; as everything has its own shadow within our Crystal Shade," the woman drew two diagonal lines down to meet almost to the center of her eyebrows under the previous lines.

The woman led her to the fountain and Grace looked into the clear water. The lines on her forehead shaped a blue rhombus standing on its edge, the symbol of the Sacred Crystal and the ancient symbol of eleven; eleven, which also represented her home province, Odess'iana.

"Eleven stands in light," the woman pointed at Grace's forehead. "Eleven mirrors the shade," she pointed at her mirror image. "A brave little guardian can face the night even without a crystal blade."

"Today, you, Grace Sessa Aredia are the youngest guardian of the eleventh province, Odess'iana," declared the man, and he bowed his head with respect. "Your large white wings, hidden in the spirit realm, will follow you wherever you go."

Grace smiled proudly. An imagination of her daydreaming mind she felt her large guardian wings are on her back, following her unseen and invisible from the spirit realm. The male stranger leaned close to her.

"As a guardian your duty is to watch the people, to listen their souls, to hear their stories and their heart's desire. And foremost, to learn more about our civilization, about our great Eecrys Aredia and her culture."

"A guardian lives so others may live," said Grace determined. "My spirit will take responsibility for my actions, my soul will be truthful and honest all the times," said the lines that she had practiced so much in her daydreamings in the hope she could say this when her dream came true.

"You speak so beautifully," the woman stroke her hair proudly. "But remember; Guardians live in secret and now you're a guardian in disguise who must act from the background. You can't show your wings and you can't tell to anyone who you truly are, not even your parents. Otherwise your words will break the secret magic of eleven."

The little girl nodded, as she understood.

"Enjoy the feast, brave little guardian of Odess'iana," the man said kindly. "Go and watch over all of us."

* * *

Along with the curious mass of people, Grace slowly wandered the streets of Odess'iana all day. Proud in her little heart, she tried to fulfill her new duty; she visited many human and Aserian performers, writers and artists, mostly those who came from Sessa Asria and Coreenthia. The traders, scientists, and explorers from Eecryssa and Sagatta, who made this long journey to voice the extolment of their great discoveries of gathered stones, plants, flowers, and beautiful jewellery to everyone, they amazed her. The pride in their life's work was only heightened by everyone's appreciation. Everyone respected each other and no one was afraid to share their knowledge. There were no secrets between the people. And just like the youngest guardian of Odess'iana, every visitor was curious and patiently ambled from one place to another to see more and more.

Her eyes caught on a blacksmith who raised his large and heavy hammer over and over again. The heated metal on the anvil glowed orange and clinked after every hit as it enjoyed the care. Behind the master, his apprentice whistled while he swept the floor.

The master carefully worked the metal piece, which slowly took the shape of a Coreenthian armband after every strong hit. Then the hammer rested for a moment, while the eyes of the master checked the armband in the hold of his clippers. Grace heard satisfied humming from under his prominent moustache, and then the master put the armband into a small bucket of water to cool it down.

Hissing steam engulfed the strong body, and then the clippers put the armband with the dozen of others on the table. The blacksmith prepared his workspace to begin his next masterpiece. He put the water bucket aside, behind him, and then carefully selected the next metal to heat. When he decided, the tendons in his hand strained as he picked up the heavy hammer.

Grace felt that the bucket was at the worst place; her instincts told her. In the very next moment, as the blacksmith raised his hammer, he already stepped back right toward the bucket before he struck down. She wanted to warn the man as she already had foreseen the Coreenthian is going to fall to the ground, while the large hammer falls from his hand and hits him. But before she had a chance to say a word, the apprentice slightly spun around and with the end of his broom picked up the bucket and with an elegant move set it away from the blacksmith's path, right before he stepped back.

The blacksmith took a glance backward, but his apprentice just whistled and swept the floor as if nothing happened at all. Grace smiled as she felt and knew; the young apprentice was an Aserian in disguise, the guardian spirit of the blacksmith.

Grace desired to speak with the Aserian so much, proudly tell him that she was the youngest guardian of Odess'iana, she was with him, one of them, at least for a day.

If I could show my shy, but beautiful large wings, she thought. But she said nothing; she didn't want to break the magic of eleven. Then the apprentice, almost unnoticed, winked at her as he swept the floor.

He recognized me! He knows I'm a guardian! Grace thought proudly. *The magic of eleven tells him who I am without a word! I'm a real guardian, like Eriana!*

Smiling, the proud young guardian walked deeper and deeper to keep the order to listen to other souls, to discover the unknown, to learn more about her own home.

"Beautiful jewellery, young lady?" a studious, yet calm tone called her, which belonged to an elegant tall woman. The traditional elegant tiara of Eecryssa, which covered her wavy, amber hair, shone in the sunlight. "Look at these polished gemstone necklaces from the Acari Mountains. Or take a look at the great white pearls from the great depth and shoals of Callao'eya. A young lady like you can get it for a beautiful smile."

The polished white pearls glistened like the eyes of her mother. After Grace presented the widest smile that she was capable of producing and accepted the necklace, the trader offered her the story of the beautiful necklace. Everything had a story on Eecrys Aredia and the necklace was no exception. Grace loved to listen to all of them, but now it was also her guardian duty to listen and learn. She was also sure that her mother was going to treasure a necklace that was more than it appears to be; a necklace with its own unique story.

"Tiny brothers and sisters were born and grow in a beautifully double-sided formed shell deep under water. We call it, Mama Yuraqilla," the woman explained. "The waves passed above Yuraqilla silently, while the pearls inside her became larger and more beautiful; she cared for all deeply. Then a young Eecryssan, Yaku, the masters of the deep water, he, who holds his breath longer than anyone, dove deeper and deeper in the cold waves. He asked Mama Yuraqilla to give him the pearls, to present them to the surface and share their beauty with others. And Yuraqilla gave their children to him, sent them to see the surface world. The woman in Yaku's village didn't want to separate the tiny white brothers and sisters, they were together, were twin souls since their birth. So they strung them together onto this necklace to be together for eternity."

Grace caressed the tiny pearls. She felt the love what grew and nurtured them.

"This is the story of their past," the trader continued. "From now on, their story, their life, their future is shared with yours or the one who will wear it. Always remember. Brothers and sisters always hold together, just like the daughters and sons of Yuraqilla."

After she said farewell to the Eecryssan woman, Grace continued her mission to learn more and to find something for her father and little Aurora, too.

"So many beautiful goods. So many," she whispered while her eyes mirrored the arven sketches, flower dyes, and paintings, tiny stone statues and little hand crafted wooden models of Ansharas and other flying craft. She shook her head, as she couldn't decide. "What should I bring you, father? What would you like the most?"

A shadow blocked the sun. It belonged to a venerable old man. The wind blew his long flowing hair and long, thick gray beard. His large and black eyes and an aquiline nose stared at Grace.

"I'm the Great Master Nervaschanzo Seranzini, the storyteller, poet, painter, sculptor, architect, artist and inventor, a true polymath of Sessa Asria. Who are you, young wanderer?" his voice rumbled quietly.

"Grace Sessa Aredia, the youngest artist from the endless meadows of the great valley of Seradelphia."

"Ah, a fellow soul who sees the world as no one else can see. I already believe you won't find the right gift here that you're looking for, young Graciana. Come. Come, sit and listen," he invited her kindly and Grace sat down on the small wooden stool, which faced the chair that the Great Master sat in. "Artists share their vision, gift it to the people. But between each other we, artists are sharing stories that we then can pass and can pass on and give inspiration. So, you'll hear the story that no one else has heard from the Great Master Nervaschanzo; the story of the crystal sunset."

The old art master coughed once before starting.

"The Divine Nervaschanzo. That's all I hear when people see my art and read the echo of my soul! Even the Great God statues of the Oval Hall of Sagatta are shy and desire the touch of this great sculptor! But how can I be divine without inspiration; an artist without a vision?" his old voice rumbled, and then he reverted to a gentler tone.

"One day a morning was half gone already, young Graciana and I still couldn't find the inspiration. I've seen days and nights as Sachylia and Carenia Seli chased each other across the sky, but the right moment didn't touch me. When one's imagination cannot provide an answer; you seek a greater imagination. But even my guardian, my own Watcher," he looked up to an imaginary face and with a pretend fury, he pointed to the air as his voice thundered once again. "Yes, you Carenian who is brilliant like me and hiding in your safe realm, you, my twin soul has stayed silent!" Nervaschanzo smiled as he looked back at Grace who enjoyed his storytelling.

"So I left my land to find my moment," the old polymath continued. "A flock of tweeting and soaring birds watched over me from the great trees and the vast skies of Coreenthia. The crystal-clear waters of the Hijazian oases eased my thirst under the shadows of the arecaceae trees and pink petals of the Yaanan sakuras danced around me in the gentle breeze. The squeezing cold of Crystana Serentis froze my breath so I could touch it, and green grass stroked my feet in the endless rich meadows of Andrenia. But none of them was good enough for old Nervaschanzo. None of them was my perfect moment. Sad and disappointed, I returned home. But I was blind, I realized." He looked up again for a moment to face his unseen guardian soul. After a thankful nod, he looked back at Grace.

"The journey was a lesson to old, foolish Nervaschanzo as the perfect moment was never gone, but waited for me. The sunrise, which was clear as the soul of the Sacred Mother looked back through my window, from above the great gulf of my home, Sessa Asria." Grace listened with great excitement while Nervaschanzo continued. "Always remember, young Graciana; never look for the moment, as the moment always finds you."

The little girl applauded and the old poet respectfully nodded.

"When you tell this story to your loved ones, please tell them you've met with the great storyteller and poet, the old Nervaschanzo, the one who has finally found his crystal sunset."

The old poet leaned closer to her.

"Time is always short for brilliant artistic souls like you and me, young Graciana. The right moment never awaits, but finds us." He spread his hands and continued. "Just look around. Moments look back all over, calling you to experience, to learn and then to later share it with others through your arts and words. And when you come to Sessa Asria someday, maybe you'll share your own story, your perfect moment with the old, but Great Nervaschanzo."

The young girl nodded at the kind old man. "I will," she said kindly.

"Now go and let your moment find you, young Graciana."

Grace admitted old Nervaschanzo was right. His story will be the greatest present she could give to her father who always loved to hear the experiences and adventures of others. Everyone on Eecrys Aredia, human and Aserian alike believed in the power of words, the shared experience and knowledge. And Grace had the talent to tell a story the same way to not lose any details or inflection from its true value. All stories and all experiences had value that served to expand the knowledge of anyone who desired to learn them. Shared knowledge and experience was one of the basic and most valuable elements of all the cultures. Without knowledge, there was no harvest, fishing, and quite simply no knowledge about their surroundings.

As she left old Nervaschanzo behind, Sachylia had already left its zenith. Under the afternoon sunlight, the young girl watched the dancers from different cultures. Grace was awed by the veil dancers of the mystical Hijaz province watching their elegantly manipulated veils move like silky water in a soft wind. They danced and shook their hips to the rhythm of the exotic music. After they finished their performance, one of the dancers, graceful and beautiful, Jameela offered to share her knowledge to any who volunteered. And Grace did; she spent most of her afternoon learning to move like the mystical dancers of Hijaz.

After the veil dance ended, Grace discovered a street, which was full of displayed fruit and foods that were grown and made in different provinces. Most of them, especially the tradition dishes of Andrenia, Atlantia, Yaana and Hijaz provinces had different tastes and used different spices and preparations than the foods of Odess'iana and Sagatta. Andrenia and Hijaz were famous for their spicy food, exotic fruit and grape drinks, while Atlantia and Yaana proudly displayed their delicious, sometimes strange fish, savoury recipes and produce. Odess'iana and its sister province Seriana delighted with their famous foods and sweet drinks. All twelve cultures were different, but the Great Deciduous Feast of Odess'iana brought the cuisine of all cultures to one place, this long street.

From under the shadow of a tarp strange fruit that looked juicy and appetizing called to her, fruit she had never seen before. The air around them was cold, frozen, and visible as if the fruit could breathe; just as Nervaschanzo described the freezing cold of Crystana Serentis. The fruits were stored in large pots full of ice and mush of snow covered their soft husk.

"This ice fruit grows only in the far northern icy province of Crystana," the trader's deep voice boomed from behind the pots. "It's cold as the name says, but it's delicious and sweet as the aya nectar." His hand, pale as the snow of Slumberous, picked up a bowl full of ice fruit and offered them to her. "Please taste. I hope you'll find them delicious."

The trader didn't exaggerate. It was the sweetest and the most delicious fruit that touched her tiny lips and ever ate. Her hand quickly picked up another, then another. The trader took a satisfied smile.

"The ice fruit, the pride of Crystana grow on the frozen hills of Carelia. They grow silently, then they peek out from underground when Crystana Serentis is ruled by the long, fair day which lasts for almost fifteen dozen days without a single night. They love our tending and we tend them gently while they bath in Sachyilia's dim life giving light. They mature slowly, turning juicy and delicious." From her eyes, Grace had seen that this story meant a lot to the man and he gladly shared it with everyone. She slowly ate the next fruit while the trader turned serious as he continued, "But when Deciduous approaches in other places, Sachylia slowly disappears on Crystana's horizon. The long day is followed by a long, cold night that sets your teeth on edge; only a true Crystanan can live in that cold. The long night lasts for the same time as the long day before it. But before the water freezes inside the aqueducts the delicious ice fruit harvest begins to bring our soul to others on Eecrys Aredia."

43

Grace just ate the very last fruit from the bowl. "Thank you," she said gratefully.

"Please remember the hard work of my people. They grew every single piece from the heart." Like two pools of water, his slitted blue eyes shone with pride as he gave a small closed ceramic pot full of ice fruit to Grace. "Share the delicacy with your family. I hope they will all find them delicious and will enjoy the fruits of Crystana," the trader added kindly in farewell.

"They surely will. Thank you very much for sharing these appetizing fruits and your amazing story, good man," Grace bowed her head respectfully.

The temptation was great; she wanted to eat just one more of these fruit, but she knew if she ate one there was a good chance that all of them would slowly disappear before she joined her family. She resisted and tried to distract her thoughts from the ice fruit.

Fluid music like the beautiest of waterfalls, teased her ears as she searched for her next destination. A few musicians from the water world of Atlantia played nearby. Unlike the traditional music of Odess'iana that always reminded Grace of freedom and sometimes the flight of an eagle, the Atlantian music was softer and slid around her like the flow of water. In due time, Grace felt the love and respect that flowed through the water music. Of course, none of these musical styles compared to the music of Serenata Merida, which was the land of music and she felt a bit disappointed that she hadn't met any musicians from that province thus far.

A Sanayra craft passed over the street where she was, as it gracefully flew toward the port of Odess'iana. The craft looked like the majestic mythological firebird it was named for; its wings glowed bright yellow and the metallic hull shined dark orange.

"Fly Aamir, fly your magic carpet," she whispered and waved with a giggle to the craft. Grace picked up this habit last Prosperous when they were in Seriana and a trader from the borders of Hijaz showed them his firebird from the inside. Just like the Anshara and other craft, the Sanayra's interior was transparent, but instead of the comfortable cushions, a large elegant Hijazian wool carpet covered its floor. Grace's mother read many tales of the Hijazian Thousand and One Dreams, which told stories about a brave man, who flew a magic carpet. And now as she knew what the basis of those wonderful stories really were she wanted to believe that her brave hero flew above her to get to and gain the heart of his beloved princess.

A sudden massive burst of flame rocketed up toward the sky between Grace and the passing firebird.

Curious, she looked for the source of the flame and noticed a strange black skinned man, who was surrounded by the crowd. The mass of spectators watched his show with awe. The black skinned man wore only pants; he held a flaming stick and a small vial in his hand. He carefully held them in front of his mouth, and then breathed a beautiful orange flame up into the sky.

Grace was enchanted. She slipped between the standing adults and other children to pop up in the front line. The black skinned man spun the stick in his hand while he danced, and then once again breathed a stream of fire into the sky. Everyone clapped enthusiastically as the man finished his performance. The fire breather searched the crowd before he looked at Grace.

"What is your name, little lady?" the fire breather asked.

"Grace Sessa Aredia of the outskirts of Odess'iana, land of myth and forgotten knowledge," she respectfully nodded to him.

"My name is Ashan Al-Karim of Jizan, outskirts of Hijaz, the land of spirits and dreams," he bowed with equal respect. "Do you wish to learn this trick, Lady Grace of Odess'iana?" Ashan asked while he began to spin the fire stick in his hand.

"Is, is it safe?" Grace asked shyly.

"If you know how to master the fire, yes, it is safe," he smiled as he stopped the stick. He lifted the stick and the small bottle to his mouth, looked up, and breathed a large flame into the air. After the flame burned out, he looked back at the little girl. "But if you do not respect its mighty power, can't accept its existence, it can hurt you; it can rule you and it can defeat you. The fire has its own wild life. You must tame it to be your friend. The question is, are you brave enough to be his friend?"

Grace hesitated, and then excitement was replaced by a cool calmness that fell upon her. A guardian never fears and she was the Guardian of Odess'iana. She also knew that her own guardian was watching over her, even in this very moment. Maybe she was in the crowd, disguised as a human.

"Yes. I'd like to tame the fire," she answered with determination and put the necklace and the pot of ice fruit on his table.

"You're a very, very brave little girl," Ashan crouched down in front of her.

"What should I do?" she asked, studying the fire stick.

"First, you must watch the wind," Ashan began. "Wind is the enemy of fire. You must embrace it and protect the flame from it. Remember. The wind must blow from behind you."

Grace nodded. She watched the flame on the fire breather's flaming stick and saw which way the wind blew.

"It's coming from that direction," she said and turned her back to the wind.

"Good." Ashan picked up a small vial of water from the table and gave it to her. "Put a small quantity of water in the bottom of your mouth. You must watch that the fluid is not on your face, nor your chest. When you are ready, blow the water out of a small opening in your lips, do it as fast as possible."

She sipped a bit from the vial and spit the water out, just as Ashan told her.

"Excellent. Now comes the fun part," Ashan continued while he took the water vial, put it on the table, and gave a vial that contained flammable fluid to Grace. "You must do the same, but now, you must move the fire stick close to your mouth when you spit."

The little girl nodded as Ashan gave her the fire stick.

You can do it. Don't fear. I'm watching over you, she heard a very soft voice in her mind, but she couldn't decide if her soul meant to calm her excitement or if her guardian reassured her.

Grace concentrated, put a small measure of fluid into her mouth, immediately looked up, and held the stick in front of her mouth. After a quick breath, a plume of fire rocketed into the sky. The flame quickly spread, and then suddenly died out. The crowd clapped boisterously. Pleased, Grace bowed to them, and then looked at Ashan to see how she had done.

"You're learning pretty well, fire breather Grace of Odess'iana," Ashan smiled.

"Thank you," she gave the stick back and Ashan put it into a water bucket.

"Wait, my little apprentice," Ashan picked up a new fire stick. "A fire breather is not a fire breather without a fire stick. This is yours, fire breather Grace of Odess'iana. You have earned it," he said and gave the stick to her.

"Thank you, Ashan," Grace nodded respectfully to him while she tucked the fire stick onto her saree belt.

"The honor is mine little fire apprentice. Never forget what you learned from Ashan," he solemnly responded.

"I won't. I promise," Grace grinned. Ashan stood, picked up her jewellery and fruit pot from the table, and gave them to her.

"The time is so young. Just look around. There are many skills that a young, strong willed girl may learn from others."

Grace nodded to him. Ashan smiled mischievously before he turned to the waiting audience. "This brave little girl has tamed the wild fires of Hijaz," applause erupted as Grace left. "Who has the bravery and courage to do the same?"

Grace looked back and saw Ashan point to a young man in the crowd. From his clothes, she immediately knew him for an explorer of the far Yaana province.

"Do you have the same bravery, young explorer? You who have wandered thousands of leagues to come before Ashan the fire breather."

"Yes. I have. I hope." Ashan and the crowd chuckled at his response while Grace disappeared into the crowd.

Sachylia looked down at her as it approached the horizon and Grace knew that she had to get back to the marketplace as father had instructed her. Filled with disappointment, she looked back at the bazaars. There were so many unusual things that she could have learned from the people here and she got so little time. But her family and the performance of the two Aserians, Azen and Vessa that she didn't want to miss waited for her.

A long walk led her back to the entrance of the marketplace. Her eyes quickly found her mother, but she didn't see her father or Aurora. Grace already suspected what happened.

"Aurora. She, she has disappeared," her mother confirmed Grace's suspicion when she joined her. "We looked away in the crowd, just for a moment and my little girl was gone. We looked for her, but she was nowhere to be found. Your father has gone to find her," she continued worried. Grace held her hand to give her strength.

"Don't worry, mother. I will help father find her quickly." The youngest guardian of Odess'iana knew it was her task to find her sister, her duty. She passed the pot of ice fruit, the necklace, and the fire stick to her, and then gave her mother a kiss on the cheek to calm her.

"Wait here, mother."

* * *

This wasn't the first time curious little Aurora straggled away when her parents weren't watching, usually under father's watch. Usually Grace felt where her sister was and there were many times when she found her before her father could. Her mother knew that she could trust Grace to guide her little lamb back to her, no matter from where.

Unlike her mother, father wasn't troubled. He knew that nothing could harm his little daughter in Odess'iana, especially under the protection of her guardian. Alas, mother was led by a mother's instinct. She was worried and Grace understood her.

"Where are you, sister?" Grace asked herself as she looked around in the dark alley that hid from the sunlight. Like a true guardian, who looks for her protected one, she had already searched many streets and alleys of Odess'iana for a long time, but she still hadn't found Aurora.

She really wandered away this time, farther than before, Grace thought and began to feel the same worry that her mother felt. *Where are you?* Her head snapped to the left and right, both paths called her. But she knew she could take only one. The question was which one was it?

"You always do what you know to be right," a hooded shadowy figure stepped out from the darkness right in front of her. Grace took a quick step back. The man wore a long black cloak with the hood hiding his head and face. Only his dark eyes were visible, icy and emotionless they mirrored an old soul. "Mother guides and protects you," his old and tired voice was followed by a soft heartbroken sigh. "But in the end, you'll be on your own."

"I…" Grace wanted to say something, but the stranger interrupted as he raised his hand.

"Hush. I'm not talking to you, my child. I'm talking to Angeni," he said almost silently.

"Angeni? Who, who is Angeni?" she asked, but the stranger shook his head. He crouched down in front of Grace and looked deep into her eyes.

"You're in a hurry, but you won't be late. Destiny always brings you where you're needed the most," whispered his calm old voice. "You always know the answer you're looking for. Never hesitate, and never fear to ask. Always trust your instincts and never forget; nothing and no one is what they first appear to be. Now close your eyes."

Darkness embraced the little girl as she closed her eyes. Her instincts told her what to do. She tried to empty her troubled mind, which insisted on believing that something really happened to Aurora.

"Where is she?" she queried her guardian in the hope that she would offer guidance. But no response came. Grace waited while all the surrounding noises faded to the endless silence, escorted by that false crystal chime that she had almost completely forgotten; yet, it still echoed in the back of her mind.

Where is she?

The vast darkness was slowly replaced by sapphire sunlight, little yellow and white jasnaia flowers in a huge beautiful garden. A little apoidea flew from flower to flower; the wind softly blew the petals in the cold air. The sniffling of her little sister found Grace's ears. For a moment, Grace had seen Aurora's terrified tearful green eyes. They reflected a large oak, the flowers, and a tiny green kimama, which circled around her. Grace felt the fear; her sister believed no one would find her and she would be lost forever. She wanted her mother and father and she wanted her big sister who always protected her.

The jasnaia garden, the answer struck into Grace's mind as she recognized the place. Her eyes snapped open to face the stranger, but he was nowhere, was gone. Surprised, she looked around, but she was alone in the dark alley.

Grace was running before she gave it thought, her steps echoed on the cobblestones. The garden wasn't far. Last Deciduous when they were in Odess'iana, her mother told her if she was separated, they would all meet in the jasnaia garden, which grew at the very top of the inner wall; the wall that always watches Sachylia when it goes down. She was amazed that Aurora still remembered this at all. But for a moment, Grace wasn't sure her guardian showed her the way. The inner voice, which guided her, now told her the answer was so different.

Maybe this is the instinct of a guardian. The magic of eleven-eleven, she wondered as she ran fast. *But who was this mysterious stranger? And who is Angeni? Is that the name of my mysterious guardian angel?*

After a short time, she arrived at the smooth foot warn stone steps that inclined up to the garden and raced up. At the top step, Grace looked around.

Aurora sat alone among the yellow and white jasnaia flowers in the small garden under the shadow of a large oak. A very small green-winged kimama flew around her. The scared little girl wept to herself while she hugged her legs close. It seemed to Grace that the small kimama was guarding Aurora.

"Thank you, Sacred Mother. Thank you, my guardian," Grace whispered as she strolled closer to Aurora, who noticed her immediately.

"Gracie!" Aurora got up in a rush. "I just wanted to hug the beautiful white tasunke," she sniffed. "He went away and I tried to find him. I got lost and I…" the heartbroken little girl wept. Grace held her close. Even without wings, she was her little sister's guardian angel.

"I'm here with you, my sister," she kissed Aurora's forehead. "You're not alone. I'll never let you go."

Aurora slowly calmed down, but still cried softly. Grace quietly began to sing.

Oh, my sister, don't be blue,
Your sister is right here beside you.
I'm protecting you; I'm with you forever,
I'm with you my kind, my beauty little sister.
Don't cry please, don't fear my dear,
You have a guide and are safe; Our Guardians are near.

Aurora wiped the teardrops from her eyes while she smiled up at her big sister. But Grace already gazed at something, seemingly amazed.

"Look at that, Aurora," she whispered in awe. "The sun goes down."

Sachylia majestically approached the horizon. Bathed in the last light of the setting sun, the sisters felt its mighty power. In this shared touching moment, their flesh rippled to goose bumps. The cold sapphire beams painted the small white clouds shades of orange and the blue streaks darkened like stained glass as the rays tinted their eyes blue. It felt like on all Eecrys Aredia, Sachylia watched just the two of them. As if Sachylia wanted to say farewell with its magnificent existence before she disappeared.

"Crystal nightfall, sister," Grace whispered to Aurora. "A perfect nightfall in light," she stroked her little sister's hair, and Aurora returned Grace's love with a hug. This was their perfect moment.

The last brightness of cold sapphire beams waved to the sisters and slowly disappeared behind the tall mountains.

Peace and silence fell on the garden. Only that strange false chime echoed once again in Grace's mind.

* * *

"They never forgot that perfect twilight they saw together," continued the misty-eyed old man while the children listened. He saw everything crystal-clear in his mind as if it happened just yesterday.

A story is not equal to experience, the wise phrase flashed into his mind, a phrase that he first heard a lifetime ago. The wise one who said this to him was right, but he just now realized it. He knew that his words could not give the children the exact touching atmosphere that the two sisters had experienced.

I will try to share my knowledge as best as I can, old friend, he thought.

"Grace and Aurora saw many sunsets throughout their lives, but this was the most beautiful sunset that they ever saw," he continued. "It was Sachylia's last present to the clear, innocent souls of the sisters. The last, but the grandest crystal nightfall of their young lives."

2 – WHAT YOU LEAVE BEHIND

"The future in a Crystal Shade is always born of pain and suffering," said the old man to the two little children. "The future, which builds from the past and present, be it a life full of joy and happiness or a life of pain and suffering. We're simply the ghosts of our past, haunting our own ruin in the future." The old man stopped, deep sorrow darkened his soul as he thought back on his life, and then continued with a faraway look in his eyes.

"In my time many said our people had no present, just a long sad past overflowing with cruelty, a void and chaotic darkness. They believed we had no future, just dreams," the old man added before he continued. "You see we forget that our present is just a moment when we make an effort to remember our joys and pains. An unavoidable moment to remember those we had to leave behind when the time came. It is a chance to regret our decisions or remember the greatest and happiest moments of our lives. But reconciliation is always followed by the glory of rebirth."

The old man studied the children for a moment and continued.

"For her soul, that beautiful and unforgettable night gave this moment. But like everyone else, she also needed to leave something behind to step further along the marked path of her destiny. She was no exception."

*　*　*

The night had fallen a long time ago. The sky was full of stars, and Eecrys Aredia's little pale astral guardian Carenia Seli watched from above, shown in all her full ghostly finery. Hazel brown eyes tried to focus, but saw only darkness and the small flames that flickered close to her.

The warm feeling, the dancing ocean of orange and yellow. It's so peaceful, Grace thought in awe, but then the smoke began to hurt her eyes. Tired, she let her eyes close to avoid the tendrils of smoke. Otherwise, she felt great, and free.

The smell of fire. And that other smell, she sniffed once into the air. Her nose took in the scent of fresh roasted meat in the air. *It's like the delicious msikwatash, with roasted beans, and corn,* she thought. The smell reminded her of the meat that her mother always made near the fire. Her father and Aurora usually ate the msikwatash with fish, but she and her mother always ate it with meat. But now, she didn't want to eat. She wasn't hungry. Her mind was scattered, but she opened her eyes again.

Everything is so peaceful and quiet. The stars are watching me. All of them, she smiled to herself. *But they seem so sad. Why?* she wondered. *Finally, the false crystal chime is gone. But what was it? Where did it come from? I don't know. I should sleep. I'm so tired,* she thought, as she desired sleep. The smoke, pushed by a light breeze stung her eyes again. She closed them and complete darkness surrounded her. *Maybe I'm going to dream about our nightfall. The crystal nightfall that we saw, my beloved sister, Aurora and I,* she thought while love filled her heart. *It was so beautiful. And it's night already. What a wonderful night it was. The perfect ending to this day; the day I was a guardian. But I promised to mother I will sleep early tonight. The light of the fire will keep the Daharra away while I fall asleep.*

Grace felt herself slowly step from reality to the land of fluid and untouchable dreams. She saw the stars in her mind. There were more than there are grains of sand on the shoreline. Not so long ago, the stars were happy, unlike now. So shy, they peeked from behind the small clouds at her and Odess'iana this beautiful night.

The false crystal chime had sounded softly again as Grace; along with her mother, father, and Aurora, had watched the opening ceremony of the Great Deciduous Feast.

That crystal music. Where is it coming from? she asked in her thoughts. The cold wind stroked her cheek as she looked around. The breeze slowly shepherded the yellow leaves along the cobblestones of the main square. The torches and light crystals were already lit on the houses and the crowd gathered. Enraptured, along with her family she had watched the noble rulers of Odess'iana, Thobadzistshin and his graceful wife Hastseolti, who stood beside him, as they prepared to open the Feast.

But instead of them, Grace looked back at the white fountain topped by a large alabaster statue stone angel statue, which cast its shadow at her. She specifically chose this place when they came in to watch the opening ceremony. This statue was her favourite. She couldn't explain why, but it always drew her here.

The statue, a mysterious High-Guardian woman stood on a pillar and embraced a baby, her wings spread defensively. Her eyes showed great love, as well as the determination and fear of one who will not lose her babe without a fight. The statue had enchanted her when she first saw it cycles ago; the motionless, winged statue that she called the

Guardian Mother. Somehow, she also felt safe here, but she didn't know why.

In reality, the statue had no name. No one knew who carved this beautiful old statue, but Grace felt that the name that she called it perfectly described it. And the cold air, the atmosphere of Deciduous that she always loved, the night and the pale glow of Carenia Seli just made the Guardian Mother even more perfect and lovely in her eyes.

In Odess'iana, most people secretly called the statue the Fountain of Time. Many have seen something in their mirror image when they looked into it. Some said old ones sometimes saw their long forgotten past and remembered who they were. Young ones said sometimes they saw their dreams, the image showed them the path to what they want or what is destined for them. And those who saw their own mirror image, they say, saw their present in the water, which meant those would remain the same throughout their lives.

Like everyone else that didn't experience the fountain's magic, Grace never questioned these legends, never questioned the words of others. However, her soul also never fully accepted them until she saw it with her own eyes. Whenever she came here, she always tried to confirm the myths of the fountain. Regardless that she had never experienced anything before, she always feared a little to face the water. Like many times before, she was curious. As always, she hesitated to look into it and kept her distance from the edge.

"Look. It has begun," whispered her mother with great excitement. Grace turned around. The rulers looked at the people from the center of the large garden as they made wondrous the ritual opening of the Great Feast. It was a tradition that was well known in Odess'iana for the last hundred cycles or even more.

In accordance with their duty as rulers of Odess'iana, every Great Deciduous Festival Thobadzistshin and Hastseolti planted a sapling in the garden. Those trees planted by the rulers before them and that they had planted in the last cycles had grown into a beautiful living heaven. Everyone watched as the noble rulers bent to the task of a gardener, but no one ever despised them for this. Throughout Eecrys Aredia, the rulers were behind many good works, but sometimes they did much more than the people had seen.

Just as many Odess'ianans had, Grace also heard the legend of Thobadzistshin and Hastseolti. While they controlled the province, they sometimes also disguised themselves and mixed in the crowd. Some said sometimes they shared their wisdom in disguise. Others said they went out to the far ocean of Aesara Alira, which was the western border of the eleventh province or to their southern border to the large gulf of Inari and its fishermen to work with them. They helped farmers or built buildings and roads along with the people.

No one ever confirmed these legends, but in Eecrys Aredia, it was the way of life. Despite their ranks, everyone was equal, even the rulers. They knew how hard the work could be sometimes and they shared the weight with their people.

As Grace saw the shovels in Thobadzistshin and Hastseolti's hands, she realized that the myths could be true. The rulers worked the hard ground with a smooth routine, just as her father and mother used to work the soil back at Seradelphia; the routine that only real farmers and gardeners would have.

She never saw the rulers this close before, but as Carenia Seli's light lit them, they seemed so familiar to her as they stood between the trees full of colourful ribbons. Grace stepped ahead few steps to see them better and look into their eyes, which mirrored their soul. She slowly touched the magic symbol on her forehead.

"The Strangers of Odess'iana," she whispered in amazed awe.

Excited, she looked at her father and mother. Deep in her heart, she wanted to tell them her great revelation, but then she hesitated. It was still today and eleven bound her. Grace looked back at the two kind rulers who dug with great joy. For a moment it felt like Thobadzistshin and Hastseolti curiously measured her from the corner of their eyes as if they wanted to see if she would share their secret or not.

Then Grace looked back at her parents who watched the rulers with the utmost respect. Like many others, her parents were also curious if the legend of the respectful rulers was true. Grace said nothing. She didn't want to strip anyone's excitement, the sense of revelation, and foremost, she still was the youngest guardian in disguise. Someday her parents may also meet with the Strangers of Odess'iana before they make their own exciting revelation. But now, the secret of the rulers would be her little secret.

With a broad grin, Grace looked toward the rulers. Thobadzistshin and Hastseolti had finished digging and they lifted the sapling and brought it carefully to its new home. They looked proudly toward the crowd.

"Eecrys Aredia gave her bounty in crops, food and fresh crystal-clear water to our families!" Thobadzistshin declared.

"We're here to celebrate the riches of Prosperous and Deciduous that she has given us!" Hastseolti smiled over the crowd and raised her arm to them. "To the people of Odess'iana, to the people of Eecrys Aredia!"

"What she gave to us, so are we willing to give back to her," intoned Thobadzistshin. "She provides for us like a loving mother, as her children it is our duty to care for her in turn. She gave us life and taught us to give life to our lands. Let this sapling be the symbol of the past, the present, and the future. Eecrys Aredia will see us through her roots and when this little tree has grown like its brothers and sisters, she will see not just the richness of our love, or our beloved city and land, but also that of generations that will care for her, our beloved mother, Eecrys Aredia."

"Like a guardian, treat our beloved home, our motherland Eecrys Aredia and all that dwell here with respect as we do not inherit her from our ancestors, we borrow it from our children," Hastseolti said with reverence. Grace felt that Queen Hastseolti looked right at her and addressed mostly her from the distance.

"I will," promised Grace almost without a tone, with pride in her little heart. As if Hastseolti could read her lips, almost unnoticed, she thankfully nodded to Grace; the youngest guardian of Odess'iana.

Thobadzistshin and Hastseolti gently lowered the sapling into its hole and covered it with soil. The lady ruler picked up an elegant dark tasunke hair pot and gave the first measure of water to the newly planted sapling in the garden. Everyone watched in silent pride. After she finished, she put down the pot and turned with her husband to the crowd. The gardeners reverted to the kind rulers that everyone knew. Thobadzistshin held his wife's hand gently and nodded to her.

"Let the Great Feast of Odess'iana begin!" Hastseolti crowed as excitement escaped her regal decorum.

Everyone cheered while flutes, pipes, drums, and stringed instruments came up. Their unique Odess'ianan tune boomed from the far corner of the sqaure. Dancers, artists, and people in beautiful masquerade costumes flooded in from the streets.

Not far from the main gates, Grace and her family stood. They had a grand view of the entire ceremony.

"The performance of Azen and Vessa will start soon," her excited mother said. She held Aurora, and kept a sharp watch on her littlest daughter. Margey wore the necklace that Grace had brought for her.

"Aurora?" Eion offered the last delicious Crystanan ice fruit to her. The little girl shook her head, and then turned back to watch the dancers with silent awe-filled eyes.

Temptation threatened Grace as her father looked at her with the last delicious ice fruit in his hand. She wanted just one more, but she

56

knew her mother had eaten the least of the fruit. Most of them had landed in gluttonous Aurora's belly. This bothered none of them at all; her sister was the youngest, she needed to eat much more, and the fruit made everyone's body healthier.

"My belly is full, thank you very much," she shook her head and played her majestic role while she forced her hand behind her back before the temptation could overwhelm her and she grabbed the fruit. She felt her mother deserved it more than she. Silently, she watched her father fondly put the fruit into her mother's mouth and the last delicious fruit quickly disappeared to dissolve Grace's temptation. A lovely smile stole over Grace's face as she saw her mother thankfully nod to her father.

"We still have time," said Eion. "What would you like to do? Would you like to explore the feast?"

"We may stay and watch the dancers' masquerade parade if you like," her mother responded with a smile, then looked at her youngest daughter and whispered into her ears. "What do you think, Aurora?" she asked, but the awed, enchanted little girl stayed silent. Instead, her green eyes, which mirrored the happy people who danced in their colourful clothes and masks, answered and quickly ended the debate; she'd like stay to watch them, too.

Grace looked around to her favourite statue once more. The little girl fell into a trance while everything went silent around her.

Let's try again, Gracie my dear, she thought to herself while she peered into the crystal-clear water of the fountain at the foot of the Guardian Mother's pedestal. The water's surface rippled slightly, blurring her mirror image, and when it cleared it was no longer Grace's face staring back at her.

A young beautiful blond haired winged Aserian woman looked up curiously, but she seemed lost and sad. Her white-feathered wings were spread wide before they lowered behind the woman's back. Behind her, the large faultless crystal watched; the mirror reflection of the night sky that watched her from above. A soft crystal chime came to her ears again, the kindest crystal chime voice that Grace had ever heard. The chime came from the crystal, its motherly voice called her.

The winged woman seemed too familiar to Grace. She was sure they'd ever met. She was a young Aserian, but she wasn't her Guardian. She felt it. Then the crystal behind the woman became brighter and brighter. It enchanted the little girl. The brightness beamed endless peace and protection toward her. It called her. But Grace resisted. She didn't want to go, wherever the voice called her. Not now.

Soft waves distorted the image, and when the water's surface calmed, the stranger's image along with that strange crystal was gone. Grace saw only her own face in the fountain. She looked up to tell her mother and father what she saw, but she wasn't in Odess'iana anymore and the fountain was also gone.

"Where am I? What is this place?" she asked quietly as she looked around. Eleven columns in a large dark hall shadowed her; an angel statue guarded each of them. "Mommy? Daddy? Anyone?"

Carvings, symbols, runes, and hieroglyphs watched her from all over the walls and columns as she slowly strolled toward the center of a hall. The entire hall centered on that horizontal and flat circular plate, full of carved regular lines; a large shiny seal embedded in the ground. Like a tired heart, it pulsed sapphire blue reaching out and called her soul with soothing crystal chime music. But as she stepped closer to the *seal*, the crystal chime music became sad and menacing. Her bare feet felt the large *seal's* surface was pure crystal as she stepped onto it. Wary, she strolled to the middle and looked down into it. Her mirror image wasn't hers anymore.

That beautiful winged Aserian looked back at her again. This time there was no trace of emotion in the woman. She seemed ruthless, cold as ice. Then after a moment, Grace was able to read the Aserian's face, even without words and emotions. Guilt and sadness exuded from the woman, it cried from her icy soul.

Grace wanted to help her, speak with her, but she remained silent.

The pulsating sapphire surface flicked to dark red and beat on like a bleeding heart. Vanishing, the Aserian woman and the mirror image were replaced by something else, something darker. The crystal-chime music became more menacing than ever before, urging the young girl to run far away as fast she could. Yet, she stood mesmerized by the pulsing crystal surface beneath her feet.

Darkness and cruelty whispered from a yawning void. She was alone in the hall, yet she wasn't and it terrified her. Someone patiently watched her from down below, from the other side of the pulsating *seal*. But not just one, thousands dwelled on the other side and only the crystal surface prevented them from reaching and touching her. These souls were not human and they were not Aserian. They were something else. They hated her. They wanted to hurt her. They wanted to kill her. Her own desperate scream echoed as a strong dark hand reached through the crystal surface and grabbed her ankle to pull her down.

Darkness crashed in on Grace as she bolted awake from the nightmare, but her eyes remained closed. Her mind grappled with the suddenness of the change.

What did I dream? she wondered. *I can't remember. I saw that beautiful Aserian woman in my reflection and then...* she paused her thoughts, but she couldn't remember the rest of her dream.

Maybe I should tell mother and father what I saw in the fountain. Did they see what I saw? Who was that woman? She was beautiful. Yes. I should tell them. But not today, she decided, smiling to herself. She wanted to fall asleep again, to dream something better than the nightmare she had forgotten.

Her body was tired, yet her soul wandered while angelic music and a choir echoed in her mind. Someone sang from afar.

"In my sleep your voice sang to me!" echoed the male's beautiful baritone.

"Please my love, fight bravely!" a young female responded lovingly.

Am I already dreaming again? Grace wondered. The music brought peace to her restless soul. The song reverberated in the darkness. But not from outside, someone sang within her mind.

"In my dreams you come to me!" called the male's baritone, her love.

"Defeat darkness, please protect me!" the woman pleaded, full of sadness.

In front of her closed eyes, she saw the two lovers, the singers, winged Aserian Viridanas, Sentinels as they sang to each other. Their angelic voices gave word to their feelings.

"Your voice calls me and you say my name!" the winged male took a step closer.

"You must embrace your destiny!" the woman held her ground. The musicians behind them melded their music to their words. Everything was so familiar to Grace. She knew the singers, she had seen them before; but in her blurry mind, she couldn't remember their names.

Don't let him go, Vessa. Grace realized that was the name of the graceful Aserian woman. *Azen loves you,* she continued her thought. The sad Aserian woman slowly pushed Azen away. A great sorrow enfolded him as his wings slumped against his back and he bowed his head.

"Your battle is waiting, my love!" still aloof, Vessa sang, but Azen stepped close, caught her hand, and kneeled in front of her.

"I will never let you go! I will never let you go, my Vessa!" the young male Aserian's angelic voice sang with fervor before he enfolded her in his arms. His wings limp down his back trembled with his warring emotions. The woman looked at him with pure love in her beautiful blue eyes. Watching in rapture, Grace saw tears in the woman's eyes; she knew why. The difference between a human and Aserian performance is; the Aserians never pretend. Their pieces were never dramatized. All of their actions, all their emotions were real.

You'll let him go, she realized as she had seen the eyes of the woman. *But why?*

"You must go," the female Sentinel sang a softer tone while the music slowly faded away. "But my soul will never let you go."

Then deep silence had fallen onto the hall for a long moment. Grace noticed a tear in Vessa's eyes.

Why do you want him to leave you behind? Grace asked herself in disappointment. The ending of the piece didn't make sense to her. She knew Azen and Vessa sang to the audience about their love, about their real feelings. She knew the two lovers would never let each other go, even if the Crystal Shade arrived. Whatever happened, their souls were connected for eternity.

Everyone clapped as the performers and musicians stood up in the Long Hall of Odess'iana to show their respect. Loud applause echoed around the beautiful, decorated hall. Azen, Vessa, and the Aserian musicians stood away from their instruments and bowed to their beloved public from the stone stage. Grace clapped quickly while she grinned at her mother, who dabbed tears from her eyes. She knew her mother was touched, as always.

Grace never understood why, but most of the Aserian pieces were based on their belief of the Crystal Shade; she just loved all the Aserian plays that told at least one fragment from that legend, that untouchable myth. It seemed its story was endless and as all the Aserian pieces were different, they always added something new to her favourite legend. This time, she missed the great battle from the play, - where the Aserians fight and defeat their legendary nemeses, the Shaina, the legions of darkness, the harbingers of death -, and she was a bit disappointed. She felt that all the plays had some sort of basis in reality, just as her mother always told her.

Someday I will find the truth about the Crystal Shade, she thought. *Someday, but not today, Gracie my dear,* the sleepy part of her thoughts argued, and her other, less sleepy part agreed.

"But why do they not stay together if they love each other?" little Aurora asked curiously, who sat on her father's knee while she crossed her arms and raised her eyebrow at him.

Good question, sister, Grace thought while she clapped and smiled at her little sister. Even if she was five, Aurora saw many things and never hesitated to ask.

Eion looked kindly at Aurora. Grace listened, also wanting to hear her father's explanation while she clapped further.

"Sometimes circumstances force people to leave someone or something behind that they love," Eion explained to his little daughter. "Someday, maybe you must leave someone behind too. Maybe you will leave your entire life behind to achieve a greater goal and protect someone that you love."

"If I love someone, I will never let that one go. Never!" Aurora stated in her small, determined way.

"I know, my little angel. I know," Eion planted a kiss on Aurora's forehead.

"I will never let you go, Daddy," she said, throwing her arms around her father's neck.

Eion lightly stroked Aurora's nose. Grace knew that her sister loved this and Aurora was already smiling. Then her little sister yawned.

Margey looked fondly from Aurora to Eion. "We should go home." Eion's tender smile answered her. Grace watched her mother lean closer to Eion and kiss his cheek. "Thank you for this wonderful night."

"Anything for my kind audience," her father bowed his head to her. "Let's go home."

Home, thought Grace, but her mind was so tired. *Yes. I should go home. Mother is waiting for me. I know she is calling me. She is calling all of us. But I'm so tired. I want to sleep in my soft feathery bed.*

The Great Hall slowly dissolved in her mind. She was awakened again, yet somehow she was unable to completely wake. Grace didn't remember opening her eyes. A few larger dark clouds covered Eecrys Aredia's eternal little guardian, Carenia Seli, and the stars. The smoke didn't hurt her eyes anymore, even if it did still whirl around her.

Where am I? she thought fondly before looking around. Somehow everything was different, even the smoke that surrounded her. But confused, she couldn't explain what.

Blue smoke? she thought in awe. *It covers everything. It's beautiful. It's so different from the blanket of orange and red silk that I'm afraid of. But why? I don't know. The blue smoke is like dancing velvet. It's calming me.*

Something splat on the ground once, and then repeatedly.

It's raining, she chuckled to herself. *Tomorrow morning will be great. I love the wet, cold mornings after night storms when the wind carries the smell of the passed rain.*

Grace looked around and noticed something familiar in the smoke. Her beloved papyrus scroll pamphlet sat on the ground under a large chunk of curved metal. Her small arven pencil sat beside it. The pages ruffled lightly in the breeze, but they stayed under cover. She watched small raindrops hit the top of the metal, slowly glide down the shiny surface, and then after a short freefall, plop into the small puddle near the pamphlet.

My papyrus scrolls are safe. I will draw on you soon. But not now. I should sleep. I hear the howling of a mingan. It is not so far. Maybe it's the Daharra. I'm so sleepy, she almost whined to herself. *I want to sleep and dream. But that night. What a beautiful night it was.*

Her soul dimly heard the wind sigh, which brought another beautiful memory to the surface while her dreams embraced her. She heard a wind like the soft stroke of wing tips, a silver Anshara.

"Ane, rhe, shaia," her own voiced counted in Aserian in her mind.

We're going home, she thought with relief. *Home.*

"Senra, 'yra, meda, vye, senia, shena, 'yren, ane'yren." As she reached eleven, something loud rumbled not so far away.

What, what was this rumbling? her thought terrified while she looked around. She calmed as she found herself in the night, which embraced the flying Anshara.

"So?" asked her father.

"Eleven moments. That's eleven thousand steps; one league," grinned Grace as she determined the distance of the far off lightning and the storm that raged. Her father proudly nodded.

Strange. I feel light. Lighter than the air, her soul thought. *Flying. Strange. It is frightening. But why? I have never been afraid of it before,* she meditated. *I know I'm safe. But I hate flying.*

Grace saw the passing darker shadows of trees below and the storm clouds at a distance. A small green orb zipped up and paced them on the starboard side of the craft.

"Look, mother," Margey looked back at Grace.

"Aurora. Look. A Guardian," Margey whispered to her sleepy daughter who rested in her arms. Little Aurora looked at the small orb and her sleepy eyes smiled.

"Is he guarding Chosovi?" her soft voice asked while the orb rounded the craft and flew to the starboard side near Aurora. The orb peeked into the craft while Aurora put her tiny hand on the transparent wall.

"They're always guarding and watching over us, Aurora," their father responded while he followed the orb with his eyes. "They're always with us, even if we do not see them."

"Come in, Aserian," Aurora invited sweetly. The orb slowly passed through the wall. Aurora opened her little palm, the green orb floated above it.

"He knows my name. He is guarding me," Aurora whispered with a smile. Her mother watched Aurora study the orb.

Grace knew that her sister was seeing her guardian in his orb form for the first time. She didn't want to say anything. She remembered when she first saw the guardian in her life and she was never going to forget the thrill of that even if she didn't remember her face.

This soul had watched over Aurora since her birth. Now, this was her sister's priceless moment. It was the moment when he revealed himself for a short time to his human charge and she finally met her guardian spirit. The first encounter took the crown on that wonderful night. As Grace watched the green orb, it told a lot with its color; unlike her guardian, Aurora's green aura guardian described a balanced, harmonious, and peaceful personality. He needed harmony in his life. He was open, extroverted, expressive, friendly, communicative, and heartfelt. One who perfectly fit her little sister.

Grace had already thought the green kimama in the jasnaia garden was sent by her sister's guardian to watch over her. *Did you guide her there?*

"He said he will be with me forever." Awed, Aurora looked to her mother. "He says I need to sleep now," she continued while she looked back at the orb, her voice, and face pouting. "Don't go, my Guardian. Please," begged the little girl, and then after a short moment she smiled. "Yes, I promise."

The bright orb circled above Aurora's palm. She giggled before the green orb raced through the transparent wall and up into the darkness.

"Ta-ta, Guardian. Ta-ta," Aurora waved after the orb. She put her nose to the transparent wall, while her mirroring eyes followed the orb for a long time until it disappeared in the clouds. The little girl yawned greatly, and then curiously watched the clouds in the hope the shiny orb would return.

"Always remember this moment, my baby girl," her mother whispered into her ear. After a second yawn, Aurora looked back at her. Her eyes whispered her little soul's desire for sleep.

Margey looked fondly at the sleepy daughter in her arms and gently kissed her forehead.

"It's time to sleep, Aurora," she whispered and sung to her.

Sleep, my darling, I will be here,
Sleep, my little angel until morn's near.
Sleep deep, sleep well, my little child of light,
Sleep well my angel, sleep well tonight.

Aurora's eyelids slowly drooped. The little girl innocently yawned while she fell asleep. Grace watched her beloved sister dive into the world of dreams in the arms of their mother. The song awoke long forgotten feelings in Grace, who also loved this lullaby. Her mother had sung this to her too when she was younger. Her angelic voice brought indescribable joy to everyone who heard it; her tenderness brought peace to everyone's heart.

A soft noise slid into Grace's sensitive ears, a cracking sound. She looked around, but she saw nothing. Then she heard the soft noise again. It was the unmistakable, delicate sound of glass or ice slowly fracturing. She couldn't tell where the noise came from. It disturbed her, her restless soul felt danger, and knew that something was not right. Her mother looked back at Grace and smiled.

"I love you, my little angel," she whispered to her older daughter.

A bright flash of distant lightning blinded Grace and awakened her soul to the blue whirling smoke that once again danced around her.

I should go home. Home, calm, she thought. Suddenly an opening emerged in the smoke and a curious looking shadowy silhouette rested on the ground. *Who could be sprawled within the whirling blue smoke?* she wondered. *Maybe they can help me and tell me where I am and how to get home. I want to go home to sleep.*

Grace wanted to move, but she felt so weak. The sapphire spiritual world swirled around her soul while the shape in front of her became clearer.

It's me. And our Anshara. I'm lying among the wreckage of Chosovi, she realized, but her soul somehow remained calm. She was embraced by endless love and peace, yet a little disappointment crept in. *My face and my hair are dirty. But the rain is cleaning the dirt. My beautiful sapphire clothes are rent and burned,* she thought with great sorrow. *My mirroring eyes are gazing toward the stars. I'll watch them for eternity. I always loved the stars. I'm watching my home, where all of us came from. I feel it, and the rain that douses the fire that burns me. Eecrys Aredia is sad, crying for me, crying for us all. But her tears will make the morning beautiful. I await that morning. But I need to go home. Mother is waiting for me. She is calling me.*

A lightning strike nearby blinded Grace's lonely little soul. In the next moment, a hooded shadowy figure crouched in front of her; that strange mysterious old man from Odess'iana. But now he had wings. The wind softly blew his ancient, worn, and ragged wings; he was an old Aserian. Like before, he wore a long black cloak with the hood hiding his face. Only his eyes were visible and gazed down at her, they watched her with love and tenderness. Even though it was dark, they mirrored emptiness and void, which scared Grace's lonely soul.

Long time no see, Angeni, the thoughts of the shadowy figure rattled around her soul. Like his voice back in the alley, his thoughts were tired and old. His shape blurred in the swirling spiritual world.

Angeni. Why is he calling me Angeni? her soul wondered, but she felt and knew; unlike before, now the stranger addressed her directly with this name. *My, my name is Grace. And...*

Her soul suddenly awakened at the thought of her own name and became desperate as she realized what had happened. Wounds quickly opened in the soul's memory. Every thought of her past poured in, the joyful as well as painful memories flooded her existence.

The first day she met her newborn sister, Aurora, the joyful days that her family spent together. The days were spent under the cold blue beams of Sachylia, in the large grassy meadow where she watched her favourite tasunkes at play. Her very first imaginary self-portrait, a stick angel with the wings she always dreamt of, the first sketch of her family and the beautiful smile of her mother. She saw her father's love when he brought a small gift to his little angel's seventh birthday. The gift garnered during the long trips with mom, dad and sister in the seventh and the eleventh provinces to discover the unknown. The sometimes defiant, if kind and curious behavior of her little sister and the memories as they happily played on the large grassy plain near their home in Seradelphia memory teased her. The moment she made her promise to protect Eecrys Aredia. She smiled thinking of the kind fire breather, who taught her how to tame the fire. And the green kimama that guarded her lost sister before they watched the beautiful crystal nightfall together. She could still hear the music and the singing in the Odess'ianan Long Hall, as well as that lovely small green orb.

Then the fear hit and the horror in the eyes of her family members.

The aura ball! It shattered! Birdie didn't listen to father's will anymore! she panicked as she remembered a loud noise; something broke away from the Anshara. The ground that screamed closer all the while she wanted to stay away from it. She feared height for the first time. She didn't want to fly anymore, but she couldn't do anything to stop her fall.

Deafening and awful screeching that shattering impact and fear was the last moment of all their lives.

That colourful cloud; the deadly blanket of orange and red silk! I'm afraid of it! I don't want to see it! It's just hurting me! Mom? Dad? Where are you? And where is Aurora? Mommy? Daddy! Sister! her panicked thoughts desperately cried, but she didn't get any response. She slowly calmed as the memories faded and she found herself in the peaceful calm blue realm. *They're gone. I'm alone. I'm afraid. Someone please. Help,* begged the lonely soul in sorrow and fear that wanted to cry, but couldn't.

Another lightning bolt stuck right behind the mysterious figure. The soul trembled and feared from him.

Please, don't hurt me. Please.

Don't fear, Angeni, came the calm tender thoughts of the stranger. *I would never hurt you.*

I'm alone. I'm so tired. I want to go home and sleep. Please, help me, the heartbroken soul thought while an all-encompassing fatigue tried to overwhelm her. *Music. I, I hear crystal music. Who, who plays it?* her enchanted soul wondered while soft clear and innocent crystal music wrapped around her trembling existence. *It is so soft and soothing, the voices of a thousand kind spirits.*

You must go now. Mother is calling you, the voice of the stranger whispered in her mind. *The beginning has just ended. The time of the one in the midst of all has come. The journey to the end is just begun.* The friendly thoughts of the stranger pulsed like blood rushing in her head, merged with the music, which came from everywhere, yet nowhere.

Sapphire light flashed in front of the tired soul. She didn't care about anything else, just the music, and the light that calmed her fear, emitted endless love, and called her.

Beautiful, her soul thought with awe as the sapphire light slowly embraced her. *Sachylia is just coming up. She makes the perfect beginning of a new perfect day.*

It's your perfect new day, Angeni, murmured the tender thoughts of the stranger as the light embraced and overwhelmed her soul. *Your life has just begun.*

* * *

"Life," said the old man. "It's a strange, fluid word in my civilization. In my time, many believed that only flesh and blood beings were able to live a real life, capable of creating civilizations, doing miracles, giving or taking the lives of other living beings, controlling the world itself and setting the rules for the future. But in reality, life itself is what your spirit, your soul is living and experiencing, your spirit's actions over all its existence, regardless that it's in a physical body or living free without any material bonds," the old man told the children. "In the Crystal Shade, most of the valiant, noble heroes were born and their real life began after they left their fragile shell."

3 – ANGENI

"As with all of our souls, hers belonged to the mother of us all," continued the old man. "She was her mother's child, but unlike other souls, she was a faultless and innocent crystal soul. The Crystal Mother called her, and yet, not as she called others. Her human life had to end so a new life could begin the life for which she was created. The life that was her real destiny."

* * *

A bright light blinded the lonely fragile soul, but as sudden as the light came, it faded away. The swirling sapphire spiritual realm surrounded the soul. Many soft shiny crystal shards that seemed like dots shone gently on the tapestry of the spiritual universe. The soul felt as if she was in a dream, yet her instincts knew she was not.

Frightened, she drifted in the river of souls with thousands more. Others left some of the crystal shards and joined the fast flowing ethereal river coursing toward the center of the realm. Each water drop was a soul. Souls of every color imaginable glowed. They also felt alone and feared the unknown as the lonely soul did.

I am afraid. I'm soft, weak, and all alone. Thousands of other souls surround me. The lonely desperate soul thought. *They're strangers to me, yet I know they're my brothers and sisters. They always were. I feel them. I hear them. Yet everyone is silent. No one is speaking. Mommy? Daddy? Aurora? Where are you?* she asked desperate, but no one responded. The crystal music called and drew her further as it drew every other soul toward the unknown flow in the river.

The music is calling and calming me. It whispers that my family is safe. I'm safe. All of us are safe. Always. Peace and harmony embrace me. I'm not afraid anymore. Mother is calling me, calling all of us. I'm her child, as all of us are. I was there before, where all of us are heading. Like all the souls in our fragile crystal universe, I was there at the creation of everything. I know that place. My soul was born there. The soul rejoiced as forgotten memories seeped in to fill her existence.

That's my home. I'm going home. Home. I know that every place she ever created is my home, because every place lies inside home. Strange, the soul meditated as she drifted along the river of souls. Around it floated millions of crystal tears, stars, projecting their multicolored light into the endless tapestry of the celestial garden, each told its story to the Creator. They all originated in the endless celestial crystal garden entombed within a large, faultless crystal; our Crystal Mother.

Thousands of Soul Rivers all around the crystal garden flowed into and out of the large, faultless crystal that sang them onward with its crystal voice to call her children home. The multicolored soul river streamed toward her, as thousands more left the crystal and headed back toward the crystal tears from which they'd sprung. It was like a large cosmic carousel that worked for eternity. The lonely soul felt that many of them were full of love, peace, and happiness, even disappointment while others were fuelled by hate and anger, but they also respected each other. Then as they approached the center of the faultless crystal, their souls calmed.

They had arrived.

I was here at the creation that started everything, but I forgot how it happened. I have only blurry memory fragments that flash in from time to time. I know I don't need to force my own soul to remember, because she is telling me everything. I'm not hearing her voice, and yet I am. It's an angelic echoing in my mind while the calm crystal music plays. Mother is not using words. The crystal music is her beautiful voice.

As the river of souls flowed into the Crystal Mother, the river separated. The light colored, peaceful souls split off to head toward the top point of the spirit crystal, while the dark, angry souls drifted down the lower flow that lead to her bottom point. As the lonely soul arrived to where the river separated, she stopped. Peace, joy and love echoed and called her from above. However, the soul also heard the painful screams far below, and feared that place.

Something stopped her. She felt that she did not belong to either of those places. The music called her existence to the center, which ended in a great bright light.

Mother is proud of us, all of us. But she tells this only to me. She has chosen me. I feel it. I'm the child that mother is proud of. But why?

The lonely soul felt her mother's invisible spirit arms draw it out from the mass of souls. She felt that the other souls watched her and they, all of them, were proud and respected her being.

Mother, thought the soul in divine happiness as she arrived home. Embraced by love and tenderness, the mother soothed her existence. They had time. They were together. Mother was glad to see her child.

Please, tell your story, the soul whispered to her mother.

The lone soul felt her mother's happiness and pride. Not many of her children wanted to hear her story. The others wanted to go home

69

after their long journey. They wanted to rest. Her curious little one was home with her and wanted to hear her story.

Everything is coming back as she shows and reminds me how she created everything, how everything had started.

Mother's crystal voice slowly shaped words within the lone soul as if it were her own inner thoughts.

Mother felt alone in the emptiness that surrounded her. The others left her a long time ago. She was a fragile soul, a lonely bright light in the night. Mother was a mother by nature; it was for her to create. And she did. She created souls who would be able to understand her. She wanted to nurture and love souls as a mother. These new souls were her little children. She had created her first two souls as opposites. They loved and cared for each other as the greatest souls for a long time. Mother was proud and love filled her heart every moment she looked upon them. Then, something happened. The souls split apart. They were angry. They didn't want to see each other again.

Since mother cared for them both, she created their own separate realms close to herself, one realm above, and one below. As she experienced previously, two different souls may not be able to live in harmony with each other for a long time. She created souls similar to both her first born, and the new souls filled the two realms. After eons, the two realms evolved in different ways; the upper realm embraced light while the lower realm was filled with darkness.

Mother wanted to build a bridge between the two realms to make peace between her children, so she did. But in the end, her children fought against each other. Mother was sorrowful that her children were trying to annihilate each other, she didn't understand the reason. She cut the bridge and separated the two realms from each other, but the war between her children didn't stop.

The lonely soul felt her mother's sorrow as she remembered.

When light and darkness weren't able to wage war directly, they hurled magnificent arrows, but couldn't harm each other. The souls were immortal as was the creator herself, but ignorant as babies, they didn't know it. In their fury, the first souls of the two realms struck with powerful lightning bolt from the heavens above, and one from hell below. The moment they touched, mother revealed herself to stop her disobedient children. She connected their two realms for eternity. But this time, with her soul.

Each word of the Crystal Mother's voice slowly soothed the lonely soul while they shared this great sadness.

The sacred crystal is the soul of the one, the beginning and the end, the creator and the destroyer. Her magnificent crystal soul's top point reached heaven and its bottom point hell. The creator knew that her creations respected her. They both fought for her, but she never understood, why? She treated them the same. Now endless peaces reigned in - hope filled - heaven, while the hate, suffering, viciousness spread through hell and reflected back to them. Mother needed to understand why her disobedient children turned against each other before she could create justice between them.

When her soul felt heaven, she was happy. It was easy to believe in hope and justice. When she felt the spreading darkness from hell, it ate at her, and she became furious, filled with endless hate. She didn't understand these emotions in herself at all. Overwhelmed by their feelings, her soul released them all, which created the crystal garden spreading around her soul. Her tears of sadness filled the crystal brine garden with millions of crystal shards, stars that left her fragile and alone.

The lonely little soul listened to the flow of thoughts and felt that her mother was helpless, afraid of her past and blaming herself for what she had done.

Something else changed that frightened mother. For the first time, she saw her own soul's shadow in the garden, her own dark manifestation. Like everything in the endless universe, her crystal clean soul had its darkness. A dark mirror image that she couldn't banish was her shadow; to forever admit darkness wherever her shadow reached. Throughout history, many have fallen under the rule of darkness, yet many of her brave light souls chased it away to bring peace to her beautiful garden.

The crystal voice embraced and touched the lonely soul. Her mother wanted to tell everything, even if it was so hard for her.

Where our crystal worlds reside and where we, the souls of both places lived under her light and shadow, the crystal garden became the battlefield of the mortal souls to wage their endless war. Our souls are just drops of her crystal tears. But many small drops can build into a river that can soon flush light or darkness from our world. We, her children became the caretakers of her crystal garden. We became the souls who determine if light or darkness was going to feed our crystal tears.

The soul felt the mix of endless love, joy, hate and anger. Her mother shared the feelings she experienced from the time she had connected the two realms.

This was thousands of eons ago, but the endless war still rages between her children, between the light and dark. Each intended to prove their loyalty to mother; each determined to revive the garden and dress up her crystal tears to their vision. They fight for the soul of their Crystal Mother. For her.

The crystal words were saturated with sadness. The soul knew that her mother wanted to be proud of her children; they were her children after all and she was their mother. She wanted to care for them, but the lonely soul felt that her mother felt powerless to stop them, too ancient to understand them.

All souls were created by the sacred soul, by mother, all lived in heaven or hell at one time. The One's mighty power gave them each an independent life to live and have a unique experience, a destiny to discover. Like the shimmering pearl in a shell beneath the ocean, each soul was housed in a physical body for one lifetime. This body was her gift and punishment to her disobedient children. It was a decision she had regretted thousands of times.

The Crystal Mother's words echoed in the lonely soul that began to understand everything that few wanted to know and even less ever understood.

Through their experiences on Eecrys Aredia or one of millions of other small shiny shards in the crystal brine, each spirit matured, gathered experience, unique skills, and grew. When the physical body died, the mature spirit returned to the sacred crystal, bringing the experiences with it, which enabled her to live, grow and share the wisdom of the one with the rest of the souls. What was infinitely more important was to understand why her creations waged war on each other.

Mother believed that her children were capable of changing their mortal lives. Their soul would go to heaven or hell depending on their actions and their soul's desire during their mortal life. All of us are messengers in our unique way. As the messengers of the sacred crystal, the messengers of heaven or hell, the messengers of the one, our actions decide our destiny.

The soul felt the endless love that her Crystal Mother infused with each word.

She knows my spirit being since I'm her child, her young spirit soul. She calls me Angeni. I know I'm not from heaven, nor from hell. Mother created my soul from her sapphire tear. She believes in me. Have I earned her trust? I will be her messenger. She has chosen me for this task. She promises that her eyes will always be on me. Mother will watch over me. I know, I will never be alone. She intends to have my soul understand all. She will guide and protect me through her sapphire tear that watches my fragile crystal shard, Eecrys Aredia. My home.

A bright flash blinded the lonely soul and it found itself shooting toward the spiritual body of Eecrys Aredia and her little night guardian Carenia Seli. The soul recognized them. She could never confuse this place with another. It was her home before. Love filled her entire being. As the soul approached her home, she saw that the endless shadow of her mother slowly followed Eecrys Aredia, but it was still far away.

I was human before. I always kept other's interests in front of my eyes; I always helped everyone as mother had taught me. Now, they must believe and trust in me or my life becomes meaningless and pointless. Their belief and love gives me light. The harmony of their spirit gives me peace and life. I need to guide and protect them well to live, to ensure darkness will never be able to harm me. That's her will. She will understand everything when I finish my long journey and return to her someday. I don't want to leave her, but I must.

A bright flash blinded the soul. She found herself in the stream of the soul river in the dancing, whirling spiritual realm. But now, the soul was alone. Crystal music was her beacon call toward a bright light.

My mortal life is beyond me. I've experienced what mother wanted me to experience. That life has ended, but my true life is still ahead of me. I'm the one who is between the beginning and the end. She is guiding me to it. I must once more meet the end to help her understand everything. I must walk my path and I must connect the beginning with the end. That's her wish. That's my life.

Other souls of different light colors of the rainbow joined the blue soul as an escort on its journey. They headed toward a bright calming light and soft crystal music that drew the lonely soul on. The other souls that guided her on the last leg of her journey belonged to this light. They were the spiritual vanguards of this peaceful realm of Eecrys Aredia. The soul felt this and rejoiced.

The soul of the One, the Sacred Crystal Mother had chosen me to represent her as executrix in my realm. In my soul, I believe I can change the world. In my soul, I believe I can defend the world with my soul, alone if necessary. I can find answers to help mother. There is hope. There is love. There is beauty. There is truth. These unite all of us, be it human or Aserian. I'm warded by mother's mighty holiness, which gives me strength and wisdom. My new name, my new rank unites everything. It may mean one, but it represents millions of souls.

I'm a Guardian, the one protecting everyone, protecting the nation that has survived thousands of eons and brought peace and prosperity to the people of Eecrys Aredia. No human being judges my actions; no human being commands me. I'm above them, I'm a higher being, but I also serve and help the innocents with my delegated wisdom. I must bring light and guidance, and ward mankind to keep the balance for eternity in peace and unity.

The Angeni soul and the souls that escorted it approached the bright light. The formation of the escorting souls quickly opened like the petals of a flower. The dancing spiritual world began to dissolve around the Angeni soul to reveal a new realm beyond it.

A gentle auric ripple disturbed the empty air in the middle of a sanctuary as a small rift formed and connected the spiritual realm with the normal realm. The soul raced out to the world that had awaited her return.

Sachylia's sunlight from the large glass windows beamed right into her, like the sun gave its sapphire light to begin her life. The swirling blue soul gave hints of the indistinguishable human form taking shape as the soul expanded larger and larger high above the ground yet still far from the immense stone ceiling. The bright sapphire aura surrounded the entire Angeni being, while it slowly pulled in to become a beautiful young woman. The semi-transparent angelic body seemed fragile, yet majestic, and graceful. Large pulsing sapphire feathered spirit wings snapped out majestic and wide as the spirit awoke like a lone phoenix from the ashes. The still hovering, slack wings and arms relaxed, the spirit soul looked up toward the ceiling.

Then the spirit body descended lightly to the cold crystal floor to rest on one knee. The Angeni spirit bowed her head; her right hand touched the smooth polished surface that supported her while she retracted her large aura wings loftily behind her back.

Now, I'm the one, the Angeni soul reborn, the Guardian of the Light. The hammer of justice to strike down evil that threatens our world from inside or without; the maker of peace, a safe haven for the lost, giving a small measure of light to the innocent even in the darkest night. I am the representative of the brilliance of the mighty crystal's soul.

The spirit felt the cold polished crystal floor under her bare spirit feet and hand as she gradually became solid. Her skin took on the flush of life, clean, faultless, and healthy; her eyes glowed bright sapphire in the light. Her long straight hair was joined, became solid, and turned to a golden blond as life filled each strand. Unruly, long locks of hair hung down in front of her left eye, which heightened her juvenility. In the meantime, the glowing and whirling shiny aura around her body flashed, and then clung solidly to her as a silk sapphire saree to cover her angelic body. Her wings glowed clean white. Her sapphire blue eyes still glowed toward the floor. Then the bright sapphire light dimmed a bit, it didn't come from the sun anymore. It maybe never did. But it was all around her and beat like a tired heart. The aura on the saree pulsed softly, flashed, and then faded away while it lost its bright color and turned white.

I'm her crystal child, the spirit soul of the One.

The woman of Grace's fountain vision looked up, the blue glow of her eyes vanishing with her first blinked. Her large wings ruffled as they came alive behind her. As her eyelids opened, they revealed young Grace's hazel brown eyes. The sapphire aura pulsed slightly in the whites of her eyes before the aura faded away. Her eyes mirrored her soul; they emitted intelligence, determination, and strength. Everything was a blur around her. The dim light was strange to her eyes.

"I am Angeni," her first utterance echoed softly from her lips, and her eyes flashed sapphire. She had not intended to speak. It was instinctive to say the name her mother had given her.

In the shallow silence, she felt the touch of the gentle cold breeze on her face and silky skin as it ruffled her hair and wings. She closed her eyes and took her first deep breath of the delectable air, filling her lungs with life. The cold air streamed in and out in a plume of mist to cool her body as life spread through her with each slow breath.

She was reborn. Everything was new to her, but also familiar. She had lived before, but this life was so different. Her soul had left this world as a young girl, crushed and broken with a sorrow-filled heart, and now, she was a higher being with knowledge, skill and wisdom, a soul full of hope, love and a strong sense of duty. All of her memories suddenly became a blur. The young guardian wanted to remember how she had come to be here; desperate to remember the place was a short time ago that comforted her with peace, love and protection. She wanted to, but she couldn't remember anything from before she took on solid form. Wherever she was now, her soul missed that other place.

Did I dream it? No, she knew she would get back there one day, but not today. She remembered only a soft, beautiful crystal music that called to her, but that memory slowly faded away too.

The young guardian angel opened her hazel brown eyes and majestically tilted her head to look straight ahead. The blurry spots before her eyes gradually became sharper as her eyes slowly adapted. A middle-aged Aserian woman crouched in front of her. Memories and experience leached into the young guardian's mind, memories she never experienced, never lived. Angeni knew the woman. Her name was Eve, the first, the High-Guardian of her people, the elder of the Aserian race; a beautiful, graceful and majestic woman wrapped in orange. She had large white wings, larger even than the young guardian's. Angeni knew Eve to be her mother, but not literally. She recognized her, she trusted her. But she didn't know why.

The High-Guardian smiled tenderly as she touched Angeni's cold face with a delicate hand.

"Welcome, my child," Eve's echoing angelic voice greeted while her eyes flashed citrine orange. The High-Guardian's voice filled the soul of the young guardian with love, gifting her a feeling of safety. She slowly leaned her head to rest on the High-Guardian's soft palm, closed her eyes and smiled peacefully while her large white wings lovingly embraced her new mother, Eve. Her angelic mother was with her. She was home.

"Welcome home, Angeni," the High-Guardian's whispered echo slowly faded. Her voice returned to normal as she tenderly stroked her daughter's hair. Peace and love filled Angeni. "Welcome home."

* * *

"Like the phoenix from the ashes her innocent soul was reborn that day," the old man told the children. "Angeni arrived home from a long and magnificent journey with knowledge, cunning, skill, wisdom and experience, though it was lost to her memories. She left our realm as a shattered soul of a child and when she returned she had become a young, mature woman; a Guardian sent to our world for one reason, to protect and guide mankind. Angeni was sent as a messenger to the Aserians, the messenger of mother, the Sacred Crystal." The old man met first the girl, and then the boy's eyes with a touch of pride.

"She was the Aserian whose rebirth had been foretold, the one born before the night twilight of the Crystal Shade. But she wasn't the only one."

4 – EVOLUTION OF A GUARDIAN

"A crystal is not polished without rubbing, and not a single Aserian is perfected without trials," the old man said. "Although she was reborn with wisdom, skills and knowledge that put her far above any human, as an Aserian the young guardian was unpolished and crude."

The old man looked at the two children.

"Do you know how life really looks?" he asked of them kindly. "Could you describe to me exactly what it is?" The two children shook their heads.

"No?" chuckled the old man. "I'm not surprised, young ones. Many live it day by day, but only a few can imagine what the real flow of life is."

"Can you tell us?" the little girl asked curiously.

"Telling is not equal with seeing, little princess," he meditated for a moment. "But there is something able to show you how life's flow moves. Come," he invited them while he slowly stood up from his chair. He shuffled to a large old wooden-framed mechanical labyrinth game that hung on the wall. The entire frame was a bit shorter than the children. The labyrinth boasted hundreds of small path segments, junctions, crossroads, and many small doors. Three wooden wheels were attached at the bottom, one small, and two large. Small polished pearls of all imaginable colors sat in a small rack on its left.

"You haven't played this for a long time, old goat," he muttered to himself with amusement. He studied the ancient game before he turned to the children.

"Aserians were the masters of life, and life is just like this Aserian perception game; the game that she and the other Aserians loved to play. Like this labyrinth, which perfectly represents life's flow, every life has a beginning and an end. There is no exception. The only question is, how long will we stay in our own labyrinth?"

The old man turned the small wooden wheel to reveal the entry point at the top while many doors opened and closed throughout the labyrinth. This also opened another door at the bottom. As he turned the wheel, the tunnels in the labyrinth changed positions and after a moment, connected again. There were no dead ends. The small wheel slowly sunk into the table to never turn again.

"As the labyrinth is randomly formed by the player, the way may become longer or shorter. All of our actions change something. Some doors may remain open for a long time while others may close after our next decision. But two doors never change; the beginning and the end."

The old man picked up a small sapphire crystal pearl from the rack and showed it to each of the children.

"Souls are like small crystal pearls," he continued. "They may reach their destination a thousand ways, through thousands of crossroads and junctions on a long journey. Some souls race through the labyrinth and live a very short life. Others play to discover every little aspect of it."

The old man turned to the game and adjusted one of the large wheels a little. The labyrinth changed its configuration. With the exception of the entrance and exit, many doors opened and closed.

"Like these two wheels, there are always two types of decisions in our life. One, which is the right one and expands our life." The old man turned the other large wheel. Different doors opened and closed. "And the other could decrease the length of our life. No one knows which wheel is the right decision. In this game, as in life, our soul listens to our instinct. Always. Each of our actions affects the path of the pearl, even if the consequences appears much later in the game, as well in life itself. Every decision has a cause and effect in the universe and every door entered opens others far-far away."

The old man put the small crystal pearl into a labyrinth hall while the children watched. The small pearl slowly searched its way down through the first two open junctions and crossroads. The old man twisted the left wooden wheel that opened and closed doors in the maze.

"Open one door and you may open many others throughout your life. Even if there are many open doors, it does not mean you will walk through all the ways and all the possibilities. Step into one way and you cannot turn back. Every door opens a possibility that may gain you sure knowledge that you lose another one. You can walk only one path at a time."

The pearl stopped at a crossroad with two closed doors while the old man looked at the children. The little girl picked up a second small sapphire pearl from the rack. As she did, the small wooden wheel slowly popped out of its place. The old man nodded at the small wheel. The boy turned it to open another entrance and exit, but it didn't change the rest of the labyrinth.

"During their long lives all Aserians consider and watch over more than their own lives, more than one pearl in their labyrinth of life," the old man smiled fondly back at the children as he remembered. As the girl moved to set the second pearl into the game the old man turned the small wooden wheel further and the open entrance and exit closed. The children looked at the old man curiously. "But first, before they start to shepherd others, every young Aserian has to face their own weakness and true potential their own way."

The little girl treasured the second sapphire pearl in her hand, while the old man turned one of the wooden wheels. Many doors popped open, including the door before the sapphire pearl in the game. Balanced, the pearl hesitated, and then slowly rolled along the right tunnel to discover the unknown. "The young guardian was a stranger in her known, yet so unknown world. In her new life, every day was a new path to walk and to discover. Every crossroad was a decision to make. A newly born life is just like a sapling in a garden on which every gardener leaves a mark as it grows. A long path yawned ahead of her, a long evolution to slowly polish her crude surface bright and refined."

The crawling pearl was mirrored in the old man's eyes while it slowly discovered new paths ahead. The small pearl had changed into a small raindrop in his mind – a raindrop escorted by countless of others.

"But first every young soul, even if they are so brave one day, has nightmares to face and fears to be conquered. It's the flow of life."

* * *

Grim cold darkness ruled the night. The wind swayed the trees. Gusts rattled the branches back and forth in the storm and heavy rain danced in the air. The swirling dark clouds raced across the sky. Their reflection mirrored in young Angeni's terrified eyes. Motionless, she had gazed at them from among her cushions in the middle of the sanctuary since the cruel storm startled her awake. The breeze, which came uninvited through the large open arch of the balcony, gently flowed over the young Aserian woman. Protective, she wrapped herself in her large white feathery wings and held a small sapphire pillow close to her chest.

"Mother? Father?" clarity and depth rang from her quavering angelic voice as she called them so silently through her fear. Her terrified eyes continuously peeked toward the main arch entrance. The satin curtain slightly, but eerily waved and separated the safe sanctuary from the unknown outside. Angeni waited for her kind mother and brave father to come and protect her, to not be alone in the deafening thunderstorm she feared so much. A beautiful lullaby, that's all she desired; a lullaby to calm her frightened soul and cradle her back to sleep to dream about something nice and peaceful to hide from this evil storm. But no one came to fulfill her desperate wish. Her soul felt safe in the hendecagon sanctuary; for her the peaceful world sat between the eleven walls and eleven pillars. Yet, a strange, binding claustrophobic feeling encompassed her. She was scared and she was so alone.

The wind howled like a grey mingan in the forest of the great mountains at midnight. The eerie scream terrified the young guardian's soul. The beautifully carved Oriental latticework doors chattered under the storm's siege. Then something in the distance, bright and sapphire, flashed outside and brought light into the suffocating darkness enough to reflect on the marble floor, but only for a blink of an eye. It was something new for her, something that amazed her young soul with its beauty for a moment. Yet, for some reason this beauty also terrified her, but she didn't know why. Then a loud clap of thunder rumbled. That gave her a silent jump and answered her question. Her trembling hands pulled the sapphire velvet pillow closer to her chest.

Like a newborn, Angeni barely remembered anything from her first days. Everything was so blurry and distant, untouchable. Everything was so familiar yet all so different, even the storm. Memories like a shattered mirror, only little splinters reminded her of the days that had passed. A middle-aged Aserian woman, named Eve, so beautiful, graceful and majestic watched over and took care of her like a mother. And that thoughtful and wise old Aserian, Aaron, so like a true protective father. But, like everything else, Angeni barely remembered even these two wonderful souls. Were they real at all or were they just a dream? Were they her parents as she thought? She didn't know, but her instincts told they were real even if they weren't here with her now. Then, where are they now? Why did they leave her alone? Did she do something wrong?

Everything from the past was like an untouchable distant dream. What was that strange pulsating *seal*, that tired crystal heart that bathed her protectively in so beautiful sapphire light? She hadn't seen it anywhere. What was that place? Maybe she was born there? Or maybe strange forgotten dreams and wild imagination merged with reality? Was it all just a dream? Was that generous warm-hearted daydreaming little red haired girl, so curious, so cute, and their parents who loved them deeply, a dream? She had dreamt about them before the relentless storm raised its clarion call. She couldn't recall who they were. They were all gone, that memory faded into the darkness to be shrouded by the veil of the forgotten.

Now, for the first time in her life everything seemed and sounded so clear. The moments that she had seen and lived now didn't want to be forgotten anymore. Rather all the moments wanted to be engraved into her mind to be part of her soul for eternity. The insistence of the splashing raindrops fell harder and faster as if the Gods poured it from vats in the heavens while the wind's howl whipped the clouds toward the unknown, didn't echo as a dream anymore, but sounded so sharp and real. As the winds howl laid siege to the sanctuary once again, the Oriental doors surrendered, they swung open to boom against the columns. The sheer curtains floated inward to welcome the wicked rain spray into the sanctuary through the balcony's huge arch. The young guardian's breaths came faster and faster; she didn't want the evil storm to come in and hurt her.

Gathering all her bravery, along with the pillow she defensively embraced, she slowly got out of the shallow circular bed. Angeni took the three stone steps down from her bed, and then a few steps closer to the balcony. Then she stopped in terror. The curtains waved as if they beckoned her to the doors that eerily banged and waited to consume her. She could go no closer. Her instincts told her to keep her distance from the balcony, but she didn't know why. Something dreadful waited beyond the balcony; she felt it and she feared it. The shadowy landscape beyond the impassable rain curtain reminded her of a town, but not Odess'iana. This was a place hidden among her fragmented first memories that her soul missed so much.

Her smooth hand reached out to touch the raindrop spray that swirled in front of her as it came uninvited into her safe haven. The first drop hit her finger; it was cold and tickled her as it slid down to her hand. Then another drop followed the first. While the young guardian watched, the raindrops quickly ran down and around her hand to continue their interrupted journey to the marble floor.

The rain blew through the curtains to spray the wild rain onto her. She closed her eyes and let her wings relax. A few raindrops silently splashed on her blond hair and white alabaster skin. Angeni took a slow breath and let the cold air fill her body. For the first time since the young guardian was reborn, she felt; she was alive.

Then the wind broke its short silence once more as it raged outside to entomb her world, but foremost froze Angeni with fear. The doors rattled faster and faster, willing her to come closer as the seemingly friendly curtains beckoned. The young guardian stepped back from the balcony to rattle along with the tree leaves that suffered outside. It felt like the great storm wanted to crush the trees, but more, to surround and shatter her safe sanctuary to get at her. The wind howled louder yet. Then the play of the silent bright lightning and the invisible, but so loud shock of the thunder stripped away her last shred of safety. Breathless and trembling in fear, she stepped back once more. She needed to leave her haven before she could be caught up and carried away by the evil wind; certainly, before those terrifying doors came to eat her.

"Come, Pilly," her quavering voice whispered to the small sapphire pillow clutched in her arms. "Let's find mommy and daddy," she finally decided.

The cold marble floor chilled Angeni's bare feet as she gathered all her bravery and stepped out of the sanctuary. Like a soft breeze, the curtain ran ghostly fingers over her shoulders as it slowly parted to reveal the long dark corridor ahead of her. Her large wings resting on her back, her white saree clung to her graceful body. Terrified and shaken, her hem rippled when took her first steps into the unknown. Columns stood silent sentry and beautifully carved angel statues peeked from the shadows. Many candles on the pedestals slept in silence. Some just put out by the wind that rushed past the curtains on the small stone windows.

Misted by errant rain, she stroked her little pillow, her only friend, Pilly who gave her a sense of safety. Her hesitant steps drew her down the endless corridor. The desperation of this fragile, mature, yet newborn Aserian woman was nearly hidden on her icy calm face. Though terrified, she was awed by the beauty as she looked around. But her curious eyes mirrored the great inner fears of the lonely soul. She tried to find someone, a familiar face in the crouching shadows, someone who could be with her, anyone. That kind Aserian man and woman she had considered father and mother. She wished her mother held her under her protective wings while her father ordered the storm with his fatherly voice to calm down — at least this is what her young soul dreamed and imagined.

"Mother? Father?" her soft angelic tone called, but no answer came. "Where are you?" she asked almost silently. Like magic, a blurry memory rushed into her mind and forced the young guardian to stop.

Grace, a woman's kind echoing voice called in her mind. The young guardian had to reach out to the closest column for support. The faces she had seen for a moment were her real parents, she felt it; she knew it. But they were human, not the Aserians she looked for. Who were they? And who is Grace, the little girl in her dream? Was she still dreaming?

As fast as it came, the vision retreated in her mind as she shook her head. So confused, breathing faster and faster, the young guardian took one step, and then another. But, as she arrived under the stone arch at the end of the corridor, her legs rooted to the spot. She didn't dare go further. Two dark motionless silhouettes waited and watched her from the large dim hall beyond. They terrified her. The silent strangers were not her mom and dad.

Angeni looked back to the other end of the long corridor. Her safe sanctuary, which was still intact, bravely stood against the wind and was already distant, excessively far. Holding the pillow tight, she gathered her bravery and looked back into the hall. The dark silhouettes that gazed at her from the night shadows terrified her.

"Mother? Father?" she called them again half-heartedly. Lightning flashed outside, the two dark silhouettes became white majestic angel statues as if to answer her call.

Ane, Rhe... her mind counted in Aserian in a little girl's voice, but she didn't know why.

Chasing the lightning, thunder cracked so loud that it startled the young guardian into gulping a fearful breath and a step back.

"Mommy? Daddy?" Desperation rising, she crushed Pilly to her chest.

Gracie, a tiny cute voice called, called for her and for a moment Angeni had seen a little girl's grin and bright green eyes look at her.

"Sister?" she whispered. Her eyes filled with tears of pain of all the forgotten memories from her previous life as that fatal night exploded to the surface. A life left behind wasn't so joyful a dream that ended in a terrible nightmare. A family left behind wasn't a dream either. Everything was real. Everything.

The young fragile angel woman collapsed to her knees, her large white wings gently draped the marble floor. For moments, not a single sound left her, yet she wanted to scream the wrenching sorrow of loss that encompassed her. Angeni's crushed soul desperately wanted to be loved, heard, but mostly to be held by someone, like Pilly in her cramped and shaking arms. She was so alone in endless sadness, only the heartbroken, painful wails torn from her soul echoed around the storm-darkened hall.

I love you, my beautiful little girl, was a kind motherly voice in her mind, as if the woman whispered in her ear now; the kind whisper so sudden opened the hidden wounds of Angeni's young soul.

"Please mommy!" the young guardian begged while her pain prostrated her on the floor. The once joyful memories became painful splinters in her heart as she remembered. For a moment, a beautiful woman, her beloved mommy looked back at her, just after giving her forehead a kiss and then smiled with a cheery smile and waved kindly.

"Please come back and love me! Please!" Her shaking hand reached out to the thin air, as if Angeni could touch her beloved mother, who was only in her mind.

Here we go! Angeni's tearful eyes opened wide as a fatherly, yet so cheery voice echoed in her mind; her strong father held his little girl to spin her in the air as they played on the grassy field.

Her back and wings strained, the inner torturing pain forced her to scream silently and weep harder and harder. "D-daddy? Daddy!" she whispered and looked up. Tears ran down her cheeks.

Don't be afraid. I won't let you go, the kind whisper echoed. Her father smiled, lightly stroked her nose in her memories; a caress that Angeni felt on her nose too.

"Please don't let me go! Please hold me just once more!" she begged the thin air. The young guardian bowed to the marble floor in endless torment. "Please!"

May I go with her? came the hopeful voice of the kind red-headed little girl. A cramped and painful scream left the trembling cherry lips of the crushed guardian as she recognized the voice of her lost sister.

No my dear. You're coming with us now, the motherly answer slowly faded while Angeni's arms held the pillow tight like she had held little Aurora in her arms to never let her go.

"P-Please! A-A-Aurora! P-Please s-sta-stay with me!" The choking words of the crying angel were swallowed by her wails that not even the downpour and cracking thunder could dim.

The tears hid the cruel world away and the great loss clouded her crushed soul. There was only pain, endless pain. "No. Please, no," she shook her head in denial. The young guardian tried to stand, to run away, out of this world away from the pain. But she had fallen back to the floor and wept. The painful scream of loss left her throat raw and echoed down the corridor while she gathered her strength once more. The strong stone columns a cold support as she dragged herself back to the sanctuary, the only place where she might hide from the pain.

"Please, don't leave me alone. Please. I'm afraid so much," she threw herself on her pedestal bed. She begged almost silently and tried to pull herself together like a weeping child among the large fluffy cushions of her little home. Her trembling arms still clutched the little blue velvet pillow close. Only Pilly was with her, no one else. So alone, she was a stranger on this known, yet so unknown world.

"Please," she asked silently once more, but her words couldn't change the past. The darkness of the night hid Angeni and her sadness from the world.

Along with the raging storm outside, the young guardian gradually calmed down. The heavenly gods had slowly ceased fire, the distant thunder now sounded like lazy stone balls rolled on cobblestones. The hungry doors ceased their shuddering, the cadenced knock of the torrential rain slowly waned, and the angry howl of the wind softened to a gentle whisper.

Dozen of candles, tall and short alike, reflected in the young woman's sad eyes. A silent tear slowly slid down her icy face; tears of prayer for her loved ones. The tear dripped past the cold blue flame of the candle lighter that the young guardian held.

"I-I miss all of you so much," she whispered on a slow breath while she knelt in front of the statue of a guardian whose wings were spread to give motherly protection. Angeni didn't even realize that she had left her safe cushion kingdom, her sanctuary to come out to the corridor, but she didn't care. Pilly, her silent guardian pillow stood guard from the floor.

"I'm sorry I left all of you behind. I'm so sorry," full of guilt and quiet tears, Angeni lit two tall candles for her parents. The young guardian sniffed, "B-but one day, we will be together. Your little girl won't leave you anymore. I-I promise."

But as the candle lighter went above the smallest candle, which stood right in the protective shadow of the two tall candles, someone leaned near Angeni's cheek and gently blew out the tiny dancing blue flame on the candle lighter.

"If you remember who they were and how they lived, then maybe they have found life again," came a young woman's soft voice into Angeni's ear. "They may have gone, but you're not alone. I'll never let you go," she added as Angeni looked back.

The bright eyes of a young, yet so beautiful, red haired Aserian Guardian woman with large white wings lowered behind her back looked back at her. The woman in the white silk saree was so familiar to Angeni; she read her soul and nature from sorrowful, yet happy green eyes. Behind her, at the end of the corridor the two old Aserians, her mother and father stood silent in the darkness. Old Aaron held Eve's hand. Endless love beamed from their eyes as they watched the two young Aserian women.

"Who are you?" asked Angeni while she set the candle lighter on the marble floor.

"You know that in your soul," the woman responded with a half-cheery calmness.

"No. You can't be real," Angeni whispered. As the stranger gently held her hand, she immediately felt and knew who the woman was; she saw it in her own mind.

"See? I'm real," the woman whispered as she gently put Angeni's hand to her icy cheek. Under the shadow of the guardian statue, Angeni hugged and held the woman close.

"Aurora," she whispered while tears of happiness filled her eyes. "Sister."

* * *

The morning had dawned cold. The sweet wind, which shepherded the brown leaves, hinted at the approaching end of Deciduous. The eyes of the young guardian mirrored the weak sapphire sunlight that glimmered through the partially cloudy sky onto her balcony. As her instinct demanded, she'd be safe if she kept her distance from the edge.

A beautiful white temple topped with a large, majestic Aserian *wing-statue* that radiated the glory of the Aserian culture, stood within the tall Citadel district of the city, which, unlike any other city, like Odess'iana, this place was not divided by walls. The Citadel was built on a tall escarpment, which had precipitous sides and was the nuclei of the large town, which radiated out onto the lower ground from the shores of the great gulf to the nearby mountains. Beautiful azure waves washed those shores in the distance and tweeting birds circled above the mirror surface of the salty water. How had she gotten here, when did they arrive? Wherever *here* is, she didn't know. But the large town where Aserian and human, like small dots filled it with life, was enchanting in the morning daylight.

"Sessa Asria. Beautiful, isn't it?" a motherly voice asked.

"It's so beautiful," whispered Angeni as she looked back at the majesty of the woman she called mother. Her orange saree gently flowed with her ethereal, graceful steps.

"Are you excited?" the High-Guardian asked and Angeni's excited nod was the answer.

"My beautiful large white wings don't have to be shy anymore. Tomorrow everyone will see them," she daydreamed. Excited she looked at Eve. "I'll try to be like Eriana, mother. I'll try to be the greatest and kindest guardian of all." The young guardian looked back at the landscape as she dreamt on. "I'll learn a lot. I'll have many friends. And I'll help them if they don't know something. They'll see I'm a kind soul. They'll know they can count on me anytime."

"I hope they will," Eve responded kindly.

"Which one is the Hall of Discipline?" Angeni asked excitedly scanning the landscape.

"That one," Eve pointed at the large winged temple. The awed young guardian and her mother watched the magnificent building in silence. Then Angeni looked at Eve.

"If I don't understand something, will you help me, mother? Will you teach me how to become a great guardian?" she asked in her shiest tone.

"I wouldn't be a good mother if I did not help you to achieve your dreams, Angeni."

As she heard her name, Angeni hesitated. She remembered and loved her human name. Aurora is called by her human name. So, why does everyone call her by a different name?

"Mother, why do you call me Angeni?" she lowered her eyes. "Don't you like my name?"

"You're the one who truly knows the answer for this question as you, your soul declared herself as Angeni," Eve's grave comment tinged with concern. "If you can't answer your question, no one else can."

Her mind tried to find the answer, wanted to remember, but she didn't know the answer.

The sapphire light shone in Angeni's eyes as the cloud that had partially covered the sun slid away. She raised her hand to touch the untouchable distant sun. Her eyes focused on her hand, which was surrounded by a gentle illusionary blue glow. It was so beautiful, but it was the same illusion as in her human life. It wasn't her aura. Why can't she see her own?

"You'll see your own evolving aura soon, after you learn to live," Eve said before Angeni had a chance to ask. Lowering her hand she looked at her mother. "One day your nature will be echoed in the color of your clothes and will shine in your eyes." For a moment, Eve's eyes flashed up same citrine orange as her saree shone in the sunlight. Angeni watched with reverent awe.

"May I have a sapphire aura?" hope shone, her eyes looked at the bright blue sun while her mind already imagined herself with flashing sapphire eyes and in an elegant blue saree.

"A spirit's nature doesn't work this way," Eve responded kindly. Disappointed, the young guardian lowered her head, her finger sadly twisted her white saree, which mirrored her innocent soul. "Your crystal clear soul must learn and evolve," her mother continued. "Your aura will blend and change along with your nature until the time you became a true adult. Hopefully, what you think, you will become."

"Then I'll do everything to have the most beautiful sapphire aura," Angeni declared proudly and with excited eyes, she studied the landscape. The High-Guardian watched her curiously and waited.

"Haven't you forgotten something?" Eve asked kindly of her daydreaming daughter. Angeni looked at her; her narrowed eyes, but mostly her frown mirrored as her mind quickly searched for the answer. What did she forget?

"Father!" her eyes opened as she suddenly realized; they must prepare for the great day. She started to hurry into the sanctuary, but after taking few quick steps, she turned around and ran back to her mother. The amused High-Guardian shook her head watching her lightheaded daughter who kissed her cheek, and then ran into the sanctuary.

Angeni saw that curious sharp green eyes studied a tiny kimama on a leaf as it slowly tried its colourful wings on one of the bushes of the tiny inner hanging garden. Aurora's curious smile showed that she hadn't changed deep in her soul, even if she wasn't the lost little child she was before, but a kind, if determined beautiful Aserian woman.

"Sister," smiled the youngest guardian as her eyes caught Angeni at the entrance of the garden. Then her eyes desperately snapped back to the tiny kimama that flitted away. "Wait! Where are you going? Come back!" she whispered so innocent and prepared to follow the kimama.

"Ah-ah-ah! Father is waiting!" Angeni sang excited and quickly grabbed her hand. Aurora immediately forgot about the kimama and followed her sister with the same shimmering excitement in her eyes.

The old, gray haired, yet juvenile High-Guardian Aaron sat behind his carved stone table in his jade green robe when the sisters sneaked into the large library to surprise their father. Angeni grinned and put a finger to her lips to show Aurora to stay quiet, whose cheeky smile agreed. So silent the two young guardians tiptoed closer and closer, sneaked column to column to catch their father by surprise from behind. Only a few more steps, just few more...

"Time waits for nobody, young ones," whispered the old Aserian when they had almost reached him. Angeni and Aurora stopped in surprise. "But I gladly do," smiled the High-Guardian as he glanced back at Angeni. Then he looked around.

"Where is your sister?" he asked surprised. Angeni looked around; she stood alone in the infiltrating daylight, embraced by the columns. "Aurora?" the High-Guardian called her.

"Come and find me!" the trilling answer came from behind one of the shadowy columns. The High-Guardian pointed at a column. A wing was partially visible. The youngest one twisted it curiously while Aaron gestured Angeni to corner the youngest one and get her from both sides. They silently moved in.

Angeni saw cheery Aurora peek out from behind the column and looked right at her with piercing green eyes. Surprised at seeing her sister's approach, the youngest immediately bolted the other way, but she ran right into the open arms of her father. She was surprised, but then...

"I got you!" Aurora grinned and hugged him while Angeni joined them.

"Let's see what we brewed all night, my daughters," the High-Guardian said as he looked at his daughters.

The excited young ones quickly picked up and put on their aprons, and then met their father at a stone table on the far side of the library and curiously peeked into the small boiling cauldron to see how their masterpiece was brewing.

Yesterday, the young Aserians had collected many fallen walnuts from the garden, then put them into the cauldron and covered them with water. The walnut simmered almost all night over the tiny blue fire and now they steeped all day. After the wooden spoon stirred the liquid for the last time, the young guardians carefully removed the walnuts from the pot and added some vinegar and a secret ingredient, Acacia, as their father instructed. Then the High-Guardian added some iron dust that Aurora slowly measured out on a small scale. After a short wait, the liquid turned a bit darker. Angeni carefully poured the tinted deep golden brown liquid into small vials.

Excited, taking off the apron, Angeni raised the first vial filled with the strange liquid to shine in by the sapphire sun. It was beautiful; the first ink that was soon going to echo the great knowledge that they would learn.

"Everyone's destiny will be revealed as they walk their long path of life. For an Aserian destiny is life itself," her father said wisely while he strolled to his table. "Always remember, protecting and guiding is a duty for which there can be no mistakes. To be a true guardian, you must reveal your fears and your weaknesses."

Angeni watched as he picked up two thick books from his elegant table. The books were new, glinted in the infiltrating sunlight. One of the covers was made of dark sapphire velvet, the other lively orange velvet – the aura colors of their beloved and respected heroines, Spirit Guardians Eriana and Iria. How did their father know these were their favourite colors?

89

"Tomorrow you'll start a wonderful journey to learn to live. Fill these pages with knowledge to reach your dreams, my daughters," Aaron gave the books to his daughters – the blue to Angeni and the orange to Aurora. They treasured the gift of their father in their hands. The young guardians lovingly stroked the soft velvet covers that their skillful father made. The place for the title was empty; left for their imagination. Beyond the elegant cover hundreds of soft white empty pages waited to be filled with knowledge. The two young guardians thankfully embraced the old guardian.

Angeni spent the rest of the day at her usual safe place away from the balcony edge. Enchanted, she gazed at the Hall of Discipline, which called her from the distance and waited for her entry tomorrow to begin her journey on the path of her long evolution. She wished the day had moved with blinding speed, but it didn't happen. Sachylia slowly approached the horizon, maybe slower then ever before.

Devious and so excited, the young guardian decided she would take the path that ran faster. She would go to sleep early so the desired day would be only moments away after she closed her eyes. A new world awaited her along with new friends, new knowledge, and new exciting adventures. Taking a last look at the great winged temple, she strolled into her sanctuary.

Inside, her eyes caught sight of a papyrus scroll pamphlet that sat on the stone table along with a small arven pencil. The breeze ruffled and swished its pages to recall a loving memory, one of the dearest of her young soul. The pages seemed empty, only one sketch on the first page; the Sacred Crystal Mother that a young girl had drawn in the Valley of Seradelphia.

"You weren't here before," she whispered in surprise. Angeni looked around, but no one was in the sanctuary, only the fresh breeze that lightly ruffled her feathers. Who brought her little treasure back to her? Mother, father, Aurora? No, they would give it to her personally. Then who? Maybe someone who is watching over her? She didn't know, but it really mattered to her soul. Touched, she held her old scroll pamphlet close, a dear memory that remained from the life she left behind while her eyes mirrored Sachylia slow dive on the clear horizon. After a long sleep, she'd greet the day she had awaited for so long.

* * *

"Look."
"There she is. That's Angeni."

90

"She seems so fragile."

"Don't speak to her unless she speaks to us."

Emotionless icy looks and whispers of young Aserians followed Angeni since she had entered the Hall of Discipline. They kept their distance and just whispered. Strolling down the long corridor, Angeni sadly hugged the velvet book with an endless desire to learn, to fulfill her dreams. Her sadness was hidden by her own angelically rigid and determined icy calm. The bands of daylight glinted on the tiny ink vial that hung from her belt.

Her soul had eagerly waited for this day. The first to begin the long path of learning to become a great guardian, the one she always wanted to be. But now, as the whispers broke the deafening silence and those icy looks followed her every step, her soul wanted to leave, run back to her safe sanctuary and stay there forever with Pilly, her guardian pillow.

The perspective of her new life offered alternately fascinated, but mostly scared her since she had opened her eyes. Her soul felt so different from other Aserians, but she didn't know why. Her spirit knew she was reborn for a reason, but she couldn't tell what that reason might be. She felt that she was a stranger amongst them and many of the young Aserian may feel the same. They were afraid of her; she felt it. Those icy eyes mirrored their fear. Was she really so different, was there something wrong with her that no one dared to tell her? No one had seen the kind soul within, who she was or always wanted to be. If only she could prove it.

Although she never met any of these young Aserians, she knew all their names as she saw their soul through their eyes… just as they recognized and knew her with a glance.

Step after step she felt like someone other then those icy looks watched and followed her, someone who sneaked from column to column. Then so sudden, someone gently pulled her right wing twice. From the touch, before she even looked back to a little human boy, she already felt who he was and had seen parts of his life in her mind, even if it wasn't clear and only for a single moment. As the boy released her wing, everything quickly faded into darkness.

"Are you the Angeni?" the boy asked, looking up at her with shiny eyes full of hope. The young guardian crouched down to him with a kind smile. Everything was so familiar to her, like it had happened a lifetime ago, but now from a different perspective. Now, as before many of the young Aserians watched her. Just her. But why?

"Yes. I'm Angeni," her soft shy, yet determined voice answered.

"Are you going to save us from the evil?" asked the boy.

"From what evil?" she curiously looked at him.

"The Shanas. The dark creatures that live in the shadows."

"The Shaina?" Angeni corrected him. The boy quickly nodded. "Why? Are they here?" she looked around, but she saw only the Aserians along with their measuring, fearful looks, and some humans who curiously watched her.

"No. But they'll come with the Crystal Shade," the boy answered. "Daddy told that you're going to protect us. Are you going to protect me? Are you going to protect my family?"

"If they ever come, like every Aserian, I'll do everything to protect you. I promise."

"Really?" The boy's eyes shone with excitement. Angeni nodded. "I, I have to tell this to my friends," the boy whispered. Crouching on one knee, the young Aserian woman smiled. But her sadness returned as her eyes followed the boy while he ran to his friends; friends that she didn't have. She felt so alone, regardless that dozens surrounded her.

Moving along with the crowd of Aserians, Angeni soon entered into the Grand Hall. In the sapphire sunlight, which beamed through the windows, her eyes looked for Aurora. For the first time in her life, the youngest guardian wanted to explore everything alone. Now, Angeni desired her sister's nearness and protection.

All in innocent crystal white, men in togas and women in elegant sarees, one hundred or even more young Aserians filled the hall. Many of them looked at her with the same icy looks as she stepped through the large entrance. Aurora was somewhere among them, somewhere in the whispering mass. But where? She hadn't seen her anywhere.

Shy and full of sorrow, holding her little book tighter, Angeni stepped back. She wanted to leave as her soul dictated, but the large metal door closed with a loud thump behind her. There was no way out. Silence fell in the hall. Angeni looked from the door to the Aserians. Their icy looks already focused on a majestic and so beautiful woman who entered the hall; her mother. In addition, her father stepped out to escort her. What are her parents doing here?

Proud High-Guardian Eve watched the students. Her elegant orange tiara glinted in the sunlight. She spread her arms and wings slightly, but so gracefully as she began in her angelic motherly tone as if she were the mother and caretaker of all Aserians. And maybe she was.

"I look upon you with immence pride and I welcome you, young Aserians! I am delighted and pleased to be here with you today, the day you start your long journey to learn how to live, how to become a true guardian. Today is a great day! We are here to celebrate the first days of your true life, the first steps you take on this glorious path. But this path won't be yours alone."

High-Guardian Eve's pride shone in her eyes.

"A guardian must perceive what cannot be seen. An Aserian must guide to help and accompany a soul on the best possible path to travel the longest and most beautiful journey in life. To be an Aserian guide in order to protect, to never endanger anyone. The life of an Aserian and their charge may start on two different paths, but one day they'll meet at a crossroad. First, before you reach that crossroad you need to open closed doors to see what lies in you own spirit, and on the path that lies ahead of you. Being an Aserian is a great, but so noble responsibility. Always do what is known to be right. Be proud and learn well young guardians. And please never forget; a guardian lives so others may live."

"So others may live," enchanted, Angeni whispered with respect. Her eyes reflected her beloved mother. In this great moment, Angeni had completely forgotten her sadness.

Learning was now their life and Angeni, along with the others, put her heart and soul into it. As her philosopher father said, protecting and guiding is a duty for which there can be no mistakes. And he was right.

The young guardian slowly realized even Aserians must learn a lot. Being a guardian sounded so easy when she read about her favorite Spirit Guardians, Eriana and Iria, although she barely remembered her favorite fairy tale. Her mind was like a newly built shiny library echoing from the emptiness, waiting to be filled with knowledge. History, literature, culture, music and many other wonderful subjects, both human and Aserian, all had a different shelf. Day after day new scrolls and books began to fill those imagined empty shelves.

The most enlightened Aserian teachers and philosophers of Eecrys Aredia shared their wisdom with the young apprentices to understand what their life and their world was all about. Every day was a new revelation, a new discovery for the young souls.

Most of the first lessons took place in the Great Library of Sessa Asria. Along with the other apprentices, Angeni looked around the large hall. Many of the books were similar to her book, except these books had a title on the cover and presumably were filled with knowledge from the first page to the last. Would her book be worthy to be part of this great library? She wanted to believe yes, she had sworn to herself to make it worthy. Her excitement and amazement slowly veiled her early sadness and those strange whispers and icy looks regardless that they all followed her.

The dark amber gold robe shone with the wisdom, inner knowledge and spiritual mind of long-bearded vivacious old Librarian, High-Guardian Abenago. He intended to bring light into the dim minds of all young souls with each of his words taught about the role of the social classes of Aserian society.

The pride of the Aserians, the Guardians with their strong white feathery wings, the protectors of noble souls, leaders and also, the artistic souls, writers, artists and poets alike. Then the warm hearted protectors of nature, the Viridanas, Sentinels by their common name, with their bony wings with sharper feather tips that picked up the colors of their surroundings, the protectors of traders, merchants and farmers. Then the silent reasoning observers who studied everything and everyone, whose life was to discover details others never even imagined, to connect the dots to find their logical way in every maze. The Carenians or Watchers with their pointed long feathers were the guiding spirit of philosophers, healers, and explorers. The apprentices slowly learned who they really were and the life that awaited them.

But there was a mysterious fourth class that neither Angeni nor the other apprentices had ever heard of or met before. As they learned, not many older Aserians had either. Very few ever met the mysterious and wise Segaran Viras, the Spiritual Vanguards, who shepherded blessed ones toward their path of enlightenment. What did they look like? Abenago never told them, and they didn't learn much more about them either. Angeni thought her mother or father might reveal more. Yet, like all their mentors, they kept the secret.

Some of the apprentices found no logic in the Librarian, who then started to speak about spirit guides, orbs, spirits and souls. Why would their brothers and sisters hide from the world and from them? It made no sense. Silent, Angeni didn't share their view. The secrecy of the Spiritual Vanguards reminded her of Eriana and Iria, the Spirit Guardians.

Maybe the Spiritual Vanguards are the Spirit Guardians, she thought excited. Maybe her favourite heroine really exists or existed.

"The spirit is a sensitive vital governing principle in the individual," the old Librarian's deep voice echoed off the shelves and books as he told the apprentices. "The soul consists of the heart. The mind, the young dim mental intellect, the will, and emotional powers. And finally the body is the contrast and gives shape to your existence."

"The spirit defines what you are. The soul defines who you are, right master?" asked shy Angeni, but full of hope from old Abenago as she tried to understand the true meaning of what she had just heard. But then, those whispers from the other apprentices came from behind her

94

once again. She felt their fear too. Her sadness wasn't visible on her calm face, but hidden by a soft sigh. Deep inside her soul, she was full of sorrow and didn't know why others were whispering about her, why they feared her. Was something she said wrong? Maybe she is not at all as smart as she wanted to be.

"It's easy to tell what the spirit and soul of others are. Everyone can judge others," Abenago looked at Watcher Panoe and Guardian Onassa, the two young apprentices behind Angeni who immediately stopped whispering. "The hardest is to know yourself," with a calm pleasant smile, he looked at Angeni as continued. "Always know yourself to make a difference, Angeni," the old Librarian said, and then he looked at the others. "Knowing others is intelligence; knowing yourself is true wisdom. Guarding others is strength; guiding yourself is true power. Never forget that."

Then his old wise attention wandered back to Angeni.

"Not every soul is dim I see," Abenago proudly smiled at her. "Yes. Your spirit is defining what you are. Your soul is defining who you are," he confirmed.

Other lessons took place inside the Citadel's huge interior hanging garden, where the Sentinels felt so comfortable. The beauty awed them, and they weren't alone. The Sentinel's tiny paradise as Aurora called the garden was magnificent and enchanting as it basked in Sachylia's sapphire light.

Angeni took huge breaths to fill her existence with the sweet scent of hundreds or even thousands of colourful flowers. The splashing crystal-clear water caressed her ears as it streamed from the aqueducts to fill the artificial lakes. This gave life to peace giving colourful Nymphaes, the water lilies that lightly bobbed on the surface.

"Take the flower, cup it gently with your hand," said radiant middle-aged Gardener Sentinel, Justicar Onessia's luscious shy voice. She almost blended into the garden in her elegant dark Peridot green saree. "What do you feel?" she asked Angeni, as well as the apprentices who all studied the water lilies in their hands.

"It's fragile. So fragile," Angeni whispered. She felt the streaming life in the tiny flower. "I fear for its life. I want to protect it even from the wind," she treasured the flower in her hand.

"Always remember this feeling," advised Onessia.

"Why?" the young guardian asked.

"You're an Aserian. You're a Guardian. The world is in your hands," she said, while Angeni's eyes reflected the water lily. "A world, a soul is a flower so fragile and this feeling will escort you throughout your life,

Angeni," then she looked at the other apprentices to address them. "But to watch over your flower, first you must be the flower to understand its life. First you must learn to understand the root to understand its blossom."

That's what all the apprentices did; they all started to learn everything about the root to understand their whole world, what they were born to protect. There was so much to learn. However not all of the apprentices agreed with this at the beginning.

"Aserians can share knowledge by a simple touch. So, why do we need to learn?" the gentle black skinned Aserian Guardian, Kien asked as they strolled back to the Great Library. Alone, Angeni closed the line a few steps behind everyone, she hugged her book and its knowledge, just as the cold breeze rippled over her.

"Sharing is not equal to experience," the wind brought the logical answer from Iris, the young Aserian Watcher to Angeni.

"A soul and spirit live to learn, but a body must learn to live," added the male Watcher, Tlanextic. "You must see, feel and hear everything to truly know what you experience."

Angeni agreed with them. She wanted to tell them, speak to them, but whenever they looked at her, she had seen that they seemed to fear her. But why?

Like they opened a curtain on a window to see an endless green meadow beyond, the words, and teachings of the Guardian Persecutor, Sophus in the Great Library revealed that Eecrys Aredia was much more than it appeared to be. There was a lot more to be seen and discover. The young apprentices needed to not just see, but also know the world their souls were eager to guard and defend.

So closely layered, seven realms existed with the one where humans and Aserians lived peacefully. The first realm deflected all the other realms from human eyes. It was Eecrys Aredia herself, all around the different provinces this realm had multiple names; Gaea, Jannah, Sehaqim, Suvaroka, and its two Aserian names, Aeta – 'home' and Capra – the 'first', like her people called her mother sometimes.

Different beautiful names of different cultures for one frighteningly fragile paradise, Angeni thought, enchanted when she first heard their names.

Then the next realm made them understand how the Aserians watched invisible and unnoticed in the background. From the wide spiritual realm, all Aserian watched over and whispered to their charges to protect and guide their conscious actions unseen. The aura of Eecrys Aredia was also known by countless names, such as Mera Amantia – the

Spirit Sea, Eren Manea, Samayim, or Dyuoka. It was also the place where the Aserians hid their wings.

"Oh, dear Sophus, don't just tell them, show them!" came Abenago's deep echoing tone. The old Librarian many times restlessly pretended he was cleaning shelves and he always added something to Sophus' teachings. Now he stood on the tall ladder, he blew the never existed dust from a crystal-clean book and put it back in its place. "Go ahead! Show them!" he egged Sophus on while he picked up the next book. "Never forget, young souls are dim and impatient; they only understand the action!" his echoing advice came from above, and then he blew the clean book cleaner. "Nowadays imagination is out of fashion," the soft defiant mumbling of the old Librarian amused Angeni.

Smiling, young daydreaming Angeni silently agreed with him, and then she looked back at Sophus who still threw hard looks at Abenago. His nature described by his lemon-yellow robe, demanded resepect in his class, even from Abenago. The old librarian ignored his unspoken demands and whistled a melody while he wiped a clean book cover.

"When you chose not to have visible wings," Sophus looked back at the apprentices, "You may divert them into the spirit sea to keep them unseen and safe." His large white wings spread wide and then flapped backward majestically. As if they dove into an invisible ocean, the wings vanished into the unseen Spirit Sea, hidden from this realm.

Old Abenago was right. That grabbed the attention of the young apprentices who now eagerly wanted to learn. The young Aserians flapped their wings back over and over again. Some of them accidentally knocked Aberago's precious books off the shelves. Regardless how hard they tried, their wings remained in this realm. Sophus smiled at their attempts while his wings, so easily and majestically, slid back into this realm to rest on his back.

"One day you'll learn how to fully enter into the safety of Mera Amentia," he said.

"What does it look like?" with her usual curiosity, Aurora asked the same question that Angeni wanted to ask.

"It's a place that flows like water; a windy realm that embraces you like an endless friendly sapphire sea. Its currents will take you from place to place much faster, you may see and step through walls and you may reach the seemingly unreachable."

The apprentices' eyes devoured him, their souls demanded more. The Persecutor continued, "When you look up in the swirling Spirit Sea, you will see a distant untouchable blurry spirit sky. This is the third realm of Sacrmera Ceatsa; the 'sacred soul garden' of Eecrys Aredia, or by its other names, Jannah, Raquia and Maharoka; that mysterious home realm of the Spiritual Vanguards."

The last words grabbed the attention of the young ones, this time even more. The Spiritual Vanguards were not simply legends; their mysterious brothers and sisters really existed. They, the great caretakers of the spirit garden watched over the first three realms and they stood vigilant guard to protect the other four realms, the realms of the Sacred Crystal Mother. Then, why did they hide?

The other four realms sounded like true mysteries, legends as Persecutor Sophus continued. Even he described the realms very briefly, as no Aserian ever stepped beyond the soul garden to see these other realms. Not even the Spiritual Vanguards.

The Garden of Kedesh, or as some called the fourth realm, Machon or Janaoka, was the outskirts of legendary Aether, the Quintessence – the fifth that divided the last two realms equally. The home of the Shaina, the fiery sixth, Mera Shatanas, hell itself and the peaceful seventh, the home of the Aserians, Mera Eecryssa, heaven itself.

Angeni was relieved to find out that she wasn't behind the other apprentices as for most of them all this knowledge was also new. Later that day with the help of Abenago, Angeni tried to find the meaning and importance of the realms beyond the third, especially the heavenly home of the Aserians where all of them would go one day by their belief. But between the hundreds, thousands of books and scrolls they had found so few mentioned the Shaina and their home realm.

What bothered Angeni the most was that there was no way to learn anything about their celestial brothers and sisters, the Spiritual Vanguards and their lives. Even Abenago became tight-lipped, which was a very rare event, when she asked about them. The few scrolls she had found had not explained why the third realm was so important and why the Aserians did not have the power to enter the other four. Seemingly, it was a sealed secret.

Then instead of her, Aurora broke the silence a day later in their sanctuary. As always, her sister never hesitated to ask questions. Usually the right one.

"Mother. Why do the Segaran Viras never appear in our realm? Are they afraid of something?" Aurora innocently twisted her wings tips behind her back, watching her mother with her bright green eyes. Angeni also perked her ears and awaited the answer.

"No, Aurora," came Eve's tenderness as she caressed her daughter's face. "As caretakers of the spiritual realms, they protect us from the unknown of the other four realms, and they protect our crystal mother from us as well. As we care for and guard this realm, it's their life's duty to tend and guard the sacred spirit garden of Eecrys Aredia. If they should fail there, there would be no one to protect the spirit realms. Moreover, if that realm fails…" The wise High-Guardian hesitated like she feared this option. "But that's never going to happen," Eve added and smiled at Aurora.

They never spoke of the Segaran Viras or their mysterious realm or beyond anymore, but the words of her mother already revealed they were not hiding. Maybe they never did. Angeni had many questions about the realms, and she was sure Aurora had too. Nevertheless, they were resigned to the fact they wouldn't get answers for some time, if they got any at all. Angeni just hoped she could meet the mysterious Segaran Viras one day.

As the first days passed, Angeni wanted to feel herself as a star in the night sky that shines along with the others. But most of the time she felt like a lone star twinkling in the darkness, or worse; the eternal daydreamer watching the distant, untouchable stars from the ground. The stars that watched and feared her, whispered about her, but never really talked to her. Sometimes she had spoken with other apprentices; it was a very rare occasion.

Angeni spent most of her time with her teachers, who did not fear her but always looked at her with a strange respect that she also couldn't understand. And of course with Aurora, who quickly gathered fast friends all around her, just as Angeni always wanted to and dreamed of. Yet, whenever Aurora wanted Angeni to know her friends better, Angeni was distant and withdrawn. She didn't want anyone to fear her, or whatever that strange thing was that the apprentices' eyes couldn't hide. Sometimes in class, she escaped to a place where whispers couldn't follow and their fear couldn't touch her; to her dreams where everyone was her friend, everyone loved her, wanted her help… just as she always dreamt. Then one cold night in her sanctuary her mother approached her.

"Never be afraid to make new friends, Angeni," her mother advised.

"This little guardian is busy," Angeni said with a cheery smile and proud elocution from among her cushions.

"This little guardian is busy avoiding everyone," added Eve with a serious, yet also concerned tone. Angeni's cheery smile disappeared. Eve saw her fear and shyness. "The question is why?" her mother asked, but the young guardian didn't respond, just lowered her head, pulled up her legs and hugged them. She didn't want to admit that maybe something was wrong with her, that with the exception of Eve, everyone else saw.

She couldn't say she felt every apprentice feared her, she did not know why. Eve raised Angeni's chin to look into her eyes.

"Aserians are proud of who they are. You shouldn't hide."

"I, I'm not hiding, I just…"

"The past is history, the future is a mystery. Live in the present, Angeni," said Eve. "Be rigid and keep a distance if you truly want and when you really have to. But please, enjoy life whenever you can. I encourage you to live. Speak to them and know them better."

Angeni's eyes asked silently as they watched her mother. The High-Guardian continued, "There will be a time, when our brave Sentinels or the wise Watchers will guide you. And there is a possibility that maybe more than one will protect you, just as you'll have to protect them."

"Protect a guardian?" Angeni's surprise rang. "Don't we, Aserians only tend humans?"

"Every soul desires protection, to feel safe. We have to care for each other otherwise who would care for us," Eve explained. "Real wisdom comes to those who listen and accept the advice of others. We must focus on our unity and equality to complement each other. We need to be protected, guided and guarded too."

Angeni understood what she said. Her true first guardian, Pilly on her bed bravely stood and watched over her even now, just as it kept her safe when she slept and dreamed. The High-Guardian lovingly caressed her daughter's cheek.

"Don't fear to know others and never try to impress everyone as you'll just contradict yourself. Always be yourself, Angeni. That's all I ask," her mother advised.

From that night, the following question bubbled up day after day; who was going to guard her and whom will she guard? Yet, sometimes she felt, rather was sure an unseen guardian or someone already watched over her. Who? She didn't know.

What was more important, Angeni slowly started to open up to the other apprentices. Speaking with them wasn't that hard after all, actually it was quite easy. Every young apprentice, even the ones who sometimes whispered about her, gladly spoke with her or even played with her. They weren't distant, nor contemptuous, rather open and friendly. Still she had seen that inexplicable fear in their eyes every day. Since she had spoken with them sometimes she had the feeling that their fear was not directed at her. Angeni felt respect and love, which shone toward and surrounded her. If she was right, then what were they afraid of? Angeni didn't ask. The answer, whatever it was, scared her even without knowing it. She didn't want to hear it or face it. Finally, she no longer felt alone and that's all that mattered. However, there was someone that she couldn't place anywhere; a young soul.

"Proud of yourself, are you?" the youngest Guardian, Aurora cheekily asked of the charming Sentinel, Jared the next day as Angeni approached them in the leaf-laden main garden in the last days of Deciduous.

"Yes. Besides, I find it very interesting. How do you explain that?" the Sentinel teased her. Raising his eyebrow, he waited for the answer.

"There are things on this world no one can answer," chirped Aurora calmly while she spread her arms. "You could find even the growing grass interesting."

"What can I say? I'm a born Sentinel," Jared proudly crossed his arms.

"Oh, poor dear," Aurora stepped close and stroked his cheek. "What a challenging life you have."

Aurora's eyes opened wide and excited as she spotted Angeni. For a moment she hesitated, but then shy, Angeni nodded to her. Grabbing the Sentinel's hand, the youngest Guardian quickly tiptoed to her sister with the young man. The three colourful feathers held by a band across his forehead gently waved after him.

"This is my beloved sister, Angeni," arriving with a great grin, Aurora introduced her regardless that both of them knew who the other was from a single look.

"Jared of Seriana," the young Aserian nodded with respect to Angeni. "Your sister talks highly of you."

"Does she?" said Angeni, and then glanced at Aurora. "Well, greetings stranger," Angeni grinned in sudden embarrassment, bowing her head slightly she already regretted she had woke up that day.

"There are no strangers to an Aserian," Jared offered kindly. "But I believe you know that." He paused for a moment before he continued at his most charming. "Something whispers to me that you're not a typical Aserian woman."

"Well, thank you. I have no idea what you mean," Angeni smiled in confusion, "but I'm sure the intent was sincere."

"A real angel woman is someone you feel you've known forever, even though you've just met," the Sentinel added, watching her intently.

"Sentinel, I believe my sister would be pleased to hear your talk," Angeni reverted to cold calmness. Deep in her soul, she wanted to end this conversation as fast as she could, but she didn't know why.

"You know you really will like me when you get to know me," he responded with a tender smile.

"Oh, I already like you," said Angeni with a cheeky smile. "You are Aserian."

"So, you are one who speaks your mind, Angeni."

Angeni looked at Aurora. "He's cute, but not as cute as he believes," she advised, but she didn't understand the hurt in Aurora's eyes. Jared would not be diverted as he stepped closer to face Angeni.

"Don't judge too hastily. Maybe fate has brought us together," he added mysteriously.

Capricious, she tried to put Jared off. "You might want to check your fate one more time, Sentinel. I'll give you time for that."

Angeni didn't know why she said this to him and was ashamed to hurt his feelings, she never intended to. Her soul loved the compliments from him, but her spirit demanded she defend herself, if only she knew why. Then she quickly turned around and left him behind, feeling him watch her with that compelling adoration. For some reason, her spirit was full of happiness, but what was the source of it?

"I'm so sorry, Jared. Did she offend you? I, I never saw her act like this before," Aurora wailed while Angeni left. "I don't know why she did that. I'm sorry."

"She is quite charming, Aurora. Icy yes, capricious, but charming," came the answer. "But shorter than I expected." The last words carried by the wind opened Angeni's eyes wide. Short? She is not short! Defiant she looked back at the pesky young man, but from the distance, the Sentinel cheekily waved to counter her furious looks. Raising her nose high, Angeni had sworn she would not speak with this arrogant person anymore. He didn't deserve her almighty presence. Of course, fate sometimes loved to avoid promises souls made for themselves.

Angeni felt guilty, not toward the Sentinel, but her sister. Angeni apologized to Aurora hundreds of times for that moment and Aurora always forgave her hundreds of times. But Angeni still regretted that day.

Angeni's little sapphire book slowly gathered her knowledge page by page as more and more vials of ink echoed their thoughts. One day Librarian Abenago advised in one of Persecutor Sophus' classes that all of the apprentices should write down all their questions, be it evident or strange, into the pages of their books. So later generations may learn how these once young Aserians meditated, when they learned and if they found the answers to their questions. Other young ones may learn from their book as well. That's what Angeni did. The pages not only gathered her knowledge, but became an echo of her curious thoughts. And she had plenty of questions, and more were added daily to the old ones, sometimes with some answers. She wasn't the only one with questions.

"Our life is already decided from birth; that's what Justicar Onessia said," Aurora chattered while her and Angeni lay among the cushions of their mother's sanctuary. The High-Guardian sat on the edge and watched her young daughters. "If it's true, why am I a Guardian?" the youngest guardian asked. "I'm always curious like Iris. I love flowers like Taze. And I will have," Aurora paused and turned secretive, winked in the dim light. "Or I already may have secrets, just like the Spiritual Vanguards," she said around a mischievous grin.

"Your soul and spirit is a protective one. You have always wanted to guard others the most," her mother responded. "But never forget, regardless who you are or where you come from, we're all the same," she added proudly.

"But there are Guardians, Sentinels, Watchers and Spiritual Vanguards. Aren't we all different?" asked Angeni.

"Everyone has different talent and desire in their soul and our spirit is determined by our thoughts," responded Eve. "All of us have hopes, dreams, fears, loves, strengths and weaknesses. These possess self-contradictory sets of who we really are," she added with great determination. "But a weapon, such as your legendary crystal blade wouldn't define you as a Guardian as every other Aserian may have and use a crystal blade. Understanding nature won't define you as a Sentinel as if you want to learn from them, you can understand nature too. Being curious and the desire of knowledge to see every aspect of life won't define you as a Watcher. But they will gladly share their knowledge, teach you how to navigate and see the big picture in the maze of logic anytime. And living in myth, understanding life itself won't define you as a Spiritual Vanguard as you can live in myth, may have secrets and may understand life anytime."

"Our soul and spirit defines who and what we are," said Angeni as she recalled the teachings of High-Guardian Abenago.

"Yes," her mother confirmed. "We all look different in this realm. Our souls are proud of what we really are and what we represent. Our wings mirror this pride. But in the second realm and beyond, we're just souls, we're all the same."

"Can I have elegant bony Sentinel wings with sharp feather tips that pick up colors of their surroundings to be one with nature, be one with the trees and bushes just as Jared and Taze hide themselves?" Aurora asked excited. "Can I be wise one day like the Watchers and understand and see the world as Iris and Tlanextic? And can I be mysterious like the Spiritual Vanguards?"

"You never will be able to deny who you are. A guardian always remains a guardian," Eve responded. "But you can and I do hope all of you will learn from the other when the time comes. Each of you balances others. The Guardians are feeling life and the Sentinels are seeing it. The Watchers are learning it and the Vanguards understand it. That's the way of life."

"Everything is balanced," awed, Angeni whispered while she peeked over the little pool in her mother's sanctuary. "Soul, spirit and body. Past, present and future. Slumberous, Prosperous and Deciduous."

Eve curiously looked at her, while her daughter continued.

"This side stands in the light, the other hides in the shade. But what lies between them, Mother?" she asked. "I see my mirror image. But between me and her," she nodded to her image. "There is the water; a strange mirror which reflects us, but it does not belong anywhere."

The mirror image watched curiously waiting for the answer. Then her finger touched the water surface and the gentle ripples distorted her image. "What lies between light and darkness, I don't know," she shook her head.

Eve smiled as her daughter looked back at her.

"Questions are the beginning of wisdom, Angeni," she stroked her hair lovingly. "You always dare to see and want to know what others will not ask and fear. But sometimes our mirror image is just a mirror image and a mirror is just a mirror. There is nothing between light and darkness. There is nothing between brilliance and shade."

But this time her mother's answer failed to calm her restless soul. Her question returned to her curious mind over and over again.

The days passed, the whispers and fear of her fellow apprentices slowly ceased. Just as she had desired so much and dreamt of, many of them became friends and asked her help daily. And many times they played the Niare e Ayeshia, the Game of Life where they always shepherded souls, tiny crystal pearls toward their destiny.

Yet, sadness returned every evening, and she wasn't alone. With Aurora, she always lit candles to honor their lost parents. They never let the candles go out; to them the light guarded the soul of their parents. They missed them, regardless how wonderful a life they had now. The sisters never spoke about the life they left behind. It was too painful for both of them.

Everyone's destiny would be revealed as they walk their long path of life, so High-Guardian Aaron said. And her father was right once more. As time sped by, Angeni's new life started to take form as she followed her desire to learn more about their belief, its past and its origin, the

Crystal Shade event that carried the demons within and which would come one day to bring destruction to Eecrys Aredia. How or when, no one knew. Every day revealed that what she believed she knew about the dreaded legend was less and less. There were so few scrolls and books about it. Too few.

"As the legends say, the evil to the core Shaina failed against us in the last Crystal Shade," the echo of rigid Guardian, Justicar Ventrissa filled the library's large hall as she extolled ancient history to the apprentices. "Not because we were stronger as they were the stronger. Not because we were more intelligent as many of them were also intelligent. They perished because we were the ones who adapted and never underestimated them."

"Never forget to tell them! An Aserian must be ready for anything!" came the voice of High-Guardian Abenago from somewhere back of the library. The shiny soft aquamarine saree didn't lie about Ventrissa's peaceful nature and clarity. Unlike Sophus the Justicar just smiled at the old wise High-Guardian and always gratiously thanked his comments.

"Questions?" Ventrissa looked the apprentices.

"Justicar. Why do we fear the Crystal Shade?" the shy question came from graceful and exotic female Sentinel Taze.

"Why do we prepare to fight something that no one ever saw?" asked Kien.

"Our ancients have seen it, Kien. We learn from their past to prepare the future for our children," came the logical answer from Tlanextic. The Justicar nodded as she agreed.

"What happens if the Crystal Shade doesn't ever come?" asked Aurora.

"It will come, Aurora. One day it will come and maybe it will be worse than our legends tell us," Ventrissa whispered, and then she looked at Taze to answer her question. "That's why we fear."

Deep in her soul, Angeni agreed even if she didn't know why. She felt the Justicar truly believed in her words.

As they learned about this legendary belief, this event, every day the eternal question returned in Angeni's being; what the Crystal Shade really was beyond the common knowledge? She felt that everyone, even the Justicar based their belief on these more than two dozen millennia old ancient myths and legends that no one seemingly ever confirmed, but believed, respected, and most feared. But not all.

"You, you don't believe in the Crystal Shade?" Angeni's dismay echoed along the temple corridor, her eyes bewildered one foggy morning.

"Not everyone does," the calm answer from Jared slammed Angeni so hard that her eyes opened even wider.

"You should truly hope the Sacred Mother didn't hear your words, Sentinel," hissed Angeni's offended fury. She looked up to the ceiling, pleading. "Please forgive his ignorance, mother. Please forgive him," she said theatrically.

"You got me wrong, Angeni," he responded, but there were no words he could utter to negate this blasphemy in Angeni's eyes. "Like everyone, I believe in the Sacred Mother," the confident young Aserian continued.

"Sure," the defiant answer jabbed while Angeni crossed her arms and glared at him.

"I also believe in the Great Spirit more than you ever could imagine. But I'm not willing to believe a myth, and I'm not willing to wait for a legend that no one ever saw, yet many fear so much because some ancient scroll says to do so."

"Beliefless infidel," hissed Angeni. Defiant, she looked away.

"Belief is not only for believers, Angeni," the Sentinel made sure he looked into her eyes. "Everyone believes in something. That's what you forget in your endless believing. If you want others to respect your belief, you must learn to respect others as well."

Angeni meditated a lot on his words even though she never admitted it to him; she realized the pesky Sentinel was right. Why should others believe in what she believed? Why demand others to respect her belief if she couldn't respect others? On Eecrys Aredia, everyone believed freely and that's what she had forgotten.

The dreaded era that may return to bring evil and darkness to Eecrys Aredia reminded Angeni of a broken vase that she had to fit all the pieces together to see how it looked before. She thought of this learning like a game. Her spirit and soul felt it could take a lifetime to find the missing pieces needed to learn what she wanted to know about the Crystal Shade. In the long lifespan of an Aserian, one could possibly discover every place and secret of Eecrys Aredia and visit everything there was to see. She just hoped she would be this Aserian who would see all.

"Where are you sneaking to, Angeni?" her father's tone held her back when she silently tried to sneak out after dawn to find her answers.

"Uh, nowhere?" she sang and quickly turned around, padding back toward her sanctuary.

"Stop right there, my daughter," the calm fatherly voice ordered. Her legs immediately rooted to the spot. Angeni curiously looked at the High-Guardian as he walked to her. "You walked this path before. You know where it leads and what lies there," he looked toward the sanctuary. "But what lies in that direction?" he curiously looked at the dark end of the corridor where Angeni was headed.

"This brave little guardian would like to go on an adventure to find her answers," she grinned proudly.

"A young one who finally realized life is not just about mindless actions and instant adventures as many believe," her father wondered, "but sometimes a world, a culture whose past must be known, its story, its secrets must be learned and revealed to understand."

"I reveal them. Then I go adventuring," responded Angeni with a wider grin then before.

"Life itself is an adventure, my dear. If you truly want to find your answers," he stepped aside. "Never hesitate, always take the unknown path regardless what others say." He smiled and let the guardian continue on her way.

Angeni spent long nights in the Great Library, her presence delighted the old librarian Abenago who was finally able to share the most precious and oldest books with an unpolished, crude soul who willingly spent time to be polished and shiny. The story about the glorious and noble winged Aserian race and their legendary lethal enemy, the evil and cruel Shaina had fascinated Angeni. Every aspect that the mentors and later the books and scrolls offered her felt true, but they didn't answer her questions like; how they were born? What the Shaina looked like? Why they turned against each other? And why did the Aserians protect mankind?

Abenago restlessly carried the books to her table night after night to reveal more and more pieces, but every detail just raised more and more questions. Without any art or sketches, the Shaina were just some sort of faceless creatures in her imagination. But Angeni did find two elements that were common on both sides in one of the oldest scrolls; facts that were so surprising and strange. Neither Aserian, which was evident to her, nor Shaina ever killed their own. Never. That was the most sacred law of both sides.

This last bit surprised Angeni. She had always envisioned the demons killing each other in their dark evil world to gain power, to rule over others or they took the life of their fellow souls for dark rituals to satisfy their Dark Lords in their hellhole. This is how many described and imagined them. Yet, this one single fact set her to thinking beyond common knowledge.

"Why does this rule mention the Aserians at all?" the young guardian's calm wonder needed to know. She could not imagine an

Aserian ever harming another. *What would the effect be if that happened?* She quickly squashed these thoughts, as she knew it was never going to happen.

While the fragments slowly shaped a larger picture, they curiously revealed the second common element. The Shaina were guardians like the Aserians, so the scrolls said. Only their teachings, their way of life was quite different in that they forced people to do evil things under their guidance. But what sort of evil, and what is evil really?

In addition, one of the books mentioned that the Aserian and Shaina had the same weakness. If they were left alone, if no one cared and no one believed in them, their souls dwindled, their existence disappeared. Angeni didn't understand how it was possible. Maybe this could be the reason why the Shaina, if they ever existed, had disappeared in the distant past of Eecrys Aredia. Maybe everyone denied them because no one wanted to see them anymore. Maybe that's why her mother suggested to not close the world out of her life, but to know others.

The next dusty scroll that she found in a forgotten corner of the Great Library of Sessa Asria revealed details that Angeni had never heard of. So, as the legends said, the Shaina lived in a terrible fiery place of death and untold horrors, Briniu Malgram, the land of evil. It was hell-land itself that the bravest Aserian, Eosh, had encased in holy light during the last Crystal Shade. This was countless millennia ago.

"Where could this Briniu Malgram be?" her soft wonder echoed and filled the Great Library as alone late night she read the scroll while the forerunner of Slumberous brought the first peaceful silent snowfall outside. "Was there a forgotten thirteenth province on Eecrys Aredia?" she wondered and tried to imagine that hellish place. "Was it a place old Aserians knew about but never spoke of? A place maybe forgotten, buried deep underground? Or was it an island with a huge evil capital, embraced by tall walls, eternal fog or dark clouds and lightning?"

Later that night, standing in the light snowfall in the library garden, Angeni looked out from under her headscarf to gaze at the stars, just like they gazed back at her through thin scattered clouds. The five starred Crystal constellation, which reminded her of the Sacred Mother mirrored in her seeking eyes. As her human mother once said, if she asked these stars, her wish would come true and she may get an answer for her question. She pulled her thick saree together as the wind softly whirled the snowflakes and ruffled her wings; in silence, she awaited an answer.

"What are you seeking?" a familiar voice asked. The fresh snow crackled as the curious *infidel*, Jared joined her.

"Answers that no one else dares to seek," her tone as icy as the cold air, but so proud, Angeni said without looking at him.

"Answers come in their time, not ours, Angeni. You don't have to seek them."

"I love to seek them," her cold defiance sharp. "Without looking for answers we would never find beauty or learn from our mistakes," she crossed her arms and watched the stars. "Now maybe their whisper will tell me what they see. Maybe they will tell me the location of Briniu Malgram."

"Why do you believe it ever existed?"

"Every legend has truth in its voice," calm Angeni responded.

"Do you believe the stars can give you the answer?" he looked toward the stars.

"Wise and silent, they see everything on Eecrys Aredia as they always did in the past."

"Wise?" the Sentinel voiced his incredulity.

"Each star is the soul of a once wise Aserian, who guides us in the unknown and shows the right path so we never make the mistakes they made," Angeni extolled her personal belief with great delicacy while her eyes mirrored the tiny bright points. "All of them are here. All of them shine on us at once. Maybe if we listen in the silent night, they would whisper all their secrets." Then her charming daydreaming slowly faded away, her disappointment slightly echoed. "But if they won't tell what they see from up there, what they've seen in the past, I don't know how to find my answer."

"Maybe you can see Eecrys Aredia as they see," Jared said her after a short meditation they slowly ambled few steps in the snow together. Angeni stopped and looked at him.

"Unlike the stars, I can't see Eecrys Aredia at once," her superior rigid voice answered.

"You can. In a place, you may be familiar with, called imagination," Jared responded and a defiant frown was the answer. "Have you ever heard the Tale of the Peregrine Clouds, the ones who had seen Eecrys Aredia in her full glory?"

"No. But I guess I'll hear soon," her smile teased the Sentinel, but her curiosity finally overcame her icy defiance. "Tell me," she asked, crossing her arms. Jared smiled as he nodded and started to tell the Tale of the Peregrine Clouds...

The night stars watched over their fragile, but breathtakingly beautiful sister, Eecrys Aredia, tiniest pearl in the night sky. Her large continents in shades of green, all connected mostly in the north, but otherwise separated by the three deep blue and vast oceans covering the fragile paradise.

Between the icy peaks of the exotic jade province of Yaana, peregrine clouds were born on the tallest snowy mountains that spired to reach the sky. The motherly wind had blown the young ones on their long journey to discover their new home. Excited and free, they travelled from west to east to reach every corner of Eecrys Aredia. The beauty of Seriana Alira, the largest ocean on the west, awed the young clouds. It was a real jewel, a shiny pearl bound by the southeastern and eastern rich shores of Yaana. But they were curious and they wanted to know what other beauty might await them. So they soared further on the endless blue sky. The greatness of the ocean beneath them reached another rich continent, which enchantingly drew the curious clouds from so far; the western coasts of prosperous Seriana and the great province of Odess'iana welcomed them. Some of the white peregrine dared to take the long journey to go south following the wild streams. From high above, along with the soaring eagles they heard the joyful tunes of the land of music, Serenata Merida. But the bravest ones went even beyond to bring rain to the western coasts and the endless forests of the most southern province, the "crystal haven", Eecryssa Hanan.

Graceful animals lived and raced across the green meadows, forests and jungles, in the rich rivers and up in the blue sky under the shadow of the peregrine clouds. They passed silently above these wonderful provinces and their diverse continent, and wanted to see more. After the long journey, the salty fresh stream of the core ocean, Aesera Alira welcomed them. Its crystal-clear water washed up on most continents and connected almost all provinces of Eecrys Aredia. Some cheeky clouds whirled north to bring permanent cold and snow to the frozen plains of icy Crystana Serentis. Others traveled hundreds of leagues to the east before they saw and crossed the prosperous great island of Atlantia. Then the reign of Aesara Alira ended as the mainland reached the western shores of the oldest and largest province of Andrenia on the north, and the shores of the mythical Hijaz on the south. And yet more clouds followed the daring waves that streamed into the Great Dividing Gulf to make Eecrys Aredia much more diverse and colorful. It separates the main land from the province of Hijaz and to create the beautiful southern borders of three provinces; the land with its bright azure waves of Sessa Asria, a land of culture, was Coreenthia. And then the tiniest province came, the land of origin, Sagatta.

The clouds had seen that only the shores of their home, Yaana didn't get the blessings of Aesera Alira and they felt sorrow for that prosperous province. But then they had seen its shores were pampered by the most beautiful treasure, if smallest ocean of all. Before the peregrines reached their *birthplace, their home, they soared over the third ocean on the southeast. Between the eastern desert shores of Hijaz and the southwestern coasts of Yaana, Alira e Ashah; the mythical and exotic ocean gave life to a thousand and one dreams with its beauty.*

Seeing all the treasures of their home, the young peregrines returned to their birthplace to along with newly born brothers and sisters visit all these beautiful places of Eecrys Aredia over and over again.

"Thank you," Angeni whispered gratefully with a warmer disposition.

"Anytime," nodded the Sentinel.

"But not too often," like a blizzard, her defenses returned. Looking toward the stars, her whisper mirrored her thoughts. "If Briniu Malgram is not on Eecrys Aredia, where could it be?"

"Ask the stars once again. Maybe the answer is among them," answered the Sentinel. Then a snowball exploded on his chest. Then another snowball came out of nowhere and smashed on Angeni's wing. The two Aserians quickly looked around; it was clear, they were under attack.

"Ha-hah! Trespassers!" Aurora's trilling came from behind her masterfully built snow castle wall, which hid in the foggy snowfall. Four other Aserians peeked out from behind the walls – Kien, Taze, Tlanextic and Iris, who all patted snowballs in their hands. "Prepare!" Aurora whoopingly ordered her tiny army.

"Don't you dare," Jared whispered warning while he protectively stepped in front of Angeni.

"Fire!" the cheery order exclaimed and relentless snowballs flew toward Angeni and Jared, who together, quickly picked up the fight against the aggressors. They were all young souls and they all enjoyed the moment.

After that joyful night Angeni started to realize, maybe Briniu Malgram was a completely different world and maybe, just as Jared said, the answer was among the stars. Literally.

A place so hot that it burnt the skin scorched the ground and boiled the life giving water. The sky was like human blood painted red by the light of the evil God, Naamare, excited, she read the next night sitting cross-legged in the library's garden and enjoyed the light snowfall. Details like this were the basis of Angeni's belief that this hell-like place could not exist on Eecrys Aredia at all. But if not on Eecrys Aredia, where could it be? And how would the Shaina return when the Crystal Shade arrived? If it ever did arrive at all.

111

Angeni's eyes mirrored the pale night escort of her home world Carenia Seli that watched her from above. She asked the stars again in the hope that maybe they would answer this time.

Is Briniu Malgram a wandering world, a star maybe, which is returning to cross the path of her home world to cast a shadow on the brilliance of Eecrys Aredia? Do the two worlds of Eecrys Aredia and Briniu Malgram meet from time to time? Is this the true meaning of the Crystal Shade? Will this evil place appear next to Eecrys Aredia like a second Carenia Seli when the Crystal Shade comes? Or will Briniu Malgram race across and scorch the sky as a shooting star just to burn the clouds before the Shaina descend upon peaceful Eecrys Aredia? Is this how they'll unleash those untold horrors on her peaceful home when the time comes?

But the stars that had seen the forgotten past once again kept their secrets. Each of her theories sounded so untouchable and unbelievable. Even she couldn't believe many of them, yet amused her. Others fascinated and amazed her imagination, but also terrified her soul greatly.

Many times after she studied the Shaina and the legend of Briniu Malgram, dreams haunted Angeni. Dreams about armies of unknown creatures gathered around a strange, yet so familiar large pulsing *seal*. Like a sorrowful tired crystal heart beats, it called them. The creatures were different, not Aserian. Faceless faces watched her with dark red and black eyes. Souls silently screamed evil and cruel thoughts of their desire for destruction and annihilation. Emotions that the young guardian couldn't even understand scared her terribly. Angeni knew in her soul that they were the Shaina, the demons, and her mortal enemy. But her mind couldn't imagine their true evil being, as she had never seen any of these terrible creatures, not even a dream about them.

Night after night, a great wind screamed and embraced the fragile young guardian in her dreams, thunder deafened her as she found herself in a dark evil deserted place; Briniu Malgram, hell-land itself. Alone, surrounded by hundreds of these faceless evil creatures Angeni's only hope was Sachylia, which always watched over her with its protective motherly light. But every time as she looked up, the red light of Naamare, the evil God swallowed the beautiful sun and put the majestic sapphire light out before it ended Angeni's nightmarish dream.

"All your dreams have meaning, Angeni," Aaron told her when she talked out her dreams after one of her terrible nightmare. His thoughts always gave her a little insight to meditate on, but did more to calm her terrified soul. "Some are the echo of your soul, fantasies, greatest dreams, or your worst fears. Like your nightmares about Briniu Malgram and the Shaina."

"Some dreams are so real. How do I know it's a dream at all?" the young guardian wondered from her cushions while she hugged Pilly. "How can I control my dreams?"

"Why would you like to control them?"

"My dreams are my fantasies, father," the young guardian grinned. Aaron responded with a tender smile and shook his head.

"Young ones," he paused thoughtfully. "You can control your dreams if you learn they are just dreams, Angeni."

"How?" she asked in great excitement.

"Observe and be patient," he answered. "If you feel you're in a dream, read something, look away, and read again. In dreams, you will see the words change, as you never can read the same twice. Some souls can't even read in dreams." The High-Guardian looked around and his eyes caught on an hourglass. "You may also look at an hourglass, look away, and then look at it again. In dreams, there is no meaning of time," the High-Guardian said while Angeni carefully listened to each word as if she heard a great secret. "But remember, visions and dreams are not the same," he warned. "While dreams can be manipulated to your will, dreams that we call visions are something else. They tell the future they hold for you or others, events that cannot be changed."

"Can I see the future?" came her wonder.

"Every Aserian can," said Aaron proudly. "Perceiving the future is our life as all our perception is a peek into the future. The difference is how much we can perceive and how far we can peek ahead."

"Can I see what the next days will bring to me?" excitement prompted her.

"Every Aserian can perceive only moments ahead," responded the High-Guardian. "Those moments could be the difference between life and death. But rare prescient visions are different."

"Why?"

"They can warn you of what cannot be avoided. If you understand them, seeing what they truly mean, you may prepare for them."

"But why can't I change a distant event as I can change close by moments?"

"Distant events are ruled by time, building up from the flow of dozens of moments that are beyond your reach. No one can change the flow of time, my daughter," Aaron's wisdom countered and he gave a kiss to her forehead. "And now the unavoidable time has come for the young Angeni to sleep and dream well."

"Tell me a story about the Great Statues of Sagatta," Angeni smiled from among her cushions, hugging her eternal brave defender, Pilly. "Please, father," she added with a wide radiant smile the High-Guardian could never resist.

"As you wish," her father said with a kind tone.

As always the beloved stories the High-Guardian told always calmed her, especially after a terrible nightmare. Before her father's story was complete, her once terrified soul had already wandered into unknown imaginings of extraordinary beauty and peace.

After that night following the High-Guardian's guidance, the young guardian turned her nightmares to her own favor, to defeat the fear that encased her soul nightly. Every time she dreamt about Briniu Malgram, Naamare didn't swallow Sachylia anymore and the faceless Shaina couldn't terrify Angeni's soul, they feared her instead. They feared the great Aserian Guardian who descended from the sky to be the nightmare of these faceless creatures. She became the one who bathed the light and glory of the Aserians onto the acursed hell-land.

Angeni thought many times of Aaron's words. She knew that they could not change what had already happened. No one could. But she still believed her father was mistaken this time and that the future could be avoided, even changed if one knew what would come to pass.

On a gray day of the third quarter of Slumberous, the time arrived for the young Aserians to learn along with humans. Men and women helped the young Aserians open their minds and hear their thoughts, to learn how to build a bridge between Aserian and human who eagerly asked the Aserian spirits for guidance and help, usually with prayers. Angeni was surprised by their wishes and how many times they asked for help, sometimes even for meaningless things. Then she remembered the times when the little girl back in Seradelphia did the very same day by day. These lessons taught her that a guardian's life is not to pamper the human and fulfill all their wishes in every second, but to watch over and to protect them even from the wind when it was necessary. And to let them act alone, to live, learn and discover. Angeni started to understand why her own guardian never appeared to her, but watched over that little girl silently from the background.

These days also revealed to Angeni how much more Aurora was drawn to the humans than any other Aserians. She cared for them a lot and tried to fulfill all their wishes from the background. Maybe her young sister understood what even the oldest Aserians couldn't. Maybe her young sister will be a great guardian one day, greater than anyone? Angeni truly hoped.

Then the strangest lessons came, taught by the graceful, strict and clever, but also warmhearted middle-aged Watcher, Persecutrix Aurilla. The citrine yellow saree gently followed each step of the creative, intelligent, detail oriented, scientific, but foremost perfectionist Aserian teacher who strolled between her lady apprentices so proudly.

"When you speak, when you gesture, your face shows joy, hope, desire, gladness, or fear, frustration, sadness and other emotions," Aurilla said to the young winged women, while they balanced books on their heads to learn a graceful posture, to stand and walk in a confident and graceful way even if these were not in their souls since birth. "When you guard, when you guide, an Aserian must suppress all emotion. You must stop gesturing. Never let your eyes betray the timing and the nature of your decisions. Never let your face tell what you think."

Blunt thumps came from behind Angeni while she carefully balanced books on her head. The noise marked that the books on Guardian Onassa's head had landed on the floor. She wasn't the first, nor would she be the last.

"In true wisdom sometimes there is disagreement, but only the sightless say what others want to hear," Aurilla continued her preaching. "The words of the wise always break down the walls of illusion while the words of the sightless only strengthen the comfortable blindness. An Aserian woman is always wise and honest, but never harsh, never blind."

Moments later, another thump came from the side as Sentinel Merina followed Onassa's example.

"Keep the head up, eyes straight ahead! Keep shoulders properly aligned with the rest of the body! Don't play *knock-kneed, pigeon-toed* young ladies, or you'll stay that way, like the Shaina!" the rigidly proud Persecutrix always warned them, while she majestically sawed the air with her tiny staff like a chorus-master. "An Aserian woman is always strong, smart, gentle and beautiful!"

"But a fragile woman can't be strong," the young Sentinel, Taze wondered shyly balancing books on her head near Angeni. Seemingly, she didn't find logic the Persecutrix's words. Nor did Angeni.

"A woman is a balanced mystery, fragile in body, strong in spirit and soul," Watcher Iris delicately responded: she, who always looked behind the meaning of words and found the logic behind everything.

"Precisely! A woman always must be a mystery man can't understand," Aurilla confirmed with full confidence. "We are the pillars of our society! Behind every great man, there is a fragile, yet strong and smart Aserian woman!" she continued with a proud smile. "Even if they never admit it," she muttered.

"If my dear Jared will be great one day, I already will know why," Aurora grinned, lost balance, and the books on her head fell to the ground. "Or not," she added watching the books on the marble floor.

The day Angeni really looked forward to was the first lesson of the Art of Defense. She hoped she would finally see the legendary crystal blade. That first day surprised her and the apprentices the most; they weren't prepared for human instructors.

Sachylia had just dawned on the cold snowy horizon when they stood around their human master, Old Shen. He meditated with closed eyes, sitting under the atrium in his dark indigo blue cloak. His face was old, long gray hair, goatee, and eyebrows all showed his age.

"I'm not interested in who you are. I'm not interested in who you want to be. What I'm only interested in is your breaking point," warned his calm, but harsh tone. The old eyes snapped open and measured the apprentices like a preying eagle. Picking up his wooden staff, he quickly stood. Short old man he was; yet, his presence radiated superiority, even greater than any Aserian.

"Strength of the body, the loyalty of the soul and the virtue of the spirit shapes the duty of an Aserian vigilant and careful. But to be prepared to defeat your enemy, first you must defeat your own limits. If you can defeat your limits here, you'll be able to defeat it anytime and everywhere."

Slowly shuffling he looked into the eyes of the disciplined Aserian apprentices one by one.

"Many of your eyes now ask; why do you need to learn to fight. There is no logic in it. Hurting others is wrong, it doesn't matter who does it," said the old master reading their eyes. "True. But you're not here to learn to fight as only the ignorant and fools fight. You're guardians, protectors learning to defend what is most dear you. You're learning to know your enemy, to understand them as evil souls who will never seek compassion and won't give you mercy."

Shen stepped up to Angeni whose eyes looked around with childish curiosity.

"But your eyes ask something else, young one. You're not afraid to seek answers," he said. "Speak my child. What do you seek?"

"Where are the crystal blades, Master Shen? When are we going to get one?" she asked as disappointed she had seen only few wooden staves in the grass.

"Why does a young Aserian need a crystal blade?" the master asked with his solid voice. "Why the hurry? Is there a clear and present danger?

Do you see anyone who threatens us? Hmmmm?" he looked left and right, then snapped his eyes back at her.

"A guardian lives so others may live. Protecting and guiding is a duty for which there can be no mistakes," Angeni said determined. "I intend to learn how to defeat my limits to not make mistakes."

"Your desire to protect others is commendable, young one," he responded. "If your spirit and soul knows what is known to be right even that wooden staff will turn into a crystal blade in your hand," Old Shen nodded at the training staves in invitation.

Excited Angeni hurried to pick up a staff and then she faced the old master.

She focused on the old mentor, and remembered how easily Eriana had fought in her dreams. *It shouldn't be harder in reality.*

"To guard others, a spirit must be vigilant, a soul must be ready for anything," Old Shen said calmly, and then like lightning from the stormy clouds his walking staff struck toward the young guardian. Following her natural instinct the agile guardian evaded the staff and raised her own to protect herself. The two staves connected with a blunt thump. The old master nodded, immediately pulled back, and lowered his staff.

"Good. Your being is eager to defend itself, eager to protect one soul; yours," he said. Angeni ventured a proud smile. Fighting and defence really wasn't that hard. "But it's not enough!" Old Shen said and with a quick movement. Much faster than the previous one, he knocked the practice staff from her hands. Her staff spun away and landed in the wet grass. Surprised, Angeni looked from the staff to her master who held his staff to her neck.

"If you can't truly protect yourself, don't expect to guard and save others, young guardian," he was calm as he pulled his walking staff back. Turning around, the old mentor shuffled back to his place while he continued, "Until you can save yourself, until you're ready to make a difference, don't dream of your legendary crystal blade or even a wooden staff."

Old Shen meant it. During Slumberous and early Prosperous, all the young Aserians never even touched a training staff, just longed for and watched them from afar. They learned discipline. They trained their endurance and practiced graceful and elegant poses, sometimes from sunrise to sunset.

"You must learn how to fight against one as well against many. Know yourself and be self-aware. Don't fear the wind, but be one with the wind," the old master repeated day after day along with more wisdom on other days. "Never hurry, but every day make just one determined step toward your goal. There is no impossible for a guardian. If there is, you make the impossible possible. For a guardian there is no fatigue, there is vitality. There is no pain, there is endurance."

Although Old Shen was human, seemingly he had more wisdom than most Aserians. He saw everything, even if his eyes were closed, but the apprentices didn't know how it was possible. Everyone respected the old mentor, regardless if he was the most rigid of all. As old Abenago told Angeni, back in his younger days, Shen was the personal guard and mentor to the noble rulers of his home province, Yaana; the land of the beautiful sakura cherry trees of which he often reminisced.

"An Aserian must learn how to use their instincts. You must know how to act from the background, become invisible or follow and find someone," said Old Shen on a foggy cold morning standing in front of a huge hedge maze that grew at the far corner of the Citadel. The hedge was the pride of Gardener Onessia, but it served a greater purpose than being a beautiful twisted plant labyrinth that she loved dearly. Two huge metal doors led into the dreaded maze, each was for one apprentice. One played the guardian and the other played the human charge they needed to find following their instinct. The young ones each drew their partner, the one they needed to find.

Iris and Tlanextic went first. The two Carenian spent more time analyzing the setup and the logic of the maze together than finding each other, which they did quickly. Then Kien needed to find Aurora, who was pretty good at hide-and-seek. The patient Guardian finally found her friend, who enjoyed the game so much that as they stepped out, she already wanted to go another round. Sachylia was already high when shy Sentinel Taze and the Watcher Panoe entered, which ended with a search for Taze who was seemingly lost in the maze – but had found a tiny flower that required her nursing attention.

The maze slowy swallowed the other apprentices; Jellia and Verena, Calei and Saths, Merina and Yuna, Iwas and Daena and the others one by one after time released them from its twisted pathways. It was already late afternoon when Angeni's turn came. The fog that had broken up in the morning had returned.

"It's fate I tell you," Jared smiled and teased to counter the glare from Angeni, who had drawn him as they two were the last pair. The courteous Sentinel gently grabbed her hand with his left, embraced her wings and hip with his right, and escorted her to the maze entrance.

"Let's pretend I already found you and call it a day," she offered in defiance of her being hustled toward the large doors.

"Where would be the fun in that?"

"Trust me. I would enjoy it," she resisted as they arrived at the entrance. "Far away from me you would enjoy it too. I promise," she tried to convince him.

"Watch your steps, little one," Jared warned her and Angeni scowled at him. She was not little! "See you inside," he grinned and gently pushed Angeni inside. As the young guardian looked back, the large metal door immediately clanged shut behind her.

The playground of a huge hide-and-seek game, the large green hedge maze reminded Angeni of the Game of Life. This time she was the tiny pearl in the labyrinth. Following her instinct, she walked path to path. As Angeni chose an intersection, heavy doors at the beginning of the new pathway closed behind her; as a decision was made there was no turning back. Like the pearl in the game, she slowly wandered to find the one she looked for. But the question was; did she really want to find him? She wasn't in a hurry. After the next intersection, she had found a tiny yellow flower on the side wall and took a huge breath to enjoy its scent. Then she took another sniff as she enjoyed the aroma. Looking up to the sapphire sun, she waited a little before she strolled further.

Infidel, infidel, where are you? her thoughts asked, but her spirit calmed her curiosity, as she didn't want to know the answer. Her instincts said the Sentinel was somewhere close by; maybe around the next corner, but where? Step after step she meditated on what would happen if she simply took the short path, crossed the maze and left Jared in this Sentinel's paradise. Maybe the Sentinel would stay here for days hiding within these beautiful hedges, waiting for her to find him. Or even an entire cycle. Then finally the crystal age of peace would shine into her life. As she had a soul and a caring consciousness, maybe she would return for the Sentinel next Deciduous to dig him out from under the snow. Maybe.

A cheeky smile crept onto her face, the thought was very tempting to her thrilled soul. She already knew at the next foggy intersection where she should turn left as her soul dictated, so she would take a right toward the exit, which called her louder and louder.

Just then, the hedge rattled behind her and a dusting of snow fell from the leaves. From the corner of her eye she had seen; no one was there. She moved one step forward to find her prey, but her instinct shouted to turn around. Defiant, she didn't care since no one was there.

Then it felt as if the hedge itself moved behind her. Angeni stopped, but she was too late. The adaptive, now hedge green, bony wings, which picked up even the tiniest surrounding details, cast their large menacing shadow as they opened behind her to reveal the preying Sentinel.

Angeni's terrified scream echoed, a flock of snowbirds scattered from the hedge maze into the air as strong arms gently captured the fragile woman from behind. As her scream faded, the young guardian already glared at the grinning Sentinel who embraced her.

"Got you," Jared cheerfully whispered in her ear.

"Trust in your instincts, never believe your eyes," said Old Shen. Shuffling and so sudden, he passed in front of the two young Aserians. Looking at each other surprised, their eyes asked the very same question. Where did *he* hide?

As the first colorful flowers bloomed, the time had finally come to learn with the straight Synoi, which was meant to represent a single staff blade. It was made of Yaanan Soideae, a grass plant with a hard hollow stem. The young Aserians soon realized without the basics they had learned for so long they would never had the proper endurance and skill to master even this wooden weapon. Its training was physically and mentally challenging. The synoi combined strong martial arts values with heavy physical elements. And the most important; it started to mold the soul and the body, and cultivate the vigorous spirit.

Most of the young Aserians never really understood why they needed to prepare that much to learn how to fight and defend themselves when there was no threat on Eecrys Aredia. Maybe there never was, only in the legends. But Angeni felt that all the training, all the meditation, all the teaching had a reason and they were just the beginning of something greater. She had seen it in the eyes of the older Aserians, like her mother and father. Many of the young Aserians clearly did not believe in the Crystal Shade or the threat it represents. They only respected it.

Curiosity led Angeni; she wanted to know what waited at the end of this long path. She followed the teachings and patiently learned with the others. Every day they learned something new and every day Angeni felt she was getting closer to fulfill her dream; to become a great Aserian Guardian. She started to feel she was slowly becoming as good as Eriana, the Spirit Guardian, who brave and alone had battled hundreds of evil ugly demonic creatures in her favorite fairy tale. However she still couldn't imagine the demons, nor the legendary crystal blade. They seemed so untouchable and unreal even in her mind. Her fantasy always tried to create a picture of these myths and soon Angeni became the greatest guardian in a place where it didn't show; in her imagination.

* * *

Darkness surrounded the young brave guardian who knelt on the edge of a jagged splintered hole in the once gleaming, debris covered wooden floor. The scanning eyes of the predator looked down into the deep dark hall levels below, she waited for her prey. Her large white wings spread wide, and then lowered behind her right before the guardian jumped into the deep darkness to face destiny.

Sachylia shone through the tinted windows on the Great Spirit Guardian Eriana, who touched ground unharmed before she majestically stood up in the ruined hall. The wind snagged her sapphire cape and ruffled her wings. The almighty being was proud, felt the unlimited power that streamed within her noble being. She was one fearless fragile angel among hundred of faceless ugly, evil demons who stared at her, wanted her, but also waited and feared her.

"Light and darkness, peace and war! These are words, nothing more! Spawns of darkness, evil to core! Tell me, why we fight this senseless war?" Eriana's crystal blade, a sharp sapphire crystal shard pointed at the closest demon while she preached further, "Thee unholy with the sinful thought! Hide in shame, now you have been caught!" The eyes of the predatory guardian snapped at another demon while she continued, "Thee unholy, hell spawn evil and cruel! Fear me, fear me you demonic fool!"

The Great Spirit Guardian measured the beasts with her eyes as she stepped among them, lowered and separated the crystal shard while her voice became deathly calm.

"When the brilliance of the sacred crystal is pale; its shade twisted and whirled; one angel's soul hidden by the veil, one, who can change and save the world."

The Great Spirit Guardian crouched to one knee while she lowered both of her blades near her and spread her wings defensively. Whispering to the faceless demons, she continued, "A fragile and brave soul, so noble an Aserian; fighting is her life, is her path. You'll face the wrath of the spirit guardian; my almighty wrath."

The faceless demons growled their endless hatred and struck at the brave Spirit Guardian. The almighty crystal blades in Eriana's hands struck swiftly over and over again. The demons scattered, turned to dust, and vanished as the relentless crystal blade hit them one by one without mercy.

The dust slowly settled as Spirit Guardian Eriana looked around the great hall. She had defeated all the ugly, evil creatures. None were a match for her almighty power. No one and nothing could to stop her. Sachylia's sapphire beams spot lit the victorious heroine.

121

"Ouch," she hissed as something blunt and wooden knocked on the top of her head. As her wandering daydreaming spirit and soul immediately rejoined the torpid body, the young guardian already knew her greatest nemesis hit her; the wooden staff of Old Shen never failed to shepherd her daydreaming mind back to reality.

"Daydreamers are dreaming about life. Guardians are becoming the artists of life," the master said as he passed in front of the young guardian Angeni who sat cross-legged on the grass along with the other meditating Aserians. Angeni rubbed the top of her head while her eyes followed the respected one who dared to end the greatest adventure of Eriana, right when she became victorious.

Along with the other apprentices who sat all around Old Shen, Angeni watched the master draw a rhombus that stood on its edge in the sand with that dreaded staff.

"Do you know what this symbol means?" he asked the apprentices.

"The secret magic of eleven," Angeni whispered as she recognized the symbol, the symbol of the Sacred Crystal Mother. She was proud that she finally knew something the others might not. Maybe this time Old Shen would be proud of her knowledge.

"Do you know what it means, Angeni?" he looked at her.

"It's the symbol of the Sacred Crystal and the ancient symbol of eleven." Angeni gathered her memories to quote the strangers of Odess'iana, then she continued, "Decisions never come from the body, they come from patience and control; one decision comes from your spirit and one from your soul. But never forget, young guardian; when you take a road, the other will fade; as everything has its own shadow within our Crystal Shade. Eleven stands in light, eleven mirrors the shade, a brave little guardian can face the night even without a crystal blade."

Angeni smiled proudly, her little *heart* and soul were so happy. Old Shen just watched her silently.

"For young souls it means this beautiful perspective, Angeni. But what else does it mean beyond a daydreamer's imagination?" His question surprised the young Guardian.

Angeni looked at the symbol and desperate, she meditated what else it may mean. She felt her cheeks flush red as the other apprentices watched her failure. "If it means else, then I don't know. I'm so sorry," she admitted and sadly lowered her head.

"Never say sorry for trying, Angeni. It's better if you fail here instead in life later." The voice of the old mentor eased her sense of failure. The young guardian nodded with respect, as she understood the lesson.

"Respectively the lines represent elements, but as a whole as they take form together, they represent the world itself," Old Shen said and then his dreaded staff pointed at the lines. "One line stands for the wind, one stands for fire. One stands for water, one stands for the ground. Between them the endless sky, void rules," he drew a line in the middle of the rhombus to create two perfect triangles from it. "However in battle it must represent one more thing. A whole living being who fights for the world itself; you, Aserian," the old master declared to his apprentices. "Your spirit must be swift as wind; your weapon must dance like fire. Your body must flow like water, your whole existence must be solid as ground. Yet between mind and body, between thoughts and execution, balance must rule. Your mind must focus, should be empty as void, your spirit and soul must be clear as sky."

The young Aserians practiced centering, distance, and correct techniques, short, intense attacks points in succession. All of the techniques that the apprentices learned and refined with one or more receiving partners taught continuous alertness and readiness. Along with the other apprentices, Angeni started to become as swift as the wind, her weapon danced like fire. Her body moved and flowed like water, while her existence was in balance and solid as the ground beneath her feet. Relentless, they all trained, sometimes against each other and sometimes one against many as Old Shen desired. In these days, Angeni had seen the returning fear in the eyes of her friends. They were afraid to spar with her. But why?

"The aasqua improves your juggling skills with both hands. It teaches a set of techniques, skills and movements combined with philosophy of ancient martial arts," stated Old Shen, while Angeni with the other apprentices measured the Synoi Aasqua, the curved spinning staff in her hands. The staff reminded her of a single wave made from wood. She had seen the aasqua many times at the Great Feasts. It wasn't really a weapon, but it was part of the Yaanan visual arts, which produced an infinite number of amazing geometric patterns and optical illusions while it spun in both hands simultaneously.

The aasqua staves slowly started to spin between Angeni's agile fingers. The shape the staffs described was enchanting and astounding to the eye.

"It's developing your muscle tone, dexterity, stamina and focus," continued Old Shen as he walked between the young Aserians who slowly attempted to twirl their staves. Angeni grinned while she spun the staves faster and faster while she described various illusory patterns with them in the air. "But foremost it teaches you to never become overconfident."

The old master's calm tone still echoed in Angeni's ears as dead silent, she already rested on the grass and counted the stars in pure daylight after one of the aasqua staves had slipped out of her hand and laid her flat. This was the first time Angeni had experienced the miraculous and fast bruise healing power of her Aserian body, but not the last.

Moments later Kien, who tried to show Taze how it should be done followed Angeni's fate. As the lesson continued Jared, Tlanextic, Panoe, Aurora, Yuna, Iwas, Jellia, Iris, Saths, Onassa, Merina, then Jared and Kien once more, then Calei, Veran and, with the exception of young Taze who was always was shy and much more careful then others, all the other young Aserians suffered the same fate, more than once. Training with the aasqua was painful. Every bruise was a mistake revealed and a lesson learned.

As her mother said, young apprentices learn from the others, especially under Master Shen's tuition. During the days of learning, Jared helped her and Aurora the most when they failed in something. He always offered his help, even if, unlike Aurora who aways took the opportunity, Angeni defiantly refused it many times. Angeni's relationship with the young Sentinel was so strange; even she couldn't understand it. Her spirit and soul wanted to keep a distance from the charming young Aserian, but somehow she also wanted to draw his attention with her icy teasing. Despite her defiant resistance, deep in her soul she considered Jared as one of her friends, if not her only true friend after Aurora.

The green leaves turned yellow, and then brown Prosperous slowly gave way to Deciduous. Finally the young Aserians began to feel the balance, control, form and calm. They trained hard daily to learn from their own mistakes to be the masters. They slowly tamed the aasqua staff. Early mistakes were left in the past as all the techniques gradually became natural, one with their being. Their eyes and Angeni's reflected knowledge and wisdom that her soul had gathered in the past cycle. Her soul and spirit had begun to grow up.

The soft wind of Deciduous carried soft music from a lyra and a kind of syrinx-pipe, meshed with that of wind-chimes and drums to tickle Angeni's ears while raindrops splashed gently on her skin. The young guardian didn't move in the rain, crouched on one knee, motionless like a masterfully sculpted graceful winged statue. Her eyes mirrored and studied Sani, the human Executor, who stood a few steps in front of her. She didn't let him out of her view, not for a second. A long wooden two-segmented Synoi Yiana straight and jointed double staff blade united in the middle where she held the grip. She held it lowered in her right hand ready to defend. Its tip slightly tilted toward the middle-aged, long black-haired Executor. Sani held the same yiana staff blade as the young guardian. The depthless, mysterious brown eyes watched and waited, but didn't betray the Executor's thoughts to Angeni.

The Executor of Odess'iana could always surprise them. He was one of the most skilled human warriors on Eecrys Aredia, and also one of the youngest in his rank. A friendly and wise soul that Angeni really respected, but she knew respect would not be enough to defeat him.

A wild soul always fights as its nature dictates; so Old Shen always said. But the Executor was so disciplined, and devious. Every time the apprentices faced him, the young human had always worn different colorful clothes just to confuse the Aserians, especially Angeni who secretly adapted her tactics to the visible nature of her Aserian masters, based on the color of their clothes. But now Angeni felt the azure fur headband - which color stood out from the different darker colored fur war shirt, breechcloth and mukluks, the standard Odess'ianan warboot – that azure betrayed the true nature of the young Executor. Angeni felt maybe she could use this to her advantage. Maybe.

Only the breeze moved around them. Sharp as polished and perfectly cut crystal, Angeni's senses felt everything all around her while her eyes focused only on the Executor. Her mind was clear and her soul sensed every little change in their surroundings, even if a leaf swished on a tree's crown. The rain slowly dripped from the top of the atrium and the leaves on the nearby trees to form puddles all around the garden. The breeze teased the small wind chime hanging at the top of the atrium. A raindrop splashed on the tip of her yiana staff blade. It slowly slid down its wooden length, crept across her hand to fall and splash on the cobblestone; the mossy stone under her bare feet felt the cold. Some of the leaves caught by the wind escaped their twigs. They fluttered to the ground, and then were rustled to her feet with the next breeze.

It was the last quarter of Deciduous and the time slowly lent itself to cold Slumberous. As an Aserian, the cold didn't really bother Angeni's body, just the rain. The feathers on her large white wings fluffed out as they collected the rain and now they were heavier than ever. But she tried to distract all her thoughts away from her soaked white saree, which stuck to her, and mostly her fluffed feathers. The young guardian breathed smoothly, tried to keep her balance, and focused on her prey, Sani.

The tones that left the reed syrinx-pipe were the echoes of Aurora's soul, heart, and mind. The youngest guardian blew the pipes with passion, her joyously played angelic music spoke of her emotions, giving heart to the music, which caressed Angeni's ears. Even happy Taze loftily plucked the strings of her lyra. Her music slowed along with the syrinx-pipe music, yet remained majestic as Kien tapped out the rapid beat. His bare hands timed the music on the small single-headed frame drum behind them. The music reminded Angeni of the flight of an eagle flying high and free.

The other apprentices sat in their white sarees under the atrium roof to watch Angeni and the Executor. On their left, Old Shen meditated with closed eyes under the covered part of the atrium in his dark blue cloak. Angeni felt that he watched her even with closed eyes.

Angeni and the Executor had faced each other since the morning. They stood among the columns of the long open atrium where the young Aserians meditated sometimes from dawn until twilight; they also practiced with their yiana blades. Sachylia had crawled up to her zenith and was already on its approach to the cloudy horizon. Its cold blue beams were a dim light on her face. Her soul and spirit in balance kept peace and unity within her as she had learned. Her body started to rebel against this seemingly endless torture since the hourglass had been flipped for the tenth time.

The young guardian had already held out much longer than any other Aserian. Yet, she and Sani still held their positions. Each waited for the other to strike, or make a small mistake the other could use. The waiting seemed endless since neither had moved since morning.

Always know and see in your mind what your opponent plans, Old Shen's words flashed into her mind.

What do you plan, Executor? How long will you be able to stand still? Angeni knew no answer would come. Try as she might, she couldn't read the eyes of the Executor.

Sani's large protector eagle spirit, Niyol watched them from under his safe shelter of the temple's atrium. Unlike any other eagle, Niyol's wing tip feathers were beautiful azure, which showed the nature of his spirit. Angeni sensed that the eagle was measuring her patiently like she was its prey.

You may watch me, Niyol. But this time, I'm the eagle and your protected one is my prey, Angeni thought while she watched the motionless Executor.

The lyra stopped and the drumbeats built to maximize the atmosphere for the syrix. As Kien hit the drum for the last time, Aurora

126

played a solo that calmed Angeni, giving her peace and more discipline. As the music soared, Angeni felt like an eagle on wing that waited for the right moment to strike, watching and waiting patiently; an eagle flying above the clouds watching its prey from a safe distance. She waited, watched the sweat soaked Executor, who returned her calculating stare.

Angeni's ears just picked up a clink. Jared turned over the wooden hourglass holder once again, for the eleventh time as the last sand grains flowed to its bottom. The rebellion of her tired body burned stronger and stronger, she wanted to strike at the Executor right here, right now. Days ago Aurora held against the Executor for a very long time, but not for this long. Unlike others who fell fast after they waited three, maybe four flips of the hourglass, her sister had held on for the ninth turn when the Executor made a small mistake that her sister noticed and struck. But Angeni wanted to do better. She had sworn to herself that this time she was going to surpass everyone. This time she will be the best; the greatest young guardian of all.

Her soggy wings were so heavy and pulled at her back muscles. Yet, her soul ordered her hands and emotions to be patient. Disciplined, Angeni forced herself to wait for the Executor to make a mistake, to leave an opening for her to attack.

There is no fatigue, there is vitality. There is no pain, there is endurance, flashed into her mind again, but she felt her body start to resist as fatigue slowly crept in. From the corner of her eye she had seen that Jared sat back and proudly watched her with adoration, as he had since this morning and every other time. Meanwhile, Taze and Kien rejoined Aurora's solo on their instruments as they continued to play.

The music cradled and pushed Angeni's tired spirit to wandering. In her mind, like Eriana, she had already fought this battle against the Executor. She had chased him through the rainy garden while they fought for every step. Right when she would emerge victorious, as if Old Shen controlled even the rain, her thoughts were disturbed when a raindrop splatted onto her golden blonde hair to snap her daydreaming mind back to reality. The drop slowly crawled forward on the top of her hair, as it reached her face it slowly slid from her forehead to slide down her cheek before it fell to the ground. Noticing how uncomfortable she was, Angeni still tried to focus. She realized that as her thoughts straggled away, she was vulnerable to the enemy. Yet the Executor didn't strike. Why? What did he wait for?

The hourglass sands poured, almost at its end again. She didn't notice as she daydreamed. Her spirit meditated while her soul and body focused. Something had changed as she rushed out of her trance. The

127

music didn't soothe anymore. Her strong feathery white wings puffy due to the rain cried to be dry, they became heavier and heavier with the overwhelming raindrops. Her body strained, was angry and her soul began to join the rebellion to end this torture.

The proud eagle still glided in her mind's endless sky. It was overwhelmed with fatigue as well, slowly flapping its tired wings. The prey was still vigilant; it knew she was after him. The prey had to distress the hunter and it was slowly succeeding.

There is no fatigue, there is vitality. There is no pain, there is endurance, she repeated to herself, but it was completely useless. The eagle in Angeni's mind saw its prey and wanted to strike to end the torture of flight once and for all. She waited for Kien and Taze's music to build before Aurora's solo would escort the imagined eagle's flight. Once more, her spirit tried to stop the open rebellion of body and soul, but Angeni knew it was too late.

The wind-chime accompanied the music with wondrous effect, then Taze's lyre stopped and Kien's drum beaten stronger, faster to lead up Aurora's solo. The eagle of the daydreamer guardian majestically flapped once in Angeni's mind as Kien hit the drum for the last time. As Aurora lifted the syrinx-pipe to her lips and trilled a swift joyous melody, the eagle's wings folded, it already dove through the clouds at its prey.

Angeni shifted and with a quick swing, she struck toward the Executor with her staff blade. The Executor had waited for this exact moment for a long time as if he knew what the guardian had planned; his yiana staff was up and had blocked Angeni's strike. Rain sprayed from the wooden staff blades as they knocked together. The drops hadn't reached the ground before the staves were in motion for a second strike.

The brave fast eagle fought her prey in the imagined sky while the young guardian tried to hit the Executor repeatedly, but he defended himself effortlessly. Angeni spun majestically, her large wings sprayed water with every wing strike at the Executor.

Undisturbed, disciplined, and balanced, Sani was quick and countered all her strikes. The Executor smoothly leaned away from each wing strike while the young guardian forced him backward with each strike. Angeni's unshod feet splashed into a puddle and she kept up the attack while their staves repeatedly crashed against each other. Aurora's syrinx-pipe music and the wind-chime faded in her mind as she focused and concentrated only on the Executor.

Did fatigue never touch him? flashed into Angeni's mind. She quickly separated the yiana staff at its center, spun both ends in her hands, and tried to connect a hit as she struck. Once again, Sani countered the sudden tactic change by separating his wooden blade with clean swiftness; crossed his staves with one quick snap of his wrists and caught Angeni's yiana. He repelled the attack, but the next blow came right after it again and again. Angeni didn't give up, but continuously struck toward the Executor.

They fought with great mastery, spinning their yiana blades in their hands, and they both struck at the slightest chance to hit the other. Between the columns of the garden, they fought on. The Executor used the obstacles as cover while the Guardian tried to slowly force him back into the open where her large wings could act freely.

In the mind of the daydreaming guardian, the swift, but tired eagle tried to fly into attack position to catch its quick prey between the rocky canyons that they descended toward. But the bird of prey quickly evaded before the eagle could catch it. The eagle became furious, railing to end this fight swiftly and decisively. Angeni finally stepped into a space large enough to finish the battle. Her rebelling soul and tired body wanted to end this fight right here, right now.

The fragile woman spun around and her wide-open wings sliced the air toward the Executor. Reuniting her staff blades, Angeni felt the Executor had already shifted to one side where she wanted him. Coming out of the spin, her staff blade came around. But her eyes opened wide as she realized Sani had crouched and the staff whistled above him. The Executor's united yiana staff was already a blur of motion. His counter strike pulled the legs out from under her.

Angeni toppled. Her staff dropped while she tried to flap her wings to regain an impossible balance. But her soaked wings were too heavy and slow. The young guardian fell back so hard that her wings splashed water out around her.

Drawing in a slow breath, she watched the clouds tumble by and let the small raindrops cool her flushed face. In her exhausted mind, she had seen the once proud daydream eagle smash into a mountainous wall of rock while her prey made a small victory fly over her shattered corpse. That's how Angeni felt when Sani stepped up and looked down at her with a gentle smile.

"The hourglass flipped eleven times, Executor," Angeni pondered. "How did you avoid growing fatigued?"

"You can't wake a person who is pretending to be asleep, White Feather," he said with great wisdom.

"Be my enemy wise, brave and strong, so when I am defeated, I will not be ashamed," Angeni quoted to the Executor with great respect.

"Only the weakness of my enemy makes me strong, and a foreseen danger half-avoided, remember that," he responded. Angeni had to smile while she nodded from the ground.

"I will, Executor." Fatigue could not hide her kindness while her fragile body enjoyed the rest and tried to ignore the dull pain in her back.

Sani offered his hand and helped the defeated winged woman up. Angeni picked up her staff blade and let her wings droop against her back. They faced each other respectfully and bowed to the other, spelling the end of this long training session. With the exception of Old Shen, who still meditated with closed eyes, everyone watched the Executor and the young guardian. From the corner of her eye, Angeni noticed that Aurora had stopped playing and smiled at her, just like Jared, who watched her with great adoration. They seemed proud of her, even though she had failed against the Executor... as all of them had.

"The one who strikes first admit he's lost the argument," Old Shen's austere voice broke the silence while he still meditated. "If you are patient in one sigh of anger, you will escape a hundred breaths of sorrow." The old master opened his eyes and stood up, his dreaded staff already in his hand as he shambled to Angeni.

"No one is interested in how long a guardian is able to stand still, Angeni. Trees may stand for eternity in peace, but in the darkest storm they get tired and in the great wind they break, like you," the old master added as he stepped close to her. "An Aserian must be one with the wind, bend with the wind like the sakura willow. No Aserian should ever break."

The old master looked deep into the young guardian's soul.

"Everything you're doing comes from your soul, Angeni. Writing words to a complete lyre piece," he looked at the musicians. "Arranging the small measure of tones to a complete composition." He paused and then continued, "Or even stroking lines to make a perfect drawing, all of them come from your soul. Your body and your weapons are just instruments to aid the desire of your soul. If your soul knows what it really wants and if it won't let itself be controlled by your body and your emotions, all instruments will work in your hands as you desire."

With a quick movement, Old Shen knocked the yiana from Angeni's hand. The staff blade spun away to land in the wet grass, just as it had that very first time. The young guardian looked from the staff to her master, who continued, "Until you control the feelings of your body and the emotions of your soul, your spirit has not grown to the task. You must see and you must trust even with eyes closed." Old Shen turned his

130

back on her and shuffled back to his mat. "Come back, Aserian, when you do what is known to be right," he ordered before he sat down.

"As you wish," Angeni said respectfully. From the corner of her eye she saw that Aurora bowed her head sadly; she didn't like when the master chastised her big brave sister. And Jared, his eagerness to stand up for her was also mirrored in his eyes. Yet all of them remained silent. They knew the old master said everything for a rightful reason.

As Angeni left them behind, she realized Old Shen was right. Unlike Aurora, Jared, and the others, who were also defeated by the Executor, they waited for the right moment to strike. But Angeni didn't attack because it was the right time. In the first nine cycles of the hourglass, she waited, but wisdom and discipline was slowly replaced by fatigue that overshadowed her body and soul. Her spirit couldn't take control. The Executor counted on this. Her weakness was in the lack of balance. That's what the Executor wanted to teach her, that's why he never let a mistake show. He waited for her to make the mistake.

Since training with the yiana staves, this was not the first time the old master had sent her away and Angeni felt this one would not be the last time. The first time the methods of her master seemed so ignominious and severe. But as time passed, she and others were sent away more and more times, the young Aserians slowly realized that their old mentor was only keeping an eye on their best interests. As Old Shen said when they first met, he is only interested in their breaking point; a breaking point that he wanted to erase from all of their souls.

A master was always right and Old Shen always did everything for a reason. Angeni felt the old master demanded much more from her and only from her. Maybe her mother, High-Guardian Eve asked this or maybe the respected old mentor saw greater potential in her. On the other hand, as she was sent away many more times than anyone else, maybe she had made more mistakes during their apprentice training, but didn't realize it until she had meditated and returned. One thing was sure; Old Shen was always right and whatever the truth was the end always justified the means.

The rigid master rarely hinted at how to correct the mistake. As he always said, one's own soul needed to find the right way. This time as Angeni slowly strolled along the temple's dry corridor, she felt that her mentor had left a hint to remedy the difficulties. Or perhaps her soul already knew the answer.

* * *

131

Thunderclouds rumbled to silence and ceased their heavenly battle. The last of the cheery raindrops slid from the leaves and the top of the temple to join the others that gathered like great family puddles. The determined and icy eyes of a young beautiful Aserian woman watched Angeni from the mirror as she looked into it. The large white wings rose a little behind her back as she sat on the bright and dry side of the temple balcony. Her eyes studied her mirror image while her soul tried to capture the moment and every little detail. Her silky white skin was like poured cream, the blond hair shone in the dim sapphire light, the look of her icy yet cheeky eyes, the shape of her soft curved lips to the tip of her nose and its shape that was not so sharp, but not round either. The woman first raised her thick eyebrow in the mirror, a sympathetic smile played on her lips. Then she tried a perfect cheery smile. Her face shape transformed from square to heart shaped, and then back to rigid square as she reverted back to cool and serious; so serious, likely for the first time in her life. A serious moment required complete seriousness from her this time, or so as she thought.

Angeni looked back at her papyrus and arven pencil that sat beside her white saree that dried on the stone ledge, then back to the mirror, then back at the papyrus. For a moment, she studied the first drawing in the papyrus scroll pamphlet; the Sacred Mother, the last artwork of the young life that she left behind.

Let's see how you rebels work while I'm away, she thought in giggles while she turned to the next empty papyrus sheet to set the second drawing into her beloved scroll, the first as an Aserian. Finally, now she had a reason, a true reason to draw in her treasure. Angeni picked up a blindfold beside her. *The heroic and resistant spirit will enjoy the deserved rest while you rebels work. It's your punishment, my dears. And I don't want to hear a squawk,* she ordered herself while she quickly tied the blindfold over her eyes.

As darkness surrounded her, Angeni sighed. Her fatigue merged with that soft torpid binding claustrophobic feeling, it had taken hold of her entire existence from the first days. Her mind projected the memorized picture onto the papyrus while her hand prepared the arven pencil. For a moment, the young guardian hesitated. She wasn't sure of herself at all. Then, the arven gently stroked the paper and the newly born black lines on the papyrus began to echo her desired vision. Like before, she didn't want to make a single mistake, but now tremendous doubts assailed her soul. She thought she was going to ruin the sketch this time, yet her spirit was strong. It calmed her while it also dictated to her body, which obeyed. The pencil moved more and more determined, faster and faster.

As the great rebels, her soul and body worked together, the spirit of the young guardian already wandered daydreamer's land in the imagined Sagattan Oval Hall. Twelve beautiful winged marble statues of the Eecrys Aredian Gods and Goddesses stood along the walls of the oval hall to cast shadows on Angeni's wandering spirit. These were the perfect statues. As she had heard a lifetime ago, they desired the touch of the great sculptor, Nervaschanzo.

Angeni had never been to the smallest province of Sagatta in her life. Her daydreaming soul built this place a long time ago from Aaron's great tales of the city of origin. The young guardian had come to this daydream so many times, but every time the imagined hall and all the statues amazed her. She loved to linger in her little fantasy world that she had slowly built from knowledge gathered. The statues and the hall became much more beautiful every time her imagination gave more and more details to her existing imaginings.

Sachylia gave its glorious light to only half of the hall, as Aaron had told her. Five marble statues were bathed in the sunlight while the other five hid in the shadows. The last two statues that faced each other stood where light and shadow divided the hall. Between all of them, at the center of the hall a large faultless crystal stood, the very same as she drew on the first page of her scroll. Angeni knew the faultless crystal wasn't in the hall in reality. But she believed it appropriate to add this little detail to her fantasy world, so the Sacred Mother could watch over all of her beloved statues. The mirror surface of the large crystal reflected a blurry figure that stood in the bright light and watched the young guardian in silence and peeked into her thoughts.

"I don't believe I ever will be ready to fight," whispered Angeni as she admitted her fear.

"Only fairy tale heroes are ever ready for a fight, White Feather. Good, noble souls always want to avoid fight, never forget that," said the Executor as his spirit strolled near Angeni. "I hope you don't mind that I called your spirit to be, our thoughts as one."

"You respect me with your presence, Executor. You call my spirit not to ask for guidance or to seek strength and wisdom, but to make me wise and to teach the lessons so that I may understand. I thank you for that," Angeni said honesty with great respect.

The Executor took a soft smile and looked at the statues.

"You're dreaming of these, White Feather," he wondered. "You're watching and admiring them. But do you know what they truly represent?"

"Each God is one of the twelve moods and major traits of the Sacred Mother; the creator of all of us, the mother and father of everyone. Each statue is also one of the twelve quarters in the three seasons and one of these Gods protect one of the twelve capitals of Eecrys Aredia," answered the young guardian, but she already had doubts in her answer as she knew the Executor never asked meaningless questions if the answer was well known, easy and straight.

"You know well what they represent for the people of Eecrys Aredia. But what do they represent for a lone soul?" asked Sani. Excited like a child who wants to prove, Angeni opened her mouth to say the answer fast, but then she stayed silent and looked at the Executor.

"I don't know," she admitted. "What do they represent?"

"Life itself that the Sacred Mother watches over from the beginning to the end. It's the path ahead of you full of opportunities, the road you're travelling full of the challenges you will face in life." The Executor looked at the statues. "These silent guardians tell you the eleven steps of one day, a cycle or an entire life."

Angeni's eyes that mirrored the statues, opened wide, excited. She thought she learned everything from her father, but now new legends awaited to expand the stories of her favorite statues.

"Come," the Executor invited her to the first statue. The female statue carved of fine snow white alabaster was the eternally beautiful and graceful Goddess Derperia Capra; the First or the Mother of all God and the protector of the first prosperous province, Andrenia.

"Capra is one my favorites," Angeni whispered as she looked at the statue that reminded her of High-Guardian Eve with adoration. "She seems so proud, but also so modest and merciful. A beautiful soul seems so wise, so clean and strong, like mother." The daydreaming young angel happily spun under the widespread wing of the statue, as if she wanted to be protected. "And like she would give motherly protection to everyone, she is spreading her wings wide to embrace the statues and embrace us all," she looked up at the Goddess from under the protection of her wing. "Capra is a true protector, like my mother and the Sacred Mother."

The Executor smiled at her and then he looked up at the majestic statue.

"In the path of life, Capra, the Sacred Mother who creates and takes away, is watching over all of us from the eternal morning light, watching over life itself," the Executor said and he looked into the eyes of the

134

statue. They seemed empty, icy as the second quarter of the cold season, Slumberous, which the statue represented. But the face of the statue filled this emptiness with warm motherly emotions. "You can't determine who she is watching over. Her eyes watch one of the statues and all of them as well." The Executor paused for a moment and then stepped in front of Capra.

"Come, White Feather," he invited the young guardian near. "Look at the other statues, look at life itself," he continued as Angeni stood near him. "From here you can't see the Sacred Mother as much as you feel and sense her presence. But as a soul is born, it'll seek her guidance and look back at Capra, look back at the Sacred Mother in every single step of life."

"Even from here, she is still watching over us from the background," Angeni whispered, in her great awe showing her back to Capra, the statue's shadow stretched right in front of her. "She is always watching over all of us."

The Executor nodded before he continued. "At birth every soul desires and deserves a peaceful new morning. A morning that Agar is guarding with his eyes as he is desirably looking toward the rising sun," he said as they stepped to the second statue of blue agate, the defender God, Dernaia Agar. Angeni watched the strong man crouched on one knee spill water out of a large amphora urn while he gazed toward where Sachylia used to rise to shine into the hall every morning.

"His soul is young and immortal, mirroring the envisioned greater future; the same that we desire in the first step of our innocent new life," the Executor continued while Angeni studied the statue. The water from Agar's urn made a swashing song as it poured into the small pool before it streamed into small veins in the ground, which encircled all the other statues in order, one by one.

"Life, wishes and dreams are like the water that surrounds the second province of Atlantia that Dernaia Agar is defending, Angeni. It is cold as the third quarter of Slumberous; born to flow along the path that lies ahead of us. Its destiny is to melt from the ice of Slumberous warmed up by Prosperous to fill the meadows and lakes with prospering life. Then as life slowly becomes old, the leaves fall in Deciduous, Slumberous returns at the end, to freeze the water lifeless again," the Executor crouched near the small pool where the water gathered. The curious young guardian followed him. "But first every life must make its first decision to step beyond," the Executor continued. "Watch the water as it pours into the small pool. The drops are making the first decision of their life flow toward Derperia Psylia through the desired path like the widest rivers of Eecrys Aredia," he looked at the third statue as he stood up.

Someday I'd like to know everything about the Crystal Shade, mother. flashed her own voice into her mind for a moment as she followed the Executor, but she couldn't remember when or where she said this. *Did I made my own decision in the past already? If yes, was this my first one? Or is it just the imagination of my daydreaming soul.*

The joyful smile of the yellow Citrine statue, the protector Goddess, Derperia Psylia greeted them.

"As you start to stream like water," the Executor continued. "Under the shadow of Psylia your soul will desire to explore the new world, to learn and to discover the unknown while your being will meet the first joys of your spirit's beginning ascension."

"Psylia always brings joy and smiles, just as Sessa Asria brought them to our young soul," Angeni admired the silky dancing winged protector statue of the third province that had watched over the young apprentices since they were here on her land. The statue beamed the joy and love in every soul of Eecrys Aredia that held families together throughout Slumberous.

"All curious young life prepares under her shadow to leave their protecting shell, their innocence behind to step into the new phase of life as Deciduous slowly ends and as the blossoming of Prosperous approaches," the Executor said.

A caring woman in jade, the Goddess, Derperia Arina looked back at Angeni with her tearful eyes as they stepped under her shadow. "Souls become balanced and colorful as sprouts are starting to blossom and life resurrects lifelessness," the Executor continued. "The tears of Arina are like the blessed rain in the first quarter of Prosperous giving life to the new flora and crops born from the melting snow and ice."

"Young romance and love is always born under Arina's sign," the daydreamer smiled.

"Like romance and love, the water of life slowly warms up as the second quarter of Prosperous approaches," the Executor said who measured the streaming water as they stepped to the fifth statue, one of the two warrior Gods sculpted from dark slate, the protector of the fifth province. " Like the people of Eecrys Aredia organize their crops and start to cultivate them to make our culture more prosperous than the previous cycle, the time has come for the great consciousness of a soul to start to learn and experience a new level of evolution before it may see the first revelations of life itself."

"My soul whispers it is the time when the strength of every soul is revealed," Angeni smiled. Every time she looked at this statue, she felt the wise eyes of this rigid statue follow all of her steps. A bit of an irony as Tari reminded her of Old Shen who was from the province of Yaana that this God watched over. Her own evolution and present is clearly shadowed by the master, just as the imagined statue shadowed her fresh, young spirit now in the hall.

"A soul becoming stronger and wiser, blooming along with the flowers steps closer to its first great revelations in life," the Executor agreed as the spirits arrived at the clear quartz statue of majestic double blade wielding Goddess, Derperia Gemiina. She divided the cycle, just as she divided the two sides of the hall with her twin blades. "Gemiina waits for us to lead our soul into darkness, the unknown of adulthood that await your discovery. She pushes us to reveal our true nature and the world as the bright and delirious childhood approaches its end."

Angeni studied the blades of the Goddess. Her left blade pointed toward the past statues on the light side while the blade in her right hand pointed toward the remaining statues on the shadowy side.

"The life that is waiting for you will be full of contradictions, just like Gemiina, who is the Goddess of the warmest quarter of Prosperous as well as watching over the coldest province of Crystana Serentis living between eternal day and night," the Executor continued. "Her mighty being connects the past, where a young soul was shepherded in the light, with the unpredictable future which lies in the shadows and where the soul will mature and grow old," he added while the two spirits stepped to the dark side of the hall.

The young guardian looked back at the statues of the past before she sauntered over to the veined green marble statue. The first on the dark side of the hall, the protector of Seriana and vanguard Goddess Derperia Cancylia heralds the end of the fourth quarter of Prosperous and approaching Deciduous.

"There is no life without purpose," Sani continued. "Like the streaming water you'll try to find on a path shrouded by darkness. A wise consciousness manifests under the shadow of mysterious Cancylia as the soul slowly realizes its true purpose."

"Cancylia is mysterious like the Spiritual Vanguards. Could their life be their true purpose? Is their life something other than ours?" Angeni asked.

"Every life is different, yet walking the same path as every soul is all the same. However, life itself is a mystery. But there is always one truth for every mystery, no more," the Executor answered. "In this part of life, all the mysterious rivers, yours and others stream further, calm in its bed like the wide, but slow rivers of Eecryssa can be pleasant like the music of Serenata Merida," they stepped to the heroic Defender God, Dernaia Lenia. Carved from the creamy tan of golden beryl reminiscent of wheat this god protected the crops all through the cycle with his holy shield.

Angeni knew why the two provinces were mentioned together in the Executor's simile. Lenia was one of the two disputed Gods, who seemingly ruled Eecryssa or Merida, but no one ever was able to decide which province he ruled and what the other God, Vira watched over. Her logic dictated the eighth province of Eecryssa belonged to him as he was the eighth statue. But then, why could no one, not even the Eecryssans and the Meridans say it with full certainty?

The veins around the statue were already wide and the water streamed into them so calm while he continued, "The water is starting to become colder as Deciduous follows Prosperous. Under Lenia, experiences may bloom into lifetime lessons, desires may become acknowledgements, and dreams may turn to glorious achievements."

"Like sprouts grown to mature plants for the approaching harvest," Angeni added.

"Yes," the Executor nodded. "And after the successful harvest Lenia lowers his protective shield for the next God to take his place. He gives a free path for you to move toward completion of your soul's ascension where all the experience will bloom to wisdom which manifests in complete balance."

"The strongest God of all, the man-of-all-work and eternally vigilant Dernaia Vira," Angeni whispered as she was swallowed by the shadow of the largest and mightiest statue as she stepped in front of it. Sculpted in an unknown stone steel blue in hue cut with delicate light streaks, Vira stood in front of his anvil holding his mighty hammer in his right hand. He hammered a sickle on his anvil to prepare the almighty instrument for the beginning of the harvest, which started in the second quarter of Deciduous. A syrinx-pipe was in Vira's belt, the instrument represented the upcoming days of joy, when the Great Fests of Deciduous would start, which also gave a hint to Angeni that this statue belonged to the ninth province, Serenata Merida, the land of music and culture. Whatever the truth was, in his quarter Vira, the multi-talented kept vigilant watch over every worker and gave strength to these last hard days to ensure the upcoming, endless happiness now eyed the guardian spirits beneath his shadow.

"With his almighty hammer, Dernaia Vira is forging all your lifetime experiences together that they may give answer to what you seek in your life," the Executor said. "It's the time when your existence will reach the eighth step three times as Dernaia Vira gives balance to your spirit, soul and body."

"Eight, eight, eight," Angeni whispered excited. She had realized this was a hint that maybe she was wrong and this statue belongs to Eecryssa. *Does it have a secret meaning? Is it a similar mystery like eleven-eleven?* she wondered. Excitement grew as she peered at the protector God who just gave her a new mystery to be revealed. Deep in her soul she feared this statue and felt resentment toward him as in the myths, he forged the Anshara hulls and other human flying craft on his mighty anvil. But as always, when the young guardian quickly stepped to the next statue to stay away from him she had already admitted whatever happened to her family it wasn't Vira's fault.

"In the third quarter of Deciduous harvest is in full swing throughout Eecrys Aredia, while Liria watches over peace," the Executor said as he joined Angeni and the tenth statue. The warrior God Dernaia Liria was the protector of Hijaz and the epitome of the first days of rest. The statue flowed with the black and green waves of malachite. He held his polished mirroring large shield in front of him to mirror those who looked at him. "Like at harvest when the people enjoy the fruits of their work and look back at the entire cycle that they slowly leave behind. In life completion is followed by retrospection that Liria mirrors to a balanced soul. Souls may know who they are, or they may pretend and live in an illusion," the Executor said and gently pulled the young guardian in front of the statue. The grin of a daydreaming spirit mirrored back from the shiny shield. "But when time comes, when your soul faces itself, you can't deny who you truly are or what to you've become," the Executor added.

"Humble winged perfection," Angeni smiled to her mirror image. Amused, the Executor softly shook his head before he continued.

"Every balance passes as night slowly twilights. As you realize past mistakes, Scoria awaits you." The Executor pulled Angeni's grinning spirit, who happily waved to her mirror image, to the eleventh statue in red-flecked agate. The spirit's other favorite, the twin brother of Derperia Cancylia. Dernaia Scoria was the warrior God and protector of their home, Odess'iana. The statue crouched in full battle armour to lay down his sword as he finished a cycle long battle and finally arrived home. Scoria protected the people of Eecrys Aredia throughout the hard days of the cycle and he represented the last quarter of Prosperous when all put down their tools and prepared for the peaceful, cold days.

"See the void and emptiness in his struggling eyes," Sani stated. "Before you can step to the final path in your life or go to bed to await your next day, you'll face this void and emptiness, a fatigue in your own spirit and soul. This emptiness can last for moments or lasts for eternity. This may swallow your struggling soul if you don't dare to dream, and to awake in the next morning to what awaits you."

The Angeni spirit studied Scoria for a long time. Great audaciousness tinged by fatigue shone in his eyes, the spirit now understood why.

"I was born under his sign," she whispered as she remembered her present and past life. She was reborn on the very same day, on her real birthday. "I respect him the most. I can feel his struggle, the weight that he carries," she added with greatest respect. In her eyes, Capra and Scoria were the only two statues that really completed each other, but she never was able to answer why she assumed this.

"Perhaps you'll carry the same weight as your soul is like his," the Executor said. "Maybe you'll be a great, ardent warrior, like Scoria. Or maybe all your life will be a struggle filled with void and emptiness."

The Executor looked at her and continued, "Whatever your life will be, in the end Sagatta, the lonely little one who stands guard between the passing and the new beginning will await you."

Across the hall from the double-blade holding, Goddess Gemiina stood the vision of sadness, the little Goddess sculpted of black and white snowflake obsidian Derperia Sagatta from whom the smallest province received its name is the forgotten. Sagatta's left side that stood almost invisible in the shadows, while its right side stood in the light.

"The eleventh, the last and the smallest, but the most important step in life is when the water of life becomes lifeless as Sagatta's arrival heralds the first day of the cold Slumberous," the Executor said as he looked at the small pool where the life of water slowly drained. "Sagatta's role is tiny, yet so great, like the smallest twelfth province where all these statues stand. Her time is the time to reconciliate, to leave your past or the day behind or to go home to the Sacred Mother."

"Sagatta has the most emotion of all," Angeni whispered as she watched her eyes. "Her left eye is full of sorrow as Sagatta regrets that the last days of the old cycle are passing. But light shines in her right eye full of happiness as she sees the upcoming rebirth of a new, Prosperous cycle."

"Like every soul, Sagatta doesn't want the past to be forgotten, but wants to be remembered," the Executor said. "Sagatta reminds us to never forget a past cycle she closed, but bravely step toward the right path which leads you to a better future, or to your next day. She reminds us, never forget a soul who is not with us anymore, but always remember the glorious achievements, the echo of every life."

The Executor looked at all the statues as he stepped to Capra.

"Agar is the beginning and Sagatta is the ending. Birth and passing are the zeroes with nine steps of evolution between them with three major steps each. All together form the eleven steps of life."

"Like the trimesters, Prosperous, Deciduous and Slumberous," the young guardian said. "Prosperous is our young age, our morning. Deciduous is our middle age, the bright noon that leads into evening as the light slowly fades. And Slumberous is our old age, the approaching twilight."

The Executor nodded agreement. "You may also find these steps in your daily life, White Feather. But there Sagatta is one with Agar where both of them, the first and the last, the brightest brilliance and the darkest shade, the beginning and the end in life form the eleventh step together to then start the cycle over and over again."

"But between Sagatta and Agar, there is Capra. She is the Sacred Mother in life. But what does she symbolize in our daily lives?"

"Dreams. Capra guards us while we sleep between sunset to sunrise, the end and the beginning."

"The guardian of daydreamers," she whispered in awe. Finally, she knew why Capra and Scoria completed each other, at least in her eyes.

"Every soul follows their heart's desire," the Executor said. "It is a hard way, but it is a good way. Richness and grace is the beauty of life which should be the path of every soul."

"Thank you for your lesson, Executor," the Angeni spirit bowed with respect.

"Now, I will leave you alone with your thoughts, White Feather, to find what you seek. As Master Shen says, sometimes you must take your path alone to see what awaits you in the next morning." The Executor's spirit disappeared as he stepped into the shadows.

There was still time to spend alone with her thoughts. After it declared its endless doubts again, her soul whispered to the wandering spirit that the sketch was halfway done. The spirit ordered discipline to continue drawing.

Countless orderly shelves of scrolls and books encompassed the young guardian's next destination after she left the Oval Hall and hurried up a long elegant spiral staircase. The Great Spirit Library of Angenius was masterfully engraved from right to left in Aserian on the wall near the entrance. Beneath it a small sign hung. *Forbidden territory! Guest spirits may enter only with invitation!* The sign, which was written with great haste, had been hammered to the wall with pretend fury right after she bowed out the uninvited and apparently lost, too curious Sentinel Jared's spirit from her spirit's library and her thoughts few days ago.

Unlike the Oval Hall and many other imagined places in her mind, she gladly shared with guest spirits during their meditations as they tried to channel their thoughts. This library was only for one humble spirit; hers. This was the place where all her knowledge was stored and hid her greatest dreams and secrets. Her deepest daydreamings and feelings were visualized in paintings, never written imagined and memorized verses and thoughts set into scrolls and books.

Large circular holes in the ceiling gave a path for Sachylia's dim sapphire light and small torches on the walls lent a cold glow to the place with their blue flames. The light reflected off gilded titles, polished stone tablets and warm wooden tables. Under some of the sun-holes, large trees grew out of the ground to majestically aspire to reach the sky, just like in the real life Great Library of Sessa Asria.

Angeni curiously tweaked her spirit wings back while she looked around. Proud of her knowledge, she always took great care of her library. Every scroll and book she read in her two lives, including many books and scrolls from the Great Library of Sessa Asria, which were here and mostly memorized. With her studies, she had pieced together a broader picture of Eecrys Aredia, its past, the cultures of the different provinces and the real meaning of her own existence.

Many enchanting paintings of imagined events and colorful landscapes looked back from the walls. Most of these imagined pictures were brought into being during meditation training. The pictures all faced their opposites; the painting of a beautiful day eyed the darkest night. The beautiful landscape of Eecrys Aredia basking in Sachylia's sapphire sunlight shone its peaceful contrast to the dark art of Briniu Malgram, bathed in the evil red light of the cruel sun God Naamare. As if they squared off to fight, the art of the noble Aserians stood against the dark portrait of faceless and relentless Shaina. Light and darkness, forgotten past and imagined future, visible, and invisible; everything that was connected to the Crystal Shade was here in one place.

The daydreaming eyes of a graceful and beautiful Aserian woman stood in an elegant sapphire saree so innocent yet so proud. Her imagined and fictive self-portrait watched over her own movements from the main wall as the spirit strolled to the polished oak table at the far end of the library. It was the work of her winged spirit's divine painter incarnation, Lady Master Angenius as she called herself in those wonderful daydreaming moments. The portrait was born from one of Old Shen's longest meditation training sessions where the spirit of the apprentices needed to face their own being to look into themselves, to see who they truly were and to know their inner being. Maybe the old master didn't exactly mean like this. However, Angeni was sure the experience of that colorful daydream was now helping her enslaved soul and body in life at this very moment.

Severity radiated from Angeni as she slowly pulled her finger along the edge of a shelf. Frowning, she looked at her fingertip. No dirt. A rigid nod confirmed her satisfaction. Then a papyrus map that awaited her on the nearby table caught those preying eyes. It was the work of the great cartographer and librarian incarnation of the Divine Angenius who gathered all of Eecrys Aredia's physical knowledge in one place, that map. However, Angeni had never seen a real map of her home world, as they were very rare. The map followed every detail she had heard and learned. She always expanded it carefully. But knowing everything about Eecrys Aredia sounded so easy when the children's tale described her home, The Tale of the Peregrine Clouds.

Angeni's eyes slowly passed over the map as if she were one of those wandering clouds travelling up in the sky from continent to continent above land and sea. Then above the Great Dividing Gulf the *peregrine clouds* stopped. One place was bare even though she'd been there for almost a cycle. The spirit picked up the arven pencil from the table to add Sessa Asria in its proper place.

"There you go," the Great Cartographer whispered proudly while she added the capital of the third province to the map. After a while, the spirit sighed with satisfaction as she finished reviewing her map. Everything seemed to be in its rightful place and followed the tale. She just hoped the Great Cartographer incarnation of hers had caught every detail properly and this small treasure of hers truly showed Eecrys Aredia just as the stars and the clouds were seeing her.

The soft splashing of the Shrine Fountain of Gracius gurgled from the middle of the library. The beautifully carved statues of her human mother and father both holding a baby girl in their arms, looked down at her. Angeni sat on the shrine's edge and looked into the rippling water. At peace, the eternal question flashed into her mind; if balance rules everywhere what lies between light and dark?

The spirit felt she still had plenty of time before the self-portrait was finished. Her mirror image smiled, she already knew how to pass the remaining time. The heavy wooden door creaked as she opened it to reveal a rarely visited place in her mind; a tiny hall at the far end of the library. Dusty and so small, it was lost in the half-light. It revealed a different life, which was half-forgotten and some parts of it so painful. Yet, just like the large hall, it delved into so many things about the past and dreams of a once little girl. At least what she remembered of that life.

Strolling to the end of the hall, where a small wooden table and chair awaited, the spirit looked around, awed, but also a bit sad. So many fragmented almost forgotten memories dwelled here; memories of her first sketches and scrolls of poems she had read and even tried to write. Sachylia's dim beams through the tiny sun-holes in the ceiling caught the spirit as she walked to the old bookshelf.

Dust whirled in the air as she picked up an old book, her favorite, and examined it from all sides. Staring at the cover, a heartwarming feeling filled her being; Spirit Guardians Eriana and Iria, the title said. The book of books that instigated her dreams when she was a little girl. A gentle breeze set the dust to whirling away from the cover, and then she hugged the book for a short moment. She wanted to open it, read it just once more to remember every little detail, but was afraid. Maybe her favorite story was beautiful because of the fading memories and her imagination as she expanded that wonderful story and world countless times in her mind. Now, she didn't want to be disappointed. Angeni fondly put it back in its rightful place.

She sat near the tiny table and quickly rolled out an empty papyrus and prepared an arven pencil. Its black tip swung like a tired pendulum above the blank white paper while she stopped and gathered all her thoughts to learn; what lies between light and darkness?

"Life is about eleven steps," her spirit's whisper reflected her reasoning. "Birth and passing are zeros, the beginning and the ending. Nine steps of evolution lie between them with three times three major steps each." With a soft sigh, she meditated again. The pencil's tip gently touched the papyrus as she continued, "Every Aserian being has one soul, one spirit and one body." The arven left the echo of her toughts slowly drawing a triangle to follow her. "Light and darkness are opposite mirrors of each other." Crumbling black lines were born as she drew an upside down triangle beneath the first one; together shaping a rhombus standing on its edge. Then she stopped for a while.

"Our souls shape the Crystal Mother, she, who gave life to the Aserians," she repeated while the pencil's tip slowly passed above the lines of the first triangle. "Then the Shaina, our dark image," the arven followed the course of the lower triangle. "Three and three. Six out of the nine that lie between the beginning and end. A third equal part remains, one more spirit, soul and body before eleven ending comes."

The young guardian studied the symbol, but rotated her head first to get a different view, then the papyrus. Regardless how she looked at it, two equal sides looked back at her.

"The crystal's brilliance is a mirror of its shadow. The crystal's shadow is a mirror of its brilliance," she whispered, and then dissatisfied, she shook her head. "Who or what are you? If you exist, where are you hiding?" But her drawing didn't give the answer.

"This is where all the knowledge fails, my dear," the spirit muttered. "Maybe mother is right. Maybe nothing is there," she added while she put the arven pencil back in its imaginary place on the table. The ancient symbol of eleven looked back at her, innocent without revealing any secret.

"Everything is told by the numbers. Eleven tells everything," the meditating spirit whispered her belief. "It's a mirror to our inner self," her cold whisper gave her inspiration. Angeni folded the papyrus in half right where light and darkness met, then flipped the paper in half and watched both sides, but she saw nothing, just the two already existing sides.

"Some say it represents the Sacred Crystal Mother and her shadow. Or the one who is watched over by her and her angels." Falling deep in her thoughts, her mind tried to recall exactly what the strangers of Odess'iana told that curious little girl. "Others say; it's a crack, a bridge linking light and darkness. A doorway..." she paused.

"A crack," the whispered beginning of revelation left her lips while her mind looked at the mystery from a fresh new perspective. The young spirit walked to the *crack* in the wall; the large arch entrance. Beyond it was darkness. Her mind began to visualize the answer and her imagination followed. "It's like we could look through the arch, our doorway that is standing between light and darkness," she realized, and then she stepped to the dark side and looked back into the light. "No one is watching the doorway, no one cares about its existence as everyone wants to see the other side; light to darkness, darkness to light."

The breakthrough was so close, she felt it. Hurrying back to the table, she picked up the folded papyrus.

"As if we would look through," she whispered, raising it toward the ceiling, into the sapphire sunlight to make the thick papyrus transparent, to see both sides at once. The bright sunbeams forced her eyes to blink while the light sparked the paper and silently revealed what otherwise cannot be seen; the triangles from both sides perfectly covered each other, shaping and giving life to the hidden third one.

"You cannot be seen, yet you do exist," Angeni whispered as she felt her restless spirit had finally found an answer to one of her many questions. She had seen a third body, spirit and soul born before her eyes. "You don't just stand between light and dark, you were born of them, born from both of us. Like an all seeing eye, you watch silently while you hide between us."

Lowering the papyrus, her spirit smiled in discovery and lone victory she had achieved without the help of body and soul. "Three sides create balance, not two," her spirit whispered. "But who or what makes all equal and complete in the eyes of the sacred one. Who or what lives between the realms of light and darkness, between brilliance and shade?" She still didn't know and maybe she was never going to get an answer for her question. Still, the thrilled happiness and euphoric touch of discovery held her as she knew; whatever she searched, it existed. It was there and she found it.

Then so sudden, doubt broke into her childlike enthusiasm. Was this possible at all? Had the young Aserian found and see what no one, not even the oldest and wisest ever did before? Or was it just a young daydreamer's imagination, something she wanted to see? The lone spirit didn't know and her soul, which was put to its slavery along with the body now, so defiant it didn't want to help her either.

"I should tell this to mother," her spirit whispered. But she feared her revelation might turn out to be nothing, just another of her daydreams. The enslaved soul grabbed the moment and immediately protested with its doubts to crush the moment further and to squash the great revealtion into disappointment. And foremost, to show the spirit the evidence she was not willing to see; "The humans are the balance," the spirit whispered. "They stand between light and darkness, they always have. That's what mother would say."

Then the calm advice she had heard a long time ago, which now sounded as an inner voice flashed into her mind to give her strength, *You always do know the answer you're looking for. Never hesitate, never fear to ask. Trust your instincts. Always.*

She didn't even remember who gave her this advice, but she felt her instinct was right this time, regardless what others said. Only the time to reveal this discovery has not yet come.

"No," she whispered; her eyes mirrored the little symbolic drawings of the ultimate discovery in her hands. "Whomever, whatever you are, you exist," her determination echoed from her angelic whisper. "I'll never stop looking for you. One day I will learn who you are. One day I'll find you."

146

The body still sketched tirelessly and her defiant soul silently protested with endless doubt, but even more against the cruel treatment. The slave driver spirit quickly cracked the whip and ordered organized discipline… while smiling; it enjoyed the rest and free meditation.

Angeni didn't want to leave her fantasy world yet; the drawing, or whatever was born line after line by her hand wasn't ready yet. A last smiling proud glance around the great library, the place that was witness to a great discovery of a young soul, she left it behind for now.

The cold sapphire sunlight from the end of the loggia called her out to the balcony. Silhouettes, two tall, and one very small one, studied her from the shadows, watched her movements. But not here, outside, in the real world. Only her consciousness manifested them as she felt their presence. Angeni knew who was watching her tireless working being, and she knew they had a rightful reason. The young guardian raised her nose so proud, but couldn't resist a soft smile as she passed in front of them.

Sitting far away from the imagined edge of the balcony at the sanctuary's stone altar, Angeni rested her spirit wings, which also felt the torture of the training. The balcony view revealed the beautiful winged white temple that had greeted her first days. This view always filled her with a rare peace and harmony. Unlike the real world, now the Citadel wasn't full of apprentices and mentors. Only a few white birds flew in the sky that she imagined there. The spirit watched and rested while the body and soul worked in balance. Then the four quick and determined vertical lines of her signature were marked as her soul and body had finished her own portrait.

The body, soul, and strayed spirit rejoined into one full existence. She expelled a breath and took off the blindfold. Angeni feared the result. Curious, her eyes examined the sketch for a long moment before her satisfied smile grew. The portrait was of the same graceful young Aserian woman she had seen in the mirror. Not a single detail missed, not a single line out of place.

"I hope my soul saw what I needed to see and my body learned what it needed to learn," she whispered to the three silhouettes she had seen in her imagination. They still watched her from behind.

"Did you have doubts?" asked Old Shen behind her while Angeni looked back. Her master and the Executor stood right behind her just as she had felt. Sani's eagle, Niyol rested on the Executor's right shoulder and studied Angeni with his large black eyes as always.

"Yes," admitted the young guardian. "It escorted me from the beginning to the end. My soul feared making mistakes. But my spirit controlled all my actions and stood vigilant guard as you taught me."

"What did you learn from it?" asked the old mentor. For a moment Angeni felt the desire to share her great discovery, but then she realized as her spirit had before; the time to reveal it had not come yet. She looked back at her portrait.

"My spirit showed what I must see, even with my eyes closed." She paused for a moment. "Even more," added with a soft smile. "My body knows how to trust in my spirit's judgment, even if it's wandering far away. But my soul felt deep doubts regardless of the outcome, yet remained disciplined." A little disappointment rang in her voice.

"Deep doubts, deep wisdom, small doubts, little wisdom," Shen responded wisely. Angeni heard pride in his voice maybe for the very first time.

"You've learned the basics of the discipline you needed, White Feather," the Executor said. "But never forget; learning never ends and always will be a companion on the long path of your life."

"I won't forget, Executor," she nodded thankfully.

Niyol screamed once. Angeni felt that the large majestic eagle praised her from the shoulder of his human charge. The large wings folded behind her back as she stood up.

"Thank you, Niyol," she crooned while she stroked the eagle kindly.

"The life of the wise will be full of doubts," Sani added.

"But there is always a way out of every dark mist, over a rainbow trail that the wise always find," echoed a calm familiar angelic female voice. All of them looked toward the source. Majestic High-Guardian Eve strolled toward them in her elegant golden saree. Her gold headdress reflected the cold beams of Sachylia into the hall, her large wings rested behind her back.

Old Shen and the Executor greeted her with a slight bow. The High-Guardian nodded to them in response.

"Their first cycle has ended. As I promised all have become disciplined and well trained," the old master said. "My apprentices know everything this old man has to share with them."

Full of surprise, Angeni stared at her old master. No one ever knew when their apprentice training would end. They lived for the day not knowing what the future would bring to their existence. She never dreamed today's long discipline training against the Executor would be her last in beautiful Sessa Asria, which she considered her second home after Odess'iana. Today was the day her beloved little book that gathered all her knowledge gets into the library of Sessa Asria and Librarian Abenago's collection.

"May the Great Spirit's blessing always be with you, White Feather," said the Executor. Niyol perched to also bless the young guardian. Angeni smiled at the eagle, and then looked at her master, who watched her seriously. His voice calm as the breeze.

"I feel your soul's desire," old Shen added. "I know what you want to hear. That you were the most disciplined and the most promising apprentice that I ever taught." He paused while Angeni waited for the words she had wanted to hear for so long. "But you're not," he added with honesty. The young guardian could only listen in silence. "Your spirit has awakened. I admit you're agile and skilled, in some ways better than most of the apprentices. I admire your confidence in yourself. But you still must learn so much about discipline. Without it, your skills and knowledge are worth nothing."

Angeni felt burning shame flow through her. Deep in her soul she realized Old Shen was right. Everything that she believed she wanted to be was just an illusion of her dreams.

"Never forget, young one," Old Shen continued. "Even well trained guardians with great overconfidence and haste fall first."

"I'm so sorry I never lived up to your expectations, master," whispered Angeni. Her old severe master shuffled closer to her and looked deep into her eyes, slowly smiled at her for the first time since they met.

"You don't have to say sorry as you never needed to live up to my expectations, Angeni." His eyes beamed at her with pride. "A good master never tries to influence his students as he knows; no soul is here in this world to be shaped and live up to another's expectation. Always be yourself and never forget; only fools and the blind want to shape others with demanded expectations."

"You taught me the best you could, master."

"I hold up high standards because I knew you'd be capable of achieving them. But I never needed to teach you anything, as you already know everything, Angeni. You just haven't realized it yet."

"I, I don't understand."

"One day, you will. But a long path is still ahead of you, young one. The entire life of an Aserian is learning and sharing knowledge, Angeni," Old Shen assured. "Be the change. Do not fear going forward slowly, fear only to stand still. Be not afraid of growing slowly. Be afraid only of not growing. Serve and guide your human charge well and one day, you may make us all proud."

"I will keep it in mind," the young guardian nodded respectfully.

"Be determined and you'll live up to your own expectation. One day you could be the greatest guardian, the one who you truly want to be."

* * *

Sachylia slowly slid toward the partially cloudy horizon, but it was still far from dusk when the noble Aserian mother and daughter were escorted by a delicate wind along the grassy garden at the edge of the Citadel district. Their relaxed wings ruffled by the cold at every step. A few birds watched them from above as they flew in formation to their unknown destination.

"It is my hope, and I believe your training has kindled something inside of you that you will experience soon."

"What do you mean, mother?" The young guardian had seen the pride in her mother's eyes. Eve seemed prouder than ever before.

"You have become something very different from the others."

"I have felt it since my birth," admitted the young guardian after a long hesitation. "My spirit is restless and my soul desires a different path. It may sound like a daydreamer's fantasy, but I'm so certain, mother. I do believe others see this in me too. Sometimes I see great respect in their eyes. But sometimes I feel they fear me, I don't know why." Angeni desperately looked into her mother's eyes. "I don't want anyone to fear me. But they do, I'm certain."

"Your soul and spirit tells you true," the feared confirmation came from the High-Guardian. "As Sachylia watched over you with her divine light when you were born, for many Aserians your birth and your presence is a sign."

"A sign of what?" Angeni asked so curious.

"The approaching Crystal Shade," answered Eve without hiding her silence and hesitation. "You could be the sacred redeemer, a savior the Aserians have awaited for so long; the Angeni soul, the incarnation of our greatest dreams and the forerunner of our worst fears. Your soul declared your being, the Angeni soul, upon your birth."

"What is an Angeni soul, mother?" The young guardian couldn't hide her curiosity.

"Life itself," Eve answered. "An Angeni soul gives hope and inspiration. It brings a soft warm light and life with its presence to every Aserian. You could be the one to bring balance into the Crystal Shade, the one whose presence also heralds its arrival. This is how the others see you. This is the legend you see in their eyes."

High-Guardian Eve looked deep into her daughter's eyes as she continued, "Believers always see signs, what they want to see in the hope their desire may come true and their faith turn real. But only you can answer with complete honesty who you truly are and what an Angeni soul is. Never let others tell who you are or who you are supposed to be. Your soul knows it, even if it hasn't realize yet, or found its true path," she said and cupped her young daughter's face. "Always remember. We are shaped by our thoughts. What you think, you will become. Be the one you want to be and let your actions and moral values define your spirit and soul."

"I will, mother," the young guardian smiled as she nodded.

"So, who are you, Angeni? What do you feel your soul wants to be?" Eve asked with motherly curiosity. The young guardian's eyes glittered; she could finally voice her heart's desire.

"I'd like to be the kindest guardian who lived so others may live. The one who will defend Eecrys Aredia and her people and learn what the Crystal Shade really is," Angeni declared, shy, yet determined.

"Whoever is truly loved by the Sacred Mother, that one's soul is always kept as a child for eternity," Eve smiled on her young daughter, and then gave her forehead a kiss. Eve's pride beamed. "If this is your wish, your true heart's desire, then that is what your Angeni soul is, regardless what others choose to believe."

Angeni's endless admiration glowed for her mother, who continued after a soft sigh.

"Like everything and everyone else, you have your own purpose, Angeni. A purpose only you live from birth and it courses through every cell of your existence. No one else's belief can change that," the High-Guardian stopped as she thoughtfully looked at her daughter. "But to be who you want to be, to step forward without fear, you must learn what that fear is and confront it. Like many others, you must learn that fear is a heavy weight you may carry from birth. Fear that you believe is a curse can be a final obstacle, a block in your being that could keep your entire existence from stepping forward in its evolution."

"If there is fear in my soul, mother, how should I defeat this obstacle?" Angeni frowned her concern before Eve continued.

"You don't need to defeat it, my daughter," she smiled at Angeni. "You do have to be aware of it to truly know yourself. You have to accept that it exists to live with it."

Eve walked to the edge of the cliff and spread her wings wide to enjoy the caress of the wind across her feathers. Then she let her large wings fall back and looked at her daughter.

151

"Come near to me, my child," she invited her daughter to the edge of the escarpment. Angeni hesitated before she took a step toward Eve and abruptly stopped as her arms and legs began to tremble.

The young guardian's vision blurred; her breath came faster and faster as she stood rooted to the spot. Bodily instincts gripped her with a terror that shook her existence. Her soul begged to stay away from the edge of the yawning drop that enchanted and started to call her, but she felt she no longer had control over her body. Forcing herself to look away from the edge, Angeni hugged her body to defend herself like a child while she stepped back from Eve, who watched her curiously.

Desperate, Angeni closed her eyes, but her mind still saw the endless, menacing drop beyond the edge. The sound of the waves that crashed on the sharp rocks deep below enchanted and called her stronger and stronger. Fighting against her nightmare, the young guardian tried to push the thought away, to not feel the terror, the calling of the dreaded depths. In her mind, the legacy of her previous life struck and she already fell into those depths while she screamed loud and desperate, until her fragile body crashed into the ground to crush all of her bones to dust. Pain overwhelmed her, as everything turned dark. Angeni saw the crushed body of her little girl self. Her little spirit and soul wanted to stay, to live, but the strength of an unknown force snatched her away from her body.

Angeni shook her head to chase the images away, but she was still on the precipice as long as her eyes were closed. She wanted to scream. Her body and wings trembled; her soul was so terrified.

"A soul may mislead others, but it can never mislead itself," she heard Eve's gentle concern as the High-Guardian lightly stepped toward her. "You are afraid of the height are you?"

The young guardian slowly opened her eyes. Eve stood between her and the edge. Ashamed, Angeni looked away. It was so easy when she thought about flying, soaring in the endless heights like an eagle. But in reality, height was the deadly enemy that always enchanted and called her.

"I don't want to fall and die, mother," Angeni's whisper quivered. "I don't want it."

"You don't need to hide your fear forever," the High-Guardian smiled as she caressed her daughter's cheek. "Remember, there is no soul without fear. Our fears make us what we are, Angeni. You must accept that. It's part of life itself."

"A guardian should be fearless so others should not fear," Angeni whispered so disappointed in herself. "Yet I'm the one who fears the most. What kind of guardian am I?"

"Only careless fools pretend to be fearless, Angeni. Guardians must know and feel fear as without fear they can't protect responsibly," High-Guardian Eve whispered while she stroked her hair lovingly. "You're a true young guardian in spirit and soul."

The crushed young guardian looked up at her. "But I'd like to be a brave guardian like you, mother," she said.

"You can be brave even with fear in your soul, Angeni. Bravery is born from admitted fear. Facing and living with it requires the greatest bravery of all." A little hope glinted in the eyes of the youngest guardian while the High-Guardian continued, "I know you believe that the others may despise you for your fear, but you don't have to. As you know, Aserians are not like birds. We rarely fly. We don't feel the necessity of it," she said, and then meditated for a short moment. "Maybe you *are* the one with the soul of an Aserian that will never fly," Eve wondered more to herself. "As it's been foretold."

"As it's been foretold? By whom?" Angeni's curiously won out. Eve smiled fondly and looked into Angeni's eyes.

"Your soul is inspired by the sacred crystal to achieve greater goals," she said mysteriously. "When the time comes, you will know all, my beloved daughter. I promise."

The young guardian nodded as she accepted her mother's skirted answer. Yet, she hesitated.

"How did you know my fear?"

"I must know what my daughters fear, Angeni, otherwise I can't protect them," Eve reasoned with a smile. "And you are the only one who always watches and kindly waves to the others from the ground."

"I never thought anyone ever noticed," she admitted naively. The High-Guardian smiled fondly and shook her head, than she lowered her large wings in sadness while she hesitated. Angeni felt that not only her soul was touched by fear. Her mother's was a different breed of fear; it bred from guilt.

"Almost a cycle has passed and neither you or Aurora has ever spoken about the life you left behind. I can understand why. But why have neither of you ever asked who your guardians were? Why have you never asked who gave your beloved papyrus pamphlet back? Do you feel resentment toward the guardians who protected when you were a child?" Eve asked crushed, and then she asked the unavoidable question. "Do you hate them?"

153

The young guardian looked at her with a pleasant smile to give her strength.

"We never asked who they were, because in our souls we always knew, mother," she explained with calm kindness. "We don't and never felt resentment toward you or father."

"You should. We failed both of you," said Eve with a severe twinge of conscience. "Although we're not your guardians anymore, we believe it's our personal responsibility to protect and guide both of you in your new life, like parents."

"You both protected us well in our human lives, guiding us with great care and were with us when we were lost. Nevertheless, the one recalled our souls to begin our new existence for a reason. It was the will of the Sacred Mother that none of us judge. We can say only thanks to you and father for always caring for us, my dear mother. I just ask you, please love us further like your daughters and please allow us to love both of you as mother and father."

Angeni kissed her mother's cheek. Love shone from the High-Guardian's eyes.

"Thank you for your forgiveness, Angeni. Thank you."

* * *

The cobblestones bathed in Sachylia's sunlight warmed the young guardian's bare feet as she ambled along the road and approached the great gulf of Sessa Asria. Her mind circled around Eve's words. What is an Angeni soul really? Who foretold her rebirth? Was someone able to foretell there would be someone with the soul of an Aserian that will never fly? Is it just a legend that has a striking similarity to life itself?

Angeni knew the time to learn those answers was far away, but she didn't distress herself. As someone dear and wise said to a young girl; never look for the moment, as the moment always finds you. She knew, one day, time would give her all of her answers.

The harsh wailing and squawking calls of the white Eyanes with black markings were carried by the sweet wind. The wind cooled her cheek and teased her wings into a luxurious stretch as she arrived at a small neat thatched house atop a hillside. Two eyes of the lodge gazed toward the gulf's clear beautiful horizon where Sachylia rose every morning to begin its long daily journey above the gulf to go down on the other side of it; the place where the sapphire sun was headed right now yet was still far from it.

The young guardian happily ambled up the wooden steps that led up to the house; she came to fulfill an unfulfilled promise she had made a lifetime ago.

"Yes, I'm talking to you, brilliant Carenian who hides in your safe realm!" a familiar old voice boomed from behind the house as Angeni slowly rounded it. "Yes, I dare you! I won't let you teach the Great Nervaschanzo another lesson!" The old master standing near his tiny wooden writing table in the garden shook his fist at the air.

Leaning on the wooden rail fence, grinning like a child, Angeni shook her head while she watched him. Her eyes noticed a fragile middle-aged woman who peaked out from the neighboring house and watched Nervaschanzo from a distance. From a glance, Angeni already knew the woman who kindly smiled and watched the master with cheeky, but intelligent eyes. She was the stubborn polymath's inner voice, the disguised guardian spirit, the Watcher that the old man supposedly to argued with.

"I write this piece as my soul dictates!" the old master raised a papyrus scroll from the table and shook it toward the sky. "I'd rather owe a journey to the devil than ignore the genius of my soul! Practice makes the master!" echoed the proud voice of the master, and he crossed his arms defiantly. The women in the house enjoyed the moment like it were already a theatre performance. Her head shook in amusement as she pushed the curtains closed to let the old man rant alone. Dramatically open wide, old Nervaschanzo's eyes glared toward the sky.

"What do you mean; every man should practice only his trade? It's art! It is imagination, you rigid, stake swallowed Carenian!"

"Behind every great man, there is a fragile, but strong and smart Aserian woman," almost silent, Angeni smiled as she quoted Persecutrix Aurilla, Nervaschanzo's guardian spirit.

"Ah, another Aserian come to give a lesson to old fool Nervaschanzo," said the venerable old giant as he noticed the young guardian when he lowered his head. "I give up. If an Aserian wants to give a lesson, an Aserian will give a lesson," he muttered in his beard.

"I can't teach a fellow soul who sees the world as no one else can see," Angeni's angelic tone echoed as she left the fence behind and strolled toward him. "Just look around, divine Nervaschanzo," she spread her arms and wings while she spun once happily. "Moments look back all over calling you to experience, to learn," she continued while she stopped and let her wings fall behind her back. "Never forget, time is always short for brilliant artistic souls like you and me."

"The eyes, the mirror of a soul never lies. What sort of evil trick is this?" the old man took a step away. "Graciana? But, but it can't be." Nervaschanzo whispered surprised. Angeni smiled and nodded kindly. "Graciana! It's really you!" The giant old man hurried and almost displaced Angeni's breath as he embraced the fragile woman with his large ham-fists and spun her in the air. Wildly smiling the young guardian looked at him. After a long moment, she got free as Nervaschanzo put her down.

"How is it possible?" he asked.

"If you borrow me a little of your time, good old Nervaschanzo, I will tell a true story that I promised long ago, in another life; the evolution of a young guardian, the one who once found her crystal nightfall."

* * *

At the end of the day, Angeni sat on her sanctuary's stone balcony altar of one of the highest towers in Sessa Asria. Restless, her hand already sketched the next page of her papyrus scroll. She wanted some reminiscence of this place before she left it for good. Her trustworthy companion, the arven pencil slowly left its black echo on the papyrus of the main temple surrounded by the large beautiful garden which mirrored in Angeni's eyes. Unlike her fantasy world, now the garden and the temple were full of life. Aserians and humans lived their daily life. Apprentices practiced along with their masters. Some Aserian and human children played hide and seek under the shadow of the large trees. Her grin widened as she watched them. The children reminded her of her left behind human childhood when her and her parents played the very same game with Aurora.

Angeni sat far from the edge of her balcony to keep her acrophobia from rising, just as she had in her spirit's fantasy world. Feeling the solid ground under her feet gave her a sense of safety. The dreaded depths didn't call her and the fear of heights didn't freeze her soul with terror as long as the drop-off was at least ten paces away.

Swift and precise, the arven pencil swiftly and precisely scratched across the surface of the papyrus. All the lines whispered that her soul was relaxed and relieved. Finally, she didn't have to hide any more secrets and she fulfilled a promise she made a lifetime ago.

Angeni stopped and proudly studied her new drawing. The lines sketched out the Hall of Discipline, the beautiful winged temple and the view of the Citadel and the library of Sessa Asria. Sachylia just

156

approached the horizon and her beams shot through the clouds to make the main temple and city swim in sparkling rivers of light. The twilight was far from perfect; it wasn't close to the crystal nightfall that she had seen with Aurora. Still it was so beautiful, the perfect ending to this day.

The sharp, all seeing eyes of the guardian spied a small fishing boat with two masts on the water; the large white triangle sails were swollen by the wind. The fishing boat approached the mouth of the Sessa Asrian gulf on its way toward the Ocean of Aesara Alira. It was missing from the sketch, but her hand already acted to correct the mistake. The pencil quickly drew the ship on the papyrus to preserve it for eternity. Then the four vertical lines at the bottom right corner marked that she finished her drawing.

The wind softly buffeted her hair, white saree, and her wing feathers. She put down the pencil and the papyrus scroll pamphlet, and then stood up in the beautiful dusk as Sachylia began to dip beyond the horizon. Angeni hugged herself while she looked down at the garden from a safe distance. A content smile played on her lips as she pulled her saree together, but one part of her soul felt great sorrow that she had to leave Sessa Asria behind. She just hoped she was able to keep her promise to Nervaschanzo and Graciana would return one day to watch the old man's greatest treasure, his crystal sunrise. For the first time in her new life, Angeni felt her boundless spirit was finally free.

Now that her free spirit was ready to declare itself to the world, something changed. Something embraced and caressed her spirit, soul, and body; a hidden power that had grown in her since rebirth. Silent, the young guardian dropped to one knee, her large wings spread wide. Everything somehow slowed around her; the soft breeze, the people in the garden, the birds in the sky, the waves on the distant gulf and the small boats on the water. Darkness fell upon her as she closed her eyes.

An immense surge held her as the tremendous gathered spirit power broke to the surface. Angeni felt her eyes flash as she pulled them open. She felt the power spread through her entire being and then a relentless invisible shockwave left her body. Her spirit declared itself throughout the unseen realms and the entire world. Angeni's soul was determined, yet for a moment she was confused. It wasn't clear what was going on around her or what played inside her being, but her spirit kept her calm.

Everything moved again while her instincts let her senses quickly spread and reach what she could not reach by touch to connect her with everyone through invisible waves. Small voice fragments broke into her mind. From moment to moment, the voices formed understandable words.

... 'yra'yren, meda'yren, vye'yren, senia'yren, shena'yren, rhe'yres! the rippling thoughts of a young boy's twenty count echoed in her mind. Angeni's vision was blurred as she watched the garden. Her eyes snapped to an Aserian boy, who now searched for the other children in the garden. Her senses told her that the voice came from him from that far away.

And when the sapphire sun goes down... Angeni heard Jared's familiar voice in her mind. The eyes of the guardian snapped to the source like an eagle snaps its eyes after its prey. Still blurry-eyed, Angeni watched Aurora slowly sneak up behind the Sentinel, who sat on the grass with his feather quill scratching on a sheet of papyrus.

... the eagle still soars on the sky, Jared's voice echoed.

The Sentinel is writing a poem? Angeni wondered.

Sky, sky, sky, the Sentinel's thoughts repeated while he searched for the perfect rhyme.

You will be a beautiful plant, little Taze, shy Taze thought tenderly while she carefully planted a sapling that she named after herself at the far end of the garden.

Masterfully carved, but seemingly the function of these adornments is chiefly decorative, she recognized the tone of Tlanextic's thoughts who studied the great temple. *Maybe Iris and I should study its history to reveal their true meaning. If there is any.*

Yuna, if you would kindly step left just once more. Come on, Yuna, echoed the determined thoughts of Kien who prepared his yiana staff and faced two other apprentices Sentinel Merina and Watcher Yuna under the atrium. *Merina, stay there.* Then Yuna stepped as was desired from her and Kien immediately struck and clashed with both of them.

Sky, sky, sky. High! Jared's thought echoed victoriously as he finally found the rhyme.

Experience comes from decisions, Aurora's thoughts returned to her sister. Not clearly, Angeni saw that her sister looked around, and then smiled as she studied her beloved prey, Jared, whose quill scratched his papyrus. *But when action must speak, nothing can replace agility, my dear,* Aurora thought happily. Angeni could swear she saw her sister flash a cheeky grin, but Aurora was calm as she ever so cautiously leaned over Jared's shoulder, and snatched the quill from his hand.

You cheeky little... Angeni's soul grinned at Jared's surprise, but her face was icy and emotionless as she listened. The young Aserian man enjoyed the fun while he stood up and tried to get the treasured quill back from her sister, who had already stepped back out of reach.

Dum-dee-dum-dee-dum. Now, I have your attention, do I? If you want this quill back, you must come and get me, Aurora's joyful thoughts rang in Angeni's mind. She portrayed the most innocent and angelic soul in the world while she waved the quill in front her face to provoke the Sentinel. Intent on catching her, he slowly approached the young guardian.

No. You're not going to get away with it this time, Aurora, was Jared's happy thoughts who could only read Aurora's actions.

And now, my dear Sentinel, catch me if you can! Aurora's giggling thoughts sped as her sister raced away and the Sentinel immediately gave chase.

Never let a moment go by, young ones, Angeni's eyes found the source. Her father, Aaron stood near Old Shen and watched his youngest daughter hide and lean out from behind a tree. On the other side, Jared tried to catch her.

A bold decision of one joyful moment may carry you your whole life, came Old Shen's wise thoughts.

Then something changed in her mind, as if dark clouds overran the sapphire sun. The joyful happy thoughts slowly faded, chaotic sounds shadowed the thoughts of the others. It surrounded and embraced the entire existence of the young guardian. The voices came from everywhere, all around Eecrys Aredia and nowhere, from all the realms and none of them. Her newfound senses could not find the source.

Angeni felt as if her existence was measured by something chaotic. Two eyes watched her, she felt it. There were no recognizable words, nor sentences, but a soft grumbling voice became stronger and stronger in her mind. Its anger became breath stopping painful to Angeni. Fear seeped into her soul; someone was listening to and watching her, just as she watched the others. Her existence wanted to scream as it began to explode from the pain, but not a single sound left her throat. Then she felt an invisible shockwave, similar to the first she realized, but much more powerful. It left her being to reach for the unknown wherever it was to chase it away to defend herself.

Just as sudden it came, all the pain, all the thoughts stopped. Angeni dropped out of the strange trance. In a panic, her quick breathes slowly calmed. The guardian looked up majestically while she threw open her wings before she folded them behind her back.

Balance slowly returned to her existence. Her eyes mirrored the sapphire sun, which still approached the horizon. Yet something was different, Angeni felt it. Her spirit was vigilant and felt that something was not right. The wind had stopped all around her. Not even a single breeze touched her silky skin.

Her curiosity could not be denied; the young guardian peeked down at the garden as her soul dictated. Bright colorful light shot out through every opening of the large winged temple in front of her. The light danced in the full color spectrum while it became brighter and brighter. Everyone below had stopped and watched the same phenomena.

The light blinded her. A strong shockwave left the temple and shattered the beautiful building like a storm wind hits a dry sand castle, crushing everything around it, tearing up trees, and throwing everyone near the temple away. Like a transparent shapeless cataclysm, the shockwave hit the tower where she stood and threw Angeni against the wall. The tall building shook hard, deep rumblings warned her as the collapse began.

As her back hit the wall, she felt the bones in her wings break before she fell to the stone. Everything shook around her while she screamed in tortured pain. The stones in the walls broke apart all around her and tumbled to the street. Just as she was coming around, the floor opened under her.

Her wings tried to open as she fell, but her back muscles couldn't follow the demands of her spirit. She closed her eyes as her worst fear rushed up toward her, the dreaded depths, and the sharp rocks at the bottom. The young guardian screamed in terror. Everything turned dark around her as her back slammed into the rock. She heard and felt all of the bones in her body explode into dust.

Groggy and wracked by excruciating pain through her body told her spirit that she was still alive, Angeni heard desperate screams echo from every direction. She managed to open her eyes. A thick dust cloud that shadowed Angeni spun in the air; it ripped and blew her beloved papyrus sketches away. Dark stealthy shadows crawled and slithered out of the temple ruins. It was like a solid whirling shadow wind that screamed an eerie, teeth-jarring howl that brought eternal terror to her soul.

All of those who just regained consciousness screamed in terror while they tried to escape. She saw the shadow wind quickly wrap around those near the temple ruins. As the wind touched its helpless victims, their pained screams built to a screech as they quickly turned into solid ash statues. Then the shadow wind's tendrils howled in search of more victims to crush them like staves break ice. A terrified human woman picked up a crying Aserian child and tried to run away, but the wind caught them quickly and finished them without mercy.

Angeni's crushed body was so weak. She closed her eyes, but she couldn't cover her ears. The eerie wind carried the desperate death screams to her ears as more souls were lost. Her heart was broken and she opened tear-filled eyes. The wind systematically destroyed everything. It ground through columns, twisted remaining trees, and turned them to dust.

Desperate, she watched Old Shen, the Executor, her mother, Eve and her beloved father, Aaron, her beautiful sister Aurora, Jared and others trying to escape.

"Go. Run. Please, run," she whispered, but their doom reached them quickly one by one. Her beloved mother, father, her mentors were no more. Horror filled her eyes as helpless, she watched the wind whip around Aurora, who tried desperately to resist. Jared tried to grab her hand, but in the next moment, Aurora screamed in howling pain as she turned into an ash statue and then exploded as the darkness squeezed her tight.

"No," Angeni's voice was weak with despair as she saw the wind crush her beloved sister. More tears appeared in her already tearful eyes, rolled down her dirty and injured cheek. The same wave caught Jared next and tore the brave Sentinel apart. Angeni's soul cried in anguish. She realized, she had just lost everyone that she ever loved within the moment of a sigh.

The wind had cleared the entire square all around Angeni leaving none alive while hundreds of shadow creatures stepped out of the chaotic whirling wind; faceless evil, each of them held whirling shadow blades. The young guardian was helpless, weak and broken on the ground crying. Her hands and legs were shattered, her crushed wings hung limp from her back. She didn't care as the chaotic shadows came closer and started to surround her. Even as her instincts told her these creatures came to kill only one soul, hers. Shocked and alone she knew there was no one left to protect her.

Then a large shadow loomed over her. She tried to look up, but the strength wasn't there as the dark figure dropped from the sky right in front of her and crouched as he landed solid on the ground. The armada of whirling shadow creatures stopped, wary, they watched the old Aserian; that strange mysterious old man from Odess'iana. The stranger wore his long black cloak with the hood hiding his head and face.

The evolution of your spirit has just begun and It sensed your presence, the tired old thoughts of the mysterious man rushed into her mind. His ancient, worn and ragged wings spread, and then lowered behind his back as he stood up. Angeni's soul could not comprehend the shape of his wings. From under his hood, he watched the armada of shadow creatures. *Your spirit just announced its true nature to the universe and It*

161

just realized who you really are. Your knowledge and your belief posses a great threat to It's existence. You must stay away from It, you're not ready yet.

Desperate and in shock, Angeni could only watch the stranger's back, who took his enemies measure in front of him while the once proud city of Sessa Asria was in ruins all around them and the ground covered in ashes.

It's feeding off your fear to manipulate you, to crush your soul because it cannot extinguish your existence now, the thoughts of the old Aserian echoed. *Listen to me. You don't have bones that can break. You're not crushed, Angeni. You never were. Everything is playing in your soul. Seek the aura of Eecrys Aredia, feel the wind to know what is real.*

The mysterious old Aserian was right. Angeni didn't feel anything, not even the wind that should caress her skin. Nothing was real, only her fear of the vision of the shadow creatures brought into her fragile and young being. The pain slowly dissipated as her spirit and soul realized it was just an illusion and slowly convinced her body of the truth.

It hid for thousands of cycles and now someone knows of It's existence. It has to stop you from revealing It's identity before the Crystal Shade arrives. It wants to crush you, break your fragile crystal reality to set your spirit adrift in the void and chaos.

The stranger looked right at the shadow creatures in front of him, who stepped closer, but seemed hesitant to fight this stranger. Two whirling dark shadow blades began to form out of the air in his hands.

"But you can't crush someone whose spirit is already dead and it terrifies you," he seethed and challenged the shadow creatures who measured him with eternal hatred. The grip of the shadow blades turned solid in his hands; slowly froze to a sharp edged, regular dark crystal, and shadow covered its entire surface which mirrored the whirling chaotic shadow creatures as they stepped closer and closer.

"I will never let you be harmed, Angeni," the stranger's tired old voice promised from under his hood, and he shifted his two whirling blades to strike. Angeni watched the stranger open his large wings, spread his arms, jump, and spin into the creatures.

The shadow blades struck true as he hacked into the first line of the horde of shadow creatures. His victims scattered after each strike like leaves after a great gust of wind and turned to dust in the air. Dozens of shadowy blades tried to hit him at once, but the stranger was so fast, he blocked all of their strikes. With his two blades, he continuously moved and sliced the shadow creatures until one creature knocked one of the blades out of his hand, right up to the air. The stranger jumped up, spun in the air and cut with his remaining blade.

The shadows that jumped after him and tried to reach him, dissolved to dust while he caught his second blade in flight. The old large wings spread, smashed back into the mass of shadow creatures while the blades danced and cut into the shadow creatures all around the mysterious Aserian. Like lightning in the greatest storm of Prosperous, he fought fast and struck hard over and over again. Angeni barely saw all of his moves. The mysterious stranger fought faster than anyone she ever knew. He jumped, rolled in the air, spun on the ground, and continuously struck his enemies without making a single mistake. The shadow creatures turned to dust sometimes more than one at a time, collapsed and exploded like grotesque clay soldiers as they hit the ground. The old Aserian ran and stabbed three of the shadow creatures that stood right behind each other on his right blade and ran with them toward the wall. The blade sliced twice and cut the other demons that came within his reach while he smashed the demons on his right blade against the wall. As the shadow creatures hit, they puffed to dust. The remaining shadow creatures tried to surround him, but his spinning whirlwind attack killed them all. It was clear; he was a true Aserian, a real protector spirit.

The young guardian's strength slowly came back, the last measure of pain disappeared while she watched in amazement as the ashes sifted down around the stranger. He stood with his two shadow crystal blades raised in his fists while his wings arched wide open in triumph. Not a shadow creature remained. Angeni could move again, as if her wounds never existed. Her wings and body healed, she stood up and stared at the stranger. She wanted to see his eyes to never forget the soul of her savior, but his hood still covered his face and he would not look directly into her eyes. She felt it.

The stranger turned fully away from Angeni and lowered his blades and wings.

"Who are you?" she asked, but she didn't count on an answer. "What are these things?"

The old Aserian glanced back, but his eyes were still covered, hidden from Angeni.

"It's the one that only you ever dared to seek and imagine," his whisper carried wariness.

The ground started to shake. The stranger and Angeni looked toward the ruins. A colossal, faceless whirling shadow creature emerged from the temple ruins and faced the stranger.

"You will leave her be!" the stranger's voice rang with hatred while he ran toward the large whirling shadow creature. It reared its long neck back preparing to strike with its twisting head. The shadow creature attacked. Large jaws arrowed at the running stranger, who lowered his blades as he ran fast. Just before the fangs struck him, the old Aserian blurred as he zipped toward his enemy. He disappeared right before the creature's mouth snapped shut where he was, and then he immediately reappeared right in front of the creature's body. The dreaded shadow blades slashed twice at the root of this evil with extraordinary exactitude. Its torso exploded to dust that spread in both directions and coated the young guardian.

The monstrous shadow creature screamed, its head snapped up while its body slid back into the temple ruins. Its ear-shattering scream echoed its pain as the body disintegrated upward.

The sky suddenly shattered, the entire world around Angeni split like a large glass ball. Bright sapphire beams of light shot through the breaches at her. The old Aserian lowered his blades and wings and finally he looked right into Angeni's eyes. She wanted to see into his soul, but she already couldn't see his eyes, as the light was too bright.

You must forget what you saw to keep your soul in peace. You must forget what you heard to not even search for it, the stranger's thoughts warned while the sapphire light blinded her completely. *It will be more cautious and you'll be safe for now. But always beware as It will look for you, Angeni.*

Angeni's eyes began to focus as she came out of the trance.

I will guard you forever. I promise, she heard the whisper in her conscience, and then the voice along with the memory of the nightmare slowly vanished.

Still crouched on one knee, the young guardian watched Sachylia disappear below the horizon with its last beams gracing the beautiful Citadel of Sessa Asria. The children still played in the garden. Her eyes followed Aurora and Jared as they childishly chased each other around the trees. Suddenly, Jared caught Aurora. She swung toward him with a grin and hugged the Sentinel as if she had caught him. The soft breeze stroked Angeni's silky skin and ruffled her papyrus scroll pamphlet on the altar. The open scroll showed the same beautiful view of Sessa Asria that she looked down on. The place she loved so much, but knew she was going to miss.

The young guardian stood up with a knowing little smile. Body and wings tired after the long day, she felt a soft pain that slowly faded away. Her spirit was at peace and was proud. Her entire existence felt safe now. Yet, she couldn't answer to herself what she needed to be afraid of. There was only peace, enduring peace. Angeni was sure of one thing; her spirit made the first great step in its evolution.

* * *

"As her spirit began to evolve, that day one mysterious door opened in her future," the old man was certain while the children listened in awe. He turned one of the wooden wheels; many doors opened and closed to shape the labyrinth once more. While the children watched the little sapphire pearl curiously rolled along and discovered new paths in the labyrinth of life. "It was a doorway that stood on the thin invisible line between light and dark," he continued. "No matter what path she chose, all would lead to that door as the cruel existence that had no name and no known past - kept it open and waited for her. There was no turning back for the young guardian. This was her life and her destiny."

5 – A DAYDREAMER'S REVELATION

"Life has always been a great revelation," the old man continued. "If we're listening patiently, it may whisper to us, may reveal the mistakes of the past, our place in the present and the possibilities awaiting us in the future. It may show and tell us what is dearest in our tiny world, in our crystal reality. And it also may reveal the fears shackling our souls, mirror fragile dreams we love and want to protect in our hearts." He looked at the sapphire pearl that slowly advanced and discovered a new path in the labyrinth.

"Just like the sapphire pearl journeying to discover the unknown, she endeavored to reveal every single aspect, every part of her life and her surroundings. And so, every day held some revelation for her; sometimes small and meaningless, other days, great and surprising. As it comes in everyone's life, for her, it was the days of the first great revelations."

* * *

I'm your consciousness, your protective spirit. But you're the one who guards me as you hold my soul in your hand. Who are you stranger to haunt me in my restless dreams? Who are you my angel of the night? My soul is filled with endless happiness when you embrace my spirit. My spirit is in peace and harmony when you whisper to my soul.

I'm alone. So alone, but I know you're always with me. We're together, forever. I'm guarding you, because I want to and as I promised. We're flying above the white dunes at night; mother is calling both of us. I'm trembling as I fear the height, I don't want to fall. Please protect me. Please, don't let me go, but hold me strong.

And so caring you embrace me so I feel safe. But you don't know who I am. I fear to reveal my soul. I don't want to look into your eyes, because I fear. But not from you. No. I fear myself. I don't want to face my soul because I know I won't like what I'll see. I don't want to see who I am, as I know; nothing and no one is what they first appear to be. Not even my dreams. Not even me.

Angeni's eyes opened and tried to focus in the darkness while her dream slowly dissipated. Since they had left Sessa Asria, her dreams had become chaotic and puzzling. At least this time she remembered everything; it all came back in her memories; the loving care and her eternal fear. She remembered her *angel of the night* the most. That unknown caring soul she loved so much in her dreams even if she couldn't remember his face. Her spirit and soul exploded with happiness when she thought of the love that she felt. These dreams always awakened something in her soul, regardless if she didn't know how to phrase it to herself. Every day she waited for the time to sleep, to dream just once more about her caring protector.

In the darkness, the young guardian sat up from her velvet cushions in her small cabin and hugged her brave guardian pillow. Her body still trembled in fear from the heights that she remembered; and yet, she slowly calmed herself. Her large wings opened wide before they retracted behind her back while she looked around. She was alone.

"Nothing and no one is what they first appear to be," whispered Angeni. Closing her eyes, she still remembered the last thought from her dream. In her mind, she had seen an old hooded Aserian rather than the protective and embracing soul who had whispered this phrase to her. He told her to always remember, to never forget this. When or where, she couldn't remember, maybe in a dream or maybe in another life.

Angeni lay back among the cushions and waited for the rocking waves, which gently slurred against the hull to cradle her back to sleep. She wanted to be with that caring soul once again, but in the darkness, she soon knew she would sleep no more tonight. Her spirit was rested and her soul refreshed. Quick and quiet she got up and left her cabin.

As they flexed, the wooden planks quietly creaked under her steps on the berth deck's short corridor past the other apprentice's cabins. The waves were gracious to sail on today for Angeni, who had some problems with the eternal heaving of the sea during the first days.

Reaching the stairs, which led to the spar deck, she stopped. A soft sigh left her lips when she had seen the common area where every other Aserian was already awake, as if they never slept at all. Aurora yawned so sleepily and played the Game of Life with Tlanextic and Iris. They had shepherded the pearls carefully, as Angeni guessed for a long time. Silent, Jared had written a new poem and meditated with a quill in his hand. Young Taze nursed a tiny flower near the table and Kien presumably meditated somewhere in the corner. From her present spot Angeni couldn't see him, or her mother and father who likely rested in their cabins. Only these seven apprentices left Sessa Asria on the same ship. Only these seven apprentices were bound for the same destination. Angeni wanted to spend time at play with them, yet she had forced herself into a voluntary exile since the first day. She had a rightful reason for that.

Night, wind and driving blizzard chilled Angeni as she stepped outside after she took the wooden stairs up to the spar deck. Taking a huge breath of the fresh air, she embraced herself and looked around. She couldn't see the stars and they couldn't see her either through the dark clouds.

The wind howled and snapped at the large sails, they billowed on the two side by side diagonal masts that were surrounded by a dark topaz blue aura. The aura flowed through the aura-cauldrons and thin veins as the will of the Master Helmsman controlled them from the stern. He navigated the ship with his will through the small crystal domes. The masterfully carved, graceful wooden-metallic hull of the ship and the two large raised diagonal masts with wing or rather fin-like sails reminded Angeni of the Cysrelus flying fishes that skimmed over the water fast, just as this graceful ship roamed the waves.

Master Helmsman Naevius, the human skipper greeted Angeni with a nod. She returned the kind gesture with a smile. The proud seaman looked ahead to master his beloved ship in the dark unknown. The young guardian strolled to the bow to continue her voluntary exile. In the last few days, Angeni preferred to spend her time alone and the bow of the ship was the best place to do that where her mind could enjoy the peace and quiet.

Peeking down from the bow the proud name of the ship, emblazoned by the blue aura, shimmered back at her from the racing surface of the icy river; *Prosperity*. The tiny letters beneath the large ones whispered her Aserian name, *Sequela*.

The *Prosperity* had gently, but restlessly plied the waves in the last seven days and nights since they left Sessa Asria along with ten other ships, which carried the other apprentices to ten other destinations in different provinces. Soon they sailed only in the company of one other ship up the huge Great Dividing Gulf as if they were bound for that mysterious place where Sachylia rose every day. For four days, the *Prosperity* and the *Celestial*, the *Peria Celestia* in Aserian, together followed and happily raced the rich coastlines of Sessa Asria and then Coreenthia where the other ship finally waved farewell to them. Alone and brave, their tiny ship chased the waking sun further right through the wide strait of Asea Marmara to reach the small inland sea of Karadeniz. It was the first time Angeni had seen the blurry distant shores of mythical Hijaz. It was like an unreachable dream as it was so far from them. Then from Karadeniz the ship reached the shores of the province of Andrenia and they sailed north up the wide Azure River, Asria where the snow of Slumberous greeted them. Now, embraced by a furious blizzard, the *Prosperity* slowly swam against the slush-clogged stream to reach their destination, the great capital of Eecrys Aredia, Andrenia.

As they travelled, Angeni's great Cartographer incarnation constantly drew and corrected the map of Eecrys Aredia in the Great Spirit Library of Angenius, following what she had seen during the day.

There was no map on the *Prosperity*. Master Naevius used his mind to remember and navigate these calm friendly waters that he had sailed from a very young age. All the rivers in which the *Prosperity* ever sailed and tracked were the corridors, and every sea and ocean this proud ship ever roamed the huge waves were the halls and rooms of Naevius' home.

The silent helmsman was skilled, a real master. He passed the control to his young apprentice, Kallina only during the day when his tired aura started to fluctuate on the masts and he needed to take a rest. During their journey, in the night when the endless darkness embraced the graceful ship he alone navigated the *Prosperity*. Now, as the cold spray tried to freeze to the masts, his glowing aura melted the ice and kept the sails dry. The forty-one steps long ship gracefully rode the peaceful icy waves by his will.

At the bow, Angeni closed her eyes. Her being felt free; it wasn't tortured by that strange, binding feeling that held her since she had arrived in Sessa Asria. She enjoyed the cradling peace as the ship hit wave after wave and the sweet cold wind hit her face and tugged at her wings. Since her soul had started to evolve and she had begun to hear the thoughts of others, her gift was very disturbing for her. Although, on the seas, she slowly learned how to focus and close these voices out, it was too exhausting for her soul. Many times, she still heard the personal thoughts of those who were close by or had strong emotional thoughts.

Her gift was unnatural, a true curse as she believed. Hearing their thoughts, she realized she was the only one who heard the voices. She also never read or heard of any Aserian that could hear the thoughts of other Aserians. She feared to share this dreaded skill with the others, they'd be more afraid of her than before. In addition, there was the endless shame she felt for learning all their deepest thoughts and secrets by no will of her own. None of those thoughts were for her, yet she heard. She heard all of them.

In her happy thoughts, Aurora was so proud of her big sister and wanted to follow her footsteps; she looked up at her with childlike adoration. Aurora loved Eve and Aaron much more than anyone else, but as she heard her thoughts, Angeni realized how much Aurora missed their real mother and father. When Aurora thought of their human parents, Angeni also turned melancholy. Nevertheless, she knew they couldn't change what had been done.

Aurora's thoughts were always filled with love, especially toward Angeni's favorite *Infidel*, Jared. Angeni finally understood why her little sister had introduced him with that enthusiastic happiness and why she had been so dismayed that day. The young Sentinel was special to her, tne first love of Aurora's life. But Angeni's capricious style had ruined her sister's great moment. What was worse, Jared fell in love with Angeni. However, the Sentinel was smart enough to hide his feelings in most cases, but he couldn't hide his thought from Angeni; the thoughts which mostly centered on her every day. The young Sentinel sometimes even wrote poems for her, just as he did now below. However, he never dared share any of those poems that were so beautiful when they echoed in Angeni's mind.

The young guardian kept her distance as guilt took over when she learned the truth from Jared's thoughts. She swore she would correct the mistake she made and somehow she would lead the Sentinel's attention back to her sister. It wasn't an easy task at all. The Sentinel was amazed and enchanted by her, regardless of what she did or how cold she was toward him.

Shy young Taze feared the legend of the Angeni soul and kept her distance from Angeni the most. However, it wasn't strange as she kept a good distance from almost everyone. The young Sentinel woman enjoyed alone time when she and her flowers could be together. The only exception for her was Kien. She looked at him as a protective brother and the young Guardian looked back at her as a fragile sister as well, one that he needed to protect even from the wind. They respected and loved each other so much, even if it wasn't always clearly visible to the eye. But it was clear in their thoughts.

What surprised Angeni the most was what Kien's thoughts revealed to her. He was a bit similar to her, a true daydreaming soul who hid behind a mask of seriousness. Since he first heard about the Spiritual Vanguards from High-Guardian Abenago, he was drawn by their legends; their mysterious life and he wanted to be a wise Guardian just like them who understood the flow of all realms. Angeni finally understood why he meditated so much. He was desirous of a higher level of perfection and balance in the hope that one day he would be the one he wanted to be.

Listening to the two Carenians, Iris and Tlanextic was the most interesting experience. Their natural eagerness to find logic and meaning in everything mirrored their souls. Where, what, how and why? These words described their thoughts the most. The two Watchers always meditated and sought answers to their seemingly endless questions, which may sound so meaningless at first. As Angeni listened to them from time to time, she learned and was amazed how they connected the dots and drew their incredible conclusions. She realized each of their questions were valid and served a greater purpose; to know the world that shaped their lives and to understand lives that shaped their world.

Angeni hated to admit to herself, but she loved to hear the thoughts of her father the most. He was a great thinker, much greater than he showed who lived mostly in his thoughts. The old storyteller's heart was full of love for her mother. During their long journey when he wasn't reading book after book or extolled wonderous tales to Angeni and Aurora, he always meditated on some gift or a verse to make Eve's day just a bit better than the previous one.

Her mother was a mystery. Angeni rarely heard any of her thoughts. Maybe the great discipline that embraced the great being of the noble High-Guardian also surrounded and shadowed her disciplined mind. Yet, when she did hear her mother's thoughts, she heard her fears and worry as well.

Eve eagerly waited to see Andrenia, her beloved home that was a part of her soul denied too long. Deeper in her soul, she was shy, fearful and just hoped her daughters and the other apprentices would love her home as much as she did. This thought returned to her more and more often as they approached their grand destination.

The thoughts of others revealed so much to her, but Angeni wished she didn't have this curse at all. Their thoughts were not hers. Their secrets and desires were not for her.

"Soon, we'll see the outlines of Andrenia," Eve said quietly as she stepped near her daughter at the bow, forcing her wandering thoughts back to reality. The excitement softly rang in the High-Guardian. Her eyes radiated how thrilled and restless she was to see her beloved home. Then her mother looked at her in concern. "I just hope you'll accept and love her as your home, just as I do. Please promise me you'll care for her deeply. She is a wonderful town, you'll see." She stroked Angeni's hair. Angeni heard a little echo of shyness in her mother for the first time.

"I promise, mother. Your home is my home," she tried to give Eve strength with her words.

"Sairvoose!" the seaman's deep whooping tone broke the windy silence as his greeting echoed from the stern to the nearby capital in the Andrenian dialect. High-Guardian Eve looked back at Naevius with excited eyes, and then quickly turned back to the shore far ahead, seeking her home.

"Sairvoose!" a soft-echoed greeting came from a distance.

"Look. There," her mother whispered excited while the *Prosperity* broke a larger wave, and the wind pulled the blizzard curtain away ahead of them. Using the clouds as a silky warm blanket, Carenia Seli spread its pale sleepy moonlight to paint a shiny blue road onto the icy river to the tiny sail, to lead it into the heart of the huge capital of Andrenia.

In the darkness, a tall beacon house reflected the moonlight to show the way. Beyond, the enormous tall outlines of the sleeping capital tried to reach the stars. Some buildings did reach the clouds. Andrenia really was the largest and most elegant city of all the twelve capitals. She couldn't imagine how a city could be more magnificent and more beautiful than this seemingly endless expanse of architecture merged into nature, yet also whispered its pride even at night.

"Beautiful Andrenia. I'm home," her mother's excitement escaped her whisper as the ship skimmed closer and closer. "Look how the great River Asria streams from north to south to divide the once two ancient cities of Andrena and Renia." Angeni took in every word while her mother continued, "She was born thousands of cycle ago, not from one settlement as other capitals, but from the amalgamation, the fruit of two tiny towns."

The High-Guardian peeked toward the western shore as she continued, "The younger, but to me the lovelier district on the western shore was once Andrena. It nestles in the forested Andrenian Chain Mountains. They stretch beyond the borders of the city to the northwestern part of the province. Those huge mountains there," she pointed, "hold the most sacred district of Andrenia. They give home to the heart of Eecrys Aredia."

"The heart of Eecrys Aredia?" This surprised Angeni. Her home world had a heart?

"It's the most sacred and a beautiful place. But you'll see, my daughter, I promise," her mother looked toward the eastern shore. "And see where those few small lights still gleam that is the older district of Andrenia. Renia sprawls across the Great Andrenian Plain that stretches flat as a tabletop beyond the city to the east and southeast."

From the corner of her eye Angeni noticed Aurora, who hand in hand with their father, looked around along with the other five apprentices watching the capital from the stern. Angeni could see her father shared his knowledge about Andrenia to her sister and the other apprentices who were amazed by the sight.

The proud little ship approached the first ice coated stone bridge that gracefully connected the two shores. Angeni was enchanted by its frozen beauty, but then worried. She looked at the two tall diagonal

172

masts, then back at the arch. It was clear they would not fit under it. She looked at Master Naevius who seemingly wasn't bothered by the approaching bridge, but masterfully sailed the ship without steering away.

Eve smiled at her worried daughter. The motherly look told Angeni not to worry everything would be all right. Yet as they approached closer and closer, the eyes of the young guardian looked from bridge to mast, mast to bridge. Just as Angeni braced for impact, Naevius' will silently lowered the huge diagonal masts.

The shiny blue aura refracted off the icicles on the masterfully carved bridge as they watched the *Prosperity* peacefully pass beneath them. The masts and the sails slowly rose to their original position, and the wind along with the driving snow caught the sails before the graceful ship turned toward Andrena's shore.

"See those two mountains on the shore?" Eve asked. "Those are the two major districts of Andrenia, the citadel and the castle districts. And tomorrow," she looked up at the large Great Aserian Temple. It loomed huge on top of the sheer walled mountain of the Citadel district on the Andrenian shore. "Tomorrow your true nature will declare itself up there. Tomorrow you'll see who you have truly become, my daughter."

From the great height, the majestic old building looked down grouchy at the tiny ship that sneaked in under its shadow. The temple had the same huge winged statue at its top that the Hall of Discipline had in Sessa Asria. Angeni was awed by its elegant beauty. For a moment as she looked up to it and as the dark clouds passed above the winged temple, she felt like the huge building would fall right at her. But it was just an illusion of her soul, which was in awe of the frosted magnificence of Andrenia.

"The rightful and fair-minded ruler, the Ceretaperia, Queen Faraa lives there along with her son, Prince Nicolas." An elegantly tall castle majestically rose from the top of the Castle district. "Like many of our great rulers, Faraa's people called her by many names; the Blessed Lady, the Bountiful Queen, the Happy Mistress or the Azure Queen herself."

"And the king?" Angeni looked at her mother.

"The queen never had a husband and Andrenia never had a king under Faraa's rule."

"Then who is the father of the Prince?"

"No one on Eecrys Aredia knows," said Eve so mysteriously. "Some say when the soul of young Faraa's love left this realm the Sacred Mother felt the overwhelming sorrow she had caused the young Princess. So she gave Nicolas to heal her bleeding heart. The prince's past is shrouded by mystery. Even Prince Nicolas doesn't know much about his past. He is called the one whose past is shaded and forgotten." Angeni watched the beautiful castle with amazement and then looked back at Eve.

"It's a sorrowful, but so beautiful legend. It must be true," she whispered daydreaming, then hesitated and looked at her mother. "It is true, right mother?"

"Who knows?" her mother smiled mysteriously, but from her eyes Angeni knew the truth was held by Eve, but she would never tell so as to keep the mystery and the legend of her home. Then the High-Guardian looked at an elegant temple, which looked down from the Castle district where to the little ship skimmed the water. "And there, do you see that beautiful temple close to that majestic saker statue, the Guardian of Andrenia?" she asked. Excited, Angeni nodded. "That's your new home, where your sanctuary will be," she continued and looked at her daughter. "As a true guardian you'll be able to watch over all of Andrenia from up there."

Tiny lamps moved here and there and awaited the ship in the little harbor now hidden in the shadow of the second, beautifully floodlit bridge that the ship silently approached. This bridge was even prettier than the one they left behind. With lowered masts and sails a few smaller brothers and sisters of the *Prosperity* slept peacefully, the calm icy water cradled them in the port. Eve looked beyond the floodlit bridge where the dim shadows delineated a small island in the middle of the river.

"Asria lovingly encircles the forested island of Amargreth," the High-Guardian remembered. "How much time I spent beside its beautiful ponds? They house many water lilies and exotic fishes. Now it's covered in snow. With the leaves gone and the trees denuded, the fishponds are presumably as frozen as Asria itself." She smiled at Angeni, who tried to see the island better, but darkness hid its glory. "But it's still beautiful. You'll see," Eve added.

Angeni looked up as the aura on the *Prosperity's* masts and sails blinked and went out, as the Master Helmsman released the crystal domes. The ship silently edged toward her home pier. As the pier got closer, the small crew prepared; Naevius readied the mooring rope at the bow while Apprentice Kallina gently operated the rudderpost at the stern.

The snow-laden wooden pier flexed as the ship's starboard nudged it. A rope sliced through the air and caught the bollard fast. The rope stretched and Angeni felt a soft twitch under her feet, which marked the end of their journey. They had arrived.

* * *

174

Pale blue Carenia Seli peeked out from behind the dark clouds, small snowflakes fell from the grey sky all over Andrenia. The Castle district where the Temple of the young Aserians' sanctuary resided slept silent. All of the apprentices rested after the long journey. Aurora, who shared sanctuary with her sister, had fallen asleep almost immediately and already wandered somewhere in dreamland.

Relaxed, but more restless and excited, young Angeni couldn't sleep. A safe distance from the edge of the long outdoor snow-laden gallery, she watched the entire city that was dusted by a layer of snow. Andrenia was much more beautiful in the snowfall than it seemed from the River Asria below where the *Prosperity* now slept in silence among her brothers and sisters. Hugging her pulled up legs, Angeni's wings wrapped around her, she waited for the dawn; her commencement day when she would become a real Aserian Guardian. And maybe, just maybe she would see the legendary crystal blade.

The soft breeze had turned the pages of her papyrus pamphlet, which rested beside her along with her arven pencil. The face of the mysterious old Aserian stranger looked back at her. The dark eyes watched her from under the hood while lightning struck silent beyond, just as she remembered him. She didn't want to forget him, whoever he was and whenever they met, if they ever met at all. Angeni couldn't remember the face of that caring angel of the night, who protected her, the one with which she felt safe. Yet, as she thought of him, her soul was filled with happiness. She wanted to know who he was; she wanted to meet him.

Her curious eyes spied a little house in the distance in front of the gallery below. Its chimney softly puffed smoke into the sky, just like the hundreds of houses around it, except this house was not asleep. A single candle flame shone in its small window. Someone was still awake in that house.

There are fifty million souls on Eecrys Aredia, but there is only one that my soul awaits, she thought. *Maybe you live in that little house, stranger. Maybe you're the one that my soul desires and calls in my dreams,* she wondered. *Maybe.* Then someone walked in front of the window and blew the candle out. The small house went to sleep.

"Good night. Sleep and dream well," she whispered with love while the gentle breeze ruffled her hair and wings. Snowflakes landed on her cheek and melted, Angeni sighed out a frosty plume in her lone peace. She didn't at all feel the cold that surrounded her. Only her breath reminded her of what cold felt like when she was still a human.

175

Her curious eyes looked right, where in the close by distance the elegant symbol of Andrenia, an enormous saker statue, or Turul as the Andrenians called it, rested on its pedestal. The statue's majestic wings spread wide; it held a large sword in its claws and screamed silent into the night. It stood guard over the entire city and its citizens since Andrenia's birth. Now, its wings and body were covered in snow, but it didn't take away from its beauty and grace. Beyond the statue in the distance, the Citadel of Andrenia perched on the edge of the tallest half rocky, half pine forested mountain overlooking the shore, the place where tomorrow her dream would come true. Still, as the moment came closer an unexplainable fear embraced her.

Angeni took a soft breath of the sweet cold air, leaned back on the stone altar and closed her eyes. She let the peace and quiet surround her; something that she desired so much. However, she felt for some time that someone watched her from behind.

"This is the life. Snowfall, quiet and peace," she whispered, intending to force the person behind her to speak.

"Isn't it a lovely night?" the voice of a *beliefless infidel* shattered her peace.

"Alas, everything has an end." Angeni victoriously smiled to herself as she opened her eyes and stared out over the city. Looking back, she faced Jared, who stood behind her in his white toga. "Well, well, well. My favorite Sentinel, and in his real persona."

"Surprised to see me?"

"Surprised? Yes. Surprised is one word that comes to mind," she responded coldly, turning back to watch the snow gently fall over Andrenia. "What can your favorite guardian do for you?"

"May I?" he asked. Angeni nodded, and the Sentinel sat down beside her. Jared watched the city along with her for a long silent moment. For Angeni this moment seemed like eternity. From the corner of her eye she had seen the young man studied her with his eyes.

"Say something," he asked her.

"What?" shy, she asked kindly.

"Well. That's a nice start," Jared smiled.

"I just love it here. It's so peaceful. So beautiful," she sighed happily. "I believe I start to see why mother loves Andrenia so much. Have you ever seen any place more beautiful? Even in snowfall?"

The Sentinel nodded agreement. Then silence again. Seemingly, it was the end of the topic, the end of discussion. But from the corner of her eye she had seen the young Sentinel look around almost unnoticed and searched for something, anything for a conversation.

"What are you doing out here at night?" Jared asked, looking at the papyrus scroll pamphlet.

"Drawing," she admitted softly and showed him the art. "Words and dreams may fly away, but drawings remain." Angeni smiled proudly in her philosophy.

"An Aserian's art is her heart," said Jared. Angeni nodded as the Sentinel studied the sketch. "Who is he?" he asked.

"I don't know," Angeni whispered as she studied the stranger on the papyrus. "So filled with sorrow and guilt, I know he is watching over me, guarding me. Nothing and no one is what they first appear to be. It was his advice in my dreams or in a once forgotten life. I don't know."

"You believe your dreams have a meaning."

"All our dreams have a meaning," she responded. "As father once said; some are the echo of our soul, our fantasies and our greatest dreams. And some reflect our worst fears. I feel he is right."

"If your soul feels this way, it might be true."

"It really matters what I feel," Angeni whispered and looked back at her art. "Whenever I remember this phrase, I see him in my mind. I know he told this to me. But when or where? I can't remember."

"Whoever he is, he is right, Angeni," Jared said. "You know what I think?"

"About what?"

"About you."

"I don't really care," she forced herself to cheek coldly, looked away and pretended to survey the city. Deep in her soul, she eagerly wanted to hear his words. *Why am I so distant?* She couldn't answer her own question. From the corner of her eye she saw that Jared shook his head with his familiar rueful smile. Angeni turned a healthy grin on him. "Tell me, what you think about me?" she asked as her curiosity overwhelmed her. Amused at her quick turn of mind, Jared shook his head while the young guardian patiently waited.

"So?" Angeni asked. She waited a long moment and saw the bravery of her friend fly away. "Can you form a sentence, Sentinel?" she teased.

"No one is what he or she appears to be the first time. Not even you."

"What do you mean?" Curious, her eyes looked for his explanation.

"Sometimes you're an insecure ice angel who is accustomed to attracting men just to leave them behind with their desire without a word. You can cut every soul with your sharp tongue and dissolve every hope in the heart of a man, especially this one. Then sometimes you're the most beloved, capricious, pleasant, timid open soul," he paused for a moment. "And foremost, cheeky spirit that I ever knew. A happy snowflake. The question is; which one are you?"

"I'm one of them for sure," she chuckled before she turned serious. "But only one will learn the truth."

As Angeni reached toward her papyrus pamphlet and arven pencil, Jared started to rub her back at the root of her wings. She closed her eyes, enjoyed it while she lowered her wings, and held her drawing supplies.

"Please stop," she asked the Sentinel softly, but he didn't. She felt all the emotions the Sentinel felt for her and it filled her with great joy. She dropped her resistance just to sense the feeling of ease spread through her body. It was that same strange feeling that embraced her when she dreamt of her mysterious angel of the night. "Good. Right there. Left a little," she whispered as she enjoyed the attention.

Jared quirked a tender smile as Angeni again closed her eyes while he kneaded her back.

"You are so sweet and so..." he whispered in her ear. Angeni's eyes flew wide open. She quickly got up and backed away while she lowered her wings behind her, in her embarrassment nearly crushing the scroll pamphlet in her hand. She swiftly reasserted her icy control.

"Don't ever cross this line."

"Are you afraid of me?" Jared asked as he took a step toward her.

"Me? Afraid?" Angeni chuckled before she glared ice. "Oh, no. I never fear. But you should." She raised her wings threateningly. "You should be frightened of me."

"I cannot fear someone who looks as innocent as you." One step and he held her tenderly.

"Me? Innocent?" she asked to cover desire while she lowered her wings.

"As the snow melts on the first days of Prosperous, your ice armour cannot hold forever." His confidence made him brave. "Innocence mirrors in your eyes. I see it."

"Uh-uh. There you're mistaken. I am not an innocent. I can... I will... I..." Her confidence rushed away and failed her.

"So? What will you do, Angeni?" he asked curiously while he looked deep into her eyes. Desperate, Angeni searched for words.

I have loved you since I first seen you, his strong thought broke Angeni's mind, made her look at him. *Your eyes. The smell of your skin and hair. I don't want to let you go.* Her spirit and soul filled with a joy that sent goose bumps over her body.

So sudden, Angeni spun out of his arms.

"Was it something I said?" asked Jared with surprise.

"Not yet," whispered Angeni and lowered her head sadly while she gathered her thoughts. Then after a long moment of silence, she looked back at him. "I want to be so good to you and to everyone else," she said, and then glanced over the city. "I want to experience and do many things. I want to tell you everything that's in my soul..." her voice caught as Aurora flashed into her mind. She closed her eyes to force herself back to the present. She wanted to say something so she could stay in his arms at least for one moment more. But she also knew Jared was not the one her soul waited. "I want to, I want to..." she paused again as her spirit conscious dictated and neglected the wish of the body and the soul. Her embarrassment slowly, but completely overwhelmed her.

"I want to dance." Her ice returned while she caressed the Sentinel's cheek. Jared was unable to stop his eyes opening wider in surprise.

"Dance?"

"Alone." Her burning cheeks didn't stop an icy grin. "Well. Not alone. Just me and my wings."

"I..." Jared was stunned into stuttering.

"Oh, no, thank you. I know where I'm heading," Angeni chuckled in her embarrassment, exaggerated her gesture to the doorway. "Where am I heading, where am I heading?" she muttered. "Good night, Sentinel." She tossed a wave while she turned and headed inside.

Why are you so embarrassed? His thoughts made Angeni stop and look back at him. "You're right. I crossed a line that I shouldn't have," the young Sentinel said. "I guess you're not going to talk to me for a long time," guilt reduced his voice to a mere whisper.

"You see it right. A long-long, very long time," her icy voice retorted. Then she paused and seriously took the measure of the Sentinel as he hung his head. Angeni's contrite spirit felt sorry for him. She knew that she might have gone a bit far this time. After a short moment, she forced a cheeky grin. "At least until Sachylia rises in the morning."

Jared's eyes snapped up to hers. Rueful, he shook his head knowing she had him going.

"You're such a little girl sometimes." His words brought back Angeni's tender smile.

"Who is truly loved by the Sacred Mother, that one's soul is always kept as a child for eternity," sang her angelic voice.

"Oh, this explains a lot. Then you must be really loved by her," teased Jared, but he couldn't stay light-hearted. "If I have offended you, Angeni, I am sorry."

"Never say you're sorry. Never regret anything you say," Angeni responded with determined kindness. Before the young man had a chance to respond, it was as if an invisible force pushed Angeni. Her legs quickly danced the happy, yet still embarrassed angel into the building. "Good night, Sentinel," she sang facetiously before she disappeared. After a moment, she peeked out. "Sleep and dream well," her song finished. She waved farewell with her right wing before she quickly ducked into the building.

The night was still young. She grabbed a music crystal from her sanctuary and turned her art supplies over to the protection of Pilly. Light-footed, she stepped, almost danced among the shadows down the long corridor. The young guardian was restless and her soul wanted to release all of the happiness that had caressed her. Her hand grabbed the closest column like she would dance with it and with a soft buoyancy the joyfully humming angel rounded it. Then her silent dance carried her toward the garden that beckoned from the grand entrance at the end. The pale moonlight duplicated her advancing shadow while the wind wafted the curtains of the windows between the columns.

"Where are you sneaking to this time, my daughter?" a familiar voice asked from behind her. Her legs immediately rooted to the spot. Smiling, she looked back at her father who stepped out from the shadows and studied her.

"To give my emotions freedom and dance out my happiness, father."

"Isn't Jared with you?" her father asked curiously as he glanced around, while sudden embarrassment embraced Angeni.

"Uh, yes, he is. Was. But he..." she blushed.

"So, you're simply running away from love."

"Me? No. Never," she denied with determined head shaking. Her father disagreed with a fatherly look. "No!" she added quickly, determined once more, trying to convince him, but as she heard her own voice, she couldn't even convince herself.

I'm old, but not blind, my daughter, she heard his thoughts.

"Maybe?" her shy voice added after a short hesitation. "Is this love?"

Aaron's tenderness touched his smile. "Never forget; Aserians hide nothing and see everything. See my daughter, not just watch."

"What should I do?"

"There is a human expression; follow your heart."

"What if my heart doesn't know what it wants?"

"It will. In time. Your spirit is strong. You're able to hide behind your emotions, out of fear. But please, don't hide your feelings. Never deny happiness and never escape love."

"I'm not escaping, just, I…" replied the young guardian while the old High-Guardian watched her with a raised eyebrow. "One part of my soul is happy that he loves me. My soul wants me to go out to the garden and dance in the snow, dance my happiness, which has embraced and caressed me since I…" then she paused with doubts.

So? her father's sly thought came through while she searched for the words. "Your voice tells me you want to like him," he calmly said aloud.

"Yes. Certainly," came her sarcastic defiance, looking away she crossed her arms.

Don't hide behind the protective illusion of sarcasm, my daughter, came his calm thoughts.

"I'm letting a moment go because I have to, father," she finally admitted and pushed on with determination. "I know how he feels, but I won't give him illusions. It's not honorable." Angeni paused for a moment and then looked deep into her father's eyes. "Aurora loves him so much. She deserves to be happy and I won't be in my sister's way."

You're an honest and clean soul, Angeni. But you shouldn't be rigid with yourself, came the old thoughts into her mind. "Sometimes you need to keep an eye on your own interest too," he continued in fatherly concern.

"When the time comes, I will, I promise, father. I know that a moment is waiting for me. My moment." Angeni sighed. "You taught me to listen to my soul and my fragile little heart. You taught me to never hesitate, but to always take the unknown path regardless what others say. That's what I do now."

The young guardian looked out the window arch toward the distant stars that peeked out from behind the clouds.

"My soul is waiting for someone else, father," she said and looked back at him. "And my heart knows it."

You're letting a sure moment go for the unknown. You're braver than I thought, his amazement echoed in Angeni's mind. "Who would be that great soul?"

"I don't know who he is at all," she shrugged her wings. "Someone who cares for me in my dreams. Even when I fear in a nightmare…" she remembered the heights from her dream. "Maybe he is someone in my future. Maybe. But I feel he is real."

"You're daydreaming as always, my daughter," he chuckled as patted young Angeni's golden hair.

"No, father!" the young guardian protested and she crossed her arms with determined defiance. "Someone awaits me. Our paths just haven't crossed yet," she declared, gesturing with her hands and her wings majestically.

Your confidence in yourself is truly respectable, she heard the pride in his thoughts. "I hope you are right," her father finally added. "Destiny decides who touches your life, but only your heart decides who touches your soul. But please never forget my daughter, true happiness in life to love and to be loved. Those who surround us give us our light. But if we're alone, our life becomes meaningless and our light quickly fades."

"I know, Father," she kissed his cheek and smiled. "I never will be alone. I promise."

"Now, go and dance out your happiness, my daughter," smiled the old High-Guardian. Angeni gave a kiss to his cold cheek and her legs already danced her out to the garden.

A few moments later, the music crystal on a small pedestal already echoed its pleasant syrinx; Lyra and crystal chime music in the garden. Angeni released her happiness as she danced. Her bare feet didn't feel the cold as they crunched the snow and followed the gentle rhythm. Like water, her delicate body flowed with her soul's hopes and desires. Her white wings like silky velvet, waved with her slender form. A joyful soul swam in happiness as her angelic voice sang.

Cold wind, soft snowfall, moonlight kiss,
He warmed up my spirit as I reminisce.
Whose face is that, who appears in my dreams,
Who are you stranger, who haunts me and redeems?

When I fall in love, I know it will be forever,
I await you stranger; even if it will take a great endeavor.
Or do I dream; never to fall in love and not heed advice,
A noble sacrifice to follow my heart; I gladly pay the price.

Are you just a mere dream, a fantasy of time?
Will our paths really cross in the future, I cannot divine.
Are you just an imagination, a mirror of my desire?
Or are you just my fantasy, as my emotions do conspire?

Your soul is calling me; you're singing familiar tones,
You're drawing me; I feel your calling in my bones.
It's a good day to love, when my soul knows the reasons why,
I'll follow my emotions, that I can't and don't want to deny.

182

I hear your call, I know my fate will be you,
Who are you, stranger, that to my fragile heart are fallen into.
I want to believe we'll be together; I can't resist the temptation,
Love is a rainbow of light, born of a daydreamer's soul revelation.

The music slowly faded away. Angeni slowed to a stop to close her eyes. Elegantly, she spread her wings, threw her hands wide and then let herself fall back. Snow exploded into the air all around her as she landed on her back. The eyes of the smiling young woman opened to see the peregrine clouds and the stars that watched her happiness. The snow that she scattered slowly fell onto her face. Her eyes caught the five-starred Crystal constellation right above her, which curiously looked down at her from between the clouds. Is it a sign? Maybe the Sacred Mother was watching her happiness, her joy? Angeni didn't know, but she wanted to believe it.

"Everyone plays in some way throughout their life," the calm, joyful voice of her mother broke the snow-laden silence. "Everyone with the exception of you."

Angeni got up, quickly shook her wings to beat off the snow, and then she looked at her mother. The High-Guardian strolled majestically in her orange saree toward Angeni; her large wings were gently ruffled by the wind.

"The Sacred Mother loves spirits like you, Angeni. Your soul and heart are open, holding nothing back. You always give all of yourself." She paused and looked down where Angeni had risen. Then looking back, she raised a delicate eyebrow at her young daughter.

Angeni glanced back at the large angel silhouette she had left in the snow. "Happy snow angel," she smiled proudly. "A self-portrait. Beautiful, isn't it?"

Eve smiled as Angeni, so like Aurora, curiously twisted her wing tips behind her back and then nestled closer to her mother, who hugged her lovingly with arms and wings. Angeni leaned her head on her mother's shoulder, feeling so safe. Her daydreaming eyes looked up to the stars.

"When I was a little girl, I always dreamt of becoming a real Aserian Guardian. Tomorrow, my dream will come true," she whispered, yet a little tremor echoed in her angelic voice. "But I fear tomorrow, mother. I fear so much, but I don't know why."

"Oh, my dear child. You fear the change. This is the one thing in all your life that your soul has been praying for. You fear the unknown and you can't go farther as your soul believes that you have reached the greatest dream of your life. But tomorrow will be just the beginning of a wonderful journey. Remember; your master training and the teachings in your long life is still ahead of you."

The words of the High-Guardian chased her fear away. "You are so wise, Mother. Thank you," she said as her heart filled with pride.

"Wise? Me?" Eve chuckled. "No, my child just experienced." She leaned to Angeni's ear to whisper in confidence. "I feared the same when I was young. I wanted to become a noble Guardian, like those I had looked up to when I was a human a long-long time ago."

"Really?"

Her mother nodded. "Tomorrow, when your nature will be revealed you'll see what you have really become. A dream will come true; you'll become a real Aserian Guardian. In that moment, the world will open its doors to show what undiscovered paths lay in front of you. As you reach one dream, another will take its place. Maybe even a greater one. And this cycle will never end while light surrounds your soul. I promise."

"I hope you are right," said Angeni with quiet fervor. "I don't want to be disappointed. But my soul fears I will be, mother. I'd like to be the one who I thought I would be, the one my soul always dreamt about." She grew sorrowful. "But I fear I won't be."

"Never be afraid of who you are, Angeni." Eve embraced her daughter. "Never be afraid to face your true being." She gave her cheek a kiss and looked up to the night sky. Carenia Seli peeked out from behind the clouds to watch mother and daughter together in the garden.

Angeni closed her eyes, certain in the safety of her mother arms as her large wings embraced her protectively. She wanted to rest, sleep in this motherly safety and dream about her angel of the night. Then after a moment, she felt the caring wings pull away and the small snowflakes fell on her cheek once again. Why was her mother not protecting her young daughter anymore?

Opening her eyes, Angeni looked around, stunned, awed to silence. They weren't in the beautiful garden anymore. Maybe not even in Andrenia. A large forest surrounded them in the snow-laden night. But how did they get there? From the wise, yet impish eyes of her mother, she read; it's her secret, she won't tell.

The old trees whispered. The misty cold air vibrated. She felt they were not alone, yet had seen no one else. She smelled the scent of the soil and the strong fragrance of the sweet flowers. Her spirit, soul and body were in complete harmony, a balance she never felt before. Endless peace ruled her existence while a caring invisible power prepossessed and soothed her entire being. This power didn't come from her mother. It came from someone else.

"Where are we?"

"The Sacred Mountain of Ram; the Gateway to the Heavens," Eve answered and looked around. "One of our ancient legends says that at the beginning of time, at this place the Sacred Mother descended from the sky in the form of a bright bird. After nine days and nine nights, she took the shape of a beautiful woman. Then from the Sacred Father, our beloved mother gave life to six boys and six girls."

"Our Gods and Goddesses, they were all born here," whispered Angeni in awe as she realized, and then excited, looked around. "The Sacred Mother, all our Gods and Goddesses walked here once, at this place. All of them."

Then so sudden, scared, she stepped back.

"No. I, I shouldn't tread on this sacred soil," Angeni stepped back once again as she realized she was still standing on it. "I'm too young. I'm not worthy to be here," she whispered modestly.

"Angeni?" Her mother raised her eyebrow looking at her. Scared, Angeni forced herself to look at Eve, looked around, and then up to the sky. Angeni's soul waited for the wrath of the Sacred Mother. The young guardian had tread where only Gods and Goddesses had treaded before. How dare she? It might be the greatest blasphemy in Aserian history; maybe the entire Crystal Garden since the world existed. Yet, the almighty wrath of the Sacred Mother never came.

"Come, my dear child," the High-Guardian's voice sang as she called her frightened daughter and offered her a hand.

Still afraid of the wrath of the Sacred Mother, Angeni sighed. Then in her childish fear, she took the first brave step onto the sacred land. She felt like she should step into a different world; like Spirit Guardian Eriana, who once stepped into the Land of the Gods.

Like a child, as that's what Angeni was in her soul, she looked around, curious, as she strolled hand in hand with her mother in the dark forest. It was like a dream and she couldn't believe she walked where many of her legends had been born. After a short walk, they arrived in a clearing circled by pine trees. A large grayish rock stood in the middle, bathed in the dancing blue light of the surrounding torches.

"What is this place?" asked the young guardian.

"The Pulsating Stone, the heart of Eecrys Aredia," her mother said, looking at the stone with great love. Angeni took a step closer to see it better. It seemed like a simple rock, a large stone, nothing more. It didn't beat, but just stood silent between the elegant torches. Yet it had drawn the young guardian's entire being. She felt a crystal-clear innocent soul

185

with all its clarity. All of these kind feelings that embraced her came from the stone heart of Eecrys Aredia.

"Come here," Eve invited her to the Pulsating Stone as she sat beside it. "Feel and hear the true language of the soul."

"The language of the soul?" she asked. Following her mother's example, Angeni sat down near the stone while her mother nodded to the stone. Hesitant and a little fearful, Angeni touched the cold surface of the stone. It pulsed beneath her fingertips.

She felt herself become overwhelmed by the beautiful emotions that dwelt within the great and endless spirit of her home world hidden within the stone. The stone shared all with her spirit and soul. It whispered to her of the peaceful and loving attentive care of the humans, Aserians, and countless other souls who called Eecrys Aredia home. For a moment she felt she was everywhere on Eecrys Aredia as her spirit became one with the Great Spirit. She saw all of the beautiful continents, all the life that the peregrine clouds have seen, and the whirling sapphire second realm, the Spirit Sea that had embraced her home like a magnificent shiny aura.

"Eecrys Aredia lives," Angeni whispered, deeply moved. "She is speaking to me. I... I hear her. I understand her. She is so beautiful."

"Every soul cries in one language, even Eecrys Aredia herself," Eve explained while the young guardian kept her hand on the stone to feel more, to speak with her home, to understand her. "We may speak different languages or different dialects, but all of us have one common origin. Love is love, caring is caring, guiding and protecting all mean the same regardless of the language. The language of the soul's origin binds all of us in peace and unity. As you understand Eecrys Aredia, you will be able to understand everyone else's soul. You will know what their need is, what bothers them, or what they want the most."

"I will be able to help everyone, even without speaking to them or knowing their language." Angeni finished with an awed glanced at Eve, but still kept her hand on the Pulsating Stone. The emotions that her home world shared kept her exuberant and joyful. Then she hesitated; maybe this would be the right time to reveal her cursed gift to her mother.

You wish to speak about your gift? Eve curiously questioned.

You're so wise mother. You always know everything before I can even ask, Angeni thought with a giggle of pride. Then her narrowed eyes and surprised frown showed she had realized that she hadn't seen her mother speaking. She heard her voice in her mind.

No, Angeni, she heard Eve chuckle. The young guardian was at a loss. "I just have the same gift as you," her mother added kindly.

"Why didn't I hear you before?"

"I learned how to live with it and how to hide it. When I want peace and quiet, I shadow my thoughts from the world. Something that you have also started to learn well on your own."

"It can be so disturbing," Angeni's voice was full of sorrow. "Sometimes there are too many voices and I cannot separate them." Worried, she looked at her mother. "I wish I could silence it somehow for eternity."

"Silence a gift that the Sacred Mother gave to your soul?" Eve chuckled. "Why would you do that?"

"Everyone's thoughts, desires and secrets are their own. I don't want to know anyone's dreams and deepest secrets. That's not honorable," the young guardian admitted.

"I wanted so much to hear this, my daughter. Your noble soul makes me so proud," replied the High-Guardian happily. She meditated for a moment. "With patience, you may learn what to hear and what you may shut out of your mind. I'll gladly show guidance, but on this long journey, you'll have to find your own path. You must be patient to see what lies at the end, to learn why you received this gift."

"It's a curse," said Angeni in defiance, as she looked away. "Everyone is an open scroll to me, even souls that I never met. But I already know all their deepest thoughts and hidden dreams. I don't want this, Mother."

"Everything has a reason in this world, Angeni," the High-Guardian cupped Angeni's cheek. "The rain falls from the sky to give life to the flora and fill the lakes for the fishes. The wind is dusting pale flowers; apoideas and other flying insects are dusting bright nectar flowers. And spirits with souls have bodies not just to see, but to feel, experience, and live on this beautiful world."

"Everything has a purpose, a rightful reason," Angeni realized silently while she looked back at the stone, which drew her spirit and still filled her with love.

"Yes. And the gift in your soul has a purpose as well, a true reason. I hope that one day you will learn why the Sacred Mother gave this gift to you. One day you'll live the moment when this secret will be revealed."

When daughter and mother returned to Andrenia the very same mysterious way as they left, the first light of the new day that Angeni awaited for so long was already close. Alone, the humming delirious young guardian strolled down the echoing corridor and danced with some of the columns that she met on her way. The pale moonlight of Carenia Seli and some torches had shown her the way back to her distant sanctuary. Her soul had waited for this moment and now she wanted to watch the sunrise from her balcony to greet Sachylia on this hopefully beautiful day. Today the all seeing sapphire eye of the Sacred Mother, she who was like a silent mentor watching over all her children's long evolution since the very first day would now be witness to all their glory. She would see what great guardians, true angels they had all become. Angeni just hoped she wouldn't cause disappointment and foremost she wouldn't be disappointed either.

In the silken darkness, a great wind ruled the night, which shepherded the sparse snow that fell outside. Some curious snowflakes swirled through the window arch as the wind puffed out the curtains. Step after step, the cold marble chilled her bare feet as she turned around the corner. Then her leg rooted to the spot. The darkness, like a silent, untouchable and invisible menace looked back at her from the far end of the next dim corridor.

Someone watched her from the black shadows. She felt it. Then she had seen what couldn't be. Shadows moved in a silent dance like they were alive. A soft echoing whisper, a whine began to echo in her mind. Someone was there. She heard its whirling cursed thoughts, which wasn't spoken in the language of the soul, but a chaotic, unrecognizable language. Who or what lied in the shadows?

A roiling, misty four-legged shadow creature stepped out of the darkness. Its body slowly whirled above the marble flagstones, but it kept its familiar shape. It looked like a grey mingan that howled to Carenia Seli when it showed its full face at night. But this creature wasn't flesh and bone. It wasn't even alive. Its soft, yet high-pitched whine menaced.

Her soul froze in fear as her young soul recognized the beast; the legendary Daharra, the dreaded shadow mingan. It wasn't a fairy tale, as she always believed. It was still night, her young soul wasn't asleep and now, the relentless Daharra came to take her soul.

The shadow creature's cursed growling pushed at her mind as it took a menacing step forward. Angeni knew she had to keep her distance and slowly forced her foot to step back once.

The Daharra barked sharply once and then started to run fast and jumped right toward her. Following her instincts, Angeni immediately crouched and spun around while her large wings flared wide to hit the beast. But her strong feathery wings, which barely reached the beast, passed through the whirling body unharmed as it jumped and passed above her. In a moment, the creature landed behind the young guardian.

As she came out of the spin, she immediately faced the Daharra once again. Its soft growling was more furious than before. Angeni trembled in fear; she couldn't even harm this beast to protect herself.

"Please, don't," she whispered in fear.

Desperate she turned and ran, and the beast immediately followed her example. The Daharra loped close as Angeni raced down the corridor. She had seen it from the corner of her eye that mirrored her fear, but foremost, the creature as it came closer and closer. Angeni smashed into the next corridor, touching and softly bouncing off a column in her rush. The shadow creature followed a dozen steps behind, but didn't catch her. It herded her. But why and to where?

Then the corridor ended for Angeni in a balcony.

"Oh, no, no, no," her whispered panic embraced her as she barely stopped at the edge. From the darkness, her mortal enemy looked back and her view became blurry. The great depths called her louder and louder. For a moment, she believed as she looked back, the last thing she would see was the whirling black creature as it launched at her. Her body waited for the pain that this creature might do with its seemingly strong jaws. But the pain never came. The Daharra stopped at the end of the corridor, kept its distance and growled menacing. Its whine was a rumble as it stepped closer to the young guardian, and then stopped again.

The first beams of Sachylia shot through the heavy clouds onto the balcony. A line of sapphire light glowed on the cold stones that separated the creature from her. The Daharra stepped back from the light as it spread in front of it.

Kill, kill her! Now! screeched and echoed a different, still chaotic voice in her mind.

An unnatural wind emerged from the corridor right behind the Daharra. Its force snapped Angeni's wings back, she almost screamed as it hurt her so much. The blue flames on the closest torches strained like they would next rush toward her for protection. Then the scared light hissed as they went silently dark, and the wind howled closer.

Desperate, Angeni fought to control her painful wings while she tried to stay on her feet so she would not fall into the endless depths behind her. A colorful cloud, whirling like a blanket of orange and red silk, swung into the far end of the corridor. Like a wide river, it raced along a stone watercourse. The dancing cloud wailed like thousands of souls in pain as it sped closer, spreading from wall to wall as it raced behind the growling shadow creature, right toward her. Angeni felt the overwhelming chaos that reverberated through the cloud, but foremost it caused an unexplainable, but great fear, which embraced and completely

189

froze her. Her desperation grew, wanted to scream, but not a single sound left her shaking lips.

The shadow creature snapped its praying dark eyes at the cloud, and then back at the young guardian. It jumped at her and the morning daylight. The Daharra began to dissolve as it reached the Sachylia's sapphire light. It howled in pain and quickly glided through the light, intent on its prey. The cloud of chaos reached the creature and with it, tried to catch the young guardian who tried to lean back and away, but she lost her balance as they both almost reached her at the same time. The ground slipped out from under her feet and she went over the edge of the balcony into the darkness below. The great depth laughed as it embraced her falling fragile body.

She had seen the creature and the colorful cloud dissolve in the sunlight right above her. Her wings froze in terror, her hands tried to reach and grab the balcony that rushed away faster and faster. She wanted to scream in terror, but couldn't. Closing her eyes, knowing the ground approached at her back, she awaited her fate.

The thin ice shattered as her fragile body and large wings crashed into the frozen fountain. The icy water rushed in to encase her being while she sank deeper and deeper. Heavier than ever, her wings soaked up the water and ice shot through her body like a thousand tiny pins. Then her cold body slammed into the hard stone bottom of the shallow fountain to crush her in endless pain.

Stunned, she opened her eyes a slit, everything was a blur and her mind could not comprehend what she saw. Sachylia's sunbeams shot into the crystal-clear water through the broken ice above.

From the blinding sapphire brilliance, through the break, a dark blurry hand reached toward her and grabbed her hand. Her eyes slowly closed as she started to lose consciousness. She felt the dark hand touch hers; for a moment, she felt safe. Her soul began to hear the echoing thoughts of the stranger, but her scrambled mind was not capable of understanding the words of his soul. Her crushed, fragile body strained as the powerful hand yanked her out of the cold water. But then, it all started to dissolve around her like in a dream.

Angeni's eyes suddenly opened. Swimming in a flux of the morning sapphire light, her eyes focused on her surroundings. She found herself sprawled among her velvet cushions in her sanctuary. Pilly, her soft and warm guardian pillow invisibly smiled back from between her embracing arms.

For a moment, Angeni felt like cold water encased her body, but her white saree, wings and body were dry. Like she overslept on her wings, her entire back hurt a little, but the pain slowly dissipated. She sighed as the memory of the shadow creature, the dreadful fall and the cold water loosened their hold on her and slid off like water from her memories. Angeni tried to remember the dream that awakened her, but it slipped between her memories. Whatever she had dreamt, it was so real a terror. Her soul feared something, but it couldn't tell her what.

The cold sweet breeze ruffled the silk curtains and her papyrus pamphlet on the stone table. It showed her last sketch; the mysterious hooded stranger. Still asleep on the other cushion bed, Aurora just turned over and covered her body with her wing, a pleasant smile giving hint to her peaceful dream.

Angeni crawled near the youngest guardian and rested down near her. As she caressed her cheek, she felt her sister's dream was joyful, something about love.

"At least you're dreaming about something nice, sister." Angeni brushed a stray hair from Aurora's cheek. "Dream well. Dream about your love."

The young guardian smiled and kissed her sister's forehead. Carefully, to not disturb Aurora's peaceful dreams, she got up and then walked out onto the balcony. Sachylia's cold dawn beams sparkled on the beautifully snow-covered city of Andrenia, which had just started to awaken. The gentle breeze caressed her face and ruffled her wing feathers while she looked around. The first birds of the day had already taken to the sky. The large bird statue was coated with snow, and still guarded Andrenia. The surface of the frozen fountain at the corner of the garden below was broken, as if someone fell through it from the balcony high above. Her eyes mirrored as an icicle fell from the bottom of the balcony to crack the thin ice armour of the fountain's pool even more.

Fallen icicles, she thought. Smiling, her eyes turned to the distant sparkling Citadel of Andrenia, the place where she would soon learn who she had become. Sachylia greeted her warmly, glowing into her eyes on this beautiful morning. The sapphire sunlight reminded her, the day she waited for so long had finally arrived.

* * *

Pleasant choir and orchestra music reverberated in the ceremonial hall within the Citadel of Andrenia. It had begun to swim in the sapphire glow as Sachylia's light filtrated through the grand open arches that crowned the beautifully elaborate ceiling. The sunlight glowed on a looming larger than life battle sculpture of the legendary Aserian

Guardian Israfil who faced the massive, horrendous horned demon Marquis Marchosias in the last judgment of the Crystal Shade. Behind Israfil, a young woman clutched her child and watched the valiant hero who fought the beast with his bare hands to protect her. Angeni felt both fear and respect as her eyes reflected the statues. This was the first time Angeni ever saw a demon and the sight of the powerful demon beast scared her, even in bright daylight. The statue of Israfil bred great respect in her as it stood for everything an Aserian's existence truly meant.

Disciplined and proud, the seven young Aserian apprentices stood in a line a few steps from each other and waited for their commencement day to begin. Ceretaperia Faraa, human protector and ruler, the queen of Andrenia stood beside Angeni's mother and father in her elegant azure ceremonial dress. Her long brown hair emphasized her regal beauty. The Blessed Lady seemed a kind middle-aged woman, exuded a majesty that demanded the respect she deserved. Full of life; her eyes mirrored her generosity and kindness. Her majestic Turul spirit, who gained his name from the protector of Andrenia, sat on Faraa's right shoulder and silently watched the ceremony with his human charge.

Prince Nicolas, an adult, but still a young child in Queen Faraa's eyes, stood proud beside his mother in shiny sapphire armour. The charming prince reminded Angeni of Jared. Young and strong, his tanned skin glowed in the blue sun. His long brown hair was in ponytail and his brown eyes were alive with intelligence... and an abundance of overconfidence. So much like Jared.

The young Carenians, Iris and Tlanextic stood at the beginning of the line. Next to them the proud Viridanas, Taze and Jared, stood before the Aserian Guardians, Kien, Aurora, and at the very end, Angeni. The apprentices all wore their white toga-like sarees that had represented their innocence from the beginning.

The human choir faced the apprentices as they sang from the far end of the hall; their song called Sachylia and hailed the young Aserians. The music that accompanied them praised the greatness of the day. Now everyone waited for Sachylia to reach its zenith above the hall to start the ceremony.

From the corner of her eye, Angeni had seen all the apprentices were calm and disciplined, yet she felt Aurora's excitement that showed in her eternally curious eyes; the same curiosity that presumably was in her own eyes too as they searched for the crystal blades in the hope that maybe, just maybe she could lay her eyes on one. But she could only see seven strangely shaped gold metallic objects on the velvet pillow that her mother held. Each looked as if two cavernous mingan skulls had been grafted to the two ends of a longer golden ringed staff, a long strange golden scroll holder; the very same she had seen once in Odess'iana when she was a little girl. Like in the past, there was nothing that reminded her of a blade or a crystal or the combination of the two.

Disappointed, Angeni realized the crystal blade could actually be a legend of the Aserians, nothing more. Maybe it was really only *her* legendary crystal blade, just as Old Shen and her mother always phrased so carefully when she wanted to learn more about it. No one ever said it actually existed. No one.

Sachylia reached its zenith and the hall lit up in its full glory as the sunlight focused on the hall. The tilted windows set into the roof bent and refracted the light so it shone only onto the apprentices, blinding them and bathing them in its brilliance.

Angeni closed her eyes for a moment. Then found she swam in the narrow beams of Sachylia, which made it impossible to see to the sides, only ahead. She felt the presence of her sister and the others beside her, but the bright sapphire light blinded her if she tried to look toward Aurora. She had to look ahead, to where the Ceretaperia stepped forward and spread her arms as she started the ceremony while the choir and music gave greater dignity to her words.

"The Sacred Mother is proud as she is watching over all of you, young Aserians." The Ceretaperia's regal voice filled Angeni with excitement. "Eecrys Aredia calls upon you in our greatest days, and in our darkest nights. Your way of life is to wisely guard our home and guide all her souls. But to protect others well, to give your very best in every way, you must first know who you truly are. Now under the sapphire light of Sachylia, reveal your true nature to the world you're willing to protect, face what your soul has become. Wisdom is the light by day. Know yourself to live wisely."

Sachylia's light held all of her with utmost tenderness while the High-Guardians strolled to the first apprentice. The young guardian strained to hear everything.

"Iris, young Carperia," Eve called to the Watcher. "Great awareness comes slowly; it's a path of lifelong learning. You're a gentle and noble soul with great wisdom and endless love of life. But now the time has come to reveal your true soul to see who you really are."

Angeni heard a strange, stroking sound that that reminded her of ice quickly freezing.

"Radiance and intelligence permeate your nature, Iris," Angeni's father spoke to her. "Logical, analytical and very intelligent. A true intellectual spirit and a good observational soul rightfully confident in her abilities and faultless perception. For you the mind is everything, full of ideas and messages to inspire others. Live and serve Eecrys Aredia as you always have. And remember, knowledge is like love. It's only good when shared."

"Thank you, exalted one."

Yellow aura. Yellow, like a beautiful Jasnaia flower, thought Angeni while she heard a noise as of crystals breaking to little pieces, but she didn't hear anything fall. What she did hear was her parents and the royals step closer.

"Carnaia Tlanextic," her mother said imperiously. "You considered your spiritual and emotional values to be more important than anything else. Is it really you, or is it what you hope to become? Reveal your nature and show who you really are."

Angeni heard that snick of freezing ice again. She wanted to see Tlanextic, but the brightness would not let her.

"An intelligent and intuitive nature eager to seek answers has declared itself," Aaron proclaimed. "A spirit filled with clarity, a peaceful soul which never fears to ask the right questions. You believe nothing merely because you have been told it, you believe because you dare to look into it. You have the ability to convey your thoughts, ideas, views and concepts eloquently and charismatically to everyone. Always give answer to those that need, and listen to the questions of those who seek knowledge."

Azure like the crystal-clear water, Angeni thought as she recognized the traits of the young Watcher's nature.

"Thank you, exalted one," said Tlanextic respectfully while Angeni heard the ring of shattered crystal. The young guardian heard the royals step closer, to Taze.

"Eternally shy, but forever caring, Taze," Eve stepped up and called the young Sentinel like she were her third daughter. "Your joyful existence has brought brilliance into each of our lives since you have come among us. But now the joyful days have ended, and you must face who you've really become."

Angeni heard that curious snick again. *What could this sound be?*

"Your nature is the sunniest of all, like a candle which can light thousands of candles with one single flame," said Aaron in a kind, fatherly voice. "Shy and sensitive within, you're happy even in your own company, but you'll never suffer from loneliness as you're always inspiring others with your presence. Warmth flows through your existence as you share and love to give to everyone. But never forget, patience yields a Jasnaia. Seek not your fears, but your hopes and dreams.

When your time comes, when you feel you're ready, don't fear to open to others as well. Serve Eecrys Aredia well, Viridanperia Taze."

Jasnaia yellow, Angeni thought with an inward smile.

"I will serve Eecrys Aredia with my best," said Taze in her shy voice.

Angeni heard her mother and the others step to Jared.

Now, this will be interesting, thought Angeni, who was most curious to know his nature.

"Jared. You were a most promising apprentice," said Eve in a tone full of respect. "But your talent and skills are not enough. The truth must be embraced to free your knowledge. And now reveal and face who you truly are."

The strange sound of the freezing ice crystals hit her ears again.

"An admired and respected creative spirit, relaxed and peaceful soul fond of nature, balanced and so strong," Angeni heard her father's pride. "You always speak from the heart and never fear to express yourself, never hide anything from anyone. Your loyalty doesn't differentiate between humans, other spirits, souls, and Mother Nature itself. It's a respectable trait. Give security, stability and balance to everyone's lives and one day you will be true Viridanaia, Jared, a great Sentinel. Serve mankind wisely, protect the weak and innocent and when your time comes watch over your charge as well as you watch over all of us."

Jade green as the beautiful and healthiest leaf, Angeni recognized the *Infidel's* aura while she heard that strange crystal clink. She had to admit that his nature described the Sentinel perfectly, but her father forgot to mention his major trait; overconfident.

"Thank you, exalted one," Jared replied.

How is our nature revealed? Angeni wondered. Her excitement grew as the High-Guardians stepped up to Kien.

"Kien," said Eve. "The one respected, admired and loved by your fellow Aserians. For a long time I couldn't discern your nature. Not because you were lost, young Asnaia. On the contrary, you've shown interest in so many things and in the end, you've connected all your gathered knowledge to the desired balance your soul always wanted. Now see for yourself who you really are. See and learn if you've become the one you wanted to be."

Angeni listened carefully. She was also curious about Kien's nature. She heard a freezing tone again.

"A real spiritual soul that your nature cannot deny," Aaron said with respect. "Philosophical, enquiring and intuitive, you know what balance really is, which you always brought among us. You have the wisdom and the sense to understand what usually only the mystical Spiritual

195

Vanguards are capable of; to understand and know what your fellow souls really need to maintain balance in life. While you live in this realm, you're drawn by the flow of the spirit realms; even if you haven't realized it yet. It is a very rare nature among the Guardians. With the bravery of the Segaran Viras, be the Aserian who protects the realms of Eecrys Aredia, guard us and share your knowledge with those eager to know more about our world and beyond."

"I will, High-Guardian," Kien proclaimed, happy pride echoed from the young man.

Purple aura of a wise soul, Angeni guessed as she heard that icy tone while her mother and the others came to a stop in front of her sister.

"Asperia Aurora, my beloved little daughter," said Eve tenderly. "You've become a charming young Aserian woman. Your open soul, curiosity for life, your kindness, good-heart and honesty cannot be denied. But is it really you or do you just hide behind a well set-up mask?"

Angeni heard that strange icy tone, but she knew already what her sister's nature was. "Amber orange," she guessed without a sound.

"Generous and thoughtful, you've become a strong joyful individual, who sometimes adventures more in the head, than in real life," said her father while Angeni smiled. "You have integrated your physical and mental qualities while you enjoy life to its fullest. Like your sister, you're a daydreaming adventurer, who hunts to fill her own curiosity, but also never fear to conquer the unknown and build the present. So please remember this; curiosity led our ancients to discover what no one had ever experienced or seen before and their daring dreams built our great society that embraces us today. Please continue this tradition further among the Aserians while you enjoy challenging and conquering all facets of all the realms. Bring joy and sunshine into the life of others and build our society, our civilization to even greater heights with your dreams and knowledge. Make us proud, my youngest daughter."

"I will. I promise, my father," Aurora agreed respectfully while Angeni heard that cracking tone once more.

Angeni couldn't help but sigh as her excitement reached its peak.

"Angeni," Eve stepped through the light barrier with Aaron, who couldn't hide their pride for her. "A promising, but unpolished daydreaming soul who must find her way toward her own balance. You have been patient; you're helpful, pleasant, and enduring. With the exception of endurance, anyone can pretend these characteristics, especially if a daydreaming soul wants to become someone so desperately;

someone who you may never have been and never will be. But now, it's time to reveal your true calling to all, even if you'll have to face disappointment."

Her soul clutched by fear, Angeni sighed as Aaron gave her the last *strange scroll holder* from Eve's pillow. As she touched the grip, which was so cold, the young guardian felt her spirit streaming through her body and her will expand into the hilt.

Majestic sapphire beams shot from the two sides of the golden hilt, then like crackling ice, water which freezes too fast, the beams morphed into solid sharp crystal, forming elegant glowing blades on both sides. The frozen crystallized aura was cold, so cold that her skin felt it. The air around the blades was foggy and gently steamed, just like her aura beneath the crystal surface.

The streaming, yet uncontrolled sapphire spirit began to glow under her skin, and then slowly embraced her entire body like an aura, which began to bleed her white saree to blue. A kind of ticklish feeling in her eyes and they flashed for a moment as her whirling spirit declared itself. Her awed eyes mirrored the sparkling sapphire color of the crystal blade, the most beautiful sapphire blue Angeni had ever seen.

She held her own sapphire crystal blade that would accompany her throughout her whole life. In her eyes, this beautiful weapon symbolized and united all the Aserian virtues; self-control, rectitude, courage, benevolence, respect, honesty, honor and loyalty.

Angeni had seen the surprise in the eyes of Ceretaperia Faraa's son, who took a step closer and watched her curiously. But her parent's eyes glowed with pride. They smiled like they had known this for a long time. Maybe they did, as old and wise Aserians saw and knew everyone's nature from a touch.

"Sapphire, like Sachylia herself. Very, very rare, young one," admitted her father. Angeni looked at him; her face aglow and embraced by dim blue. "You're a young caretaker, young Sachylia Asperia, a balanced and generous existence sustaining and respecting life itself; even if you haven't realized it yet. A calm and strong intuitive spirit with a peaceful, yet cold sensitive soul, you have a caring and loving existence ready to help others with your intelligence, inner knowledge and wisdom. You live in the present, but so brave you dare to seek the past, as well you're vigilant, willing to watch over our future. However, daydreaming souls are sometimes lost in the drift of time and imagination until finally they can't find their true place in their own time. So please, hear me, my daughter; never forget who you are and never forget where you come from. Remember always."

"I will, father," said Angeni with respect. Then suddenly the two solid crystal blades crackled as they turned back to a whirling aura, which immediately streamed back to the grip. Her spirit was overwhelmed by fatigue, exhausted by the crystal blade. Her instinct recalled her shiny aura from the grip into her body. The hilt of the crystal blade was lifeless gold in her hand, while the uncontrolled aura glowing all over her body faded away.

With great respect, Angeni bowed her head to her parents, who responded the same.

Sachylia crept past zenith and the brilliant light around them suddenly dimmed. The apprentices proudly held their closed blades, all their togas and sarees matched the color of their natures. Angeni felt more happiness than she knew what to do with, although she hid it well. Her icy face had shown no emotions.

High-Guardians Eve and Aaron strolled back to Queen Faraa, and Prince Nicolas in the middle of the hall while the choir's calm music again caressed Angeni's ears. The ruler stepped forward along with her son to greet them with respect while the choir sang quietly in the background.

"Protecting and guiding is the greatest responsibility of all that any spirit may receive," the queen said. "A wise and noble way of life for which we're all grateful. The Sacred Mother who inspires us each day reminds us; light dispels darkness as wisdom dispels ignorance. A wise soul never stops learning, but always seeks knowledge. Learn to speak and act wisely to enrich Eecrys Aredia. With your thoughts you make our world."

As the Queen spoke, Angeni felt the young, charming Prince. His eyes showed a soul so caring; he watched her and only her. But why?

"Anywhere is good, but home is best," the Ceretaperia continued after a short pause. "From this time, my home is your home. My joy is your joy. My pain is your pain. I thank you for sharing your lives to guide and defend ours," she decreed with sincerest respect. "Welcome home, Aserians. Welcome home."

* * *

"As time carried on, the two pearls, the lives of guardian and protected one come closer to each other," the old man noted while the children watched the labyrinth game. He slowly turned the small wheel on the game to open another entrance and exit, but it didn't change the rest of the labyrinth. Excited, the girl looked at him as she prepared the sapphire pearl that she treasured in her hand. The old man smiled and nodded. The girl let the pearl go to start and discover a life in the labyrinth.

They watched the two small sapphire pearls slowly roll along on their separate paths. But the old man in his mind saw the spot on the board where they're paths would cross for them to meet in the future.

"You two walk the same path," he whispered to the pearls. Just like in their lives, they still had a long way ahead to reach each other.

"The charming young Prince was the one that she dreamt about," the little girl declared and crossed her arms, and then she hesitated and curiously looked at the old man. "Right?"

"He was the caring knight, who waited for his beautiful angel princess," the boy added excited.

The old man simply smiled at the children whose eyes watched him curiously and waited for his answer.

"Unlike fairy tales where the prince and the princess always met, under the brilliance, the shadow tales are shaped by the erratic path of life, which has moments both joyful and cruel."

"In a good tale there always must be a brave Prince who meets the beautiful Princess," the girl raised her nose in protest.

Amused, the old man's soft smile turned to her.

"The princess and the prince do not always meet in their lives, at least not literally," he continued. "But if they do, the prince may not be a prince, nor a knight at all, maybe just in his soul. And a princess might not be a princess, just a crushed fragile soul with nothing left but her dreams of a better future." The children listened to his explanation. After a soft sigh, he continued, "Sometimes our desire to believe and our great hopes, other times our desperate moments and our loneliness create the princesses and knights of our dreams."

"So one day she will meet the brave knight she waited for," the boy said excited and waited for an answer.

"The Prince is *her* Prince," the young girl declared in her tiny determined tone while her furious eyes turned to the boy. The old man smiled before he continued.

"Destiny always brings us where we're needed the most. And brings us mostly to the one who needs us the most." The old man looked at the two sapphire pearls. "Destiny held someone for the young daydreaming guardian. Someone her life would connect to for eternity."

6 – ECHOES OF THE PAST

"Just like water and fire, light and darkness, brilliance and shade, every element in the universe has an opposite, even if we cannot see or have never heard about it," the old man said while he shuffled to a polished oak table, the two children hurrying behind him. As they stopped at the table, the old man picked up two pieces of flint. With the precision of routine, he started a fire under a small clay jug full of water. Content, he watched the flames lick up the sides of the jug.

"Perfect." The old man sat down on his chair and studied the two children. "Everyone, be they living, spiritual and even non-living is born or created for a reason. There is no exception. Some people never know what this reason is, why the sky is blue, the grass green, or why birds fly or why they even exist. They never search for the answer, as sometimes they are too lazy or worse, too blind to even see it. But those who search for answers have a chance to see the real purpose of their life and the lives of others."

The old man studied each child individually.

"Yet even if you know, one question always remains. Do you truly see the real purpose or are you just living in a fragile crystal reality that you created in your belief or what others created around you to fulfill their expectations?" He turned and gazed at the small blue flames heating the jug. "All of us are living in the echoes of the past and only time can give the answers for our questions."

* * *

The heavy snow of Slumberous melted outside in the sparkling sunbeams. Like a cheeky old friend loath to leave, Deciduous returned after the commencement day to take a good look at Andrenia before it finally left once again, this time for almost an entire cycle. The icicles finally succumbed to water drops, which like naughty children jumped one after another from the highest spires to gather in large puddles on the ground.

Like icy flames, the swirling azure aura stream of the crystal blade reflected in Angeni's eyes. Along with the other young Aserians, she studied the noble open weapon in their old mentor, High-Guardian Michael's hands. The bright glow of the blades glinted on his majestic azure battle armour.

"So ancient and deadly, even the oldest Aserians fear its power," his imperative tone assured them while he watched the blade glow in his hand. Angeni felt from his voice that he truly respected and feared the power of the blade. "Even water freezes solid by the touch of these noble blades." Old Master Michael turned his blade by increments. "It respects and is harmless to its master, yet it turns the soulless to dust. Every living soul becomes solid crystal reflecting their nature with a simple cut. But a fallen enemy is no longer your enemy. Every soul must go home, must be released from their crystal prison." His intelligent brown eyes looked at the young Aserians. "None of you ever dare practice with it against each other. None of you ever dare to touch the blade of another," his deep and harsh echo demanded while his eyes flashed azure. His voice put fear into the heart of Angeni and the other young souls. He made it clear; he was not exaggerating the dangers that an open crystal blade carried within.

All of the young Aserians nodded. They understood, and the master continued.

"In time you'll learn to master your blades alone without endangering anyone." His crystal blade suddenly lost its solid shape and the whirling aura returned into the elegant golden hilt to the sound of cracking ice. "But for that you'll have to learn how to master your spirit and reveal its full potential."

The High-Guardian clipped the empty golden hilt to his belt.

"Life is not about finding yourself, but about creating yourself," his voice softened as he paced in front of the students. "It's always easier to destroy than build," he said, then a glaring bright azure aura embraced the High-Guardian; his battle armour instantly morphed into an elegant azure robe. "But creating or giving life is much more elegant and beautiful."

The young Aserians were awed by what they saw. Angeni realized that her mother was right; the commencement day was just the beginning of a wonderful journey and the world just opened its doors to show what undiscovered paths lay in front of her.

"You must tame and train your spirit so fatigue won't ever touch you," the High-Guardian said. Opening his right palm, it glowed in his aura. "And you must feel how to stream your own spirit, so you may create and give life by your own will." A tiny azure pot flower took form as it was born of his shiny aura. Satisfied, the old master watched the tiny plant, which had just spent its first moments in its new life, then walked to the window to put it among the other tiny azure flowers that were bathed in and enjoyed Sachylia's cold light.

The first days of the master training wasn't so different from the first days of their apprentice training with Old Shen. They did not even touch their crystal blades, just watched them from afar as they rested side by side on a large carpet. Just like in the past, it had a rightful reason, so the old High-Guardian told them.

"Be patient. Slow water can wash the shore away," their mentor always said while the young Aserians sat on the ground and concentrated to give life to the first aura orb of their lives. But in the first days, all of their attempts failed as each try exhausted their untrained spirit.

An old friend also returned; the Synoi Yiana jointed double staff blade. The High-Guardian wanted to see what they had learned in Sessa Asria. Angeni intended to show him to prove what a great guardian she had become. So did Aurora. As they faced off, Aurora knocked the staff from Angeni's hands with one sudden, but fluid motion, just as Old Shen always had and as she seemingly learned from him.

"Ha-hah!" Aurora's proud enjoyment of victory echoed in the hall. She couldn't enjoy her moment for long. With childish glee, Aurora ran to hide between the columns of the hall as Angeni chased her and tried to grab her wings. At the very last moment, Aurora had escaped from the pretend wrath of her sister to the only place where Angeni couldn't follow. Up.

The youngest guardian had cheekily smiled from above while she majestically flapped her large white wings and cheekily waved to her big sister.

"Come down right near to me, little Aurora, oh, my dear." She glared up at her sister with her eyes flashing sapphire.

"Oh no, my sweet, defeated sister, I'm fine up here," came Aurora's bubbly response, hovering above her grounded sister.

"Aserians must bury the hatchet if they wish to live in peace," the remonstrance of High-Guardian Michael insisted, who watched them and wasn't pleased with the undisciplined young one who still needed to learn a lot.

Andrenians taught them to focus and to improve their dexterity with their traditional game, called target archery. It was one of their skill games where the archer needed to shoot fletched arrows at targets set at various distances, shooting through rings and the tiny ears of amphoras without damaging them. Many Andrenians were the master of this game, and could hit their target even when they rode on the back of a racing Tasunke. Young Prince Nicolas was one of these masters.

The Andrenian wooden reflex bow that he wielded required tremendous strength. Elegant bracers protected his forearm from the stinging slap of the bowstring and the fletching of the arrow. Angeni watched the young man in his sapphire cloak masterfully shoot arrows from the back of the Tasunke right into their target and he never missed. It was likely he would want to amaze her, and only her with his skill. The young guardian read from his eyes that his soul desired speech with her. Yet, he never said a word, and always kept his distance.

Day by day the warm-hearted old High-Guardian Michael, who wasn't as rigid as he first appeared to be, taught them as if they were his children. A few days after commencement, the time had finally come for the young ones to make the first step. To see what their spirits were truly capable of, learn how to hide their wings and step into the second realm of the Spirit Sea that Persecutor Sophus had told them a lot about in the past.

Like every other young Aserian, Angeni awaited this moment so much, to see what the aura of Eecrys Aredia looked like. But it wasn't that joyful a moment as she'd always imagined. She spent only few moments in Mera Amantia before she escaped back to the first realm. The sight of what awaited her, terrified her deeply, but she didn't know why. It was as if a little girl's young soul had left her body to shapelessly float in this strange realm.

The young guardian slept terribly for four nights. She had awakened in tears with Aurora's arms around her trying to solace her beloved sister. The Spirit Sea burnt into her mind; a place which whirled in beautiful sapphire, but everything twined and raged, which reminded Angeni of her first memories; the doors that wanted to eat her as that great storm raged and embraced Sessa Asria, the time when she realized what she had left behind. She didn't want to enter and face the Spirit Sea anymore. However, High-Guardian Michael didn't give her a choice.

* * *

The thunderous sapphire Spirit Sea twined above the shell of Eecrys Aredia, which gave safe ground to every spiritual being in the second realm. Its walls of tall and small houses were like untouchable blurry silhouettes, shiny surfaces of rivers that were like passable paved roads rippled in the never-ending tempest. So distant, high above in the sky, the third realm of the sacred soul garden silently watched the spirit body of young Angeni, who stood in the Mera Amantia's streaming aura of Eecrys Aredia. There was life up there where the Spiritual Vanguards lived. She felt it, just as her soul felt her mysterious brothers and sisters watching her from above. Right now, even at this moment. However, she

203

had never seen them. Maybe they peeked from behind those racing spirit clouds; she didn't know. Their home was like an untouchable haven, even from the second realm.

There was something so touchable to Angeni even here; any dreaded depth in the first realm was also a dreaded depth here, which called louder with its enchanting whirling sapphire streams and waves.

Invisible, her sapphire silhouette merged completely into the blue Spirit Sea; her entire being used the silent waves like a covering blanket. No one had seen her here and no one was able to see her from here when she lurked in the first realm. Like a loving mother, the sapphire aura of her home world protected her shiny and fragile sapphire spirit in this realm and beyond.

Angeni relaxed, she felt the strong wind tug at her spirit wings. Then she let her spirit body be embraced and caught by the wild twisting streams, just as she had learned. She felt her invisible body merge and blur, becoming one with the current. Like a leaf on the surface of a fast river, her soul moved toward the destination that her will desired.

One with the silent storm, her disciplined mind controlled the flow. It was like flying in a dream; she was like the wind, soaring close to the ground to not face the dreaded height. Passing through the silhouettes of large and small halls, wall after wall as if they were open windows, the long outline of a crowded corridor welcomed her. The sapphire soul streamed between the living colourful silhouettes of human beings and winged Aserians, who glowed in the color of their nature; they all did their daily tasks in the first realm. Then the corridor quickly ended. She soared through the next wall into the temple's vast interior hanging garden aglow with the colourful auras of the living trees and flowers. The soul almost touched the surface of the fish lakes as she soared over them, just almost. Then the streaming soul glided into another corridor, which finally revealed the place where her disciplined will ordered the streams to carry her in this endless dreamscape.

The sapphire soul strained her entire existence, and within a blink of an eye, Angeni took solid form. Like a stone skips, splashing and racing over the crystal-clear surface of the lake, flapping her large feathery wings wide, the young angel woman emerged from the second realm.

Feeling the solid ground under her feet once again, she set down on one knee. Agape and delirious, Angeni looked around the hall that silently welcomed the little intruder. Her wings lowered behind her while she stood up and smiled, satisfied. For the first time in her life, she was really in that place where she desired to be. So much practice finally fructified and she hadn't fallen in the middle of the fish lake as she had last time, nor smashed into her *favorite* tree in the garden like she'd done twice before that.

The fear, which embraced her spirit that the wild Spirit Sea bred in her days ago no longer existed in her soul. No more fear, only her strong disciplined will controlled the streams, just as High-Guardian Michael taught them these last few days. One thing still hadn't changed since the first day. Her spirit was so exhausted; she wanted to go home to a deserved rest.

It was already late afternoon when she stepped out of the Citadel with Aurora. The cool atmosphere of returned Deciduous hit Angeni. It always reminded her of what it had been like to be a human. But in the distance, she had already seen the dark snow clouds gather on the horizon as Slumberous prepared its forces to retake Andrenia from the gentle intruder for the rest of the trimester.

There was one rule outside the temple for the young Aserians, so their Mother and Father said. No wings allowed to be seen. Hiding their shy wings in the Spirit Sea, the sisters as well as the other young Aserians happily merged with the Andrenian crowd everyday to learn about their new home. And they tried everything to make each of their days memorable.

Like children, the young Aserians played hide-and-seek, discovering even the most hidden corners of the Citadel and the Castle Hill as they tried to find better and better hiding places. Angeni had found the best place of all, the second realm, which hid her perfectly. Day after day, she felt safer and safer there; she didn't fear it as before.

"Angeni?" Jared's call echoed in the spirit realm while Angeni, the hunter, studied him from the Spirit Sea. *Where did that cheeky little rascal hide this time?* she heard his thoughts. Unseen sapphire eyes watched the green winged silhouette that searched a small alley. It was time to take friendly revenge for an old grievance. As the Sentinel stepped in front of her, only Angeni's hand gently reached out behind Jared in the first realm. With a quick jerk, she snatched him into the second realm.

Before that moment, Angeni had never heard a grown up Sentinel scream. Now every time she remembered that wonderful moment, she smiled with exquisite satisfaction. She couldn't forget those hard looks eager to take revenge when his terrified scream slowly faded away.

Every afternoon the sisters visited the young baker in the Castle district. Senet worked and lived only a couple of houses away from the Temple, which was the home of the young guardians. The kind man, who thoroughly believed they were human, always gave them fresh bread and special flat nut cakes that he filled with different delicious secrets;

cheese, beans or even sausages. While they filled their bellies, Senet couldn't stop talking about his young wife Xeana. He felt so blessed because destiny, or rather the loving work of two guardian spirits, as Angeni began to believe, brought this beautiful and beloved woman to him.

Saying farewell to Senet, the two young women happily crossed the long main street that throbbed with life. Hand in hand, like real loving sisters they strolled under the shadow of the majestic Temple of Dreams. As the wind embraced their sapphire and orange silk organza, the looks from some young Andrenian men showed that they desired to hold them as their eyes followed the two beautiful women. Like every day before, Angeni just smiled to herself. If these men knew they were Aserians, not even stealing a kiss would enter their minds. Leaving the heartbroken men behind with their disappointment, but eternal hopeful thoughts, they turned into a long elegant ambulatory; the Corridor of Wishes as the natives called it. For the eyes it didn't differ from any other trellis and flower-roofed ambulatory in the district, only its legend made it different; as Senet had told them.

"So this is the place where all our dreams are listened to, and later come true?" Aurora whispered. In the middle of the ambulatory a few steps ahead of Angeni, Aurora looked around at the hanging masses of flowers. Then the youngest put her hand on the yellow wall to make her wish, just as the baker had told her.

"I wish something great for the humans," Aurora's sweet mysterious voice came as a whisper. "And something really nice for my dear brave Sentinel," she giggled. "I hope he will be able to handle eternal love," she grinned back at Angeni. "Do you make a wish, sister?"

"Yes," Angeni chuckled. Standing in the middle of the corridor, she quickly looked around, but no human was around. "I wish to have beautiful wings this big!" Her large wings flared out from the second realm so wide the tip feathers of the giggling guardian's wings almost reached the walls on both sides. Regardless how hard she tried to spread her wings wider she couldn't quite reach the walls. Then she gave up and lowered them. Disappointed, she looked left and right to judge the measurement between the two walls.

"Someday, but not today," she whispered and her wings majestically disappeared into the Spirit Sea.

"Come on, sis. Seriously. Wish something," asked Aurora in innocent kindness. Then she gently took Angeni's hand, led her to the blue stone wall, and placed Angeni's hand on it. "Please."

I wish answers, to know everything about the Crystal Shade, her soul desired as her palm touched the cold wall.

"What did you wish?" Aurora sparkled with hopeful curiosity. But cheeky, Angeni raised her nose and with majestic steps, she slowly walked away.

"Wings, wings! Large feathery wings!" Angeni carolled happily, almost dancing out of the ambulatory onto a wide tree-lined lane that extended around the top of Castle hill to encircle it completely.

"It's not fair. Please, sister. Please, tell me." Aurora hurried after her. "Please?" She begged with her eyes.

Angeni stopped with a sigh and looked at her.

"I wish..." she started, but Aurora's eyes opened wide with merriment and she leaned in fast to whisper to Angeni.

"There he is again," Aurora sang. She peeked past Angeni, and then looked back at Angeni's wry smile.

"I know," Angeni had been tracking Prince Nicolas from the corner of her eye since they had stepped onto the treed lane. Silent, he watched her from a distance like he had sometimes done since he had seen her on commencement day. It's as if he would like to talk with her, but didn't dare.

"Don't you go and speak with him?" Quiet excitement compelled Aurora.

"Let's see..." Angeni though, and then looked at her sister. "No. This humble little woman has pride and won't go to him," she raised her nose imperiously.

"You should, sister. He may be shy, but he definitely waits for you to address him," Aurora said, then for a moment she peeked beyond Angeni. The Prince looked back at her. "He seems to be a kind young man, even if he is not the bravest."

Angeni carefully closed her mind to not hear what he thought. Her curious eyes already searched for something along the soggy pathway of the treed lane to distract herself from the Prince's presence.

"As father used to say; time waits for nobody. But I do," Angeni stated proudly while she happily noticed a reddish brown chestnut on the ground under the shadow of a close by tree, which slept its quiescence. "If the lovely Guardian won't go to the Prince, because she won't," she declared. "The Prince will come to the lovely Guardian," sang her angelic voice as she hurried to the tree to pick up and examine a large shiny chestnut. "I'll give him some time," smiling she picked up more chestnuts one by one from among the wet leaves. "Or eternity to gather his bravery."

Cheerful snowflakes silently drifted inside in the sanctuary. The invisible hand of the chilly breeze of returning Slumberous billowed the silk curtains aside to touch and caress Angeni's icy face. The young guardian rested on her knees, her eyes closed, concentration evident by the crease in her forehead as she focused her steaming spiritual power inside her body. Deep silence had embraced her and day was replaced by night when Sachylia went down. Only the aura around her hand gave a hint of light to the hall. In her mind, she imagined she was giving life to lifeless and shape to shapeless. And the tiny sapphire orbs obeyed. They rose from her palm and flowed toward each other. Together they built the beautiful shape that she had imagined and that her will ordered. A small faultless crystal's beginning was born above her sapphire glowing palm.

A few chestnut stick dolls sat on the shelves and held their breath, awed as they watched their young mother. Angeni concentrated harder, her brow puckered, but it was all ruined when she felt someone step up behind her. The partially formed crystal above her palm cracked and collapsed as she lost focus. The solid pieces flowed back to orbs that merged into her palm. Angeni sighed, defeated, sorrowful for her tiny build-up of power that her chestnut children won't see now in its full glory.

"Knowledge is power, and practice makes the master. Persistence always rewarded," came the soft, but oddly craggy young male voice behind her.

"It's like I hear my old mentor," she mused while she stood up gracefully and turned around to face Prince Nicolas, who stood behind her in his dark sapphire cloak. "But thank you. I'll keep it in mind," Angeni smiled, and then was all seriousness. "How can I help you on this late night?"

"The High-Guardians ask for our presence. Please, come with me," a royally mannered summons was still a summons. Angeni quickly picked up her cloak and pulled her hood up over her head. The golden hilt of her Crystal Blade clicked onto her belt as she took it from Guardian Pilly. The noble weapon rested on Pilly every night.

The young guardian followed the silent young dignitary. The Prince didn't say a word as they strolled along the corridor, just sometimes took a quick glance at her from the corner of his eye. Angeni curiously took his measure, but stayed silent to keep her headstrong promise; the Prince will come to the lovely Guardian, not the other way around. If he wants to speak someday, he will. If not, nothing will change.

After a long silence that only their echoing footsteps broke from time to time, her curiosity began to win. A cheeky thought flashed into her mind and she opened her mind just for a moment to hear what this mysterious young man may think. But she was surprised to hear silence, nothing else. His thoughts were disciplined, much more disciplined than any other human she had ever encountered before. It's as if he knew she could read his mind and carefully tucked his thoughts into the shadows.

Rascally snowflakes whipped around them as they stepped out of the temple. The snow, which covered the cobbled road, crackled and crunched under their boots. The slush dimpled in their wake. Only the joyful wind of Slumberous broke the silence of the sleeping street now and again enjoying its endless freedom. It cheekily whistled as it roamed between the neat little houses that rested in their cold white coats. Torch flames waved, the playful breeze rushed ahead to search for new playmates. With a happy whisper it snagged Angeni's cloak to reveal and stroke her large wings for a moment, and then circled once around the Prince and swayed further to play with the trees and bushes in the large castle's garden where they were also restlessly headed.

Carenia Seli's pale blue face was obscured. Yet, it curiously tried to peek into the anteroom as the heavy oak door creaked upon opening to let Angeni and Nicolas inside. Their sapphire cloaks were caked with snow as they escaped the blizzard, whose snowflakes heartily played outside with the wind. Angeni shoved her hood off. Her and the Prince brushed the snow from their clothes before they entered the castle's pristine grand lodge where Eve and Aaron awaited them.

"Mother, Father," Angeni greeted her parents respectfully.

"Aen Celestias," Nicolas addressed them. "We are here as you requested."

"Mother, Father. Why have you asked for our presence?" Angeni asked with curious respect. Regal High-Guardian Eve's eyes took in the two souls.

"Every soul seeking itself must face the answers they have sought," she answered mysteriously. The Prince simply nodded as he agreed.

"The Crystal Shade," Angeni realized in a whisper as her excited soul bubbled.

"Yes," her father confirmed. "But please remember; a knowledge revealed and seen cannot be buried in your soul," he warned. "If you open this door to see what secrets hide behind it and you shed light in the darkness, you cannot turn back. The question is not do you want the truth behind the legend, but are you ready to face it?"

"Yes, my father. I'm ready," Angeni answered, determined without hesitation.

"So shall it be," Eve agreed while she stepped close to Angeni and Aaron stepped up to Prince Nicolas. The High-Guardians fanned out their large white wings and with a quick snap, they completely enclosed the young ones.

Darkness entombed Angeni. She felt the feathers of her mother's wings smooth against her body. As always, she felt so safe in the motherly embrace, and then her mother's large wings released her.

They weren't in the grand lodge, not even in Andrenia anymore. The silent tempest twined, an endless grim blue realm peacefully swirled around them. A place so different than the Spirit Sea with no visible walls, silhouettes, height, or depth that Angeni felt was all elusive surroundings. They existed and were invisible in this strange realm all at once.

Angeni's body and wings glowed in the sapphire of her streaming aura, but unlike in the Spirit Sea, here she wasn't invisible and everything was so peaceful. The twisting shades of blues in the realm didn't hide her, but gently wrapped around her. Looking around she had seen her mother's winged spirit body glowing citrine orange, Aaron in jade green and the human, Prince Nicolas in sapphire. He had the very same aura as her. Like her parents, the silhouette of the young man watched her. Calm radiated, not a single trace of awe or surprise. This wasn't his first time here, wherever here was, or so it seemed.

A lone majestic azure spirit being stood in front of them; its large spirit wings gently floated in the endless realm, like plants bow and wave to undersea currents. All around them, unseen thousands of other souls watched them, but mostly Angeni. She felt it.

Looking into the spirit being's eyes Angeni recognized his soul, even without meeting him before. He was Aen Segaran Viranaia Remiel, the respected elder of the Spiritual Vanguards.

We sensed your presence, the Vanguard greeted them; he didn't speak, his thoughts echoed throughout the spiritual realm. *Aen Celestias,* his unspoken thoughts greeted Eve and Aaron with true reverence. *Young ones,* he nodded to Angeni and Nicolas, who bowed back with great respect.

Remiel, Eve's thoughts greeted him respectfully. *We greet that place where you and I, we are one.*

The Spirit Aserian nodded thankfully, and then he looked at Angeni. Silent and awed, Angeni still looked around like a child who just took her first steps in a new world, discovering the unknown.

See our beautiful and beloved home, which is everywhere and nowhere, his thoughts echoed. *We greet you in the sacred soul garden, Sacrmera Ceatsa, where all rivers and fields flow together all around Eecrys Aredia.*

The sacred soul garden, Angeni's amazed thoughts echoed like she would shape the words. She took a step forward gawking like an explorer who had just stepped onto undiscovered land. After a long moment, she looked back at Remiel. *My soul knows you. I feel it. Although, I cannot remember. Have we met before?* her angelic voice echoed in the spiritual realm.

We have all met before and we always will meet once more. That's our way of life, Vanguard Remiel's thoughts replied. *We are those who stand between the passing and rebirth. Guardians of the barrier, we divide worlds and realms to protect Eecrys Aredia and the Sacred Mother as well, shepherding the newly born souls to their home and passing souls back to the Sacred Mother so they can rest.*

You guided my soul to the place I was needed the most, Angeni's response resounded.

The Spiritual Vanguard bowed his head solemnly.

As the Sacred Mother wished and desired, his mind and eyes on Angeni. Imperative, the elder looked back at the swirling realm. The silhouette of a vast place began to grow and take shape into a large hall behind him. *And now, we guide your souls and give you safe passage to the place where time and truth meets. As your mother wishes and desires.*

Eve nodded thankful and respectfully. Her and Aaron with a quick flick covered Angeni and Nicolas once again with their wings to then, after a blink of an eye, flicked back from around them.

The cold air and solid walls bit in as Angeni looked around the large torch lit hall. Only a tall black monolith stood against one wall, protected and bracketed by eleven braziers that threw dim light across its glossy surface.

"Where are we?" Enchanted, Angeni moved slowly toward the monolith as if it drew her closer.

"The Hall of Origin in the Temple of Sagatta," her father answered. Angeni's eyes opened wide, surprised. Within moments, they had travelled to the heart of the smallest province.

"That's hundreds of leagues away from Andrenia," she whispered, realizing the true meaning, importance, and possible dangers that could

211

lie in the third realm. It really was everywhere and nowhere all over Eecrys Aredia.

Angeni stared at the monolith. She did not recognize it; her father had never told her about this part of Sagatta in the past. Her eyes questioned her Aserian parents as she looked back at them.

"This is the Stone of Origin; a silent legacy and a forgotten legend," her mother beamed. "An ancient storyteller, ready to reveal the past with its silent wisdom." Angeni felt High-Guardian Eve's pride as her mother glanced from the stone tablet to her as her parents approached her and the monolith. Ever watchful, the Prince silently followed them.

"Always remember," continued Eve, "the present battle of the past conquest has always been the key to determining the future."

"It's now time for you to know the past, so you may find your path in the present to determine the future." Seriousness lowered Aaron's tone. Uncertain, Angeni looked at the monolith and bit her lip. It sat there, silent, like an old grouchy man from ancient times, impatiently waiting to tell its ancient story with all its wisdom.

The young guardian gathered her bravery and looked back at her parents. The prince behind them watched her with profound respect, but stayed silent, as did her parents. Ready to open an invisible and untouchable door to reveal and discover the past, Angeni turned and stepped into the band of darkness right in front of the monolith. The truth she had desired so much for so long was right in front of her. It awaited her, only her.

In the dim light, she could only see the tablet's dark surface. Of its own accord, her hand rose. Her forefinger glowed sapphire, giving her light in the soft darkness. The tablet unblemished sheen reflected back, at least for a moment. Sleepy and shy, Aserian hieroglyphics hinted at their presence and then glowed under her aura light to reflect at her as they awoke one by one like they could burn into her aura. As her hand slowly passed over the monolith from right to left, the letters began to shape words, and the words finally shaped sentences. She started to read.

As every cycle ends in itself, all the stories must be told from the beginning to the end, and all Crystal Shade must be known to never forget the mistakes, the echoes of our past.

Mankind had once been their own angels and demons on the ancient motherland and forgotten paradise, Mer Gaea. The spirit land home to millions of great souls was a paradise where mankind evolved peacefully for so long. In time so few were innocent and so many lived to see death with the desire aimed only to kill their brothers and sisters. Loving and destructive nature was in their souls. Their voice first whispered so silent, no one even heard. But then, the whisper became louder and louder, turned heaven to hell as their voice called for the era of the Crystal Shade. Souls killed each other without remorse, without mercy, crying heartbroken for their fallen loved ones, never wanting to let them go. But no spirit vanished; no soul is swallowed by the silence until not a single soul remembers them. Too many still remembered the lost ones.

And the fallen ones returned. Innocents, boundless spirits in the shape of winged angels descended from the sky. The restless ones gave demonic shape for their obtrusive, raging evil nature. They wanted to rage their war on to take revenge for the lost ones and to redeem their own cursed souls. Mankind didn't want to cry and suffer anymore and the angels heard their call, becoming the guardians of the souls who created them. Their light drove darkness from the sacred land and for so long, peace and prosperity ruled. For so long, no distance was too far and no goals were unreachable. The stars were touched; they were in mankind's hands. Living in a dream, everyone thought peace would last for eternity, and so it seemed. But they were wrong.

Forgotten by time, but never banished the Crystal Shade has returned. Shadowy evil followed in its path to take back what they believed to be rightfully theirs. Light and darkness, brilliance and shadow divided the world. The unwary and unprepared fell when the night twilights in the Crystal Shade. The cruellest gave life to Naamare who purged the innocent, scorched the lands to ashes and destroyed once beautiful Mer Gaea. But the world didn't end as so many believed, as it never ends in the twilight of the Crystal Shade.

Naamare, the destroyer of light was the life giver of darkness. Her dark radiance created the second world from the sparking ash. Like a cursed distorted and twisted child, the hell land of untold horrors Briniu Malgram grew and evolved under the dark red sunlight. Human souls were crushed and shattered, tyranny, pain, and suffering embraced, turned, and silenced them on that cursed land. With no hope and no escape, they were enslaved to serve the dark masters as humble servants. And so, every soul forgot how to resist, how to fight. Slowly they too turned dark as night and evil as their masters. In time, once proud and beautiful Mer Gaea became a myth and so, forgotten, but her soul was never destroyed as so many believed. Light was encased, bound in darkness and awaited the return of the Crystal Shade, as evil had waited before.

And so, the dreaded shade must return. The ground opened and the wind blasted the dirt away from the sacred ruins of Mer Petraea, revealing the tear of the Sacred Mother, which called and awakened every silenced soul. At the dawn of the Crystal Shade, light and darkness clashed as the guardians

213

descended from the heavens to battle the demons, to fight for mankind once again. The unbreakable human, Aserian chain was forged, and they marched against the armies of the Overlord Ashmedai. They fought so heroic to bring light back and chase darkness away.

The battle raged for countless days and nights, thousands of noble and evil souls vanished forever. But the Overlord Ashmedai, he whose soul and blade glowed in the red shade of Naamare, seemed invincible. He awaited the Crystal Shade in his cursed lie and was prepared for the arrival of the dreaded era, which would strike fear even into the darkest of souls, but also respect. The horde of darkness slowly decimated everyone who opposed his mighty will. But nearing the crystal twilight when all hope seemed lost, a young Aserian, Eosh, whose soul and blade was born of the Sacred Mother's sapphire tear, returned from his death. Emerging from his senseless destruction, he descended from the fiery sky to face the tyrannous and cruel Overlord to end this seemingly endless battle at the sacred place of Mer Petraea once again.

Hope glinted in the eyes of the lost one when in the twilight; Eosh had merged his soul with Ashmedai's rotten red soul at the tear of the Crystal Mother. So brave, he fought the Overlord and pursued him alone throughout the forgotten Garden of Kedesh, right to the heart where everything begins and ends, where good and evil must face each other; Aether, the Quintessence. Eosh's sapphire blade struck the heart of the demon and destroyed his relentless fiery soul. As the Overlord fell, the young Aserian's glowing spirit cleansed the darkness and his soul gave life to a bright young sun, Sachylia. Naamare was swallowed and the sapphire light encased Briniu Malgram, sending the spawn of evil back to their brimstone hell. In the noble brilliance, Eecrys Aredia was born, a beautiful third world full of life to be a haven for the shattered and the safe home for the lost ones. Everyone who looks up to the daylight sky at Sachylia sees the glory of that day, the moment when peace embraced the youngest paradise born under her light.

A home world guided and guarded by the light vowed to never make the same mistakes again, to never forget, and fall once more. However, we all know as time passes, the glorious present will become the forgotten past. Fairy tales may turn into history and history may turn into legends, myths, and fairy tales or they vanish for eternity. So let all who read this know; the evil souls never rest and Briniu Malgram is preparing in the shadows, ready to emerge from its dark prison to bring the unimaginable horrors to young Eecrys Aredia. Always remember the courage and valour of those who have been forgotten and be vigilant, prepared for the day when the Crystal Shade arrives once more.

"Our past. It's so, so sorrowful, and still so beautiful. It frightens and also amazes me," awe oozed while Angeni drew her hand away from the stone. She watched the letters slowly seep back behind the gloss as the tablet returned to the slick silent monolith it was before. She realized what she had read. Her excitement built, however, part of her soul was disappointed. There was no third side, as she believed she would find.

"We, we must tell this to the people, Mother," the young guardian's husky reply silenced her excitement as she looked back at Eve. "To everyone. They must know the truth."

Tinged with sadness, Eve shook her head.

"They all know what the truth is, Angeni," she said sadly. "Everyone learned it, just like you. Sadly, very few believe it."

"Our civilization has been built and is living on the ruins of our legends," added Aaron. "Our past, our own history has became our fairy tales. For them our truth is their myth."

"Just as the Stone of Origin had written," realized Angeni.

"All of our teachings and our beliefs are centered on the Crystal Shade," Aaron's tired old eyes mirrored his daughter. "But many, mostly the young believe only what they see and experience, not what they read or hear from the elders. For them the Crystal Shade is just the theology of our society, a myth teaching morality and a fearful legend breeding solidarity."

"Why can't they believe?" asked Angeni disappointed. "We also haven't seen the Sacred Mother. None of us have, but we still believe and pray to her. Every one of us."

"Each day they see the miracles that the Sacred Mother has wrought," determination pushed the Prince to join them. "They see her life giving sapphire tear Sachylia as she watches over all of us on Eecrys Aredia. She gives us plenty of crystal clean water and good crops to eat and drink the wind to cool our fervid days, storms to never forget what darkness is. She gave the sky to the birds, the ground to the humans and animals, and the oceans to the fishes. These wonders make them believe. What else could give us all these miracles if not the Sacred Mother?"

Angeni listened in silence.

"Nicolas is right, Angeni." Sadness tinged, Eve's voice faltered. "If humans and even the youngest Aserians did not see Sachylia by day and the stars at night, they would forget about the Sacred Mother as well." Aaron put a calming hand on Eve's shoulder, cooling her sadness. "And if humans could not see us, Aserians, they would think us a legend too. They would name our voice and our guidance as their own thoughts, strange voices in their own minds."

215

"But, but it's all here," Angeni looked back at the sleeping monolith, desperation flowed into her. "It's all right here," she gestured at the tablet before she looked at her parents. "We should at least try to tell them so they may understand our fears."

"You can't convince those who live blindly, believe only to their eyes, but are unable to truly see," said Aaron sadly. "Should they understand a fear that no one ever saw? Should they understand a cruelty and a darkness that no one can imagine?" Grim, he continued, "The Shaina are the evil, this we know. The darkness holds them fast, so the legend says. No one can truly know what their existence really is until it is met. And if anyone does, they will regret for a lifetime that they ever had doubts, so our mind says."

Eve pondered the monolith.

"We must always consider what to reveal," she whispered. "Eecrys Aredia is the home of wounded souls. Most of the humans should never learn what strength lies within their souls. Like those who created us, the humans would destroy our home."

A multitude of questions in her eyes, Angeni turned to Eve.

"If humans felt their power, even just once, Angeni, they won't let it go as most of them simply couldn't. Only the most disciplined and strongest willed humans with the cleanest souls ever become rulers, or permitted to bear a crystal blade. Those few rise to our ranks as true protectors of Eecrys Aredia." The High-Guardian looked proudly at the Prince. "Like, Nicolas. They all spent their lives preparing to defend our home. But they also know when to make battle sacrifices, when to lay down a weapon, and when to let power go."

Angeni nodded, she understood their concern. Her eyes looked back at the monolith. It still called her even though she had revealed all of its secrets. "My soul whispers that there is more between these ancient words. These lines have a much deeper meaning."

"Your soul has not deceived you," Eve watched her with approval, stepping to her. "You will learn everything when your life crosses the path of truth. Everything that you read was just the beginning of a long journey."

The Prince hesitated, glanced at the High-Guardians, who pleasantly nodded to him.

"There is something else I'd like to show you, Angeni," he said at his gentlest. "Please follow me." She curiously looked at her parents whose pleasant nods said; go bravely with him.

Silence fell over the young guardian and the Prince as they left the Stone of Origin and the High-Guardians behind to stroll along the long

216

dim marble corridor. Once again, the Prince, who led the way with slow leisurely steps, said nothing. Only the crackling flames of the torches breathed, as if they gossiped about the two young ones. Curiosity led Angeni to follow this mysterious, but seemingly shy young man. She felt the young man's excited heartbeat in his throat, but it didn't reflect on his face or in his eyes. Then the Prince stopped under a large arch that led into the next dim hall on the right side of the corridor.

"If you would," courteous, he let her step in first. Angeni stepped closer to the arch to see what waited inside.

"The Gods and Goddesses," she whispered as the entrance revealed the Oval Hall of Sagatta and the resting statues on the far side. Awed, the tiny angel stepped under the huge shadows of the motionless giants who slept so peacefully in their grand dwelling. The hall was the same as she had imagined from the tales of her father. Excitement glittered in her eyes. The twelve statues stood in light and darkness in the same order. Yet all of them were much more beautiful than she could have ever imagined, especially her favourites, Capra and Scoria. Now at night instead of Sachylia's cold rays, blue torches gleamed on the statues on the light side.

A crystal-clear gurgle brought Angeni's eyes to Dernaia Agar as he endlessly poured water from his large amphora urn into the small pool, so *life* could embrace the other statues one by one through the tiny veins. The veins glowed dimly as only a few light crystals lit them from below, making the circle of life that they described much more beautiful. Shy, she put her hand under the life-giving crystal-clear cold water to feel that it was real. The water coursed over her silky hand and the drops slowly slipped around her fingers. She felt like a dream had come true.

Enchanted and agape the winged daydreamer wandered into the middle of the hall, which unlike in her dream was empty, to be among her favourite Gods and Goddesses. She felt as if the giants would awaken to greet her. But no, they just watched with motionless eyes.

From the corner of her eye, Angeni had seen the Prince hesitate, his eyes on her before he looked back at the statues. His soul showed amazement. It was clear he had not seen these statues before. A shy young man he was and now he gathered his bravery and thoughts to break the heavenly silence.

"The tales we love the most mirror who we really are in our daydreaming soul," looking around, his reverence quietened his words. "Your father told me this hall was one of the tales which is a reflection of you. I can see why you love and dream about this place. And now, I may understand you better and know who you really are."

Curious, Angeni watched him stroll to an empty book pedestal on the light side of the hall. He pulled an old book out from under his cloak. It had no title, just an elegant decorative cover.

"This fable-book is one of the oldest on Eecrys Aredia," the Prince said as he placed the ancient book on the pedestal. Opening it, he slowly turned its rustling and frayed brown pages. "It is so fragile. It is rarely opened to share its ancient tales. But when it is, when young souls of Andrenia need dreams, the childhood of those who read it or listen to its tales is heightened." He looked at Angeni as he continued, "It holds so many ancient fables teaching morality and the highest values with tales you cannot dislike. It also shepherded me to be who I am now in the present." His hands carefully turned the pages to the last story. "I've seen a tale mirroring you, Angeni. If I may, I'd like to share one of my favourites with you, the shortest one, so you may understand me as well."

Curious to learn the Prince's intentions, Angeni silently stepped to the pedestal, hesitant, she looked at him.

"Please, Angeni," he needed her to understand his soul and the desire that drove his life.

Angeni's hand smoothed the surface of the ancient parchment. She felt the soul of the book was more than millennia old, even much older. The tale had no title; the elegant letters on the page innocently looked back at her, ready to tell their ancient wisdom. Reverence softened her voice as she started to read.

When the young world is out of balance, the beginning is already forgotten and the midst is ready to see the end. The era where the two is divided into three, in the crystal garden where every world vanishes before a young world destined once again to be swallowed by the cruel shade. Reliefless, the people forgot who they are and where they came from; sorrowful they do not live the right way. As the dawn rises, the path of two sapphire souls cross, their spirits rise from the emerging chaos of the approaching twilight. A soul with a past shaded and forgotten is amended by a soul who has wings but will never fly to be the light in the darkness of the Crystal Shade. The youngest guide by heart and protect the elder who embarked on a journey to cleanse the world of the chaotic shadows.

Reaching the bottom and gently turning the old page, Angeni touched the fragment of some missing pages. Only a sentence or so less was visible, *Changing woman becomes the...* she read the tiny fragment, then the next one. *... and destroying the monster threatening...* Then she continued to read the last undamaged page.

... when the blue star spirit dances in the plaza and removes it's mask. Very soon after this, all ceremonies cease. The separated shall be one and those who are at peace in their hearts are already in the Great Shelter of Life. Yet, there is no shelter for evil, and vengeance served for all time right before chaotic darkness embraces us. Light rain blue fire, doom and death in the time of the great trial and finally the evils flee to their own destruction to banish the Crystal Shade forever.

Angeni turned to the very last page; it was empty. She was surprised and Nicolas vindicated as her touch gave life to the page, which was much older than the rest. A message awoke from its long sleep and bloomed on the paper under her finger. Like sapphire fire, the letters burnt and fed from her aura as they silently spoke to her.

Nothing and no one is what they first appear to be. Not even you, Angeni.

The young guardian sucked in a shaky breath while she pulled her hand away from the paper, letting the words slowly fade.

"It's not possible," Angeni whispered. Shocked to see the Prince's surprise, who had also seen the unexpected. "Who, who wrote this book?"

"I... no one knows." Bewildered, he had to move in and look closer at the now empty page. Shocked silence sat heavy in the hall. It seemed like all twelve majestic giants behind them held their breath and awaited the explanation.

"It is you, old Aserian, who is protecting me unseen. You're not my imagination or a fantasy," Angeni could barely breathe. "You told me this phrase in my dreams or in a once forgotten life to never forget. Why?"

"But this book could be thousands of cycle old," said Nicolas bewildered. "It could be as old as Eecrys Aredia herself or even older. How could anyone, even an Aserian know you'd ever open this book?"

"Perceiving the future is a guardian's life as our perceptions peek into the future. The question is how far ahead can we see," she recalled the knowledge her father once said. "His old *Prescient-soul* may have seen our path; the events ruled by time that no one can change, yet everyone can prepare for the time beyond our reach."

"Why does he speak through a fairy tale?" asked the Prince. "It makes no sense."

The young guardian's eyes looked around the hall that symbolized the circle of night and day, life and death, beginning and ending, where time passes, then is swallowed and forgotten by time.

"Fairy tales may become history and history may turn into legends, myths, and fairy tales or they vanish for eternity, so the Stone of Origin said," her whisper just reached Nicolas. She turned to him. "A story told by history can distort and change, its essence and truth may vanish in time or may turn into a tale just like the Crystal Shade. But a story-must-be-told turned to a tale is treasured for all eternity, spread word by word. Also, words may change, but it essence stays as no one wants to change it, but will instead tell it to generations to come to learn, to always remember."

Angeni looked Nicolas in the eyes and continued quietly, "You knew this tale was about us. That's the reason you've looked at me so strangely since you first met me."

The Prince nodded and chose his words carefully.

"When I was a child my mother always read from this book, she read the Great Tale of the Sapphire Souls, as we called this nameless tale," he began. "The story of the bravest two who will defeat the Crystal Shade and bring eternal peace to Eecrys Aredia so no one will need fear again." The Prince's eyes examined the fragment of the missing brown pages in the book he loved so much. "However, mother always filled the missing pages with life and imagination night after night." He loved the queen's life stories. "Maybe that's why I loved to hear this tale the most. It was never the same. Only the beginning and the ending, and those tiny hints in between."

Angeni smiled as she watched the daydreaming Prince. He was just like her. He lived in his dreams.

Nicolas looked back at her, "When my crystal blade revealed my nature for the first time I felt I should be one of these sapphire souls; I'm the one whose past is shaded and forgotten." He glanced beyond Angeni. Eve and Aaron watched them from the shadowy entrance. "And some who grew up on these tales in the past thought the same," he smiled at them, and then looked back at the young guardian. "Then on your commencement day I saw you, Angeni. Since that day, I have lived in a fragile crystal reality ready to be shattered to reveal a terrible nightmare we can't avoid that's ready to trap and rule us all. I truly believe you're the guardian who will amend my soul. But I also fear, because if this is true, the Crystal Shade is approaching as well."

The young man touched her hand while he bared his soul by looking into her eyes. His touch revealed a clean and so disciplined spirit to Angeni. His was a daydreaming soul without a guardian spirit who patiently waited for someone, the one exact Guardian to guide him for the rest of his life. He wasn't shy, as he seemed before, but a brave soul who feared terribly for his people and their home. This was the reason he distanced himself from her. He had hoped he could delay the inevitable. Then after a moment, Nicolas removed his hand, a soft sigh escaped as he looked at the ancient book.

"But I still don't know how you can be the one who has wings but will never fly. It doesn't make any sense," a little hope crept into his voice; he still believed that maybe everything from his favourite tale was all just a coincidence.

"It does make sense," Angeni glanced back at her mother, who knew this all along. "Believe me. It does." Then she looked back at the Prince whose despair was real.

"If this is all true, it would be an honour if you would be my guardian spirit, Angeni," he asked with utmost honesty.

"No, brave Prince," she said. "The honour would be mine," she nodded slightly to accept his request. Her pride tinged with sadness, Eve stepped closer.

"The dawn of the dreaded era must be close as the path of the two sapphire souls has finally crossed," her regal bearing overshadowed her sadness. "But every first step to victory is through our faith. Amend each other and be our light in the darkness of the approaching Crystal Shade."

* * *

"Faith is one of the greatest things in life," the old man continued while he poured tea for the little children and himself. They thankfully nodded as they accepted the small delicate cups. The old man put down the jug and savoured a sip from the small cup before he continued. "The greatest is believing in love or in a grander, better future. They are all based on faith. But belief without knowledge is a dangerous combination which may blind us with its sonorous promises."

Serious, he leaned closer to the children. "Always remember; nothing and no one is what they first appear to be. There is no exception, especially not under the illusionary brilliance and shadow of the Crystal Shade. Everything has a shaded meaning with only one truth, regardless what you read, hear, or see. It is a delusive mirroring perspective that hides reality from your eyes; a crystal reality ready to encompass you to distort your judgment with its brilliance to then blindly lead you upon a shadowy path that will divert you from the truth."

7 – DEMENTED ORCHESTRA

"Fantasies and dreams are the cornerstones of our lives," the old man ruminated while the little children sat on mats in front of him and drank their tea. "Small and also great achievements, sometimes entire civilizations were born from them."

"Why?" asked the little girl. The old man chuckled softly.

"Why? Good question," he responded. "I believe it's in the nature of every reasonable being. Sometimes they need imagined stories, dreams and fantasies more than bread."

"But we can't fill our bellies with dreams," said the boy.

"That's true, little knight," the old man agreed. "But without dreams and fantasies we're just forgettable lifeless empty shells, a spectre haunting this world without leaving a single memorable mark on it with our silent whisper. Whoever forgets how to dream, young and old alike, could turn out to be an empty spirit with a dead soul whose body alone lives on without any emotion or true purpose."

"I like to dream," said the little girl.

"Me too," the boy added quickly.

"Never forget how to dream, young ones," said the old man's fatherly verdict. "Dreaming never depends on age, regardless what others say or want you to believe. You see, I was a great dreamer when I was young, and I still love to dream in spite of my age," he said proudly and blessed the two children with a gentle smile. "Your joyful dreams and fantasies are the food that caresses and spoils your fragile soul. You can be anything in them; beautiful princesses or valiant knights, facing adventures that you never dreamt of before and living on wonderful and magnificent fantasy worlds that no one can take away. No one."

The old man sipped his tea and continued.

"The world of imagination can be your hiding place when you're alone, when your life seems hopeless, or when you want something so desperately, but know a long path is still ahead to reach it. Dreams will give you the reason to live on even in the most desperate moments as they are something always worth fighting for."

He looked at the crystal chrono device while his voice softened.

"But unlike a dream world, life is not that simple, and it always holds its own surprise for us. Life is a relentless hunting shadow that chases us wherever we go. In the most unexpected moment, it shatters our crystal reality with its icy cruelty to banish everything we ever desired and dreamt of. Sooner or later every knight and princess must face the blinding illusion that they live in or worse, a deceiving dream world what others have created around them." The old man sipped his tea and continued, "Only a shattered mirror is able to reveal who we really are and who we never were."

The little girl sadly twisted her princess dress with her finger. The old man's smile was as gentle as the hand he laid on her head.

"But not everyone's dreams can be shattered, little princess."

"So, I can be a princess?" Exquisite hope in her eyes, she looked up.

"In our world, you're the princess of kindness and happiness." The old man looked at the boy. "And you, the knight of bravery and honour. Being a princess and a knight in your souls and hearts doesn't need a title. Your inner spirit and your actions tell others who you are and what your soul stands for."

"And if I want to be an angel princess?" asked the little girl, her eyes glistened.

"If you act like a happy angel, who is merciful and full of life, smiling and caring for others with all her heart, others will know this about you without words." The old man looked at the little knight. "And if you are brave and honourable, everyone will look and treat you as a knight of the light, even without shiny armour or a crystal blade."

"I can still be a knight if I lay down my sword?" he asked while he put his wooden weapon on the ground. The hope in his eyes was tinged with curiosity when he looked up at the old man.

"How do you feel?" asked the old man.

"Like a knight, without his sword."

"But you're still a knight inside," the old man answered with all seriousness. "Only the bravest souls can lay down their weapon willingly. Not many can do that."

Proud, the little boy looked at the little girl.

"May I keep my crown?" she asked, still fearing her treasure and her dreams would disappear.

The old man lifted the little girl's chin and smiled.

"You may keep your crown, but remember. Even if someone takes it from you, if you're a princess inside, you will remain a princess. No one can take away who you really are, what you have lived and experienced."

A short moment of silence to gather his thoughts, the old man's sigh lightly shifted the steam from his cup.

"On the world many soulless beings try to shatter the dreams of others just to achieve their own. So please, always be careful to not be soulless when you're trying to reach your dreams, because you're not the only one filled with hopes. Many also want to change people, enforce their ideals on another soul, or demand one act, as they desire. Yet, no one was born to please others. Always know who you are as if you don't know, who else would?"

The old man put his tea down as he continued.

"Dreams are like starlight. Some of them are so pale and never seen, while others must take a long path until someone sees their brilliance in the endless darkness. But dim or bright they might vanish if the dreaming stars are shattered and cease to exist. As the starlit sky of dreams turns silent, a cold uncertain world remains for us; grim and dark places where we just hope we may live another day." The old man leaned toward the children to make sure they understood. "Stepping out of the safe dreams to face the cold cruel reality is the hardest thing in life, even so for a young daydreaming guardian."

* * *

A woman's silky hand with the palm open reached forward, embraced by a gentle glow. Cold like her nature, dozens of sapphire orbs, smaller than almonds began to form from the icy aura. Turning her hand upside down, they fell to the ground right in front of her bare feet. They bounced few times in silence, and then rose to float above the ground. The orbs quickly spread out around the guardian until they were dozens or more paces off and hovered into position to surround her from every direction.

In the dim large hall, Angeni crouched on one knee in her dark sapphire crystal armour. She separated her closed crystal blade grip and held it tight. Sachylia's cloud filtered rays peeked through the sapphire-tinted crystal windows. The sunbeams glanced off the golden ornament on her left and right pauldron guardbrace; the golden number eleven set eleven above eleven together represented Odess'iana. The large feathery wings spread, and then as one of the circling orbs slowly approached her left wing tip she pulled her wings majestically behind her back. The orbs slowly circled Angeni.

The polished dark crystal mat surface that enveloped the floor, every wall, and column of the training hall was cold under foot. The entire hall reflected the glowing aura orbs as well as her armour's mat surface. Angeni closed her eyes, concentrated, and waited. Soft waves of cold air on her icy skin preceded one of the orbs as it changed course and sped toward her.

The hunter's eyes of the guardian opened and snapped toward the racing orb, the primary blades glowed sapphire as they came alive from both grips. Fast, the guardian leaned away from the attacking orb and the swinging crystal blade slashed at it as it passed. The orb exploded into smaller fragments that innocently dropped to the cold stone floor in apparent death.

The rest of the orbs vowed cruel revenge for the fallen one, Angeni felt the intent. They immediately attacked her and two of the closest orbs immediately followed the fate of the first. The edge of the crystal blades had sliced with precise strikes as the guardian spun around. The large feathery wings flared and hit another two prowling orbs to send them reeling across the hall.

The single blades spun once in Angeni's hands and struck, but the orbs scattered all around into the air. Two desperate orbs running for their tiny lives were too slow. A silent popping scream as the sapphire blade jabbed them before they had a chance to reach safety and like two tiny feathers in the air, they whirled to the floor.

The rest of the orbs didn't rest. So furious, they tried to ram her wings fast to take revenge for the fallen. Angeni snapped her all seeing attention to them and spun to evade, she pulled and forced her wings close behind her before they had a chance to score. Her white feathers vibrated unharmed as the orbs passed above and below them.

More orbs charged at the Guardian, who reunited her grip and opened the blades from both sides of the golden hilt. The dual blade spun once in her hand, sliced ahead, spun once again and jabbed the two that she reached for ahead of her. Then with a swift crouch, she separated her grip by pushing the two halves in either direction. The two blades spun in her hands and sent two more orbs to the ground.

Icy sapphire aura shot out from the back of the blade hilt's ornament, right above Angeni's gripping hand. The back of her hands felt the cold as the aura crackled to shape the deadly backward secondary blades quick as thought. The Guardian twirled the two dual blades in both of her hands. She struck with the primary blade and sliced two lurking orbs as well as another two with the backward blades when she pulled them back fast after her strike. The remaining orbs raced away from her once again to keep a safe distance.

Angeni's smile was sly while she tried to follow the orbs with her eyes as they circled around her. The Guardian flared her wings wide to startle the orbs a little then retracted them immediately behind her back. The crystal blades crackled as they lost integrity and went silent. Sachylia's pale sunlight danced on the golden grips as she held them close to her, defensive, waiting for the circling orbs to strike.

225

Many orbs had already fallen, but this was just the beginning of their heroic fight and Angeni was well aware of it. Like the edge of invisible striking blades, the orbs started to besiege the guardian from multiple directions so incredibly fast and relentless. But her crystal blades swiftly riposted their attempts and knocked many back to keep them away, while others sadly fell. The guardian continuously changed the form of the crystal blade, from single to dual, dual to single. One, two, sometimes four blades defended against the attackers as the primary and secondary blades in both grips lit up and faded away over and over again as her will changed the shape of the crystal blades.

The Sapphire Guardian never stopped for a single moment. Her spirit was swift like the wind; her existence was solid like the ground. Her mind clear as the sky, the angelic body danced like water between the orbs while the crystal blades danced and flickered like sapphire fire. She defended herself from one side as well as from two or more sides simultaneously, as if she fought two or more armed opponents at once.

Still the orbs didn't give up. They wanted to go home to be one once again with the Great Spirit of Angenius; they all knew just one of them need to reach her to end this battle. The relentless crystal blades were always in their way, between them and Angeni, to stop all of their desperate attempts. Once again, many brave orbs fell silent in the siege. Regardless of their heroic tactics, they couldn't breach the defence to get home to be one with the young guardian's spirit. Then the siege stopped and the remaining orbs once again circled around Angeni.

The guardian's eyes flashed sapphire once and only for a moment as she focused and looked around. The cheeky little orbs circled her peacefully like they had nothing better to do than glide in the fresh air at a safe distance. Only their silent whistling missed that they pretended they knew nothing and they're not even here, look elsewhere.

Every time they surprised her with something new, and this tactic was definitely new. They were intelligent, just like her, and adapted with all the knowledge her spirit ever learned. She tried to imagine herself in their place to learn what they would try to achieve next with this pretend innocence. She didn't know which one would strike next or from where. Then she suddenly realized; the two orbs she had swatted away with her wings were not in sight. So, where were they?

Angeni snapped her attention up, her eyes opened wide, surprised. In the very last second, she crouched and rolled away as the two sneaky orbs struck from above; their battle cry unspoken to make their silent run even more heroic. The large wings flared as she came out of the roll to regain balance. Her eyes on the tricky orbs had already seen that they wouldn't give up.

The sneaky orbs almost hit the ground before they sling shot right toward her without any loss of speed. She watched them suddenly evade and realized they had double fooled her. These two played the real bait.

Her eagle sharp eyes snapped to the right while the blade closed in her right hand. The aura crackled as the small crystal shield flashed from the top of the blade hilt and came alive just as her will ordered. But it was too late, the armada of the orbs already raced toward her from every possible direction. There was no time to deflect them all.

The sapphire aura flashed and embraced Angeni's entire body as she stepped back so desperate was she to stay away from the miniature army that could easily defeat her. Then a bright flash and she disappeared to appear crouched dozens of steps behind the tricky orbs. She left only a thin sapphire trace between the two points as she dove into the Spirit Sea and gave herself to the safety of the second realm's raging currents for a moment.

The orbs faced her quickly while the bait orbs joined the relentless and unstoppable floating army. Their flags united, they were ready to defeat their mighty enemy; her. And they had every chance of this, as Angeni knew. They had defeated her many times before just to teach her something new.

Angeni felt it was now her turn to strike. The primary blades opened in her hands and the orbs split formation to arrow at her from both sides. The young guardian sprung up from the floor and her legs already carried her fast right between the striking orbs. The white wings flared as she spun between them and the crystal blades that were already in motion. As they sliced, sapphire fate reached the slowest orbs. They fell slowly to the mat crystal ground like tiny raindrops while the rest tried to evade the sudden spread of feathery menace.

As she came out of the spin, her body flashed to dive once again into the Spirit Sea to gain some distance.

But the remaining orbs had adapted and were already after her, ready to corner the guardian when she reappeared. The sapphire blades came alive once again, as she defended herself against the striking waves of the remaining orbs. Like sparkling blue rain, the sliced orbs fell to the mat where her feet danced majestically, and never stopped. Then she slowed to a stop.

Only one orb's glow reflected in her eyes, the last that luckily escaped her almighty blades. Desperate, hopeless, and so alone, it circled around her. Angeni felt bad for this brave little one, yet she knew it wouldn't stop trying to return into her Great Spirit.

The sapphire blades closed as Angeni united her grips and waited for the last strike. She didn't need to wait long. The aura had barely dissipated in the golden grips and the heroic tiny orb sped up. Instead of striking right toward her, it dove toward the ground to strike from below. The guardian spun backward to keep the orb away, her wings flared open while the large aura shield crackled to life from the united grip.

The little hero evaded her slicing wing, passed under the feathers to face Angeni when she came out of the spin. Between the guardian and the orb, the sapphire shield rose and struck the tiny hero with tremendous force. Silently screaming, it ricocheted away to fly across the hall. Angeni watched it shrink in the distance while she crouched out of the spin and pulled her wings back fast.

Her sapphire eyes flashed victorious. Her delicate fingers spun the united grip in her hands. She savoured the crackling sound as the united shield collapsed and the dual blade form shot out in mid-spin from both ends of the united grip. Then the dual blade stopped vertically, right when the orb stopped. One final desperate attempt, the orb shot back toward her. The glowing sapphire blades curved back and stretched out to become an elegant bow. An energy string manifested between the tips as Angeni's fingers pulled back the thin air and a sapphire crystal arrow took shape in her hand.

Angeni's eyes narrowed as she aimed toward the orb and released the arrow. The arrow shattered the air and its tip punctured the small orb in flight. The mortally wounded hero split into smaller drops that fell silently to the floor. After a moment, the crystal arrow innocently exploded to tiny sapphire orbs as it hit the hall's dark mat crystal surface, which prevented the walls from being blasted to dust by her deadly power.

Deep silence fell over the hall to honour the fallen. Only the ice crackling of a closing crystal bow broke the silence before the deadly weapon went silent. Angeni stood up and clipped her grip onto her belt. She looked around the battlefield, which was filled with the scattered glowing remains of the heroic, if defeated orbs. They had fought well.

Closing her eyes, concentrating deeply, her aura flashed all around her body. Her will called the orbs home, and they happily obeyed. They rose all over the hall, and then raced back toward the Great Spirit to be one with her again as they had always desired. She felt the knowledge that her aura orbs had gathered during their short independence. They silently whispered every tactic they saw and experienced to her spirit and soul to later learn from the mistakes she had made during the exercise.

The mat crystal walls watched her, awed as the battle armour's dim luminescence glowed like deep blue flames around her body and with a bright flash; it morphed into her ruffled sapphire organza strapless gown. The elegant cloth came alive as a soft breeze found its way into the hall and fanned its silky hem. Angeni opened her eyes; her smile satisfied, her spirit, which was still fresh, was full once again as her aura glow faded away.

Her loyal scroll pamphlet and arven pencil awaited her in the shadow of a dark mat crystal column. The drawings of the crystal blade, born in the early days of her master training looked back at her as a reminder to tell what this noble, but deadly weapon was capable of, what forms it could attain. She had studied this drawing many times to never forget. Although, she had to admit that in the last trimester this was merely symbolic. Her soul and spirit knew all and were now merged to the blade that followed only her will. Angeni crouched down to pick up the pamphlet and the pencil. As she touched them, they lost integrity to morph into a sapphire orb that slowly merged into her hand to be one with her spirit.

Everything was from the same spiritual material, both living and lifeless, so she learned from High-Guardian Michael. Unlike her clothes or armour that was a projected shell of her spirit's existence, she needed to learn how to give separate life to objects, to give them an independent spirit and keep them together without her. Regardless of long hours of practice, she still couldn't create objects larger than a lifeless crystal and she couldn't give life, not even to a tiny kimama. As her mentor taught, it was easier to practice with existing objects, to turn them shapeless and recall them from the spirit later. Soon her pamphlet, pencil, and even Guardian Pilly became her loyal helpers in the learning.

The blue aura slowly faded into her hand. Standing up from near the column, her eyes glanced at the only exception that could never turn shapeless by her will, but would always hang on her belt. No one ever said who created the crystal blades. And strangely, no one was able to make them shapeless again. Not even the most skilled Aserians, regardless of their hard focus. The crystal blade would always fuse their aura into the golden hilt to shape the deadly blades. Only the aura of Eecrys Aredia could change the elegant hilt in the Spirit Sea to travel along with the drifting spirit. It was like the hilt of the crystal blades were born and constructed from her home world's aura, so Angeni believed.

Soft clapping reached her sensitive ears. She looked back at Jared, who stood in his green toga, leaning near the next mat surfaced column with a grin.

"Someone is taking her training too seriously," he called pleasantly.

"Someone must," she answered proudly. Daydreaming she looked up to the tinted ceiling windows as she continued, "Maybe somewhere up in the endless darkness the Shaina are preparing their legions to strike at us. Maybe one day Briniu Malgram will appear in the night sky to shadow our home for all eternity."

She glanced back at the young man.

"Maybe the Shaina and all of our legends are real. Why do you dismiss the possibility?"

"You said it, they're just legends," said Jared.

"Every legend is based on something," Angeni smiled back.

"Like your favourite Spirit Guardians, Eriana and Iria."

"They exist." She paused, looking back toward the ceiling daydreaming. "They always did, Jared. The Spirit Guardians are out there, somewhere. They still fight the Crystal Shade for all of us. I know it's the truth. I believe it's the truth."

The Sentinel smiled and shook his head. "Eecrys Aredia grew older, yet sometimes you are still that little girl inside your soul. Sometimes I wonder how you turned into a Guardian."

"I put on my kindest smile and said please," she answered with an angelic grin.

"New days, new surprises. Angeni can say the word please," Jared teased the young angel woman who smiled at him. "I hope you know believing blindly can draw you away from the truth."

"The truth makes my belief strong, my dear beliefless infidel," Angeni responded. "You should try to believe in your dreams too. It refreshes your spirit and your soul. It is something that does not depend on age, or experience." She twisted her wingtips behind her back, a cute quirk that she knew would soften Jared's heart and help her end this debate. She predicted it would only be a few moments before he admitted she was right. But she was mistaken.

"Hiding behind your innocent charm is not going to make you right, Kachina," he chided, calmly amused calling her spirit in his Serianan dialect. Now knowing she would have to take the long way to convince him, she pinned him with complete seriousness.

"Everything has a reason, Jared," she said stepping closer to her friend.

"Like everything in your world," responded the calm Sentinel.

"You read my mind," said Angeni with pretend awe.

"It's an easy read. You know that," Jared laughed and teased.

"My world is your world," she purred while she looked deep into his eyes. "You know this young woman is right. You feel it, otherwise you wouldn't be here talking about the legends and myths that I believe in," she continued as if she was the last innocent in the world, but Jared put on that insufferable smile.

"Without charm, little one."

Angeni's eyes flashed indignantly. She dreaded to think this nickname would be with her for life even if she had the average height for a female.

"I'm not little," came her defiant protest and crossed her arms as she turned away to hide behind her hidden weapon if charm didn't work.

"Defiance won't work either," came the man's soft tone behind her. Angeni's eyes opened wide, then threw a glare back at the smiling young Sentinel. With majestic steps, she slowly rounded on the Sentinel.

"Fighting evil, defending good, defeating darkness, helping the innocent and ensuring justice," reverted to daydreaming, she paused. "It would be exciting and so romantic, don't you think?" she finished in trepidation.

"Excited and romantic?" Puzzled, Jared raised an eyebrow. The daydreaming angel nodded, then he continued, "In fairy tales, war always sounds so romantic and exciting, I know," the Sentinel said with a touch of concern. "But where someone must live in fear just to be saved I don't believe it can be either of them. I don't want to see anyone hurt or fearful. Why do you want that, Angeni?"

"I... I don't want..." she stuttered then stayed silent; feeling like her reasoning was dashed with one single sentence. The Sentinel was right, they didn't know what war was and deep in her soul she feared it. But why had she never thought of this perspective before?

"We live for a reason," whispered Angeni. "Just look around," her voice echoed as she looked around the large hall. "Why else would we train from dawn to dusk preparing for something that will never happen? Why do our souls fear a darkness and evil we have never known before?"

"It's our philosophy of living wisdom to prepare for everything," came his answer.

"Our philosophy follows the path of good, biasing us from evil, something no one has experienced, but a wisdom told by the legend of the Crystal Shade," she said determined. "A philosophy of yours is a legend of mine, both dwell in the very same roots in the forgotten past."

231

"It's not that simple…" the Sentinel whispered, then turned quiet and thoughtful. Proud of her logic, Angeni watched as the sparks of wisdom started to light his spirit; she had so longed to see this. "But I have to admit, your explanation rings true," he finally admitted looking at her a little embarrassed as if he'd lost a sparring match. "Do you know what concerns me?"

"That this fragile woman is more intelligent than you ever believed?" she teased with a shy grin.

"That it's just another one of your myths, little one that no one is ever going to confirm," came his answer, which met with the resistance of a fond smile "But no."

"Then what concerns you?" Angeni looked curiously at him, crossing her arms.

"There is something in your eyes."

"Dust?" she asked innocently as she rubbed her eyes.

"No," smiled Jared and stepped closer to the young woman who looked at him. "Your eyes are mirroring something. Something that I can't name or explain."

"Humble wisdom," Angeni grinned.

"Definitely not," came the teasing, and then the Sentinel turned serious. "In the past you have spent long nights to search the answers to learn more about the demons of Briniu Malgram and the Crystal Shade. But then so sudden you became silent and didn't search for answers anymore." The Sentinel looked deep into her eyes. "Every time I look into those eyes they mirror silent answers that I fear to ask because I would fear to hear. Your soul whispers you do know you're right, but I can't explain why. And that scares me, because I know I must take up the question; what will happen if you know your legends are not a dreamy myth as I believe, but a cruel nightmare ready to come true?"

All of Angeni's kindness suddenly disappeared behind her icy mask.

"You're not lost like the others," she replied. "You can ask questions, regardless of your knowledge. So please know; we can never avoid the Crystal Shade. The time to face the truth is maybe closer than anyone ever believed," her angelic whisper echoed around the hall.

Shaken in his belief for the first time, the young sentinel nodded, silent.

"And now, if you will excuse me," she whispered.

Sorrow sat heavy on Angeni's soul as she left the young man behind with her pretend harsh theatrical exit, but otherwise, maybe he wouldn't take her seriously. A twinge of conscience had embraced her, but she had to break the young man's safe crystal reality. She knew it was necessary to

232

wake him up, or at least breed curiosity in him to later ask more questions, so he would not just learn the truth, but also would come to accept it.

The dim cold sunlight sifted through the dark clouds to glitter on a silent silver Kerecsen craft as it majestically passed over the Citadel Temple and shadowed the young guardian who walked down the stone steps. Angeni stopped as the craft blocked the sun for a moment. Her eyes mirrored the graceful metallic saker as it climbed higher and higher with leisurely wing flaps. Then her attention was drawn to dark heavy clouds on the horizon beyond the craft. A massive storm approached. Lightening danced between the shadowy clouds; so strange, none were followed by thunder.

Another strange storm, Angeni thought with misgiving, knowing it would arrive soon, hopefully before she reached home. The wind already carried the sweet refreshing smell of the imminent rain as she took a huge breath of the cold air of early Deciduous. She already waited for that loving feel, the stroking of the rascal raindrops on her skin. But unlike her, her large white wings weren't impressed and defiantly dove into the safety of the Spirit Sea to stay warm and dry. Her body flashed to give life to a thick hooded cloak to cover her thin gown. Letting a childish smile escape, she pulled her dark blue hood up and stepped out to meet the approaching rain.

The birds came in low, darting to safety. People took in clothes, children, flowerpots and rushed into their homes. Doors and windows slammed shut one by one. It was clear; every soul respected, but mostly feared the recent nature of Eecrys Aredia. In recent times, every storm seemed so strange and even more unpredictable than the one before. During Prosperous, many deadly storms seared the forests and destroyed crops before the harvest began. Even the almighty lightning that Aserians could not even save other souls from, acted so strange. Unlike before, now many times they were silent and struck not just the tallest buildings, which drew the destructive energy to calm it with their rods, but to trees and smaller houses as well in the wake of terrible destruction. Every storm made Angeni feel like something unstoppable approached, and that restless Eecrys Aredia would feel it. And maybe she did.

In the shadows of the neat houses, the young guardian was soon alone as she strolled down the serpentine walkway that ran from Citadel Hill to the tiny valley extending between the two mountains of Andrena's shore. The wind heralded the approaching storm, pressing her cloak close, its hem snapped as she pushed against the gusts with slow steps. The young guardian opened her mind to feel and know what her charge,

Nicolas did. An echo and joyful, if so hollow flute answered and she knew the Prince was still on an obligatory music lesson; something this young guardian will miss as she wants to keep her hearing. Smiling, she shadowed her mind to leave the joy of music to Nicolas. She knew she had plenty of time.

The darkest clouds had already reached Castle Hill when she began to climb the long narrow steps leading up to the Temple road and home. As if she was a child again, she enjoyed the first raindrops to hit her skin. First slow, then faster and faster. The heaving wind already swirled and raced the brown leaves along the cobblestones. At the top of the steps, Angeni turned to her favourite Chestnut tree-alley.

Lightning flashed silent in the distance one after another. The rain pinged faster and faster, as alone on the road she ambled home. Angeni smiled as the young chestnut trees happily whispered while they waved in the wind enjoying the fresh water and the loving caress of Mother Nature. Then, a bright flash, so like a sapphire arrow from the sky, a lightning bolt crackled. It's tip split a young tree in half a few dozens of steps from Angeni. Large white wings emerged from the Spirit Sea as the horrendous explosion hit and froze her spirit, terrifying her soul and rooting her to the spot.

Engulfed in flames, the tall slender tree flayed in the wind, one of its thin branches sparked and dropped to the cobblestones in front of Angeni, the tree spirit's wail assaulted her mind. She felt the endless pain that overwhelmed the young tree, its scream for help and mercy in the language of the soul as the relentless fire licked the branches and leaves. Raindrops merged with her tears and slid down the icy face. The frightened tiny angel watched the flaming death of the once proud tree. No one could do anything to save the young soul that never had a chance against the almighty wrath of Eecrys Aredia.

Why, why are you so furious? her scared sad thoughts asked while she wiped her tears away. *What did that beautiful young tree do against you? Does your wrath signal the approaching Crystal Shade? Is it really approaching, as we believed and so you feel? Did we not care for you enough? Please tell us, how did we hurt you?* Yet, Mother Nature raged all around the scared guardian and blew the raindrops onto her face in answer.

Her ears still rang from the strike as the burning tree's painful and heart-smothering death keen faded in her mind. However, the faded ringing slowly gave way to a soft crystal chime of a thousand crystals merging with a deep menacing hum like the deepest voiced bassoon. It echoed in the back of her mind, yet she felt it had come from a great distance. Her soul became restless and disturbed hearing this. She looked for the source, but never found it. What was this rumble and where did it come from? Angeni didn't know. Yet, deep in her soul, she knew she had heard a similar calling chime before. In a previous life?

That strange deep bassoon echoed in her ears, it wrenched her soul to sadness. Her feathery wings began to fluff out. Reflected on her eyes, she watched the rain gradually try to extinguish the silent tree's dead corpse; where the brilliance of a young joyful life was moments before, now only void and emptiness dwelt under the shadow of smouldering death. For the first time in her life, she thought; if this is what her lifelong dream, the dreaded Crystal Shade truly carried within then she didn't want to know the truth anymore.

* * *

The storm still raged outside while Angeni stepped into the temple's pristine grand lodge. Her wet cloak gently sloshed off the raindrops before it flashed blue, lost its solid shape, and merged into her body, leaving only her dry organza gown. Large white wings shattered the air as they emerged from the Spirit Sea, stretching wide, curious to see if it was safe and dry now to relax majestically behind her back.

Strange sounds erupted as the sad bassoon and crystal chime still echoed in her ears, it called her from somewhere close by. Angeni took few steps and looked around to find the source of this strange music. But the lodge was empty, no one played.

Where is this music coming from? she wondered. Her footsteps echoed in the lodge as she ran up the stone stairs. Angeni tried to follow the music, which seemed to come from upstairs. She searched corridor-by-corridor, sanctuary-by-sanctuary, chamber-by-chamber, hall-by-hall, but not a single soul resided in any of them. And that demented, dark music still called her like it was always just one room ahead of her. Then the music came from the lodge once again.

Statues watched her silent and curious and remained motionless as she arrived back on the ground floor. Under their shadows the desperate young guardian looked around again and again, her terrified eyes frantically searched for the source. Where is everyone, where'd they go, where is this menacing music coming from? She didn't know, but it was everywhere and called her wherever she went. The music restlessly played, its dark demented tones reverberated from everywhere all around her, from every statue, corner, wall and hall. Terrified, Angeni realized; the demented sounds played within her own mind.

"No. Please, don't," she whispered terrified. "Mother? Mother!" Her desperate voice called as she began to search for her corridor to corridor, hoping she could answer where this demented music came from. She desired motherly protection and just hoped her Mother could explain this phenomenon. Maybe it's a defect in her, like the acrophobia, or something worse. But once again, no one was around. *Where is everyone?*

Then after a few empty halls and sanctuaries, disciplined, she was slowly able to suppress the strange menacing call in her mind, just as she always had with wandering thoughts of others. Regardless of her efforts, like a sad oppressed soul it still played like a whisper in the back of her mind. At least it didn't bother her anymore and her soul began to calm. She was a lonely strolling shadow on the empty corridor when she heard a soft familiar hilarious chuckle. It came from the half open door at the end of the corridor.

The young guardian gently pushed the oak door to peek into the large hall. A huge rotating ball of mirrors focused and reflected light from some light crystals to illuminate a large city model that stretched across the center of the room. Aurora and enthusiastic Iris and Tlanextic studied the city. Amber aura embraced the youngest guardian's hand; she concentrated and her aura slowly moulded itself into a small orange flag with a pole.

"Every soul has a pair they can't live without," Tlanextic said to Iris with his wise, calm voice. "Taze spends all her time with Kien. And Aurora ambushes Jared at every opportunity."

"I love those moments," Aurora chuckled. She stood the orange flag proudly on the tallest tower of the city model. Her lips blew it slowly to give life to the tiny orange flag, and then gazed at her handiwork with a satisfied smile. "There you go," she whispered.

Amused, Angeni peered at what she could see of the city as she silently approached the trio. The city didn't remind her of any capitals and its style didn't resemble known provincial architecture.

"So who is Angeni taking care of?" asked Iris.

"All of you," Angeni said kindly, her smile broadened as she sauntered closer.

Aurora spun around, surprised, her wings flared wide to hide the city model.

"Stop right there, trespasser!" she ordered. Surprised, Angeni's leg immediately rooted in place. "What brings you into this forgotten, but forbidden little corner of Andrenia, my dear? Shouldn't you be," Aurora searched for a thought. "I don't know; somewhere else?"

"Have you seen mother?" Angeni asked softly, trying to hide her inner fear.

Aurora slowly looked to the left and right, then looked back at Angeni.

"No," she tweeted with a superior, icy tone. "But please give her my best wishes, when you find her."

"Where is everyone?" Angeni asked.

"Preparing for the Foundation Ceremony. Go and find them," determination tinged Aurora's response.

"Today is the Foundation Ceremony?" Angeni whispered, realizing she had completely forgotten about it. Since this sense of duty had embraced her, her days started to blur together with similarity. She also realized in this case her Mother and Father would not be back in Andrenia before evening. She hadn't even remembered where they went. A soft sigh barely hid the quiet demented music in her mind. Angeni looked curiously at her young sister, who still watched her silently, and seriously waited for Angeni to leave.

"What's that behind you?" Angeni asked.

"Nothing," Aurora innocently shook her head.

"Then what is that large town?" Angeni tried to peek beyond Aurora's large wings, but the model was almost perfectly blocked from her vision. "I don't recognize any of its architecture."

"Something that only initiated ones are worthy to see," came the answer. "You're not worthy."

"Then initiate me," asked Angeni. "Please, sister."

The youngest guardian just watched her, protected her secret with a hard stare.

"Please?" Angeni asked once again so kindly.

Aurora eyes shot left and right, yet her wings still covered the model. Iris and Tlanextic seriously nodded to Aurora as they decided. The youngest guardian looked back, her narrowing eyes still measured Angeni for a longer moment in silence. With a flourish, Aurora lowered her wings to reveal their secret. The youngest guardian quickly spun to the city model and theatrically spread her arms.

"Behold, my dear!" her regal voice chased itself around the hall as she proudly presented the city. "See the rise of the new dawn of mankind, the capital of the thirteenth province; Yavrora Gaea!"

"Aurora Land?" Angeni, who raised an eyebrow, stepped closer.

"Or Dreamland," Aurora added, looking back at her. "Or something else. It's still not decided," her pretend regal tone faded away. Angeni smiled at Aurora's childish glee.

"The thirteenth province was your sister's dream, Angeni," Tlanextic said.

"We believe it's appropriate to name it after her," Iris added with eternal calm.

Angeni took a good look at the city and its surroundings. The districts, towers, and roads showed the detailed work to anyone who saw it, right down to the smallest statues and trees. The young guardian crouched down as she followed the long, but strangely designed aqueducts that she hadn't seen in any known architecture; large mirrored panels ran in rows along both sides.

"We just solved how to turn the thirteenth province into a flourishing and prosperous capital," Iris' pride glowed. "Even if it is buried in the unsettled frozen northern plains."

Angeni looked at them curiously.

"Yavrora Gaea would be the twin sister of Crystana Serentis," Iris explained.

"On the western shores of the ice gulf, Satara'eya," added Aurora.

"The land of the long day and night," Angeni whispered, awestruck studying the detailed city. "The icy plains where the cold sets your teeth on edge," she added, and then looked at Aurora. "That would be a huge venture."

"Life is challenge, my dear," was her sister's pretending icy response. Angeni studied those strange aqueducts, which already carried a trickle of steaming water from the nearby by fountain as if the small mirrors had heated it by themselves.

"Those aqueducts will bring the fresh mountain water from the Hills of Carelia," explained Tlanextic.

"Carelia? That's where the ice fruits grow," Angeni mumbled, remembering the story of the trader who once shared with a little girl in Odess'iana. "But during the long night the water freezes inside the aqueduct," she looked back at the Watcher. Tlanextic nodded.

"That's the reason why the Crystanans have to melt ice into the cisterns beneath the city," he said. "But Iris developed a new irrigation method to bring the water to the surrounding lands too even during the cold long night."

Iris smiled at the strange steaming aqueduct system. Beautifully carved built-up prisms covered both sides. Tiny crystals hid beneath the transparent prisms.

"During the long day these prisms will gather Sachylia's light, focusing the beams to melt the frozen water," Iris said with modesty; only her eyes mirrored the depth of her excitement. "The small heating crystals draw their life from Sachylia through the prisms. They store the heat of the sunlight and when the long day ends, they will continue to prevent the water from freezing far into the night." Iris watched the aqueduct. "Be it long day or even the coldest long night the twin cisterns will always be filled with fresh water."

"Twin cisterns?" Angeni asked.

"Tlanextic recognized that unlike most of the provinces, there are no thermal springs in that region," said Aurora. "Otherwise Crystana's people wouldn't need to melt and heat water for their daily usage. So he meditated further." Her eyes gleamed proudly at Tlanextic.

"The first cistern would be the same as the one storing the cold water." Tlanextic pulled a small building away at the end of the aqueduct to reveal his masterpiece, the divided twin cistern structure beneath it. "But the second cistern's bottom would be paved with heating crystals, using the same method we used with the aqueducts. The town's cisterns always will be filled with fresh cold and hot water."

"These inventions may also help the other citizens of the icy plain," Iris added.

"It sounds so simple," Angeni whispered surveying the intricate model before she gave her attention to the two Watchers. "Why did no one ever think of your idea before?"

"Beauty lies in simplicity," Iris answered. Enthusiastic, Tlanextic nodded agreement. Awed by their logic, creativity, but foremost, the endless modesty, Angeni studied the miniature aqueduct and the cistern system, knowing this was simple only for the two Carenians.

"Like Iria," Angeni whispered, realizing her sister was trying to follow the life of her favourite Spirit Guardian, who always dreamt to build for mankind.

"Good examples, better and higher always give great dreams," Aurora nodded with a proud smile.

"So where's Eriana's citadel?" Angeni scanned the city with childish curiosity, feeling like she looked at a fairy tale town of Spirit Guardian Iria.

"Eriana's citadel. Let's see." Aurora's eyes reflected the city as she studied it building to building. "Where did we put it? Where did we put it?" she asked herself, and then looked seriously at Angeni. "Nowhere," and she was dead determined. "Those who do not build can't have a city, not even a small house," was the unexpected answer.

"Then where will I live if I visit you?"

"You're not permitted to enter," Aurora's icy response surprised Angeni.

"What? Why?" Angeni asked.

"Province Charta, point one, appendix A, like Angeni. Ardent warriors are not permitted to enter within the gates of Yavrora Gaea." Aurora haughtily raised her chin. "Weapons never bring peace, but only destroy." Her eyes glanced at Angeni's crystal blade that she always wore so proud, the only weapon in the hall. Then she looked back at her beautiful town. "Building is a life achievement of our dreams and mere fantasies." The ire and superiority in Aurora surprised Angeni. "As Father once said so wise; whoever searches for war may cause war itself. And I feel that Father is right," she added determined.

Whatever this phrase really means, Angeni heard Aurora's thoughts, merging with the suppressed menacing voice in her mind. *When you lay down your weapon, I'll tell you where we built it,* came the silent defiance, while the youngest guardian crossed her arms staring at her.

"In the moment you put down your crystal blade just for one day, you will get an invitation from the wise ruler herself. From me!" Aurora grinned and pointed to herself. It didn't last long; Aurora the serious and majestic came next. "But until this happens, you may sadly watch the prosperous city from the other side of the gates." Aurora paused, and then looked at her city. "Gates! We need more gates," she realized and turned to Tlanextic.

Angeni shook her head as she saw the excitement and desire to create in her sister's eyes.

"We need large impressive gates there and there so the people can approach from every possible direction," Aurora pointed at two parts of her city.

Tlanextic and Iris opened their palms. A small azure orb above Tlanextic's palm and a yellow one appeared above Iris' palm. The azure and yellow auras slowly formed into different types of gate models in their hands.

"These two statues are not just decorative," Tlanextic said as he gave the small gate model to Aurora. "They will guard the entrance vigilant and echo the prosperity of your city."

"Our city. Our city," Aurora admonished. Her eyes beamed pride while she took out a wall segment, gave it to Tlanextic, and set the gate down in its final place.

"I added some flower trellises," Iris introduced her segment as she gave her model to Aurora.

"Beautiful feasts are always in need of more flowers. An excellent thought, my dear." The youngest guardian giggled while she placed Iris' gate in its place, then she slowly stepped back. Her pride grew as she studied the model. "Beautiful isn't it?" she asked happily, twisting her wingtips behind her back in excitement.

"Yes. Beautiful," Angeni said with respect and awe before her cool demeanour covered it. "But you should quit dreaming and start to take life seriously someday, sister," she said soft and clear.

Aurora spun around, more determined than ever, like she expected this response. Iris and Tlanextic hastily occupied themselves with the model.

"No sister," Aurora said in a weird combination of determination and kindness as she stepped up to her. "You should start to live someday. You take your life too serious, preparing to defend Eecrys Aredia from an ancient legend, which may never come." She majestically rounded on Angeni, while she continued, "But I!" Aurora glanced at her loyal partners and corrected herself. "We! We want to see the rise of flourishing cities! We want to make people happy all over Eecrys Aredia! That's our life! We three will establish a new province where great feasts, justice, eternal peace and beauty will rule," she dreamt aloud.

"Not only beauty exists on this world, Aurora," Angeni countered just as determined.

"As Master Shen used to say; everything the Sacred Mother created has beauty, but not every soul may see it," Aurora carolling tone quoted. "Knowing is never as good as love, and loving is never as good as enjoying. Don't let daydreams imprison you."

"The Crystal Shade is not a daydream," came Angeni's calm answer, her eyes flashed sapphire to give measure to her words. Aurora remained calm. "You do not know what I know and have seen, sister. Life is not as simple as you would like it to be."

"Ancient Yaana proverbs, next chapter, life really is simple..." Aurora started.

"... but our spirit and souls insist on making it complicated," Angeni finished along with her. "As a guardian I live so others may live," Angeni added determined.

"How can you want to protect life if you slowly forget what it is?" asked Aurora. Silent steps carried her to Angeni. Angeni stayed silent, only a soft sigh left her lips. Those beautiful green eyes still watched and patiently awaited the answer; an answer that she could not give.

"I believe you're right," she whispered after a long moment of silence.

"Her majesty's sapphire eyes are finally open," Aurora smiled, and then like she realized something she had forgotten, she raised her hand to gesture Angeni to wait. The youngest guardian sauntered to the side table nearby, which was a jumble of scrolls. Searching fast, she picked them up one by one, checked the seal on them, and put some back on the table in the same order. With a grin, her hand worked fast rolling out the scroll on the table. A quill quickly grabbed from the nearby inkwell already scratched elegant letters on the paper. Angeni watched her curiously as the young one finished the writing, blew at the paper to dry the ink fast, rolled the papyrus up and along with the scroll in her hand; she marched back, passing it to her sister.

"To never forget. Wisdom Verses of Master Aurora, first edition. Freshly dedicated," the proud, superiority announced. "Let's consider this an experienced, lovely soul's gift to an inexperienced, lonely one."

Angeni smiled to herself as her eyes mirrored the tiny seal silently whispering its name; #11 – Angelic Wisdom to Daydreamers. Her silky hand slowly rolled out the elegant scroll to reveal the letters to her eyes, which desired to read this written wisdom.

> *When wind caress, the sun shiny and bright,*
> *It's a sign our spirit and soul is swimming in light.*
> *Life is the day where brilliance, peace might reign,*
> *Sometimes it is shadowed by storms, clouds, and rain.*
>
> *Spirits are born to dream, live, love and see,*
> *Always know what a beautiful life it may be.*
> *Eternal daydreams may blind you, shadow your present,*
> *Please never forget what makes life so pleasant.*
>
> *A single light may give you the most beautiful day,*
> *Walk with opened eyes; never let a moment away.*
> *Always balance between reality and sweet dreams,*
> *Live a great life; always let your soul gleams.*
>
> *Live to dream, dream to live, never forget,*
> *Don't have an empty life you would ever regret.*
> *Drop your soul bonds; let your spirit free,*
> *Or be a lonely star on the sky's endless tapestry.*
>
> *Your ever caring and loving little sister, Aurora.*

An ink drop slowly crawled down from the last drying line. Touched, Angeni rolled up the scroll and kissed Aurora's cheek.

"I will keep all your words in my mind," whispered Angeni, treasuring the touchable and palpable echo of Aurora's life; something that she didn't have.

"The youngest guides by heart and protect the elder," Aurora said proud and determined, crossing her arms. Angeni's beautiful eyes opened in surprise as her sister quoted those strange lines from The Great Tale of the Sapphire Souls without her realizing it. "Live and love. Enjoy every moment. That's my gift to you," the youngest added regally and raised her nose.

"Thank you," Angeni nodded to her. Aurora slowly opened her palm that glowed in orange and a tiny shovel manifested in it.

"Come, sister," Aurora grinned, passing her the shovel. "Let us set the foundation stone of Angeni's tiny village."

Angeni smiled and happily joined the others around the model city where the almighty, but so generous ruler of Yavrora Gaea gave her a handful of land on the barren, icy outskirts. Looking at the shovel in her hand and the land where she would have to build, reminded her of the childhood of a little human girl and a life she had started to forget. So ironic, as a child she wanted to be an Aserian Guardian so much. Now, the Aserian Guardian started to miss her childhood, maybe more than ever the time when she lived to dream and dreamt to live. She slowly realized being grown up and taking life so seriously, she had forgotten how to dream, how to live.

During that stormy afternoon a tiny village was born. It started to take beautiful shape building after building, road after road following the conception of the great architect, Master Angenius. But in the back of her mind the suppressed strange crystal chime and that deep bassoon still echoed menace.

* * *

It was late evening, but the crystal chime and that throaty bassoon still played. But a while ago the music started to reverberate and now the young guardian felt as if a great orchestra played somewhere in the back of her mind led by an invisible conductor who fanatically conducted the same tones over and over again. Now, along with the wandering, uncontrolled thoughts, the great music feast in her mind was suppressed to soft silence, allowing only the addressed thoughts and deep emotion to reach her soul. Yet the music was still there and played so soft and menacing.

The long Crystal Hall, the castle's great lounge for ceremonies for exceptional occasions now echoed from the emptiness. Mirrors on the walls and the crystal ornaments of huge chandeliers reflected only two souls who stood in the pale moonlight; the young guardian who prettified Nicolas, set his collar to seem untouched.

"You're a very confident young little man, aren't you?" Angeni whispered, looking into his eyes.

"I try to be," grinned Nicolas.

"Just try it further," the icy, yet smiling answer came as she pulled the hood onto his head.

"So, where are we going?" Nicolas asked curiously of the woman who set his hood perfectly.

"Tonight, you're not the Prince, and I'm not your guardian spirit," she whispered while she pulled her hood up over her head and her eyes flashed blue from under it. "Tonight you'll be just a man who enjoys life. Tonight, I'm your conscience; your cute inner voice. You may call me, Grace," she introduced herself kindly.

"So, where are we going?" Nicolas asked again, amused. "Grace?"

"Wherever we go, we must go with all our heart; enjoy and remember every moment of the journey," she measured the Prince with her eyes. Then with a very quick move she snatched Nicolas' crystal blade from his belt.

"Hey!" Nicolas tried to reach his blade to get it back.

"Ah-ah-ah!" Angeni raised her hand to stop him, while her eyes flashed sapphire. "Bladey goes to sleep now," her voice carolled while she clicked her own blade from her belt as well. With both blades in one hand, her free palm glowed sapphire and Pilly began to take shape. A fond smile for her 'old protector friend', the young guardian walked over to a short, elegant table and put the pillow on it. She trusted the blade grips to Guardian Pilly's heavenly, but foremost soft protection. Nicolas' frown reflected in the mirror while he watched her silent and curious from behind.

With a childish joy the young woman set the neat little pillow and the blades straight, like they were a part of the Hall's decoration, and then she looked back, serious, at the Prince. "For one beautiful night, we enjoy life unfettered. For one night, you will be a simple ordinary human who will learn what life really is. What the life of an ordinary human could be," she slowly turned to him.

"Sounds intriguing," Nicolas still eyed his blade. The polished golden hilt reflected him from afar. "So? What does one, who is not a Prince do?" he asked, looking back at Angeni.

"Talk to your angel, listen without fear, and I will give you a message," she breathed while she leaned to the prince's ear. "Loud and clear!" her angelic voice boomed suddenly. Nicolas jumped before his wounded, martyred grin started and her echo slowly faded in the hall.

"And what do I get? A cheeky female conscience, great," he said. Angeni looked up and raised her hands to the masterfully painted ceiling that told the story of Andrenia's rise.

"I told you, Almighty, that he would not appreciate your idea. But no, you always know everything better than humble me," she implored, and then smiled at Nicolas. "Tonight, there is no guardian to accompany and surround you, just another human that you'll spend a simple night with."

Serious, the young guardian stepped close to him, her wings suddenly snapped wide, and then wrapped around the Prince. The surroundings morphed around them, the Vanguards gave them safe passage through their sacred realm as the guardian desired. Then the whirling realm slowly dissolved around them and moments later she pulled her wings away from Prince Nicolas.

Drizzle fell from dark clouds where they stood on one of Andrenia's narrow streets. Soft thunder rumbled from afar; the storm slowly moved away from Andrenia to soon leave only the clear sky above. From the far end of the street, the large and beautiful Hall of Andrenia called them with its warm lights aglow in its windows. Many humans strolled through the grand entrance into the building, all of them eager to see the Foundation Ceremony of Andrenia and the heralded performance of the talented hall singer, Ourania.

With a mischievous smile at Nicolas, Angeni's wings disappeared into the Spirit Sea.

"You've called off my appearance here to bring me to the ceremony that I originally needed to attend?" he raised an eyebrow looking from the entrance to his home, to Angeni. "I will never understand the logic of Aserian women."

"Tonight, you will not enter as the Prince of Andrenia; no one will know you're even here," Angeni whispered. "You and your humble Guardian are far-far away on a secret, world changing official matter."

"Right. What's the point of this?" Nicolas hand went to rest on his hilt, and missed.

"To see a different side of life," said Angeni, smiling. "No one will give you special distinction in the hall. No one will stand up and applaud you when you sit down before the performance starts." The young woman rounded on Nicolas. "Today, you're a mysterious stranger from…" She meditated a moment. "From Odess'iana! One who'll enjoy the performance in peace with another stranger, Lady Grace of Odess'iana."

Wary, the Prince looked deep into her eyes.

"What happened to my rigid guardian and who are you, stranger?" he asked seriously.

"Truth melted my frozen heart, my rigidness is no more," Angeni admitted theatrically.

"So, finally you listened to someone. Aurora?" he asked and the young guardian's smiling nod was answer enough. "Admit it. You're trying to impress me," he smiled at her, and then looked at the hall entrance. "I'm flattered," added cheekily.

"An Aserian never intends to impress you, little man. Just bless, guide and protect you," Angeni responded with pride. "But tonight, you're protecting me," she pointed at herself. "Tonight, you'll see the difference between life and *life.*"

She pointed up to where the moon had just begun to eclipse. "See? Tonight we're not the only ones pretending to be someone else. Carenia Seli is also hiding behind a mask."

Nicolas watched the blue celestial escort with awe, and then turned to Angeni who lifted her nose and offered her arm. "Please, kind stranger. Will you escort me into the hall?"

"With pleasure," the Prince's charm warmed Angeni's soul while he twined her arm in his.

Approaching the hall, Angeni had seen Nicolas' eyes study their surroundings. This time he didn't need to greet anyone, just simply strolled toward the grand entrance. From the embracing touch, she sensed the young man was truly happy, like a man free of shackles, without the mantle of royalty that weighed his whole life. Yet, something still bothered Nicolas, yet with great self-control he hid it very well from her. Maybe the fact that the hall singer, Ourania was to sing for the rulers of Andrenia and now then she had a chance, the Prince would not be here on this great night, at least not officially.

The entrance of the Great Hall restlessly swallowed the visitors. A Janitor stood guard in his flowing silk and silver clothes and greeted the happy flow of men, women, and children one by one.

"Greetings on this beautiful night," Angeni stepped up to him.

"And such a beautiful day for the Foundation Ceremony," the Janitor responded, looking at the night sky, and then back at them.

"Will the rulers of Andrenia be attending tonight's performance?" Angeni asked while the Janitor greeted a passing couple with a kind nod.

"Unfortunately, young lady, Prince Nicolas is unable to attend this performance. But our beloved Blessed Lady will grace us with her ever-inspiring presence."

"I'm so sorry to hear of the absence of the Prince. He must be very busy," Nicolas whispered with a hidden cheeky smile while the Janitor silently greeted a young family entering the hall.

"But I sincerely hope, young Lady and Sir, that the performance of Ourania will compensate for his absence," said the Janitor kindly.

"It surely will, good Andrenian," Nicolas' respect rang true from under his hood.

"Please enter and enjoy the performance in the Hall of Andrenia," the Janitor gestured them inside with a flourish.

"Thank you," nodded Angeni as Nicolas grinned before they entered the large hall.

You honour us, and Ourania says thank you for your presence, the thoughts of the Janitor addressed her. *Our doors are always open, and we will gladly do anything for you, Angeni.*

In the Great Hall, two empty seats silently called to them and offered their comfort among the throng of people. The interior of the hall reminded Angeni of the great Long Hall of Odess'iana, but this hall's stage crowded the entire opening along the Azure River's shore. The beautiful floodlit bridge connecting Andrena with Renia with its elegant stone body was the foreground. Across the river, the Andrenian Castle Hill was visible, which gave majestic background to the entire hall full of beautiful statues and paintings. Its small domed ceiling was painted to show that both humans and Aserians protected Andrenia.

Like colourful statues, hundreds of dancers stood motionless and silent in their rich costumes on the stage and waited; as did the dancers on the stages set up on the shores of Andrena and Renia. Musicians sat to both sides of the stage and waited to start. Not a single note left their instruments, just the echoing overlaid crystal chime and deep bassoon played in Angeni's mind.

Then a soft torpid feeling took hold of her entire existence, something she had felt in the past, back in Sessa Asria. A claustrophobic feeling, as if she were forced, trapped and held here in this realm. Yet, her instinct knew she was safe, and no danger threatened. Still, she felt the illusion that space and the other realms beyond, which surrounded her became shallow, smaller, and shadowy. Angeni slowly stretched her fingers in an attempt to break the torpidity in them.

"Do you feel the difference?" Angeni asked Nicolas, to distract her being from that suppressed menacing music that still played softly in her mind and the sluggishness that slowly faded away. Yet, that strange stifling feeling stayed.

"I always imagined how this hall and the ceremony would look from a different perspective," the Prince whispered while his eyes slid over the crowd, and then up to the royal box. "I've always sat up there." He looked at Angeni and set a pleasant smile. "Thank you."

"Don't thank me yet," she smiled. "The end of the night is far from over." Angeni pulled two small baskets from under her cloak. "Ice fruit?" she offered one of them with a wide smile. Nicolas happily accepted and took a bite of the tantalizing fruit.

"I didn't know Aserians ate," he whispered as Angeni took a bite of a fruit. It was delicious and sweet as aya nectar; they grew every single piece from the heart, so a kind trader had said to a little girl in the past.

"That's the human way of thinking," she answered happily. "We don't need to eat, but we can. And I love to eat." She grinned and quickly finished the small ice fruit with relish and picked up the next one from the basket. "Nothing can compare to ice fruit. Except frozen whipped cream with spice and cocoa," she added dreamily. "That's my favourite."

A few moments later, Ceretaperia Faraa and her escorts, Eve and Aaron arrived on the royal balcony. Everyone in the hall looked at the ruler with loving respect and enthusiastically applauded her. The queen was dressed in shimmering silver, a gem between the two High-Guardians, who stood vigilant in their elegant clothes of tinted citrine orange and jade green. Faraa's Guardian Spirit, Turul rested on the balcony rail and awaited the performance as well.

"So, this is how everyone sees her," amazed and proud, Nicolas clapped. "It's so different."

"See?" Angeni was also amazed by their majestic appearance. They were elegant, three gems out of the thousands, and her mother, Eve was the most beautiful. Her elegance was heightened by a diamond crystal, large as a fist, it hung around her neck like a pendant and refracted soft moonbeams into her eyes just as her mother looked down at her for a moment. Angeni noticed the Queen's pleased smile too as her eyes fell on the young Guardian and her happy son in the crowd.

Thank you with all my heart, Angeni, the Ruler's pleased thoughts rang clear. Then Faraa looked up to Carenia Seli; already half hidden behind the lunar eclipse. On the two shores and the bridge, all torches blinked out as one. Only the pale moonlight glowed over Andrenia. The drummers' earthy beat rolled with the ruler who strolled to the edge of the balcony. She majestically spread her arms and the drums stopped. Deep silence fell on the hall.

"I look with pride at you, the people of Eecrys Aredia!" she called in her regal voice. "A prosperous nation was founded at this place a millennia ago, on the day our ancestors settled on the two shores of this rich and beautiful land." Faraa looked up at the moon, which looked back at her with pale moonlight. "On the star trail, Carenia Seli is shy, spending her time to prepare and greet us on this great day with her new light. She has the honour to tell the tale of light and darkness which lives from mother to daughter and father to son!" The ruler looked back at the people as she continued, "Let happiness, peace, and comprehension be in our hearts and souls! We greet you with dance, fire and celestial light, summoning the spirit of ancestors and asking for the blessing of the Sacred Mother in merriment and in plenty! Bright lights of the ceremony shine in all of our eyes. Many happy returns, happy birthday, Andrenia!"

The drummers awakened their drums to beat fast and loud as the ruler's voice faded. Flute, harp, lyre, and syrinx players of a celestial orchestra joined and the dancers came alive. Whistles shattered the night sky as volleys of sparkling fireworks launched from the shores of Andrena and Renia, and from the beautiful floodlit bridge behind the stage. The tiny rockets crackled as they exploded into a thousand colourful shiny flakes, punctuating the rhythm of the traditional drum, choir, and the dancers.

Fire dancers clapped their hands and stomped their feet in pairs, following the ancient Andrenian music on the large stage. Cold blue fire rose up all around them at the edge of the stage, flaring with the rhythm as they portrayed the birth and rise of Andrenia with their dance. The music drove them, continuously changed with the style of the dances as history came alive on the stage; the greatest moments and turning points described by the dancers and the music. Men, women, and even young children danced happily together and separate to the music and fireworks. Then colourful, elegant flags marched in, swung majestically, and danced with the rhythm, together and sometimes separate.

Angeni had never seen most of these dance styles, but it enchanted her. Like everyone else, she was swept away by the complexity and emotions. Her eyes mirrored the dancing flags, waving to the exploding fireworks that spread thousands of trailers. They fell to Andrenia one by one to tell of the peace that ruled Eecrys Aredia. And Nicolas; his face glowed with joy and happiness as he beheld the happy families from Andrenia and distant lands here to see the great ceremony.

"If you don't know what you really care for and love, you don't know what you defend and what you must fight," Angeni leaned in to whisper. The prince nodded understanding.

As the finale approached, the dancers had already danced the present era in quick and cadent Andrenian dance style to the fireworks that flared with them. Twelve flags waved in the colors of the twelve provinces. Blue sparkling wildfire, like waterfall poured from the bridge and the hill behind to raise the dignity of their performance.

A saker cry reverberated in the air to call attention as twelve mechanical bird craft, Anshara, Kerecsen, and Sanayra at different points on the horizon appeared above Andrenia. Each of them glowed in one of the twelve colors of light auras to represent the twelve capitals of Eecrys Aredia. They all flew closer together and met right above the bridge of the Azure River. The beautiful fireworks shot up to launch the large birds as they majestically rose up to the stars, where Carenia Seli was almost fully in the lunar eclipse.

Angeni, Nicolas, and the crowd were awed by the light show and the escape of the crafts' glowing hulls into the dark sky. The dancers followed the thump of drums while the craft curved downward. The music soared as fast as the craft, whose aerial acrobatics stole the gasped breaths of the audience as they approached their finale. The silent birds joined formation to show their unity to all. Dancers waved the flags of the twelve provinces from the stages and greeted the large metallic birds that flew together symbolizing the united twelve provinces of Eecrys Aredia.

As fireworks were launched from all around, an azure aura orb shot into the sky above the castle and transformed itself into an enormous saker, which opened its wings, just like the statue that protected Andrenia. The huge aura wings stretched wide and the bird silently screamed toward the audience. Angeni knew that only High-Guardian Michael could create something of this magnitude.

The aura bird faded away and as the last colourful fireworks had exploded, the dance had ended as complete darkness shrouded Andrenia. The crowd erupted into cheers and applause as the performers left the stage. Deep silence fell over the hall as the shadowy figure of Ourania stepped onto the dim stage.

The young woman seemed fragile in her golden saree, which glinted in the pale moonlight only for a moment as the last sliver of Carenia Seli disappeared and the entire stage was plunged into darkness. Complete silence ruled; even the wind held its cheeky breath back in excited respect. Then Ourania's angelic soprano climbed clear and beautiful across the Azure River as she began to sing.

When the last hope of light fades away and darkness embraces my eyes, I know celestials are guides, and our mother watches from the stars. My greatest dream came true; in my dreams I called you my stranger, my eyes are full with tears; I begged, I called you in my prayer.

The luscious tones stroked Angeni's ears, slowly cradled her. Her eyelids drooped, flickered, and then slowly closed as if forced by an invisible power to fall asleep so sudden. She felt her consciousness ebbing away, all her thoughts faded. Darkness held her for a moment, and then her eyes snapped open as her conscious expanded to see everything she could not see with her own eyes. A foggy dark alley, so cold and strange flashed in her mind like her eyes had seen it, but the shiny white of her eye reflected the hall and the singer whose song continued.

You're an adventurer, a wanderer; you call everyplace your home, but maybe this is your day to settle down, please call my home as your own. Your duty, your life is calling, I feel it day by day; all joy must have an end, you always leave everything behind for duty, you're not senseless, please don't pretend.

A lonely old Aserian stood in the middle of the alley; his sapphire crystal battle armour gleamed proud in the dim light. His lined grandfatherly face unfamiliar, his gray hair waved in the cold wind gusts that brought the beautiful song of the hall singer, so menacing.

Our moment is past, you must go to your battle, there is no time to say goodbye, when you disappear behind the mountain, my soul cries, my heart will die. Your fellow traveler is the soft caressing wind, the only one to whisper in your ear, you must bind to someone or one-day sorrow will fill your eyes.

The old guardian's eyes glowed bright sapphire as he looked up; immense solitude seeped from his tired soul; an unknown soul that Angeni couldn't read. The dim light glinted as his hands adjusted golden crystal blade grips while shadowy silhouettes approached him out of the swirling white mist.

251

As you look away, the memory of your face fades into the shade, I beg, I want to be with you, open your heart, don't play masquerade. Look at me stranger, look at me with your beautiful eyes, open your soul; look at me and show the light in your eyes.

Sharp metallic tools, axes and scythes, now weapons with a dull glint in the starlight; dozen of men and women alike surrounded and closed in on the old guardian in the dark alley. Even the wind held its breath, scared for a moment at the evil and darkness that oozed from their souls.

The light in your eyes whispers, you are brave, the lonely one, living in solitude, my heart is alone just as yours; you're not the only one. You live in the shadows; surrounded by darkness and fear, I feel you're my strong knight, whose soul echoes crystal-clear.

The dual-bladed sapphire crystal blades came alive in his hands and struck without hesitation as the humans rushed at the old Aserian with a raucous battle cry. His age was not visible in his movements; he evaded the dashing sharp axe and struck back fast. The closest soul screamed as the deadly blade went through his chest without any great resistance and like blood would spill, dark ruby red crystals quickly embraced the wound. The sapphire blade pulled back fast, but the crystallization didn't stop on its victim. Like quickly freezing and crackling ice the ruby spread beyond the wound to encase the entire body of the screaming man who had dropped to his knees with the deadly pain. His suffering didn't last long; the blade struck once again, fast to shatter the crystallized body and release him from the torment.

Angeni instinctively tried to look away to not see his end, but she couldn't turn away from the vision playing in her mind. The relentless crystal blades danced in the night struck over and over again and showed no mercy. Archaic weapons and old tools turned to dust, screaming souls crystallized bodies shattered, red and black crystals bounced on the cobblestones to clink like the menacing crystal chime were the cry of the fallen dead souls.

Warriors must have a bright guiding star in the dark sky of night, I know you'll save us from darkness and will come back to me, my brave knight. You always fight darkness; you always protect us from a fall, fight bravely to ease the darkness around us all.

The screams slowly faded, but the chime still echoed. Noble sapphire light sparkled on the thousands of shattered rubies, garnet and black tourmaline crystals that rested on the cobblestones around the old Aserian Guardian. Then the light faded on the shattered souls as the blades closed in his hands. The old eyes were full of sadness that desired the endless peace that only the stars in the stormy night sky could give as they shyly looked back at him.

I promise, I'll be your bright guiding star in the dark of night, my soul is with you, you're not alone, my strong knight. Your bright guiding star will lead you back home, wherever you are, be it the closest lands or distant continents afar.

The illusive fog slowly encased the distant vision like she had fallen into an endless mist, then her eyes opened wide as her consciousness smashed back into reality. Silent and terrified, she gazed ahead when she found herself in the hall once again. Carenia Seli's eclipse had almost ended and its pale light shone on Ourania as she sadly sang in the pale moonlight.

As celestial light always returns; I know you will come back to me, when I see you again, in my happiness I will fall before you on bended knee. As Carenia Seli to Eecrys Aredia, in darkness I'm your light, when I see you again, my heart will beat again, my soul will be bright.

The fragile singer drew out her finale' with so much hope in her voice. But the strangely echoing deep bassoon and the crystal chime shadowed this hope with its much more menacing chime in Angeni's mind. The uncontrolled emotions around her of the people, who enjoyed the ceremony, broke her mental barrier, the inner music became louder, and louder regardless how hard she tried to suppress it. Helpless, Angeni looked up to her mother who always made her feel safe; her eyes begged for help. Concerned, Eve already watched her from above, and then quickly left the balcony.

Everyone stood with a roar of applause, but the scared eyes of the young guardian, just mirrored the hall as they frantically scanned for the source of this untouchable voice that called her. The clapping slowly faded until only the invisible dark duet played in her mind. Her eyes snapped to Nicolas. He didn't applaud like the others, but also shook his head like something was bothering him; his eyes also searched the hall for something unseen. The young guardian stared at him in disbelief as she realized…

"You hear it too," her voice was barely a whisper.

"Where is it coming from?" troubled, Nicolas looked at her.

"I don't know," Angeni responded. "But at least I do know why an orchestra is playing in my mind," she realized the menacing music Nicolas heard, the same rhythm merged with hers to give life to this invisible dreaded orchestra that only they could hear.

Her soul desperately fought the chime that raged like a wild beast. As people started to leave the hall, the mental barrier slowly eased the pressure and her soul finally shut the demented orchestra back into the shadowy basement cellar, left to play its menacing music where she couldn't hear. As her mind cleared, Eve and Aaron stood behind them, watched them.

"Come with us," her worried mother said. Silent, they followed the two High-Guardians out of the hall. The young Guardian still felt that strange claustrophobic, feeling stronger than ever while the orchestra of the damned softly faded to a whisper in her mind.

The cheery voices of the people slowly faded as they left them behind to traverse a long corridor.

I hear what you hear, but I can't see what you've seen, Eve's concerned thoughts addressed Angeni as they stepped into a dim, finely decorated, but empty lounge. "Please tell me, my daughter," Eve looked at her while Aaron closed the doors behind them.

"Spreading darkness, cruelty and death," Angeni whispered in the pale blue moonlight, which flowed right at her through the windows. "A true nightmare where the people were evil, Mother. They were soulless, senseless and brutal beings; I've seen it in their eyes." She stopped, thinking of the senseless death she had seen, and then continued terrified. "But a brave Sapphire Guardian so old and tired fought the souls wearing the mask of evil from the shadows to corrupt our beautiful land."

"Eosh," Eve whispered quietly, looking ahead of herself.

"Eosh?" Angeni's surprise made her pause. "Is he still alive?"

"That's impossible," the bewildered Prince added. "He lived in the twilight of the last Crystal Shade. That was dozens of millennia ago."

"He is the Sapphire Guardian that you saw," Aaron said with a soft sigh.

"The lone guardian whose eternal soul has kept Eecrys Aredia in the light since the last Crystal Shade," Eve added.

"How can you be so sure in this, mother?" the stunned young guardian asked. "It all sounds like a legend, so impossible."

"He is my wise and noble father, Angeni," Eve answered after a short hesitation. "Only your father and I know his true identity."

Angeni's words trembled as she whispered, "But why did the humans turn against him if he is so noble? They were not demons. They didn't even resemble the statue of Demon Marchosias. Why did he kill them?"

"He killed humans?" Nicolas' whispered as he looked in stunned disbelief. "Why?"

"Please never judge when you don't know the premise, that's all I ask." Eve paused for a moment, then her voice turned serious as she continued, looking at both of them. "Maybe you'll have to do the same when the time comes."

"Please mother, please don't say this," Angeni stepped back and shook her head, shocked to hear this from her. "I won't take anyone's life away. Never."

"It never will be your choice, Angeni," Aaron responded sadly.

"You taught me every life is sacred," Angeni retorted. "I'm not willing to hurt anyone."

"You can't protect everyone on Eecrys Aredia if you're willing to protect her," said the Prince full of sorrow as he turned to Angeni.

"How could you say this, Nicolas?" the young guardian asked bewildered.

"He is right, Angeni," added Aaron determined. "Please never consider that it is expedient for you as in this time the need of the one must be sacrificed, so others may live."

Angeni bowed her head sadly, but inside she started to admit that her parents could be right.

"You've seen what our present or what our future might be," Aaron continued. "Eosh will share the rest of what you need to know as even if we explained, you won't believe since one cannot imagine it fully until you see it for yourself."

"Like everyone else, my father has waited for you, the Angeni soul for a long time," Eve said, proud of her daughter. "Now the time has come to share his wisdom with you. For your end is just the beginning."

"But I'm not the Angeni soul that others wait for. You told me, mother; what I think, I will become, so my actions, my moral values will define my spirit and soul."

Her mother stepped close and gave her a motherly smile and caress.

"My beloved daughter. Who you always wanted to be is what the Angeni soul always meant; the guardian who lives so others may live," she whispered calmly. "We never wanted to shepherd, but wanted you to find who you truly are."

Silent, Angeni watched her parents. She felt like she'd been pushed into a whirling surreal and cruel world, which slowly entombed her to never let her go.

"Won't you come with us?" she asked after a long moment. Deep in her soul she feared to step into the unknown and leave the protection of her parents, to leave their safe life behind.

"Eosh has prepared us, so we do know what to do," said Eve. "But you must learn from him. His wisdom will reveal why you walk on this world."

"How will we find him?" asked Angeni, but deep in her soul, she didn't want the answer.

"He will find you," Eve responded. "When he does, you'll have to leave everyone behind. Only you two may hear his words. No one else."

"Why?" asked the Prince.

"In the times ahead of us there is no place for doubt and no time for convincing," Aaron responded. "The true nature of the Crystal Shade cannot be told, but must be seen to understand. Events will dissolve doubt and will convince the beliefless. However, your path is different than theirs. It always was different." Angeni and Nicolas understood and nodded to Aaron.

"The Segaran Viras will give you safe passage to Arabah in the northern territories of Hijaz province," Eve determined. "Then follow the call in our realm to reach Aysdemera, the place where past, present and future meets."

"Why can't the passage lead us to this place?" Nicolas asked. Angeni looked at her mother to hear the answer.

The same reason some old Aserians were not able to protect their human charges in the past, Eve glanced at Angeni; her face reflected the guilt and pain within before she continued. "Aysdemera is the beginning and the end; one of the twelve sacred places where the will of the Sacred Mother rules beyond our realm. There the Spirit Sea is dark and shallow, only our spirit wings may hide safely. A repulsive power, so overwhelming and strange embraces and binds our spirits. A mute and shy place hidden encased from all realms forever, destined to keep its silent secrets from all souls as no one may ever pass, no one may ever see what lies in those twelve places beyond this realm."

"That strange power that I've felt many times and I feel now," Angeni realized, still feeling that unexplainable claustrophobic hold that embraced her now, the same that her soul had felt every day in Sessa

Asria. Eve slightly nodded. "But what is calling us, mother?" the young guardian asked.

"A sacred place once tasted the darkness and the cruelty, echoes the voice of the past to remember, to never forget," Eve's sadness made her voice rough. "Aysdemera is waiting to reveal its buried secrets in the dawn of the Crystal Shade."

* * *

Thousands of heavenly lights mirrored in her curious eyes as they searched for Briniu Malgram in the endless star trail, but only peace ruled above. The home world of evil hid behind one of the enchanting masks up in the crystal garden, so Angeni believed.

Watching the stars, the crystal chime and the sad bassoon still played as the restless conductor led the demented orchestra in her mind like compass needle drew enchanted Angeni toward their destination. A mournful breath left her angelic lips; she knew the warm safety of home, like the stars, was so distant.

Gusts of dry wind hit her icy face as she looked back to the horizon, her sapphire cloak's silky hem softly tugged by the breeze. Dense sand blew up, shot through with silent lightning on the dark skyline; the same strange phenomenon that had besieged Andrenia, like it followed them. The unknown path ahead of them now seemed much more terrifying than it ever seemed from a distance. And that claustrophobic feeling, the strange force encased her being, trapped her in this place unable to access the Spirit Sea save for her wings.

The cool delicate grass rustled as the seven wanderers caught up on Angeni and stopped to watch the distant heavenly battlefield.

"Awakening tempest," Kien said quietly while his homeland was struck by the raging elements, heat-laden chain lightning ripped along the horizon without a hint of thunder. This storm was something that he had never seen before.

"Maybe it will pass in front of us," Tlanextic quietly hoped while Aurora's majestic wings emerged from the Spirit Sea. The wings rose a little, so the feathers could gauge the wind's intent.

"It's coming right at us," Aurora said with certainty before she sent her wings back into the safety of the second realm so no rain may touch them. Jared studied the distant raging nature of the storm he knew best. Angeni had read from his soul, even he wasn't sure what this storm would do, or where it was headed.

Worried, Nicolas looked at Angeni from under his hood. "We're so close to our destination. We should go on."

"This storm is too unpredictable," Jared finally said. "We would be safer on low ground to let it pass." He looked down on a lush grove valley. Shy Taze nodded agreement.

"Embraced by the valley, it seems sheltered," Tlanextic added as he studied the large grove ahead.

"I agree," said Iris.

Angeni looked at the prince, who watched the horizon from under his hood. Eagerness to go on oozed from his soul.

You should listen to us, little man, Angeni addressed her thought to Nicolas.

Maybe you're too cautious, Angeni. It's just a storm, Nicolas's thoughts answered while he watched the lightning on the horizon. *Your great awareness may lead to the wrong assessment.*

Being wrong is a human trait. Aserians never make mistakes, Angeni asserted. The Prince raised and eyebrow at Angeni, but the young guardian watched him without emotion, imperative. Reluctant a moment, Nicolas nodded to Jared. With the two Sentinels in the lead, the eight wanderers descended into the valley while lightning struck in the distance to light the way. The sand and storm swirled and raged closer along the horizon.

Please never question me again. Never question any of us, Angeni's thought reverberated with her displeasure to the Prince who strolled beside her.

My apologies, came his swift thought. The young guardian nodded to him as they descended below the valley rim.

The first of the arecaceae trees gently swayed in greeting to the eight wanderers as they gained the valley grove just as the storm hit and raged all around the valley's rim. Angeni shadowed her mind to put the demented chorus back into its basement prison to play sorrowful music there. She knew for a time they did not need to know the right direction. Finally, she could enjoy the peace that the Prince enjoyed a time ago by suppressing it in his mind. Only one needed to hear this cursed music. Only one needed to lead the way to Aysdemera.

"What can be so charming in a children's book?" Jared debated from the lead with Aurora under the shadow of the trees, arm-in-arm.

"It's a book full of mystery, enchanting charm, great romance, sad drama, eternal war between light and darkness and more mystery," Aurora extolled with childish glee, and then looked at him. "Uh, did I mention mystery?" Jared just shook his head and smiled. The youngest woman set an offended, rigid look at him. "Don't tell me you never read it or you will shrink in my beautiful eyes, my dearest Sentinel."

"Your sister said the same," smiled Jared. "But neither of you ever told me why it is so different?"

"It is the only book on Eecrys Aredia that never ends," Aurora explained haughtily. "With the last pages missing, you, my dear must imagine what happens next. That's the best part of it."

"We're likely to stay here for some time," Jared said. He tracked the clouds as the storm looked to pass near their safe haven. "Tell me the short of it." Jared looked at the woman.

"Why should I tell you?" Aurora frowned at the young man. "Different people have different visions when they read. I can't and won't give away my inner vision. Aurora's vision is Aurora's dreamland and Aurora's dreamland is Princess Aurora's impregnable castle," she chirped, her raised nose betrayed her pride.

"Then at least tell me your ending. What's your ending, Princess?" Jared asked curious. Aurora looked at him. Angeni had seen her sister's eyes narrow, watching the Sentinel to see if he was worthy to know her inner most dreams. The youngest guardian sighed.

"A so beautiful and heart-smothering dénouement," Aurora started, and then she paused to continue defiantly. "That you won't ever hear, my dear. If you want to know the legend of Eriana and Iria, be a good Sentinel and read it," and she looked away.

In the shadow of the soul crystal Eriana has finally found salvation and peace and Iria has forgiven her, Angeni thought as she remembered her ending.

The storm slowly moved closer, it would pass near the beautiful grove the group delved deeper into. Then as the whispering trees spoke with the wind, it slowly revealed an enchanting shy oasis that hid from the outside world. Ancient ruins peacefully loitered with nature a long time ago. A bubbling rocky waterfall called them to a small lake. Between the trees an elegant and proud, yet tiny and broken old pavilion offered a shelter, it called them without a word. Its masterfully carved columns were embraced by nature and curious green grass peeked out from its cracked stone floor to be the soft blanket and pillow for the wanderers.

"We should ride out the storm in this beautiful paradise," Taze whispered shyly, amazed by the natural wonder of the little oasis, which was a real heaven for the Sentinels. Angeni turned to Jared while the young man watched the storm clouds rage up beyond the rim of the valley. Furious winds shrieked and lightning struck rapidly outside their safe shelter.

"The storm passes slowly," he said. "We will be here for a long while."

"Then we should enjoy the momentary rest," Nicolas said. Angeni agreed with a nod. Aurora stepped ahead, awe in her eyes, she grinned at the beautiful waterfall, and then the young Aserians.

"You thinking what I'm thinking?" she asked them. "Let us explore every part of this tiny paradise."

"I'm with you," Jared replied with a weary sigh.

"Oh, my little Sentinel. You sound so tired," said Aurora with playful concern.

"We follow Angeni. Even the strongest tasunkes would be tired," Jared cheeked back before he turned a gentle smile to Angeni. The young guardian smiled and shook her head at the truth of it while Aurora and the others spread out to discover the delights of the grove oasis.

Angeni glanced back at Nicolas who already sat in the green grass and ate a fresh Andrenian fruit he had fished out of his small pack.

"A peaceful night is it, stranger?" she asked, sitting down near him. Nicolas looked at her with full mouth, slowly checked the fruit, and then swallowed it before he nodded with a smile.

"You also seem tired," Angeni said with care. "Rest, Nicolas. I'll watch over you."

"I will, when we arrive," he stubbornly responded. "I cannot sleep while this music is echoing in my mind. Even if it's so soft."

"Maybe we will also need all of our strength there. We don't know what waits for us," Angeni said quietly.

"I know," responded Nicolas' quiet thoughts. "Dreaming and facing our fantasies are not the same are they? It is becoming harder and harder as we get closer," he said and ripped another bite from the fruit before he looked around. "I wish we could stay here."

"I know how you feel," Angeni whispered with a weary sigh.

"You should take a small measure of rest yourself," he chided fondly. "Your face is dirty and you also look tired. You should refresh yourself."

Angeni's eyes glanced at the small lake. Its gently surging water had drawn her eyes since they arrived. She looked back at Nicolas.

"Don't go anywhere, little man," Angeni threw back in pretend seriousness. "Don't even think of it."

"Why would I go, my guardian? While you're around me, I know nothing, not even the raging storm can harm me," he smiled, and then slowly finished his meal.

Pale moonlight burnished the young guardian as she crouched at the lake's edge and plunged her hands into the cold water, enjoying how it encircled her fingers. She gently splashed her face clean, and then she stopped. From the rippled water Carenia Seli's pale face watched back from beyond the dark churning clouds, along with a young Aserian woman, who stared back from the water with fear in her eyes. A fear that chilled her to the soul she had refused to admit through their travels. Facing herself, she could no longer deny it. For the first time all her knowledge, the truth she had sought to learn now terrified her. She wanted to turn back, to be safe at home. But she knew there was no turning back now.

She looked back at Nicolas. Curled up on the grass carpet, he already slept under the protective cover of the broken pavilion. Angeni smiled fondly as she strolled back to him. Sapphire light glowed around her hand as her aura shaped a folded sapphire blanket.

"Sleep well, stranger," she whispered so caring as she covered Nicolas. Her palm glowed once again as her aura gave her eternal guardian companion pillow shape along with a second folded sapphire blanket. Angeni sat on the wild grasses near the Prince and settled in comfortably. Her eyes awed at the small friendly oasis bathed in the moonlight that gave them safe haven.

"You're right, Iris. This architecture is very different," Tlanextic was awed as he studied the old ruins with Iris. "Five-six millennia old, even much older."

"More. Just look at those beautiful carved arches. They appeared seven or eight millennia ago in the southern territories of Hijaz," Iris' excited awe rang true. "This place amazes me. All of the details tell the story of its past."

Storm hurt us. Fire. Burning fire. Taze's fearful and heartbreaking thoughts made Angeni immediately look at her, but it wasn't the thoughts of the young Sentinel. These words were the feelings of a yellow celandine flower. It reached Taze's soul, who knelt near the flower on the shore and had touched it. The plant's fear of this strange storm became Taze's fear. The shy Sentinel smiled with empathy as she leaned close to the wildflower. "Don't worry, little one. I'll protect you," she whispered calm and peaceful before she tended the beautiful plant.

Then Angeni's eyes caught Kien. The young Aserian meditated once again to reach the balance he always dreamt of, to someday not just see, but also truly understand the world in which they all lived. Angeni knew that he already understood the world much better than any of them.

"And there flies a Sentinel!" Aurora's excited chuckle declared from somewhere.

"No, Aurora! Wait, wait, wait!" Jared shouted. In the next moment, a splash sounded from the lake. Soaked through, the young man slowly rose from the water, glaring up at the top of the waterfall while his wings appeared in a menacing hunch.

Carenia Seli's pale light brightened Aurora's wide grin. In the shadows, she stood naked at the edge of the rocks, waving cheekily down at Jared. Then she raised her proud chin, spread her arms and wings.

"Watch and learn, my dear," came Aurora's boast and she majestically dove from the rock. Her wings retracted and disappeared as she fell and her lithe body cut into the waves. It was a long moment before her head broke the crystal-clear lake. Aurora took a large breath and shook out her shiny red hair, laughing as thousands of water drops flew away from her. The Sentinel tried to catch Aurora, but she dove into the waves. She broke the surface a little away, cheekily waving to him.

Watching the playful souls in this endless peace, Angeni realized they were all children at heart and maybe this joyful night was the last for all of them before they were forced to grow up. They could not comprehend that peace and harmony were a mere illusion that could disappear from one moment to the next. The young souls didn't know why they came to Aysdemera. There had been no time to explain or ease their doubts about the truth of their legends. They came because they were told to escort her and Nicolas to Aysdemera. For now, a fragile crystal reality surrounded them ready to be shattered and banish the dreams they lived for. Even worse, it was her cursed fulfilling dream that would shatter theirs. It was all her fault.

Sad, Angeni lay down on the grass and held Pilly close under the blanket so her brave guardian may protect her from the cruel illusive world. She closed her tired eyes to hide from grim guilt and shame. Maybe if she hid, all of their dreams could live on. In her soul she hoped if she kept her eyes closed long enough, maybe they'll all awake back in Andrenia where they would live their hearts desire. She felt the tear roll down her cheek, but she didn't care. She shed one silent lonely tear for a shattered dream that may never come true because of her dream. Another tear came, and another. The young guardian kept her eyes close and prayed for the dreams of others. Like a warm blanket, her own dreams slowly embraced her.

In her dream, she was in Andrenia with the others in a world where everything was simple and as happy as they all imagined. They lived for their dreams while all of their actions reflected their love for life. All their dreams came true. Imagined towns came alive, poems and wisdom brought light into everyone's life. Even a tiny chestnut family became larger day to day. Mothers and fathers protected their happy children who all lived for their dreams to then become parents as well to see their children reach what their souls desired. Peace and harmony wasn't an illusion here. They all knew none of them need fear the Crystal Shade, none of them. But then a cruel bright sapphire light blinded the dream world, and shattered all their dreams.

Along the valley rim, a few of Sachylia's beams shot through the dark clouds on Angeni's eyes to awaken her. The sun slowly rose, bringing its first tentative light to the valley. Angeni closed her eyes again; maybe she hadn't closed her eyes long enough to make her wish come true. She sighed and had to face reality. She wasn't in Andrenia with the others as she had hoped and desired deep in her soul. The trees of the grove looked at her along with Jared, while the suppressed orchestra of the damned still played in the cellar of her mind, eager to show her the way.

"Angeni. The storm is over," the Sentinel whispered.

She stood up and looked around. Everyone was ready to go. Guardian Pilly and the blanket soon became one with her spirit while the prince stepped close. Their eyes mirrored Sachylia together as it climbed higher and higher behind the clouds.

"Every dream-filled night must end once," Nicolas whispered with sorrow. The young guardian silently nodded and took a last sad glance at the beautiful oasis. This peaceful little corner would be forever treasured in her heart. She didn't want to go. She didn't want to know what the Crystal Shade was. She wanted to go home.

But then she opened her mind to let the conductor and the orchestra play aloud, to show the way.

"Let's answer whatever calls us out there," Angeni said quietly to the Prince so the others would not hear. As if a strong power forced her, she turned and took the first step. Then the next one and the next as the chime and bassoon drew her. The large trees of the grove watched as these joyful young souls left the safe haven the valley had offered. Joyful leaves stirred underfoot and happily danced into the air as their steps scattered them. The same steps ushered them all closer and closer to the relentless place that stood somewhere in the distance and waited with a large hammer to shatter everything they ever knew and believed. The trees cast lonely shadows on the wanderers as they marched away. Angeni fell deep into her thoughts to search for a way to save all their dreams, and to keep them alive.

Systematic, she tried to find not just any solution, but the right one. After a few steps, she had decided. Only two of them would enter Aysdemera delve into whatever awaited them. Her mother said, only she and Prince Nicolas could meet Eosh, only the two must hear what he had to say. Then she realized no matter what she asked or ordered, the others might agree, but they would still follow them unseen like true guardians. She would do the same, but maybe not. Would they stay behind? She had to try to protect them. And maybe, just maybe if she asked them so nice, they would listen.

Thick greenery slowly opened onto a large drop-off to reveal a huge valley in front of them. Angeni kept away from the edge and kept an eye on the threatening clouds as they majestically plumed on the horizon throwing lightning beyond. Below, a beautiful city rested within a grassy canyon embraced by two rivers born of a huge waterfall that poured behind the rocky crags into a moat-like basin. As the rivers arrived on the outskirts, huge amounts of the water roared over the rocky ledges to thunder far below in the churned up mist. Tall and small buildings alike stood proud to offer safe haven and a place to live and dream to its citizens. Dozens of aqueducts carried water through the city like arteries, they supplied its lifeblood. Brave bridges spanned above the depths to hold the main land and the grove full of giant arecaceae trees together.

A soft, warm wind caressed Angeni's face, ruffled her blonde hair and white wings. With the others, she studied the city of Aysdemera. It seemed an ordinary bustling town in the center of a huge living oasis like the one they had left. So beautiful and enchanted this place the restless demented orchestra called them to like an awakening tempest.

* * *

"Dreams sometimes couldn't be achieved without shattering the dreams of others," the old man told the children, putting his tea down. "Always carefully define what your heart desires as distant, unreachable dreams always seem so innocent, enchanting and sweet. But sometimes the sweetest dream is a true nightmare ready to unfold."

"Many say that life can be easy and we are the ones who make it complicated," the old man walked with the children to a small stone table. "That can be true. But I believe life is capricious, like the Crystal Shade itself," he picked up a colorful seven-sided fortune crystal. Three facets were sapphire; another three cut from ruby, and the seventh, a transparent diamond mirrored the curious faces of the children as they looked at it.

"The subtle, unpredictable way of life is akin to this Andrenian Septagon; it can show what your future could be. Peaceful and bright, what you desire," he said, pointing to the sapphire facets. "Or the darkest day, which like a sudden tempest, is ready to swallow the clear horizon," he pointed to the ruby facets. "You never know when the tempest will arrive to darken your life and surroundings forever."

The Septagon's first stria lit up in sapphire at his touch. "Life is about decisions of good and bad, quite often without realizing it. As the sun crawls up into the sky, you never know what destiny was dealt for you or those around you for the day," he said as an image of beaming, sun-dappled people appeared in the facet.

"Heavenly life," the old man thought aloud before he looked at the children. "Some bring you wonderous days beyond your dreams."

The crystal glowed blue as he touched the first ruby facet, which morphed into a picture of a cruel, dark place where people suffered.

"Infernal death," he whispered, and then continued to speak to the children. "Sometimes decisions throw you into a horrifying day that'll haunt you for the rest of your life no matter how hard you want to forget, or how much you regret the past."

The old man looked at the crystal chrono-device. The dreaded shadow slowly crept over and covered the tiny, fragile orb so dear to his heart.

"From that moment on, you desperately wish for the sunny days knowing nothing will be the same again." He looked back at the children and touched the second sapphire facet. A happy young couple appeared; a lovely, red-haired angelic woman's arms circled the man's elegant blue wool uniform. The moment the woman kissed him was frozen for eternity in the crystal.

The old man smiled fondly at the picture. He knew those on the crystal; he and his beloved wife.

"Well, I never looked good in any picture. She always raised the quality," he said with a chuckle. He knew the kids believed he spoke about his wife, but this time his words had a double meaning. The picture didn't show everything or every person.

In his mind, just as in that long forgotten moment, the crystal had shown a third person standing behind them unseen to watch over him. Content, the old man continued.

"Everything happens for a reason, even if you can't see it for a long time. Every day can be the last of a once joyful life. Every day may reveal the true shades of a destiny we can't avoid." He set his arthritic finger on a ruby facet. The old man watched a grim picture of suffering, cruelty, and killing glow into shape. "Many believe in a fate laid out where every event happens in only one way that leads to this unavoidable destiny we can't escape. Never determined, destiny always changes, feeding on past actions and mistakes that sooner or later catch up to you."

The old man studied the two children. He became very serious.

"We may spend an entire life living in light or in the shadows." He pointed at the sapphire and ruby strias, and then to the diamond facet of the crystal. "With faithful dreams we can give life to our destiny walking on the path of fate. But a fate born from fear always creates nightmares."

* * *

The brewing storm slowly blanketed the awakening city. Heavy raindrops fell to beat the dust up from the cobblestones. Morning seemed so far off, sunlight barely sifted through the clouds, and gave the strange impression of evening's approach instead. Beneath the dark shadows of the grove of sprawling arecaceae trees, two wanderers approached the waterfall city of Aysdemera.

Unseen and invisible as true Aserians, the others followed the Sapphire Guardian and Prince Nicolas. Even Angeni could not see them and only felt their presence. They were here, somewhere in the grove and silently watched over them. Only Nicolas' false whistling interrupted the silence and the enforced peace, which ruled Angeni's disciplined mind. She didn't need to follow the menacing music anymore. But the strange claustrophobic power that latched onto her entire being was stronger than ever; the kind of power that only allowed her wings to be hidden in the shallow Spirit Sea.

A deep horn sounded from the distant city to greet the travelers as Angeni and Nicolas stepped out from the shadows of the arecaceae trees. The long majestic stone bridge arced above a large waterfall connecting the grove with large closed storm gates, which protected the town along with the tall walls. Carefully stepping in the middle, the young guardian forced her eyes down to not even think of looking beyond the edge. Yet she heard the rumbling crushing torrent that came from deep below to drown Nicolas' hollow whistling. In her vivid imagination she had seen the great drop and the churning waves beneath calling to her already terrified soul.

Seventy steps long, so she estimated before they stepped off the bridge. As her count reached one hundred at the middle, she already knew her torture would be longer than she had prepared her trembling being for. Maybe she should simply take larger steps instead of shakily padding along.

Yet, another greater fear struck her as the large gate loomed closer and closer. The once bright path that her dreams had laid in the past, and now, ahead of her was shrouded by darkness. The place where this road led seemed so menacing, like the great mass of dark clouds gathered on the distant horizon. Her spirit feared the answers that might await them. Although terrified of the unknown, they drew doggedly closer with each step. What if the Crystal Shade is here? She didn't want it. She wanted to avoid the unavoidable, wanted to turn back and go home, but she continued toward the gates.

None of this fear showed on the guardian's emotionless face. Only her icy eyes that concentrated ahead of her mirrored the pacing sapphire sandals that may have betrayed her. A loud creak drew her attention as the large storm gates unsealed and grated open. For a moment, her soul was terrified; what might the open doors reveal? An ancient temple full of secrets, crazy demented people or hordes of demons? Her eyes narrowed as she watched the entrance, which came closer with each step. As the gates opened wider, it also revealed the peaceful old, if lively town of Aysdemera beyond.

"Are you scared?" Nicolas asked smiling. He glanced at her hand that rested on her crystal blade.

"No. Excited," Angeni responded with her fear buried under the harshness.

"I wonder if we're ever going to find Eosh." The Prince's eyes studied the huge town ahead.

"Have faith, little man. Sooner or later, he will find us," Angeni almost sang her response. "Whenever that will be," she added almost silently. She let out a grateful sigh as the bridge ended and her feet felt the safe solid ground of the large forefront that extended out in front of the town's entrance. An aged woman, her shiny silver hair and elegant red silk robe bathed in the dim sapphire sunlight. Her deliberate, yet leisurely pace brought her out through the gates.

"Greetings travelers! We have been expecting you," the woman spread her arms and bowed respectfully. "I'm Lilis, the Prime Conciliatory of Aysdemera," she introduced herself with a grandmotherly kindness tinged with the strength Angeni saw in Lilis' eyes. "So, as I've been told noble and distinguished souls will visit us from the greatest province of Eecrys Aredia. I've been asked to lead you to the Temple of Salvation where we've arranged a small welcoming ceremony for your arrival."

"Thank you for your kind welcome, Prime Conciliatory," Angeni replied. "Please lead us to him."

"As you wish," the old woman bowed with respect and showed the way.

"See? He already found us," Angeni whispered to Nicolas cheekily as they followed the Prime Conciliatory.

Soft rain barely made a sound on arabesque linen awnings that stretched between many of the ancient rooftops. Despite the imminent bad weather, some traders still offered their merchandise, musicians played, and Hijazian veil dancers twisted to an earthy rhythm. The water flowed and babbled within the aqueducts throughout the town like arteries in a living being. The soft swishing reverberation coming from the distant waterfalls was a natural calm background in Aysdemera. It sounded like the whisper of a thousand kind spirits. Angeni could understand why they called the town, the Spirit Voice.

A strange instinct made the young guardian's entire being tremble; her eyes studied everyone around them, hoping to glimpse what was causing her unease. Her instincts knew what this acrid feeling was, but she couldn't define it, couldn't even describe the feeling to herself. An Aserian had no fear, yet a deep primordial fear churned within her. Her soul cried for vigilance; her spirit sensed that everyone on the streets was watching them. Just them.

Fear is only as deep as the mind allows; nothing should be feared, but understood, so Old Shen had said in the past. Does her initial fear breed more fear that slowly choked her? Or was this feeling an illusion manifested due to her doubts and wishes to stay away from the answers she feared so much? She didn't know. She silently followed the friendly chatty Prime Conciliatory and Nicolas and slowly started to believe her fear may not be justified at all. Everything was so peaceful and normal all around them. It was an ordinary stormy day in Aysdemera where people went about their daily life.

Citizens took plants in, retreated into their homes and closed their windows to keep the approaching storm outside. Soon, only Angeni, Nicolas, and the Prime Conciliatory walked the empty alleys that the young guardian found so familiar and pulled her aside bit by bit. Her vision of where that mysterious Sapphire Guardian, Eosh appeared came sharply to mind. The battle she saw had or would happen in one of these empty alleys. Yet, everything seemed peaceful and orderly. Only the storm winds built up nastier with time. Since Angeni had seen the dark horizon, she knew the worst was still ahead. Her cloak was already drenched and she could feel the cold water soak through her clothes.

Only a few of Sachylia's sapphire streaks punctured the dark clouds before the thick brewing mass slowly blotted out the sunlight to stain the sky dark as night. Angeni, Nicolas, and Lilis had walked a league, even more as they passed through the long streets toward the Temple of Salvation, which stood at the far end of Aysdemera; so Lilis said. Like a true guide, the wise old woman kept their interest on the long journey as they chattered about the city and its culture. The Prime Conciliatory extolled the town's accomplishments while the guardian's eyes studied the architecture. She began to understand how Iris and Tlanextic could be so awed by the beauty of buildings as they always were, and presumably were now somehow hidden as they followed.

A new empty shelf had been moved into her Great Spirit Library with a hastily written label, Aysdemera. Angeni's great scribe incarnation made notes to fill the shelves with knowledge while in the corner of her mind, her restless divine painter incarnation, Lady Master Angenius already made quick sketches of these beautiful buildings to later paint for all eternity. Silently awed, the young guardian usually lagged behind, always noticing a much more beautiful building than the one before.

As they went deeper and deeper, the buildings had become older and older as if they stepped into the past. The style slowly changed from clean, elegant, and modern to crude, mythical, and so ancient. Still beautiful despite their age, the old buildings were covered by groomed moss. Mother Nature embraced the unharmed columns and had protected them for a long time with elegant woven vines. Beautifully carved statues stood silent in the rain on the facades and in the parks; ancient, weather battered. Like true caretakers, the raindrops lightly misted the pale green skin of the ancient copper statues and cleaned the cracked wounds of the old sleeping stone giants. Their motionless eyes that had watched the same beautiful scenery since it sprouted and had seen generations grow up under their cool shadows, now followed the three souls as they passed in front of them.

The rain fell steadily heavier. Like mischievous children, silent raindrops screamed their joy as they slid down swaying leaves, creaking signs, old tiles, and sleeping statues alike to then gather in puddles on the cobblestones. Lamp flames waved so furiously to misdirect the cheeky wind that searched for new playmates all over town, spun the empty roundabouts and swung on the swings like invisible children on the playground. A soaked polished pebble hopefully watched the three souls approach its hopscotch marks and silently called them to play, but only the young woman glanced at the child's game with a pleasant smile before all of them strolled further.

The storm flashed the extent of Eecrys Aredia's fury; sapphire lightning shattered the sky to reveal a grouchy old building that watched the visitors' silent padding across the huge square that sprawled up to the front of the hallowed building. Darkness swallowed the last hint of bright light and two moments later thunder rumbled as Angeni counted.

The Temple of Salvation was the most beautiful and seemingly oldest building of Aysdemera. The broad entrance of the elegant white alabaster temple opened onto the square, but the building ran back under a large swath of falling water, right into the rock wall behind the waterfall. A maze of stone aqueducts sprouted from the rumbling waterfall to deliver its water to the other districts. The rest of the water flowed from either side from beneath the temple into two rivers. Shadena and Shadana, the younger and older sisters as the Aysdemerans called them, began their calm journey to encircle the whole city to slowly broaden out to feed the waterfalls at the city gates.

Peaceful azure light drew the eyes to the small stone windows of the temple. Shadows passed inside the warm building from time to time and soft music sifted outside.

"So, this is the end of our journey, the place where we will learn everything," Angeni murmured with a wary eye on the temple. Fear jolted through her entire being.

"You'll learn everything you need to know," the Prime Conciliatory said. "The question is; are you willing."

"We're willing," affirmed Nicolas, but this time Angeni wasn't so sure, and stayed silent.

"The desire for knowledge is always the first step to making everything better," the wise old woman looked at the silent guardian. "Listening is the key that can unlock the truth within you."

Soft sweet steam swirled in the heavy air and brushed Angeni's face as they stepped through the main entrance of the temple. In the young guardian's daydreaming illusion it felt as if she had stepped through a barrier that divided ignorance from knowledge. A loud thump echoed as two men closed the polished oak doors behind them to deny the cold storm entry.

A grand hall welcomed them; the most beautiful that Angeni had ever seen. Arecaceae trees stood proud on balconies, native plants gave a naturally peaceful look with hundred of blue-flamed torches to accent the tranquility.

The temple contained a small part of the great waterfall that they had seen outside. The two rivers, Shadena and Shadana flowed in as one and divided here at the bath before it flowed out as two under the temple. The large aqueduct that snaked along the ceiling reminded Angeni of a stone tree branch that split off at sixty-degree junctions from the main aqueduct. The main branch caught the falling water near the ceiling at the far wall, and then divided in the middle to feed the two closest corners of the wall. The aqueducts diverted water to the widening terraces, plants, statues, and fountains of the higher and lower balconies before they delivered their refreshing content in the middle of the hall to fill the large bath with crystal-clear water. Steam rose sleepily as underground thermals heated the water and the gleam of peaceful azure light crystals lit the bath and the small waterfalls below.

The whole place was reminiscent of a huge oasis. Many people from different provinces rested on cushions; some talked and others played instruments. Wild and exotic music, but somehow also so soothing, the gloomy tones followed the atmosphere of the raging storm.

A sudden burst of lightning split the storm outside to flash bright inside the room with a crack of thunder two heartbeats later. Angeni wished Sachylia would shine through the glass ceiling. How wonderful this place would be in the sunlight, she couldn't even imagine.

"Welcome to the Temple of Salvation," Lilis offered with reverence. "While we wait for him, please have a seat, warm your hearts and dry your clothes." She gestured to a low table. "Eat and drink. Please, enjoy our hospitality."

"Thank you," Nicolas said as a man arrived with two steaming goblets on a silver tray. Like a good master of the house, Lilis gave the fresh hot nectar to the two guests. The masterfully cultivated arabesque goblet warmed Angeni's hands as her fingers twisted around its heated body. The sweet smell of the steaming white drink reminded her of a drink loved by a little girl a lifetime ago. A sip and the nectar began to warm her soaked and chilled body. It was the sweetest and most luscious Ambrosia she had ever drank. Like soft silk, the ground almond that infused the milk stroked her throat.

"If you need anything, just tell me," Lilis offered. Angeni and Nicolas nodded their thanks, and the Prime Conciliatory strolled away.

"I don't believe they know Eosh is an Aserian," Nicolas whispered to Angeni while they strolled deeper into the hall.

"Mother said no one knows his true identity," Angeni whispered. "They also are not aware that I'm an Aserian." She glanced at the goblet and sipped the hot nectar to pamper her spirit and body. Guilt began to seep in. Her sister and the others waited outside, somewhere on the streets in the storm. But she knew if she wants to protect them and their dreams, they shouldn't meet Eosh, as her mother also said. This time there is no time for doubt, no time to convince. Now true believers must hear the truth.

* * *

Golden blond hair shone with azure light as Angeni's head broke the crystalline surface of the bath. Taking a huge breath, she relished the fresh steamy air. Water drops glistened in the air as she shook her head. Diving into gentle waves, she swam under the closest tiny waterfall. The crystal-clear grace poured over her head and neck, warmth stole over her silky body to cleanse and refresh. Soft music reverberated through the swath of water to stroke her ears and she pushed herself away from the wall. The water gently flowed around her hands and embraced her body as she dove back into the waves and swam to the darker side of the bath.

No shame felt as a man covered the slight woman with a large fluffy white towel as she climbed out. No one turned away from others on Eecrys Aredia, even if they were a bit different, less or more attractive, every soul was special and unique in essence. The man left while Angeni pulled on her strapless sapphire gown, slipped into little elegant gem-clad sandals, and flicked her cloak over herself. The crystal blade clicked onto her belt and she carefully covered it before she stepped out of the darkness.

Silent admiration warmed her soul as every man watched her with hope and desire, just as they had while she swam; or so it seemed. The wet, cold stone silently tapped under her sandals as she sauntered alongside the bath, thinking in rhymes and enjoying the distinctive attention that some women attract.

Graceful fragile body, hidden angelic existence,
Desire love, silky caress, dream of me from untouchable distance.

272

But then her eyes caught on a shadowy figure who sat cross-legged at the far end of the hall. He watched her differently. He studied her with great interest from the shadows. The dim light illuminated only the man's sharp eyes until a mischievous lightning flash from outside revealed him for a moment. The aged human in an elegant dark red hooded doublet smoking an intricately carved pipe had a face so old, yet unfamiliar. Certainly not the old Aserian from her dreams, nor Eosh. As the bright light faded, darkness enshrouded the man, but his deep brown eyes still followed the guardian.

Strolling toward the velour cushions, Angeni's attention turned to Nicolas, who sat in the corner of the temple gazing at the only living being, who drew more attention than herself.

A golden veil fluttered through air as the exotic Hijazian dancer flowed across the floor like swirling rain in the gentle wind while she followed the delicate music that reverberated around the hall. Silky tanned hands moved like calm waves of a mythical and exotic ocean, slender hips shook like a joyful leaf in the breeze, ebony hair flowed through the air and golden belly chains clinked pleasantly as the beautiful woman accentuated the black-skinned drummer's gentle rhythm. Her wriggling faultless dance amazed everyone. For Angeni it was a dance so familiar, that a little girl once tried to learn it at the Great Feast of Odess'iana.

The young guardian sat down on a cushion far from Nicolas, so as not to bother him. But with a keen eye she watched the Prince who definitely enjoyed the distinguished attention. The dancer slowly caressed his face and teased her veil around his head; this dance was only for him, no one else.

The storm still raged outside; a lightning bolt struck again, and as Angeni counted, two moments later thunder clapped loudly. So strange, it's like it couldn't come closer or move farther away, but whirled and concentrated in one place. Restless, she hoped that Eosh would arrive soon.

"You seem to be more than you appear, young lady," the old voice of Lilis noted as she sat beside her.

"You're not the first to say this, Prime Conciliatory." Angeni smiled to herself and pulled up her legs to hug them. Like a distant relative soul, so much like her mother, Lilis was wise and kind; she could read it from her eyes.

"Please, call me Lilis," she insisted. "Lilis means, the woman of the night."

"I'm Grace Sessa Aredia of Odess'iana," Angeni introduced herself with a slight bow of her head. "Please, call me Grace. It means..." She paused for a moment. "Well. Grace." She shrugged and smiled.

"There are no secrets in front of me. I know who you are, my child. I knew even before you came here. I bow to the divine in you." Lilis smiled. "But no one mentioned your friend's name. When I asked, he called himself 'the mysterious stranger of Odess'iana', whatever that means," she said amused.

"My mysterious stranger," Angeni smiled to herself. "I never thought that playful night would mean anything to you, little man."

"You're not a couple, I can see that. Yet something binds you," said Lilis.

"How do you know that?" In her curiosity, Angeni rested her head on her knee, feeling so peaceful, like a child.

"I'm old, but not blind," Lilis said with a knowing smile. "You're here and he is there, yet he glances at you many times, protecting you with his eyes with caring."

"Does he?" asked Angeni in surprise.

"Just as now," Lilis said softly as she turned her back to the young man. Angeni snapped her attention toward Nicolas, who immediately looked at the dancer and drank his hot Ambrosia like he'd been doing it all along. The young guardian's fondness infused her smile.

"Do you love him?" Lilis asked.

"Everyone who knows him loves him," she chuckled to avoid giving a straight answer. A black-skinned man stepped up with a silver tray and offered goblets of warm Ambrosia. Like a child, with bright eyes Angeni quickly grabbed the goblet and thankfully nodded.

"You didn't answer my question," reminded Lilis, picking up another goblet from the tray.

"Me? I'm different. It depends on my mood," Angeni grinned, while she enjoyed the warmth of the goblet in her hand. "Let's see." Her preying eyes narrowed as she looked at Nicolas, then at the twisting dancer, and then back at Lilis. "No. He is not my favourite person today," she teased.

Lilis stared intently as she shook her head in a grandmotherly way. Angeni knew she couldn't avoid answering, but hesitated nonetheless.

"I honestly don't know." She glanced toward Nicolas. "Our paths may be joined, but that doesn't mean our lives and fates are the same. I feel responsible for him, but my soul is drawn to another."

"Feeling responsible is one of the signs of care and love," Lilis said, looking knowingly into Angeni's eyes. "Sometimes even a seemingly meaningless moment can forge two souls together for eternity, even if the fruit of that night can't be fulfilled until some distant future," the Prime Conciliatory assured her.

"Or can never be fulfilled," Angeni added sadly, staring at her drink before she took a sip. "Faithful dreams may vanish when the path of fate leads us to our destiny."

"No one tells who we are or what life we should live," Lilis said thoughtful. "We control the life that the Sacred Mother gave to us. There are no boundaries for our dreams, not even for our lives."

Angeni smiled tremulously. She felt maybe the old woman was right.

"May I read your hands to tell you what lies ahead of you?" Lilis offered kindly.

"No," Angeni pulled her hand away. "I know what lies ahead of me. I wish I didn't," her conviction came out harshly. By Lilis' face, she saw that her words cut deep. Unbearable guilt built in the guardian's soul, she did not mean to hurt the feelings of this kind soul who had just offered aid, and wanted to help her. "I'm sorry, Prime Conciliatory if I offend. I really am."

"If you don't want to see, this old woman won't force you," Lilis responded softly, but also tinged with sadness. "You're a good-mannered, kind young lady who cares for the souls of others, regardless of how well you know them. In your eyes, all souls are the same, because you know we are the same since the beginning. You recognize the goodness of others."

"The spirit in me meets the same spirit in you," said the young guardian. "Within each of us there is a place where peace dwells."

"Please promise me, you will never forget these words," Lilis entreated.

"I promise," she swore softly.

"You see what others feel and show regret when necessary," Lilis continued. "I accept your apology."

Angeni thankfully nodded, then she looked toward the far end of the hall where the shadowy figure still sat, smoked his pipe, and watched her, just like before. The young guardian felt that the man did not intend to disguise his interest in her.

"May I ask who is he?" Angeni asked.

The Prime Conciliatory looked back at the old man, and then at Angeni with a soft smile.

"Who do you think he is, my child?"

"I don't know. But I feel him studying me."

275

"Your senses do not betray you," responded Lilis. "He could be a wise man, curious to know who you are, where your soul comes from and where it is heading," she added quietly before she shrugged. "Or a simple aged man who just watches a graceful young lady who might remind him of the dreams of his youth. The real question is not; who he is? The real question is; how you see him?"

Angeni looked at the old man and then back at Lilis.

"It wouldn't be appropriate to assume. I should meet him, and learn the answer for myself. We all live in oneness, one family, and one heart of compassion."

"Wise answer, my child," the old woman's growing respect echoed. "You are one of the rare ones to want to know the person before you judge."

"So, who is he?"

"Who knows?" Lilis smiled at Angeni's sudden grin. "Maybe he is the soul who accepted his path, someone who doesn't believe in the change. Or maybe everything we see and might read from his eyes is just an illusion."

Angeni watched the old man for a moment and realized that Prime Conciliatory might be right.

"Like him, I know what path lies ahead of me," Angeni whispered with a sorrowful heart. "But unlike him, I desire the change as a dream I wish I'd never dreamt slowly becomes reality." The young guardian looked at the old woman with desperate eyes. "I see a destiny unfolding I wish I never knew, walking a path which leads to a place I don't want to go. I want to wake up before the nightmare binds me, but I know I can't."

"Never determine your future, even if you know your destiny; there are several paths to choose from, and limiting yourself to one would be nearsighted," Lilis said wisely. "The desire is the first step to make changes. Perhaps the Sacred Mother guided you here for you to find the path you seek in your soul."

Angeni looked at her hopefully and after a short hesitation, she offered her hands to the old woman to read from. "Please tell me, is there another path for me."

The Prime Conciliatory waited for a moment, and then nodded to her.

"You have seen the reality of the living," Lilis purred in so sweet and enchanting voice, looking into her eyes. A touch, not much from the old woman and Angeni's entire existence cried in silent despair, shouted to see what she must see and do.

"Now, see the dream of the dead, Angeni," came the dark whisper as their eyes locked; Lilis knew exactly who she was, even before the touch, so the young guardian learned as a soul hidden revealed herself.

Angeni's mind suddenly opened as darkness and evil bubbled up within the old woman; her soul wasn't as human as it appeared to be. But a soul born among the flames on the wastes of eternal darkness. Hot falling ash burnt her ash grey skin, pain-riddled, echoing screams welcomed her soul when she was born long ago of a red heart full of dark wicked thoughts; hell itself. Moments from a long demented life played in her mind; an elder soul embraced and worshiped by thousands of evil creatures. An evil that reached out from hell with its cramped, fiery hand as a twisted invisible storm of darkness entwined and choked Aysdemera like thin grasping vines.

So naive, a young guardian, and a man came as strangers to this forsaken soulless place swallowed by darkness, awaiting someone they didn't know like so many other souls before. Mimicked serenity and blind trust, not much was needed to lure them into this enchanting nest. No one waited for them here. Only death, as the bearer of illness and disease, the woman of the night, Demon Matriarch Lilis, had welcomed them.

Angeni's terrified eyes flashed sapphire blue; just a moment had passed since she had been touched by the demoness; the guardian yanked her hands away. She rose and stepped back from her so desperately fast that she stumbled. Large white wings flared out of the Spirit Sea like a fearsome being to break the surface of the calm where nothing was before. A bright aura surrounded her entire body as the silky cloth of her cloak immediately morphed into protective crystal-blue armour. Dual sapphire blades came alive in her hands as she instinctively grabbed and separated her crystal blade as she crouched and her wings flared wide.

The empty goblet of Ambrosia that had been kicked aside still bounced on the marble floor when the Sapphire Guardian was ready to defend against the Demon Matriarch. The healthy skin of the old woman turned dark and creased, her hair the slate grey of ash; a real demon, Matriarch Lilis stood in front of Angeni in her true shape. Lilis was much older than she had disguised herself, but was nothing similar to the distorted pictures that described the demons. The Matriarch had no horns as the statue of Marchosias presented the demons, nor knock-kneed and pigeon-toed as Persecutrix Aurilla always told the young ones. Despite her age, Lilis was majestic, even graceful in her dark robe, but also very fearful at once.

The sapphire blades struck at the hell-spawn, but red blades came alive as the Matriarch defended herself, spinning her united elegant golden hilt out from under her robe with a fluid strength, almost knocking the blades out of Angeni's hands as their blades crossed. With the same buoyancy, Lilis separated her grip and slashed toward the guardian in a glowing red arc, which forced Angeni to leave her offensive stance and step back fast. The red blade passed in front of her, it was hot enough to burn her skin as it passed close to it.

From the corner of her eye Angeni saw that Nicolas realized what was happening and grabbed for his blade, but he touched only thin air, his blade was gone. Looking up, surprised at the dancer. Two polished elegant daggers that the woman had hid under her veil were pushed to his throat. Every single soul was demented in Aysdemera, man, woman and children alike, as was the beautiful enchanting face that turned a glorious and biting smile on Nicolas.

Between the columns, the battle raged on. The sapphire blades crossed the striking ruby blades right in front of the guardian as Lilis cut toward her with incredible speed. The crackling scrape that didn't fade away, another one came as the Matriarch pushed the young guardian back with each of her strikes, forcing her to continuously defend herself. The crystal blades clashed swiftly with the fury of the demon Matriarch's attack.

The old man still smoked his peaceful pipe in the darkness; those cold eyes still studied her moves. Her mind focused on the battle as the Matriarch spun her blade fast and jabbed toward the guardian who blocked in the very last moment and riposted unharmed.

Her instincts told her to escape into the Spirit Sea, but she felt that claustrophobic binding power that ruled this place. The same rules applied to the Matriarch. But it was clear to Angeni that the old demon didn't need any celestial power to defeat her. She was well trained and much more experienced.

Her every strike forced Angeni farther and farther away from Nicolas. Fear shone in his eyes as the demented crowded around him, but had not yet struck. They simply kept Nicolas contained in the brightest corner.

As Angeni spun away from a deadly strike, she saw that the pipe smoking old man's place was vacated, as if bored of the fight. But where was he? And who was he? Maybe he was a demented soul like Lilis, and everyone else in this forsaken place. Her spirit was prepared to fight against two, but the mysterious old man never came. Only Lilis' burning red crystal blade came, which just thrummed past her ear as she came out of the spin.

The guardian united her hilt fast to block when the Matriarch's blade hit the sapphire blade with such tremendous force that it kicked the golden grip out of the guardian's hand. The glowing aura blade dissolved as the noble weapon's grip glinted and flipped in the air above and behind the guardian. A deadly slash just passed in front of Angeni when with a desperate large flap of her large wings, the fragile woman pushed backward into the air toward the spinning grip. With unflinching determination, Lilis pulled her blade back for the next strike.

Angeni's hand caught the grip in midair; the glowing dual sapphire blades came alive while she arched toward the floor. As her feet felt the ground, almost spraining her ankle from the impact, she spun around and her crystal blade grated against the next deadly strike. Yet again, the ruby blade pulled back and struck.

A giant flap of her wings gave Angeni greater forward momentum after she leaned back from the quick jab. Terrified, Angeni watched Lilis' deadly red blade pass right over her head and swung further to bite into a pillar where the main aqueduct divided in two above the bath. Like quicksilver, dark red crystallization spread out from the scar across the column's live moss surface to quickly cover the pillar.

Lilis struck with the same ferocity with the other side of her dual-blade, but the sapphire blades blocked it once again, as Angeni twisted herself out of the spin. The momentous unrestrained blade fight between the two women raged between the columns of the hall. The weapons continuously changed shape, the blades crackled and screamed as they connected.

The hell-hot blade seared her silky skin as Angeni leaned away from Lilis' sudden stab that passed near her ear, and then pulled back fast. The spreading ruby ate at the column, a crack soon followed. Behind Lilis, the pillar exploded into thousands of fragments from the heavy weight. The aqueduct that it held up shifted and swayed. The twanging restraining chains couldn't hold the full weight of the heavy stone sections and water.

But the battle didn't stop. Desperate, Angeni leaned away from the quick stabs that came faster and faster. With a thunderous roar that overshadowed the crystalline clash of the blades, one end of the aqueduct section dropped as its chains snapped. The aqueduct segments fell behind them one by one, quickly pulling the other segments down from the ceiling. Icy water flooded the floor and waterfalls spurted from the cracked segments. Lilis pushed until Angeni was under the last section of the aqueduct. The collapse rushed closer and closer to them.

Sapphire and ruby blades crossed as the next section smashed to the floor so close, followed by the groan of the last section that overshadowed the guardian. Confused and desperate, Angeni couldn't decide where to focus; on her enemy, or the aqueduct about to fall from above. It quickly became clear that each action of her enemy was well calculated, and she had let the Matriarch force her into this choice.

The stone aqueduct above Angeni cracked with a reverberation that echoed around the hall. It trembled as it began to shake loose, and then come loose with the pull of the fallen sections. Angeni spun backward and tried to hold her flaring wings close to her back while the Matriarch suddenly stopped.

The last chains that held the heavy aqueduct segment snapped just as Angeni spun out from under the deadly shadow. The heavy segment and free flowing water fell between them with a thunderous crash. The marble floor shattered to cover everything with dust and water. The waterfall that poured into the hall from the top of the building to fill the aqueduct now poured the frigid water over the two celestial beings. At an impasse, they each lowered her weapons and watched the other over the flowing water that separated them.

A glare of hatred beamed from flashing sapphire eyes as they watched the blurry demon behind the newly formed waterfall, the downpour did nothing to cool her temper. Water drops crystallized ruby and sapphire as they touched the glowing crystal blades. Small red and blue crystal fragments bounced and tinkled on the remains of the marble tiles that the deluge of cold water hadn't quite reached.

"I hope you regain your self-possession now, my child," Lilis' nature defying kind motherly tone chided. "And now, you'll listen."

"We don't have anything to say to each other," Angeni glared through the waterfall.

"We are the same," Lilis answered. "We were friends, two equal souls as one not long ago. Why can't we live in peace?" she asked softly, almost desperately.

"We're not one. How dare you, demon?" Angeni's superior inflection railed while her wings soaked up cold water. Her hands held motionless blades tighter, discipline ruled her being. As she had been taught, she stepped left from under the waterfall. The matriarch followed her carefully, but kept her distance. The blurred face and red eyes of the demon watched her through the deluge of water separating them.

"I'm so disappointed, Angeni. You show yourself to be a caring being, saying words that sound so noble, but everything is an illusion embraced by emptiness. Everything you've told me was a lie, even the promise you made moments ago," Lilis retorted spitefully. Her words jabbed harder than any crystal blade, but Angeni didn't show it on her face.

"I didn't know what you were. But I do now, deceiver," Angeni countered defiant and determined, but deep in her soul she knew the demon was right.

"When your soul is happy, my soul is happy. When your soul cries, my soul cries. When you laugh, I also laugh. When your eyes drop tears, my eyes drop tears. When you are friendly, I also am friendly. So, when you want to kill me, I want to kill you. What makes the true difference between us, Aserian? What?" Lilis asked softly, carefully studying the young guardian who did the same.

"You're a murderer, killing innocents," Angeni's instinct dictated while she watched the matriarch's hand tightened her grip. "I know everything about you! I saw what you are!"

"A distorted image built from the endless hatred and prejudice which embraced your whole life," Lilis appealed calmly while she shook her head. "You were the one who raised a crystal blade against me, just as you hypocrite Aserians have always done against my kind throughout history. If I wanted to hurt you, both of you would be dead already."

From the corner of her eye, Angeni saw that Nicolas was still surrounded, but other than he was scared to death of the blade still pushed to his throat by the charming dancer, he was apparently unharmed. "As a guardian of mankind, I swear I won't let you destroy Eecrys Aredia for your blind belief," the Matriarch continued.

"You're bringing darkness and suffering to Eecrys Aredia," Angeni whispered in soft surprise as Lilis' words sunk in. "You bring destruction to this beautiful paradise! Not me!"

"Why would I destroy my home, Aserian?" asked Lilis quietly.

"No," came the denial from Angeni who eyed the demon through the waterfall. "How dare you? Eecrys Aredia never was your home," she hissed furiously, defying the blasphemy. She held her blade tighter, but her strong spirit ordered obedience to not strike first, otherwise the argument would be lost, an argument that may cost her life, as Old Shen forever taught her.

"The blind believer will never listen to words, but must learn from experience," the old woman chuckled to herself, like someone who realized something. "So the Messenger of the Sacred Mother said; an elder may stop you, another may kill your soul," Lilis whispered, and then spoke up. "I have walked my path. I do not want to change, my child. I know what your Angeni soul will become in its blind belief; the destroyer of Eecrys Aredia, Aserian, and Shaina alike." Lilis held her grips much tighter hearing a small degree of desperation in her tone. She prepared to strike, so the young guardian felt. "I'm not willing to kill you, Angeni, but in the name of the Sacred Mother I will stop you," she decreed while her eyes flashed red. "I'm so sorry, my child."

The ruby aura flashed and embraced the Matriarch's entire body; a bright flash and she disappeared. The falling water exploded into Angeni's face.

The illusive time slowed all around Angeni to show her every detail of this deadly, but seemingly magnificent moment. The red blade sliced through the waterfall followed by the striking demon. The slow water drops hissed on the blade's hot surface before they lost their liquid shape to turn into solid ruby crystal. The tiny fragments bounced down from the striking blade to start their fall before they plopped into the water at their feet. Although the moment seemed endless, it happened within a blink of an eye. As the ruby blade came closer and closer a glowing sapphire blade came up to defend her being from the deadly strike. A sweet clink and the two crystal blades met, forcing her mind to drop out of the enchanting trance.

The Matriarch's eyes glared red rage as the blades held for a seemingly eternal moment before they were drawn back fast to collide again. Under the falling water, the battle between the Sapphire Guardian and the Matriarch now raged unrestrained. Each swing sliced through the waterfall, and scattered crystallized drops around them.

Angeni didn't let the demon control the fight anymore. Belief and will of survival gave her strength while the crystal blades clashed and crackled. The guardian defended herself and waited for the right moment to end this battle.

The deadly ruby blade shattered the air toward her head, but the guardian leaned away just in time. Her cheek felt the burning heat as the blade passed, and then pulled back to strike again. Angeni had doubts that she could keep up this pace much longer, she trembled inside, and her muscles continuously overextended with the strength of the Shaina Matriarch's strikes. Her spirit couldn't order discipline anymore; her rebellious soul and tired body needed to end this fight.

The menacing deadly blade flew toward her, aimed right between her eyes. The Sapphire Guardian leaned away, feeling the heat on her forehead as the blade jabbed. Enough! Angeni reunited her sapphire blades as she spun, her flaring wings sliced toward the Demon Matriarch. They sprayed the mass of water that they soaked up and had slowed her down, were now liberated. Angeni had seen Lilis pull her blade back and step away to dodge Angeni's wings. She shifted to one side, where Angeni wanted her.

But as she spun and showed her back to the Matriarch, doubt and fear flared in her spirit that chilled her entire existence. If she were mistaken, she wouldn't come out of this spin alive, an eternal mistake of a young fool, inexperienced and unfortunately, impatient and stubborn Aserian Guardian. She, who trained so hard, but never heeded advice, lived only to spin into a painful death and fall in her very first battle.

She remembered how many times she had imagined what fighting demons would be like. She never thought that someone she trusted and liked, even for a short time could turn out to be her most deadly enemy. Everything seemed so easy in her dreams. So easy, but in reality she couldn't defeat one, never mind the hundreds she had faced as Eriana, a true master of the crystal blade in those dreams. It was clear, the Matriarch played with her. The young daydreaming guardian was no match for the experienced old demon. Unlike her fairy tale heroine, Angeni's good and noble soul wasn't ready for a real fight.

She didn't want to die. She wanted to live, so desperate for one more moment, just one more. Her body trembled in fear and waited for the deadly pain that would slice into her body any moment. But the pain never came.

Coming out of the deadly spin, she snapped her eyes back at Lilis to see that the demon's blade didn't streak toward her. Her fear and doubt suddenly dissolved as her blade came around, her large white wings snapped behind her back to not leave herself vulnerable. The moment she desired to live would become the last the Matriarch would live. The Sapphire Guardian pushed her blade determined and strong toward the demon. The old woman's eyes slowly closed like she wanted to embrace death.

Matriarch Lilis screeched as the icy sapphire blade ripped through her chest. The demon's muscles stiffened as her skin began to quickly crystallize outward from the wound. Her eyes flashed blood red. A dark scream left the throat of a dying soul as the demon woman dropped to her knees. The demented blade fell from her cramped hand and the golden hilt splashed and bounced on the floor while the last measure of aura faded and the weapon closed.

Lilis snatched Angeni's hand so tight to make her feel the agony she felt. Hope, a shred of compassion, pride, sorrow and a tiny bit of love lived in this dark soul; love for her people, which she feared and love for her home. And an endless fear not from death, from her, the Sapphire Guardian; the evil destroyer that she may become, so Lilis deeply believed.

I can't kill you, but I hope I stopped you, the Matriarch's thoughts came through while the crystallization reached the hand that gripped Angeni tighter. The screaming old woman gathered her strength to look into her eyes to share the last, somehow peaceful thoughts with her. *See and live, I beg you; save yourself to save us all. May Kasdaye kill your soul if I have failed.*

Angeni shivered at the old demon's last thoughts. All the darkness in the Matriarch slowly faded as the crystallization infused the dead body and encased the demonic soul.

"You'll not use the name of the Sacred Mother again to justify your lies," Angeni whispered, harshly, she overflowed with fury and hate.

A fallen enemy is not an enemy anymore, but a desperate soul trapped in a fragile crystal prison waiting to return to the Sacred Mother, High-Guardian Michael had taught. A soft sigh left her lips as she took a final glance at the silent defeated demon; a tiny shred of sorrow in her soul for the woman who was so friendly and kind moments ago, like a true mother, and also her mortal enemy, now dead.

The Sapphire Guardian spun for one last noble strike to set the trapped soul free. Her large wings flared and rose as they passed above the silent Matriarch. Her golden grip glittered in the air as it filled with the deadly sapphire aura to come alive once again. Like ice breaks into slivers, the lifeless ruby statue exploded in a thousand pieces as the relentless sapphire blade struck with tremendous power. As the crystal pieces bounced on the floor, they cried final respect for the defeated imprisoned soul that had finally been set free to rest in peace for all eternity.

Nicolas! She looked back realizing she had committed the greatest mistake a guardian can make, leaving her protected one alone, and in grave danger.

"She killed her. She wanted to save us all, and she killed her. Killer. Senseless Aserian killer," whispered dismay struck Angeni as the people around Nicolas stared in shock at the young guardian. Tears filled the dancer's eyes as she stood away from Nicolas.

"Angeni!" helpless and desperate, Nicolas shouted as two men grabbed him and held him down while the other demented citizens around him sprouted weapons seemingly from out of nowhere. They were hidden in plain sight, merged into the surroundings like they were part of the temple and its objects; under the cushions, or near the candelabra in the shadows as if they were a part of it. Old sickles, scythes, hatchets, tools so innocently designed to help people now glinted deadly in the lightning lit hall.

"His death will be your failure, Aserian!" the dancer cried. Her dagger shone as she prepared to take revenge for the Matriarch. Too far away, shocked by her mistake and bound by the invisible curse, the young guardian knew she couldn't do anything but watch. The woman's blade shot into the air. Terrified, Nicolas looked into her beautiful, seductive eyes, too late knowing what her true motives were.

A recognizable whistle shattered the air. Purple and a green arrows bit into the marble tiles between Nicolas and the demented ones. The dancer stepped back as the ground started to crystallize in a small radius, and the surface turned to dust to reveal raw earth beneath.

Everyone looked up to the six Aserians who stood along the side balconies in glowing battle armour, their majestic crystal bows aimed at the demented souls. An errant breeze ruffled their large wings; their faces calm, emotionless and unreadable. Another arrow appeared in Kien and Jared's hands as they cocked and aimed once again at the milling demented ones below.

"Leave him be!" Kien's strong voice broke the silence as his eyes flashed purple. But Angeni felt his hidden fear. The fearful thoughts of all the Aserians crashed into her mind;

What are they doing? Who are these people? How did they even think of this? all of their thoughts echoed almost at once, but none of their emotions were visible on their icy faces as they aimed their arrows at the demented.

I won't hurt anyone. Never, came the last thought, Aurora's.

You don't have to, because we won't fight, Angeni thought determined while she forced her mind to keep the rest of their thoughts away. "Let him go!" she ordered the demented with her powerful angelic voice.

"We won't obey a killer," a man hissed with burning hatred. Still held down, Nicolas stared terrified at the dagger the exotic dancer handled a few steps away from him.

"Leave peacefully. We're not here to fight any of you," the guardian offered. Her voice softened as she continued, "We must bury the hatchet if we wish to live in peace."

"This hatchet awaits you, Aserian," said another, who hefted his hatchet in irony.

The sapphire blades suddenly went lifeless in Angeni's hands as they closed.

285

"No," her angelic voice came soft and determined. "None of us will fight the other."

"It won't be your choice," the dancer's sweet voice purred while her hand held the tiny dagger. Her eyes turned the darkest black for a moment, announcing whoever she had been; she was not that person anymore. Raising their weapons, the demented took one step ahead while the Aserians aimed at them from the balcony. Angeni had read from their eyes they would not fire, they would not kill. The light caught on the beautifully chiselled dagger and reflected in Nicolas' desperate eyes as the exotic woman raised it. The young guardian realized; she had made a fatal mistake by hesitating.

The glass ceiling suddenly exploded into the hall. Everyone looked up and braced themselves as sharp fragments shattered on the marble accompanied by an old Aserian, gliding down with open wings to land among the demented ones. The Prince pushed his captors away, and scrambled to get as far as he could away from them. The large old wings stretched and threatened while deadly sapphire blades opened in his hands. A feather floated silent in the air. While he slowly straightened up, his wings relaxed against his back. Angeni knew and recognized him; Eosh.

You must fight if you wish to redeem their souls, his old thoughts addressed her while the demented skittered a step back from him, growling their hatred, they completely forgot about Nicolas.

"No," Angeni whispered and stepped forward to follow her soul's desire. "We will not harm these people! This ends now!" Her eyes flashed sapphire to show her determination.

"As the demon said, it won't be your choice," Eosh's old, tired voice replied softly without emotion. The terrified, shocked thoughts of the Aserians broke into her mind once again;

But demons are just myth. It can't be. Angeni was right all along. They're not a legend, their desperation echoed when she finally shoved all their voices away. She saw the fear in the eyes of the young Aserians. What they had heard and seen now dissolved all their doubts and convinced the beliefless, just as her father had said.

Like a hunter, the old Aserian watched the demented people edge closer. The sapphire blades patiently steamed like ice, motionless, prepared. The old eyes reflected the deadly tools that waved in the hands of the demented as they stepped closer. Then metallic gold glinted as Nicolas' sleeping blade appeared from under the robes of a demented man.

The old Aserian immediately spun and struck at the man first without hesitation. The deadly blade jabbed into the chest of the first victim. The golden hilt bounced on the marble floor as screaming in pain, the man had dropped it. Burning red garnet started to spread from the wound as the blade pulled back fast while Eosh spun once again as the rest roared and attacked him. The sapphire blades struck relentless, passing through their weapons, turning them to dust before it struck into their soft flesh.

Shocked, Angeni's eyes barely kept up as watched the demented souls quickly succumb one after another. A deadly orchestra of the fallen, desperate voices sang of excruciating pain. Their shattered crystals bounced with hollow echoes on the marble floor. Disappointment infused, her young soul had wanted peace and now all of them would die by the hand of the old Aserian. He fought so majestic and deadly; a true master of the crystal blade, just like the fallen Matriarch. His age didn't hamper his skill. Watching him, Angeni realized she never had a chance against Lilis. But then how did she survive? How did she defeat her? Maybe the Sacred Mother watched over her and guided her hand. Maybe.

Shocked, Tlanextic slowly lowered his bow first. Then the others followed his example one by one. Angeni held her golden grip tighter, she wanted to end this senseless killing, but she did nothing, just watched stunned.

Please, don't hurt the humans! Please! she heard Aurora's crying thought horrified by the death of these people and she wasn't alone. A rolling tear sparkled on little Taze's cheek as she looked away to not see while Iris shook her head bewildered. The fear in strong Kien's eyes matched Jared's eagerness to stop the killing. Their eyes described all their conflicting emotions, even if it didn't show on their face. Motionless, they watched the massacre in dismay from the balcony as the old Sapphire Guardian butchered those who never had a chance against him. He battered and sliced all of them one by one standing between him and Nicolas. Increasingly tiny crystals skittered across the floor.

As the deadly blades shattered a black tourmaline statue of a fallen man, something metallic and shiny glinted, spinning fast toward Nicolas. The glowing crystal shield clinked in Eosh's hand as it came alive. Two tiny daggers fell harmless to the marble floor before they had a chance to reach the Prince. The old Aserian lowered the shield, snapping his attention to the last demented one. The dancer stood a few dozen steps away as the elder already marched toward her, relentless with not a hint of emotion on his icy face.

"No. Please don't. Please don't hurt me," the dancer's voice trembled so desperate as she backed away, quickly turned, and tried to run away.

The golden grips glistened in the dim light as the old Aserian spun them in his hands, the shield and blade closed while the hilts reunited with one gentle move. Sapphire blades shot out from both sides of the hilt. So fast, Angeni couldn't even see it, the blades folded back while an energy string materialized between the two tips. The will of the old Aserian gave life to a crystal arrow between his fingers as he cocked and aimed. The arrow already split the air to hit the escaping dancer in the back. A scream so horrifying echoed as she fell to the marble floor. Obsidian raced to swallow her beautiful silky body spreading out from the wound. After a time, the painful death scream faded as the crystallization consumed the woman.

Eosh stopped beside the horrified, silent statue of the fallen one. The sapphire blade sliced the air and struck hard and merciless, shattering the once beautiful woman into thousands of pieces. As the tinkle of the last crystal fragment faded away the deadly blades finally closed. The old Aserian's emotionless eyes reflected the obsidian splinters.

May your soul rest in peace, Rana, a grandfatherly pain echoed in Angeni's mind. *Sorry I couldn't protect you,* his deep regret came through; regret Angeni couldn't see on his tired, cold old face. Standing among the thousands of shattered crystals the old Aserian clipped his silent blade to his belt. The splinters silently cried disturbed as he picked up Nicolas' blade grip.

Angeni watched, silent and shocked as the elder Sapphire Guardian approached her. An Aserian who killed humans that he was supposed to protect; what kind of guardian is he?

Please don't despise me, my child, the old Aserian's tired thoughts addressed Angeni as he stepped up to her. The young guardian looked away; she didn't want to look into his eyes.

"I might have been able to save them," she whispered sadly. Eosh sighed heavily as he looked deep into her eyes. His soul's pain and regret rested there.

"I wish you could, but no one can save them anymore," he said with his old, grandfatherly voice. "I only redeemed their souls, which burnt them by darkness from the inside. They were already dead."

The young Aserians slowly wakened from the shock. Silent, they spread their wings and jumped down from the balcony to join Angeni. Their wings stirred the air as they back flapped before they touched the ground in dead silence.

"You need to learn so much, young Angeni," the old Aserian quietly said to her.

"I do not wish to learn how to kill," responded Angeni almost silent and let out a calming sigh. She felt like she was in a nightmare from which she couldn't wake. But she knew everything was real and there was no room for disobedience.

"Don't ever drop your vigilance for the desire of seducing women," Eosh reprimanded the Prince, passing the silent crystal blade back to him.

"Thank you for saving my life," Nicolas said grateful.

The old Aserian nodded, then looked at the young guardian. "I'm also telling you this, young Angeni. Never leave your protected one alone," came his old tone. The young woman just bowed her head, knowing the great mistake she committed.

The young Aserians gathered around them with fear in their eyes, fear of old Eosh. But with a glance from the old Aserian all of them knew who he was and they need not be afraid of him.

"Time is short," the old Aserian said to them. "You must leave. Now," he ordered. The young Aserians looked surprised. Jared threw a quick bewildered glance at Angeni, who nodded to him slightly.

"No," Aurora's desperate whisper broke the tense silence.

"We're here to protect them," argued Kien.

"We won't leave them behind," Tlanextic was offended. The young Aserians nodded their determined agreement.

Your sister and your guardians are just like you, Angeni heard the old guardian's thoughts, who smiled with a touch of awe. *Just as my beloved daughter told me. Faithful and loyal, brave Aserians in soul. But all so very young.*

"Where they go, we go," Jared was brave and determined as he looked at Angeni. The young guardian knew the imperative voice was addressed for her; he won't leave her behind. Eosh smiled.

"You remind me of my own protector and friend, Israfil," he said, stepping to Jared.

"The one who defeated Marchosias?" Kien asked, amazed while Jared challenged the old Aserian with his look.

"But that was many millennia ago, Master Eosh. How is it possible?" Iris wondered.

"The past doesn't really matter now. Only the present and the future count," Eosh responded with a kind smile. "You know my protector from our history. What you don't know about him is that he knew when he had to leave me behind. He knew when our path must be separated and when we must be united."

Angeni felt that she must make the final call and Eosh awaited this from her. She stepped to Jared, and then looked at the others.

"Never consider that it is expedient for us. This time the need of the one must be sacrificed, so others may live," Angeni quoted her determined father. As she looked at Jared, her eyes flashed sapphire. A moment of restrained denial filled the hall.

"I understand," Jared finally nodded with respect.

Eosh looked at the youngest guardian who still hesitated; her eyes showed her desire to go with her beloved sister to protect her and to be protected.

"You need not worry, young Aurora," caring, like a true grandfather, he looked into her eyes. "I will protect your sister," he said.

"But--" Aurora started, but Eosh raised his hand.

"No, my child. This journey is only for them," he said. "You must tell everyone what you've seen, the darkness you have witnessed. You must ensure the safety of the others, as well assure that everyone will learn what has transpired here," Eosh looked at the young Aserians as he continued, "Young brothers and sisters in arms, watcher over and defend each other. Reach the border of Arabah and ask the guidance of the Segaran Viras. They'll help you reach all provinces to warn everyone in time. Tell them to prepare to defend their safe haven as well as ours as the time has come. Don't hesitate, don't delay, my children. Go, now," he commanded.

"We will do as you order," Kien confirmed. Jared nodded along with the others in their agreement.

"Please take care of her," Aurora's whisper was full of love.

"I will. I promise."

* * *

The paved and masterfully chiselled marble hallway led deeper and deeper under the Temple of Salvation slowly turned into a harsh and soggy rocky cave-like corridor. Sleepy dripping stones danced motionless in dim sapphire light that shone from Eosh's hand as he lit the path ahead of them. Cold water that had found a new way out of the flooded hall peacefully trickled under their feet as it discovered the dark path along with the three souls. Damp, moist air that hadn't carried any voice for a long time now echoed the distorted tone of the trespassers.

"Those people, what took hold of them?" asked Nicolas.

"Yfrit spirit demons, night shades," the old Aserian answered. "The cruellest and most vicious of all. It's breeding in humans with tempting words and sinister actions, re-shaping the soul itself."

"Do not speak of evil for it creates curiosity in the hearts of the innocent," Angeni quoted one of her father's proverbs. The old Aserian's nod confirmed before he continued.

"Words are much more destructive than any weapon that touches a soul," he said. "Purring words of a demon are always used to confuse and shake belief. They use perceived weakness of the strong, weak, wise and naive alike. They're breeding desire, temptation, conflict, and hate that may overwhelm any sanity. Capable of killing the innocent Jinni spirit in anyone, leaving only darkness in the soul. Evil soon takes control over them."

Eosh glanced at Angeni as he continued, "Demons will use every trick to turn you against humans or even each other. They're even willing to sacrifice themselves just to achieve their goal."

Those strange last words of the Matriarch still haunted the young guardian, but the words of the old Aserian finally calmed her spirit.

"Always use faith as your shield against their words," Eosh advised.

"How did the good vanish in them? Why can't we save them?" asked Angeni so quiet and desperate.

"Evil cannot be killed in a soul once it has tasted darkness," the grandfatherly voice responded. "Every soul is like a candle light in the darkest night. When light dies only the memorable darkness remains," Eosh's sorrow echoed in his voice. "Only the strongest willed human may give new life, a new light to their own souls. But their conscience will never let them live in peace. They can't hide from the darkness of how they lived, what they did, and every thought. Many who couldn't live with the thought, took their own lives, even the life of their entire family and friends in the fear they had spread the evil to their loved ones." The elder guardian sighed as they walked deeper into the cave corridor. "Without the desire to change, the evil spirit demon will never let the good one be reborn."

"For them, there is no redemption," Angeni realized. Eosh nodded.

"The temptation is always stronger than the desire to change," Nicolas mused.

"Every soul can break by feeling the power, the temptation," the old Aserian continued matter-of-factly. "First regrets vanish to slowly be replaced by desire. For them there is no way to turn back. And evil spreads like wildfire as sinister words breed these demons in other souls as well."

"Every soul?" asked Nicolas.

"There is good and evil in every soul, maybe even in us, Aserians," old Eosh continued. "All souls are the children of the one. We're different, yet we're the same."

"We're the same," Angeni remembered what Lilis had said, but then she quickly tried to dismiss all her words. "Where did they come from?" she asked. Her soul wanted answers; there were only questions in her restless spirit. "Why can't we use our power here? What is that strange storm above Aysdemera?" she paused for a moment, looking at Eosh. "Is the Crystal Shade really here?" she summarized all her questions. Her tone was troubled saying the name of the most dreaded legend that amazed her and she respected, but her entire existence was awash in fear. Eosh smiled at her.

"You remind me of my beloved daughter, who took up the same questions when we walked here ages ago," Eosh remembered with fatherly pride. "Your curiosity is right and I would be very disappointed if you did not ask these questions. But be patient, young Angeni. Words can't describe what you must see and experience on your own."

"Where are the other Aserians?" asked Nicolas, but the old Aserian gave no answer. Silence spoke louder.

Strange insects, nothing like Angeni had ever seen before crawled in the small cracks as the sapphire light reached them. Their sinister souls betrayed just by looking at them. Black creatures with two claws and strange tails with a sharp needle at the very end of it tried to stay away from the light or stalked them motionless with their diminutive black eyes. And strange footless, long thin creatures crawled in their dark scales; the air slowly scented by their thin tongue, which darted out of its small mouth, making a sibilant sound.

"Stay away from them," Angeni quiet tone warned, feeling the evil inside them. The Prince immediately stepped aside from the creatures, like the ground burned his feet.

"Will they come after us?" Nicolas asked looking around, his hand rested on his blade, then suddenly he stepped to the left as another strange insect with dozens of legs appeared and raced along the wall right near him to disappear into a crack.

"Sooner or later they will," was Eosh's calm response. "But our destination is not theirs. Where they came from is where we're going."

"Why? Where are we going?" Angeni asked.

"There," Eosh said as the cave corridor slowly opened into a huge cavern, revealing the outline of large underground ruins of an ancient city asleep in the darkness. A large broken stone arch guarded its endless dream at the tall ledge. Dense white mist shifted everywhere, like a loving blanket embraced the old buildings. Water poured through various small furrows that it had restlessly dug out over the millennia to feed many broken aqueducts and flood other parts of the beautiful, if ruined old buildings. Silent conquerors, wild plants covered most of the cracked walls. Creepers, like veins ran through the whole city. Almost palpable darkness spread from the place and slowly oozed beyond the arch; the suppressed damned orchestra of crystal music and sad bassoon that still played restless and so soft, called from here.

Awed Guardian and Prince asked the same question in thought. Where are they, and what is this place?

"A mare of the last Crystal Shade, a haunting echo reaches out from the forgotten past; Mer Petraea," the old Aserian answered their silent question.

"The sacred ruins where light once emerged to defeat darkness," Angeni whispered enchanted. Eosh nodded. "And so, the dreaded shade must return," she started to quote the Stone of Origin as she stepped ahead to see the sacred place. "The ground opened and the wind blasted the dirt from the sacred ruins of Mer Petraea, revealing the tear of the Sacred Mother, which called and awakened every silenced soul."

A tired breeze touched Angeni's cheek when she stepped through the arched gates; the stroke of forgotten painful memories, darkness and death, which ruled Mer Petraea.

* * *

"At the gates of Mer Petraea her pearl rolled through a door opened for a long while. The past's echo waited for the young guardian along with the mist to embrace her, to never let her go," the old man sighed. He stared down at the Andrenian Septagon for a moment. Three facets each of light and darkness showed different pictures; heavenly life, happiness, salvation and infernal death, cruel suffering, and sorrow. But the last, the diamond facet glowed back innocent and empty. By the old man's touch the last stria filled with life; one side of it sapphire, other half ruby.

"The choice between light and dark, life and death. Tempting," he whispered. The old eyes reflected the silent chrono-device as he looked at it. "You're not making my life easier, are you, old friend?" he asked quietly. "Even if you do know I won't take sides, except the path which is never offered and no one can see." His determined whisper became a sigh as he looked back at the children, who watched and waited curiously.

"Our life is the mirror of the choices we make. Sometimes a good choice which may light our life is born from the echoing shade, the sorrowful experience of many wrong ones," he said with a soft sigh as he continued. "But sometimes the choice you believe to be right could be the worst of all, which could determine the rest of your life."

9 – FALSE LIKE A KIMAMA

"We never know what evil really is until we face it directly," the old man said.

"But she faced demons," insisted the little girl. "They're evil."

"Indeed," the old man appreciated her bravery. "But even if you believe you had seen what evil really is, sometimes you must realize there is always a greater one." He frowned at the enchanting chrono contraption in the middle of the floor. "At the very moment when you face the darkest shade, you'll realize what the breaking point of your existence truly is. Looking into its eyes, it will sear the spirit and shatter the soul so you never forget," he added with a broken heart, and then he looked at the children. "Sometimes the greatest evil is like your shadow, closer to you than you ever imagined."

* * *

Angeni felt the slippery moss-coated stones under her feet. Her eyes intent on her tiny sandals, they took small silent steps as she followed the dancing pale shadows of Eosh and Nicolas ahead of her. Torture of a terrified soul and a personal long path of hell, a thin stone path stretched ahead of her spanning above Mer Petraea; a hell that others simply called a bridge. More than a hundred steps and it's like they still strolled at the beginning of it. Where ever it led in the fog seemed farther after every step, so Angeni thought. Does this bridge have an end at all or does it span into eternity?

The vaporous air danced all around in thick white mist that lightly stroked her wings and skin while it revealed bits of the forgotten past all around. For her, every step revealed more ancient and decayed cobblestones of hell along with tufts of grass and moss. Everything was bathed in dim sapphire aura light that shone from Eosh's hand. Then a bar of shadow slid across the stones as they passed under an ancient arch. Her curiosity overtook her terrified soul and she looked up. Out of the mist, ancient runes and hieroglyphs covered the stone banisters and the walls of the arch. Echoes of a forgotten past had been engraved into the stone to share with the reader as they descend deeper and deeper in the heart of the ancient city, so Angeni believed.

She quickly snapped her attention back to the cobblestones. The last thing she cared about now was ancient knowledge or the grand view that surrounded them. The bridge was thin and ancient and the great depth called her. Seeing the condition of the ancient overpass, she was certain it would collapse under her. Before every step, she believed the next step would be the fatal one when the stones crumbled and the darkness would swallow her screaming being. Or the next one. But the ancient skyway was solid. For now.

The crashing torrent of the underground river that wildly flowed far below all around the ruined city called her with its perpetual rumble. In her mind, she imagined thousands of possibilities as she fell into the darkness followed by the debris of the collapsed stone bridge. She just prayed for one of the deep river channels to be right under her when the bridge finally gave out.

But she knew she wouldn't be that lucky. If she were, she would bounce off a sharp rock before the final splash. Then the ruins of the bridge would fall on top of her to cover her for all eternity. If there were no sharp rocks, the water would be shallow. A blunt splash, and then would come the rumbling debris grave.

As the countless vivid possibilities flashed into her terrified mind, she knew her chances were very slim if the ancient patchwork, after millennia of restless standing, simply lied down to rest. But nothing was enough to convince her to think otherwise, even if her soul knew she couldn't die from it. Just be buried alive for eternity. As she estimated, the bridge arched seventy-five steps above the ground, maybe more. That would give her enough time to scream louder than ever while she flashed back her young and beloved life three times before she reached the dark and sad place that would be her grave.

Her soul soon joined the inner rebellion that her slightly trembling legs and terrified spirit led under their flag united. The endless depth whispered for her to look down. The darkness laughed at her weakness. The mist gently swirled aside from time to time to show her, only her what waited below. That strange claustrophobic feeling that encased and weighed on her entire being just made it worse. It's not like the Spirit Sea could make it different, which was shallow at this cursed place, just like the churning river that awaited her terrified soul. Then after the next step, it felt like the playful wind would resurrect. In her terrified mind, she already had seen the wind gently embrace her body, playing with her feathers and wings; then a friendly gust, a push, and screaming as she already plunged down beyond the ledge. Yet, only a soft breeze moved to caress her face.

She just wanted to know which sentence, which word of Eosh's convinced her to take the short way, instead of the safe, low ground path that snaked down below. The old Aserian first didn't even believe she feared heights. He'd lived for so long, but never met any Aserian who feared it. Then a pleasant smile from the old Aserian, some kind words, a nod full of pride from her, and then she found herself marching along the ancient patchwork.

Why her pride beat out her fear to make it look like she could defy her acrophobia, she didn't know. She'd never been able to do that for herself. Since they were now in the middle of the bridge, it didn't much matter, regardless how many times she thought back to the last moments she spent on safe ground. There were only three ways to go; ahead, back, or over the edge where her sharp rocks and favourite shallow river waited. She was sure at the middle of the arch all three would have the same distance to solid ground. But for her, the greatest distance was between the bridge and the dark cruel depths. Her terrified soul knew with the help of the ancient bridge, that she would be forced to take the long path below.

The whole journey on the bridge from hell fanned her inner rebellion with each step. Drawn by the depths, she felt the urge to run down the bridge and jump into the chasm just to finally be free of this endless fear. But her eyes focused on the cobblestones while she controlled her trembling legs and held her wings tight to not obey the call of the depths. She kept her self-control. Barely.

Tight-lipped, and grim, Angeni took the steps one after another but her terror didn't show on her cool continence, not even in her eyes. She glanced up once again to see the end of the bridge, but she had seen only the path of hell leading into more infernal mist. Eosh looked back at her. From his eyes, she knew the old Aserian was proud of her; this was the only thing that calmed her three-fold existence a bit in her internal hell. It seemed Eosh was also amused about her fear, but hid it very well. Then the young guardian looked down once again to watch her *favourite* cobblestones, which like an endless orderly army, marched under her feet.

"So ancient and beautiful," Angeni heard Nicolas' awe which broke the silence from time to time, but she just forced her eyes to not look at the great view. "How did you hide this place from everyone?" he asked fearlessly while Angeni had seen as his dancing shadow ahead of her look down at the silent sleeping ruins below.

"Every citizen of Aysdemera knew of this place, but its horrifying legend kept them away," Eosh responded. "Only few dared to ever come deep below. Those few became the protectors of Mer Petraea," he paused. "Brave souls, who all gave their lives that night to protect this place from darkness. I wasn't able to save them, only kill them," his grim voice whispered.

Silence fell as they strolled further. Once again, Angeni was left alone with her marching cobblestone army. One came after another, but then they slowly started to take on a dark red pulsating light. And it became brighter and brighter after each step. The dancing dim shadows of Eosh and Nicolas suddenly stopped in front of Angeni.

The young guardian stopped and looked up to see the source of the bright red light, but foremost to learn how long her torture would be. But the bridge ended few steps ahead of her in a large sanctuary on the top of a large rock mountain that loomed from the center of Mer Petraea. Eleven vine wrapped columns surrounded the sanctuary; an angel statue guarded each of them. Carvings, symbols, and hieroglyphs told their stories silently all over the vegetation free wall opposite the end of the bridge. The entire hall centered on that horizontal and flat circular plate, full of carved regular lines; a large shiny seal embedded in the ground. Like a bleeding tired heart, it pulsed a menacing dark red. Angeni knew she had seen it before. When or where, she didn't know. The *seal* caused both fear and respect in her soul.

"What is this place?" the young guardian asked while she hurried to the safe, solid ground drawn by the beautiful ancient sanctuary. Within, she praised the Sacred Mother that she had kept the path of hell intact under her beloved little soul. Feeling the ground under her feet, her spirit and soul relaxed, but her ears awaited the rumbling sound of irony, as the bridge would collapse now that all of them left it behind. However, it never happened.

"Where the past, present and future meet in one place," Eosh answered as they moved deeper into the sanctuary. "Eecrys Sacreren, the Crystal Gate, the Tear of the Sacred Mother," Eosh said. "One of the twelve most sacred places on Eecrys Aredia." The old Aserian leaned closer to Angeni. "Close your eyes and listen," he whispered.

Angeni closed her eyes, but heard only a very soft crystal chime echo in her mind different than the one that called them here. It thrummed louder and louder. It reminded her of the clearest flute; a chiming voice that trickled like a waterfall where crystals flowed instead of water into a large crystal lake. It was kind and pleasant; caressing her soul like a loving mother cups her child's cheek, enchanting Angeni with every variation.

"It's so beautiful," she whispered, opening her eyes the soft crystal chime slowly faded to a soft reminder in her mind. "Where is it coming from? Whose magnificent voice is this?"

"It's the voice of the Sacred Mother," Eosh whispered. "She is calling us through her tear and also warns us of the approaching darkness of the Crystal Shade."

"How did darkness start to spread?" Angeni asked quietly.

"Ask the tear itself. It will tell you," Eosh added while he gently took Angeni's hand and led her to the cold crystal surface of the pulsating gate. "For the tear there is no time. It witnessed everything and it will gladly tell you who brought darkness to Eecrys Aredia."

As her delicate hand touched the gate, an extraordinary power spread through her existence. Like a living being, the gate revealed its past in her mind to tell what rankled this old, tired heart. A sudden flash and the crystal gate that reflected her curiosity pulsated in dim, peaceful sapphire under her feet. Angeni looked up.

Everything seemed so surreal and dream like. Eosh and Nicolas were gone. The misty soft blanket gently shifted around the sanctuary. A dark silhouette stood in the middle of the large crystal seal with his back to her. Angeni cautiously approached him from behind. As she tried to look into his face, the silhouette looked away as he raised his hand high.

The young guardian looked up at his hand where a tiny diamond crystal refracted light into her eyes. It was so familiar; she had seen this somewhere, but where? And that claustrophobic and soft torpid feeling, the strange force encased her being and took hold of her entire existence. It was so strong.

The crystal became brighter and brighter, it enchanted Angeni with its light. The sapphire glow under her feet flickered, and then beat faster and faster. Angeni looked down at the man; finally, she saw his face and looked into his eyes. She knew him, even if she couldn't read his soul with a glance. He was that mysterious hooded stranger from her dreams, the one who always guided her; at least so she believed.

As it pulsed, the sapphire gate changed to spinning hell red. Desperate, Angeni looked around while the crystal music and that menacing bassoon chime rang in her head, commanding hundreds of red, black and other sinister coloured orbs to rise from the crystal surface all around the stranger. Demented screams filled the sanctuary. Evil and darkness oozed from the small demonic orbs; the same that glowed from below, beamed from hell itself.

Terrified of an evil she never experienced before, Angeni reefed her hand off the surface of the gate and crashed back to reality to hyperventilate in sheer panic.

"Why did you do this? What evil have our people done against you? What?" her lips begged for answer with hatred and great dismay.

"Do you know him?" Eosh asked with surprise as he felt Angeni's torrent of feelings. The young guardian nodded while she slowly calmed down.

"He is," she paused to bite down her ire. "He is an old Aserian who guards me in my dreams, he watches over me. At least I believed he did," she whispered looking at the Prince.

"No, that's impossible. Why would he do this?" Nicolas said bewildered, while Eosh looked curiously at the young guardian.

"Angeni. Whoever you believe him, whoever he appears to be in your dreams, he never was your guardian." He looked deep into the young woman's eyes. "If he were an Aserian, he wouldn't be able to open the gate to hell. No Aserian can."

Stunned, Angeni stayed silent. She didn't know what to believe anymore.

"Is he a demon?" the Prince asked after a short moment.

"Maybe the last demon of Briniu Malgram," confirmed Eosh.

"What was in his hand?" Angeni asked, while her mind desperately searched her memories for where she had seen that diamond crystal.

"A morsel of the Sacred Mother's tear; the crystal key," Eosh responded darkly. "A seal to heaven and hell, a key to life and death, a dark keeper of silent secrets."

"The will of the Sacred Mother," Angeni whispered. The old Aserian nodded. "Mother said there are twelve places where this mute and shy power rules. Are there twelve keys?"

"Once in the past, twelve teardrops were born of twelve tears to keep balance; twelve teardrops gave life to this world," Eosh answered. "In the hands of good, they sang to heaven. In the hands of evil, they whispered to hell. But in time, all but one teardrop vanished, destroyed. As some legends say; the last demons of Briniu Malgram and their servants destroyed them to strip Eecrys Aredia of almost all heavenly life. But they spared one crystal key as they knew, just as they can give life, even one can control all the gates to heaven and hell; even one can bring darkness to Eecrys Aredia in the next Crystal Shade."

The old Aserian let out a ragged sigh.

"But the spirit of the other eleven still rules, their shattered bodies dispersed, buried throughout our lands. Even in their death, the mighty power of their spirit still rules all of the realms. Even in their death they still echo and reach us to rule from the forgotten past, just as they also reached you at the outskirts of Odess'iana," he whispered to Angeni. The young guardian sadly nodded, she knew one of these tears was the reason no one could protect the once young girl and her family.

"Who had the power to destroy these sacred artefacts?" bewildered, Nicolas wondered.

"There are no indestructible artefacts, only in the fairy tales," old Eosh smiled. "Like any crystal, the tears can be shattered easily. That's why we keep the last one safe; to keep Eecrys Aredia alive. But only my daughter knows where it is and where the last tear was the last night the gate was opened. She is the guardian of the last crystal tear."

Angeni looked up, finally realizing where she had seen it.

"It was with Mother in Andrenia, I saw it," she whispered, remembering when her beautiful Mother looked down at her during the Ceremony of the Foundation Day; the shiny crystal key, like an elegant, large pendant hung from her neck and refracted right into her eyes.

"Then another key must exist," Nicolas determined.

"Sounds so impossible after all this time, but that is the only logical explanation," Eosh agreed, and then the old Aserian frowned, his voice full of disappointment. "But then, this old Aserian also has been mistaken before. I also believed all my life that the shade of the Sacred Mother opened the gates to hell when the time comes," he took a soft sigh. "So many things have changed. So many," responded the old Aserian with deep sorrow.

"What is the Crystal Shade really?" the young guardian asked. Eosh hesitated to gather his thoughts.

"I've had time to meditate on this, but I still cannot give a simple answer to your question." He paused with a soft sigh. "Some days I believe it's the way of life itself with all its brilliance and shade. Other days, I believe it's an ancient fairy tale told so well everyone believes."

"Fairy tale?" Angeni frowned stricken; she never thought this old Aserian would commit blasphemy. She forced silence.

"A world, its history is always shaped by the words of the greatest storytellers," Eosh answered, and then looked at the Prince. "Some may be rulers with rank or lineage, but they all tell stories that others will remember. Good or bad, only time tells. Maybe that's how the legend of the Crystal Shade was born. A story shaped by words, so enchanting, giving the hope we desire and making us face all our fears. A tale everyone wanted to believe in and now, finally come true." The old Aserian smiled to himself while Angeni's intent eyes watched him. "This is just a strange fantasy of an old man who lived too much, my child. What I can say for sure; the Crystal Shade is the unavoidable change itself."

"Change?" Nicolas raised a dubious eyebrow.

"Regardless how hard you fight, how much you want to protect your loved ones, nothing and no one will be the same after the dawn of the Crystal Shade," the old Aserian's sorrow echoed in his voice. "Your

301

friends may become your greatest enemies, your loved ones may never see the next sunrise. Everything you ever knew, everything that you are could change within a moment. Just as you have seen already."

"But how can the Crystal Shade be here?" Angeni's desperation echoed. "Naamare doesn't shine on us and Briniu Malgram is also not visible, or wandering in the star trail."

Eosh's grandfatherly smile beamed at the young woman.

"I believe it would be better if the ancestors told this answer with their own words. Come," the old Aserian invited them to the walls covered with ancient hieroglyphs and writings; runes so ancient and strange, yet so familiar to the soul. The soft pulsating red light lit the young guardian as she crouched near the wall with Nicolas close behind her, studying the symbols, which were eager to tell the story of a long-long time ago. But they remained silent to Angeni's soul.

"I, I can't read them," she looked back with childish desperation. Eosh smiled kindly down at her.

"Because you're trying to find your world in the symbols instead of trying to understand them and their meaning," he said patiently. "Every word that a soul writes, another soul can read."

"The language of the soul," the young guardian whispered awed and Eosh kindly nodded.

"It has been the same since the beginning of time, yet many used different symbols to visualize the voice of the soul. You must feel to understand, see their meaning to read all of them."

"These symbols, even the words they shape are sounds and look like Andrenian," Nicolas said, stroking the runes one by one as he tried to read them. "But they're so ancient and different. I can't understand them."

"The ancient language is the one that can remember, a language that can tell," the old Aserian said grandfatherly. "Andrenian is the language of the soul, the oldest language from all the others ever born."

"Then why can't I read it?" asked the Prince curiously.

"Time, like every language, it has also changed and evolved. But the Andrenian language never forgets where it came from, always shows its noble and unique traits to every generation by its runes. Never forget; a world, a culture always lives in its language. This language never let it be forgotten."

Angeni looked back at the symbols; they still looked like the same ancient mystery to her.

"Open your soul to read and see the past," Eosh crouched near Angeni. He placed her hand on the stone wall.

Angeni slowly moved her palm to the first symbol. She cleared her open soul and focused as she tried to understand the echo of the forgotten ones. Then after a short time, the symbols began to silently whisper their meaning in her mind as her hand passed over the symbols; she couldn't understand how this was possible.

"We are," she whispered, reading the first symbol. "No. We were," she corrected as the symbols from right to left began to reveal their meaning in her being. She heard Eosh step back to leave her to read while her hand passed over the symbols one by one, silent and slow. As her hand passed over more symbols, her soul translated faster and more confident. A story so ancient, which happened dozens of millennia ago on a different world began to reveal itself. A soft cough came from behind her. The young guardian looked back to see Nicolas smiling at her.

"Oh, sorry," she whispered sheepishly, and began to read the symbols aloud from the beginning.

We were always proud, noble, daydreamers and caretakers. Nothing could stop us from reaching what our heart desired. Mer Gaea was our home, we never denied our beautiful world, but we knew our souls were born elsewhere. We followed our beliefs, the desire of our hearts and our souls. We followed the voice of the Sacred Mother that called to us in our dreams since the beginning of time through her pulsating crystal heart. Dreams led us; dreams to find the place where all of us originated.

We traveled faster and farther, spreading across our beautiful lands. Before long, we could see the day when our reachable continents would be exploited, and then there would be nowhere else to go. Then we reached out to the stars and swam among the waves of the silent sea. Our soul became one with the thousands of stars; finally one step closer to fulfilling our dream. One step closer to home. A small star reached a tiny one. It was so beautiful.

There was no one to stop us, so we believed. Many gave their lives to fulfill our dreams, but their sacrifice wasn't in vain. We kept their memories, learned from their mistakes and we never forgot them. We, the brave, swam further in the crystal garden to find the path toward the Sacred Mother, to find our way back home. But now, everything is only a painful memory.

In our desire to achieve our dreams that made the grand unity of our civilization, we forgot how to fear. The Reapers of Darkness were gone; we banished them generations ago, so our legends had said. We forgot; everything has a shadow we must fear. And the forgotten shade arrived. We couldn't avoid our fate. Horror descended among our once proud and noble people. Mer Gaea had seen the burning of Aredia Seli where only the voice of the dead echoed in the stormy red wind. We retreated to our home, the only place that always loved and protected us; even when we wanted to leave her behind to fulfill our dreams. We believed at home, we'd be safe. We believed they'd spare us. But we were mistaken.

Our beloved home couldn't protect us. The vanguard night crystal sadly watched as our beautiful civilization was annihilated by the darkness. They were evil, cruel, and relentless, struck us without mercy. But these were not like the ones the legends describe. They did not die. Our souls were crushed; tears filled our eyes as horror, senseless cruelty and endless pain embraced us. We saw our beautiful guiding star, Asria's eternal azure light extinguished within a blink of an eye. Just as our dreams were shattered and gone as they appeared. Our lands burned like hell and marked our unavoidable, sorrowful end.

Fear embraced us, crushed our fragile hearts. Trembling, we believed everything we lived for would vanish; our dream to find the sacred one will never be fulfilled. We believed life and great sacrifice of generations was in vain. But we were mistaken.

Our dream had been fulfilled in the ruthless horror and suffering while our beautiful civilization fell to ashes and the Reapers of Darkness spread across our lands. Mer Gaea was scorched and her dead shell was embraced by the silent darkness. As the night twilight in the Crystal Shade most of our souls returned to the Sacred Mother. Most of us reached our dream and returned home where we always desired to go.

There are few of us left. We know we will soon be gone. We can see our fate as we had seen the fate of others, as we had seen the fate of our home. Only we, a handful of keepers are left who once lived in the light, but now will be shrouded by darkness. Our memories will fade, will be unreachable and forgotten like a dream we always loved and always lived. Our achievements will vanish in the darkness, as we know it. A dream will stay in the light, but someday our legacy will awaken. We'll be here to light the lost hope when the shade arrives again.

The young guardian reached the last symbol; she lowered her head with a weary sigh.

"Who were these keepers?" Angeni asked looking at Nicolas. "Did the Aserian Guardians call themselves keepers in the past?" She was thoughtful as the forgotten past was revealed to her.

"They stepped out onto the crystal garden. But how?" Nicolas questioned. "What did they know that we don't?"

Angeni couldn't answer. She looked back at the symbols that echoed the past.

"Why would anyone ever want to leave their home?" she asked of herself in dismay. "We were born here, we live here, and we die here. Our home is our responsibility."

"The Sacred Mother punished them because they wanted to leave the home she gave them. Their dreams destroyed their home," Nicolas said softly.

Angeni nodded in agreement and turned to the next wall to read further. These writings were different, someone else wrote this. After a short time, her soul began to understand the strange words and was horrified to realize, these memoirs were written by the Reapers of Darkness. She read with greater reverence and fear as her mind built the story from the fragments she read.

Pride, honor, and strength ruled Briniu Malgram since Namaare gave her life. Our heart always has beaten so proud when we looked up to our beautiful burning mother. She gave us strength, forged our people and our empire strong with her red glow. The Sacred Mother watched over us every day, gave us unfettered life as we served her. But we learned to never forget the horror, the pitiful weakness, which encased and destroyed our enemy. They believed us invincible, but they were weak and unprepared. We learned from their mistakes. As humble servants of the Sacred Mother, we never forgot the winged destroyers, but awaited their arrival.

We loved our home world; we always have as the one gave it to us. We never wanted to leave her for pathetic dreams, but always wanted to protect her. Discipline ruled our spirit and obedience hardened our souls. We knew they would come back. And the shade truly has come, as we predicted. The winged destroyers descended to bring light to our dark skies, to destroy everything that we ever built and achieved. Moreover, we failed. Prideful overconfidence caused our downfall. Our knowledge, our strength, what we believed in wasn't enough. Their weakness was their dreams; yet, their dreams gave them strength.

We know our fate. We are being exterminated. Our empire is gone. Nothing will remain of the proud world our hard work built together. We will all vanish. But we do not fear; we never did. The winged destroyers are hunting us, coming to exterminate all of us to erase what and who we really are. Light will dilute our proud dark hearts; we know soon we all will return to our beloved Sacred Mother. We'll go, but we'll go with pride, which always will remain in our dark hearts. We know weakness, heavenly manipulation, unconditional obedience, and control will embrace the souls left behind. False, illusionary peace will greet the weak children in their sanctified heavenly theatre. But we'll not see that time.

So much sorrow and so much irony. Here, in our proud Mer Petraea where we once defeated the destroyers long ago, we failed against them. Our pride, in which we blindly believed, bred our failure, the same weakness that the destroyers called dreams. We're the same, but we were too blind to see. We're the same as we always were, and maybe we always will be.

But it has no real meaning now. The winged destroyers came for us. As the legends described them, they're relentless, showing no mercy to our kind. But in this war, we're also the same. Cruel, relentless, we show no mercy. They lighten our once dark, beautiful skies, extinguished the fire on our beautiful lands and destroyed our order, our pride, and all our achievements. Naamare's flaming guiding star does not shine upon us anymore. We know we have failed. The Sacred Mother was with us, but we let her down. Our great pride failed her. But we know she will help us as she always has with her children. In time, maybe she will forgive us.

Our dark legacy, which will have no great expression or the excess pride that we had will hide in the shadows long after we are gone. But no light can extinguish darkness completely, as we yet believe. Awakening is unavoidable when the shade arrives once again, as it always has. The legacy of the keepers will be here to welcome darkness again when our time comes. We have the suppressed legacy that the winged destroyers can't banish and abolish as they did with our home; the knowledge of what they fear and what they can't kill as the knowledge is in all of us.

Briniu Malgram is gone, her fiery heart turned icy and so cold, as the sapphire light shines on her once blood red lands. A lifeless heart is beating now in the cursed place of Eecrys Aredia, which was born of her. But our soul is like a tear of the sacred one. For us time has no meaning. The echoing legacy of the past will awaken. The winged destroyers will await the return of the shade, this we know. And our souls will be prepared. We will take our revenge for the lost souls and we will melt the cold heart and ice mask so Briniu Malgram may live again. We, the keepers will bring balance to our world as we always have. That is our legacy in the Crystal Shade.

"It can't be," Angeni whispered shocked, looking back at the Nicolas.

"It's impossible," the Prince added, while the old Aserian stepped near them.

"A world corrupted by forgetting, destroyed by fire," Eosh said. "A world of dark midnight destroyed by cold and ice. But a third world, so beautiful born from their ash."

"Eecrys Aredia is Briniu Malgram?" asked Angeni while she still couldn't believe what she read.

"So is Mer Gaea," added the Prince. The old Aserian nodded to them. Enchanted by the magic of the past, the young guardian looked back at the wall.

"Echoes of the forgotten past, stories of keepers of light and darkness, keepers of humanity," she whispered.

"We're the destroyers in their eyes, just as they're the destroyers in ours. Fascinating," Nicolas quipped cynically.

"We're the same; we all have dreams and pride. Why can't we live in peace?" Angeni quietly asked the same question the Matriarch had asked of her. "What compels us? Why are we doing this?" she wondered without answer.

"Please never forget the past, always remember, that's all I ask," Eosh requested as they watched the ancient wall. The young ones nodded with respect. "Come," he invited them with a grandfatherly kindness. "I have to show so many things to both of you that you should see and learn about our world."

The old Aserian led the two curious young ones to an arch, which opened to a larger hall. Images of fighting angels and demons in the agony of their long forgotten war adorned the eleven immense columns. Tiny blue flames danced alone in old oil lamps to give light. Pulsing like a tired heart, the menacing red light sifted into the hall to shine on the orderly shelves that gave home to ancient books.

Angeni's eyes mirrored a strange device as they stepped within; thousands of energy orbs formed the mass of a majestic miniature galaxy under the tip of the long tapered crystal shard. Each star a tiny orb in this chrono device had different colors of the rainbow that mirrored in her awe-struck eyes. A crystal shard hung over the middle of this small universe, casting its shade like some large mystical sundial. The ancient chrono device looked the same as the sketch she drew about the sacred one; the shard represented the Sacred Mother.

"What is this?" asked Angeni enchanted as she slowly approached the device.

"An ancient storyteller," the old Aserian commented while the young guardian and the Prince stepped closer to the device. "It tells of the eternal battle fought under the dreaded Crystal Shade. Like the stars that shine down at night, it is telling the birth of civilizations that held days of pride and glory, and the twilight of worlds, which had secrets and mysteries no one's ever going to hear." Eosh stepped close; his eyes mirrored the tiny colourful orbs that curiously watched them. "Every world had a champion whose soul gave life and light to these worlds. But sometimes one star on the sky, one civilization suddenly vanished from

307

the crystal garden and lost souls began to haunt the vast dark space. Souls joined those millions of others, who haunt the ruins of fallen and long forgotten civilizations banished by the Crystal Shade."

Then the old Aserian sighed, his face sorrowful, "But as capricious the Crystal Shade is, maybe everything I know is wrong and what I tell you is not the truth I believe it is. I'm not sure anymore," he admitted, doubt rang in his old voice as if his greatest belief had been shattered.

"What do you mean?" Angeni asked while Eosh sadly studied the chrono device.

"Something has changed," the old Aserian's voice was full of trouble. "Maybe everything I believed I knew about the Crystal Shade for two dozen millennia is false. Maybe I lived my whole life in a blinding crystal reality just waiting to be shattered at this moment."

Baffled, Angeni and Nicolas waited for an explanation.

"The Crystal Shade shouldn't be here. Not now. Not at this time," desperation edged Eosh's voice as he stared at the chrono device. "Like every hourglass, it has its own restrictions on when the previous era ends and the next one begins. By my belief, it should be cycles away."

His eyes mirrored the crawling shadow's edge in the device that just approached a small sapphire orb.

"The shade is barely reaching Eecrys Aredia, but darkness has already spread beyond these walls. This means, I've been mistaken," he shook his head dismayed. "My device is worthless. It cannot foretell the Crystal Shade's arrival as I believed."

Angeni felt his deep disappointment. She felt sad for Eosh; the old, but so noble soul who had created this device long long ago to give hope to everyone, a way to never forget and time to prepare. Only now many millennia later did he realize his greatest invention was a failure.

"There could be thousands of answers for a question but only one is the truth itself," Eosh lowered his head in sadness. "It seems my answer for the question wasn't the truth, but an illusion that may now cause the fall of Eecrys Aredia."

"We're not going to let that happen," Angeni's determination and friendly hand on his shoulder caused Eosh to look up and nod thanks.

"Our hope now lies on the shoulders of those brave Aserians who will warn everyone about the Crystal Shade. I can't do anymore for our people."

"They'll succeed. They'll warn everyone in time," Nicolas tried to reassure the old Aserian. Angeni agreed. Eosh stood straighter and nodded.

The young daydreamer looked back at the chrono device and studied it with silent glee. Eosh stood beside and watched her while Nicolas looked around in the hall.

"I was right," Angeni whispered with childish awe. "Each star is the soul of a once wise Aserian, who guides us in the unknown to show the right path so we never make the mistakes they made. All of them are here. All of them shine at us at once."

"You have imagination, my child," Eosh remarked. Angeni looked at him curiously while he continued, "You've heard thousands of stories about the stars, and yet, you created a new one, which better describes your dreams. My daughter said you've always walked on a different path. She was right."

Angeni stood prouder when she turned to Eosh.

"In a way, you're right, young Angeni," Eosh paused and looked at the miniature universe. "Your beloved stars are the souls of our brothers and sisters that defeated the Crystal Shade on their own worlds." His eyes mirrored a shiny sapphire orb with a warm smile. "But they're not dead. Their souls still protect their worlds until the twilight of the Crystal Shade."

"I'm not the one who creates new tales of the stars," Angeni was amused.

"All the stars are born from pain, death and suffering the Crystal Shade carries within. There is no exception," the Prince and Guardian listened in awe. "If you defeat the Crystal Shade, young Angeni, your clean soul will shine down on Eecrys Aredia too, even if the world you knew will be no more." Eosh let out a soft sad sigh.

"How?" asked the young guardian. Nicolas watched them curiously, awaiting explanation.

"You ask many questions, Angeni. But you never asked how it is possible that Sachylia glows in her glorious light as she does now."

"I never asked because it's evident. Our crystal mother created her to guard us," said the young guardian proudly, and then deflated. "She created Sachylia, right?"

Amused, Eosh nodded.

"Of course she created, my child," the old Aserian's pride grew. "But Sachylia is also a sign of a long forgotten victory over darkness. With its light it tells the story of a young, romantic warrior, who had to leave everything and everyone behind to give light to his world."

With grandfatherly pride, he looked at the young ones as he continued, "My life is told by Sachylia, as yours might be when your time comes, young Angeni," Eosh said quietly as he remembered his long life. "In the end your soul may tell your story to Eecrys Aredia."

"I, I don't understand."

"You will, my child. That's the life of your Angeni soul," Eosh responded kindly.

"What do we, guardians really do in the Crystal Shade?" she felt that this was the right question to ask.

"Attract trouble?" Nicolas quipped with a grin. Angeni smiled impishly as she looked at him. "Apologies. I spend way too much time with Angeni," he added, but Eosh didn't even try to hide his amusement.

"Who attracted more trouble in the beginning? The eternal question in the crystal garden, oh my dear Prince," Angeni stepped to Nicolas speaking with a deceptive calm tone, slowly caressing his face. "The fragile, needing to be a protected one? Or the humble, but almighty guardian?" Her wings spread wide, and then lowered behind her back. "In time so few were innocent and so many lived to see death with the desire aimed only to kill their brothers and sisters, "she started to quote the Stone of Origin theatrically as with majestic steps, she slowly rounded on Nicolas. "Loving and destructive nature was in their souls. Their voice first whispered so silent, no one even heard. But then, the whisper became louder and louder, turned heaven to hell as their voice called for the era of the Crystal Shade."

Her eyes flashed sapphire to give measure to her words, then she continued, "Souls killed each other without remorse, without mercy, crying heartbroken for their fallen loved ones, never wanting to let them go. But no spirit vanished; no soul is swallowed by the silence until not a single soul remembers them. Too many still remembered the lost ones. And the fallen ones returned. Innocents, boundless spirits in the shape of winged angels descended from the sky. The restless ones gave demonic shape for their obtrusive, raging evil nature."

She stopped, looking at the Prince. "Your foolishness gave life to the heavenly angels and the evil, ugly demons. But the Sacred Mother, so noble and wise, created your silky winged beautiful guardian to protect you from your foolish actions, little man. Never forget that," she added with controlled coolness. Amused, Eosh smiled as he shook his head while Angeni continued, "So who attracts trouble? Tell me, my dear Prince." The young guardian crossed her arms and glared at the Prince while Eosh silently chuckled.

"You're right," said Nicolas shaking his head amused.

"Your guardian is always right, little man. Remember that," speaking the same cold tone Angeni raised her nose in playful superiority, keeping the amusement she felt inside hidden.

"But when the shade arrives you would be right, Nicolas," added Eosh.

"Would he?" Angeni snapped her attention to Eosh. She had noticed Nicolas' superior smile appearing on his face.

"Light gives you truth, Angeni," the old Aserian replied. "But as dusk falls and darkness arrives none of these rules apply anymore."

"We are to protect them. Nothing can and nothing will change that," Angeni's certainty hit immediately.

"That's true," Eosh admitted. "But when the shade arrives, none of the humans will be safe around any of us. Chased by the darkness, Aserians may attract more trouble to humans than all the humans brought on themselves together in the last two dozen millennia."

Angeni and Nicolas stayed uncharacteristically silent.

"In those times we, Aserians are much more fragile than ever before," the old Aserian added.

"Fragile?" Angeni's curiously went up a notch raised her eyebrow to Eosh.

"You can be a superior being, Angeni. Compared to the humans, you are," Eosh admitted. Nicolas looked at him immediately.

"Please, don't elevate her confidence that is already brighter than Sachylia itself," he pleaded with a cheeky edge.

"What is true is true, my Prince. Accept that fact and your life will be easier and much more beautiful. I promise," Angeni responded with a wide grin.

"Young ones," Eosh whispered amused, shaking his head at their banter, and then seriousness set in. "But as everything else is balanced, your existence must also have its shade."

"Now I'm listening," Nicolas grinned. Angeni responded with a fond smile.

"Even if you are the most skilled Aserian Guardian, or the most helpful and beloved person, like every soul yours can be easily shattered, even without a crystal blade. Those who surround us give us our light to become the light." Eosh looked at the closest oil lamp where the little blue flame peacefully danced in the darkness without fear. "Our souls are like the tiny flame, which declares itself proud between the shadows with its noble light," he said, then looked back at Angeni. "Even one angel is capable of stopping the demons from spreading darkness, and brings peace to Eecrys Aredia. Even one," he said with complete certainty. "But

311

as balance rules in the Crystal Shade, one demon may turn the tide and can plunge our eternal light into darkness as well. Never forget that, Angeni."

He took a soft sigh as he continued, "But if no one believes in you and not trust you, your life becomes meaningless and pointless," he said and gently turned the oil lamp down; the tiny blue flame almost vanished, slightly flickered. "Your light will fade. It will be swallowed by void and emptiness."

Then the old Aserian gave mercy to the flickering light and turned the oil lamp back up; the little flame happily danced. Angeni smiled fondly, remembering the words from her father before her commencement day, when she tried to escape love. She just realized what her father really meant.

"Never be alone, never be unguarded, Angeni," the old Aserian looked deep into her eyes as he continued.

"I'll protect her," Nicolas insisted.

"Ah, that would be a strange new world, right little man?" the young woman responded calmly, crossing her arms.

"Oh, I would love that world. Trust me, my humble guardian."

"I'll leave you the dreaming, but one day when you awake, you'll see that the silky winged one is polishing your crystal reality to shine in the background," the young guardian declared.

"Even if it sounds strange, for the first time, he is right. He can protect you," Eosh said and the Prince thankfully nodded for the confidence. Silent, Angeni studied the young man with her eyes from top to bottom, from bottom to top, and then looked back at Eosh.

"No, he can't," she responded calmly, but Eosh raised his hand and the young guardian went silent.

"What you believe is merely his fantasy can easily turn into reality during the Crystal Shade. I know he will do anything to protect you. And you know that too," Eosh finished with certainty.

"A fragile human, even if he is as well trained and courageous as Nicolas can't protect me from a demon," Angeni spouted in surprise, but was quite determined. "I'll not let him drift into danger, which would certainly cost his life because of humble me."

"But I…" started Nicolas, but Angeni snapped her flashing sapphire eyes at him.

"Oh, I know you would protect me," she added kindly, and then renewed the seriousness. "But it's not your task and never will be to fight for me, little man. Don't even think that."

"But…" Nicolas was determined to argue.

"You don't want to face the wrath of your mighty guardian, do you?" Angeni questioned as she stepped closer to him, her eyes flashed again and her wings snapped wide. Reluctant, Nicolas shook his head, but Angeni felt regardless of his honesty, he would never comply with her order.

"Please don't be harsh with Nicolas," Eosh interrupted. Angeni looked at him while her wings lowered to her back. "The bond between the two of you is very strong. Whether you like it or not, Nicolas will protect you when necessary. You may order him, but as you read from his eyes, this is the only order he will surely disobey."

"I'm his guardian and we're going to keep it that way," Angeni's determination returned while she glared at Eosh.

"You can't order a real man to leave a friend behind, even if that friend is an Aserian Guardian," said Eosh calmly. Angeni felt the old Aserian was right. "Humans are not as fragile as you believe."

"But they..." started the young guardian.

"They need our guidance, our protection," continued Eosh. "But they have great strength, more dignity and bravery than you would ever believe and imagine. Sometimes greater than we Aserian have."

"Sure," responded Angeni defiantly, and then looked at Nicolas. "Just take a look at my brave strong prince," she added cynically. Nicolas responded with a gentle smile.

"We don't need to protect them from the wind, Angeni," Eosh insisted. "What do you believe my protector Israfil was? Aserian or human?" The old Aserian waited with a treacherously kind smile.

"He was an Aserian," said Angeni in an instant as the winged statue of Israfil who fought his eternal battle against demon Marchosias in the commencement hall came to her mind. But as her words left her lips she felt that Eosh directly asked this question, and she was wrong.

"Or an honourable human soul who fought bravely like an Aserian," responded Eosh. "Statues usually represent our bravery, our actions, how others saw us. But they rarely tell who we, what we really were. Not our origin, but our actions that show who and what we are, young Angeni. Never forget that."

The old Aserian looked at Nicolas with great respect in his eyes.

"You never met the bravery and courage that lies in them as these noble traits cannot be seen in peacetime. But in the Crystal Shade, you will," he said, and then looked back at Angeni. "Sometimes the protected one needs to protect the guardian. If this time comes, because it will, never hesitate to trust Nicolas; never hesitate to ask the help of any human. Please promise me."

"I promise," responded Angeni after a short hesitation. Her instinct told her Eosh knew what he was saying; yet, her soul couldn't accept everything immediately. Everything she learned now was the opposite of what she learned. She wanted to say something; so sudden a soft beating sound hit her ears, and then deep silence.

Eosh suddenly raised his hand to stay silent, his other hand already rested on his crystal blade grip. Angeni noticed the change immediately, as did Eosh and Nicolas. The bright light that came from outside wasn't that menacing red as before; calm sapphire light beat softly. The silky fingers of the young guardian slowly twisted around the golden grip while she and Nicolas hurried after the old Aserian out to the crystal gate sanctuary.

Angeni read the intense surprise in Eosh's eyes as the gate pulsed sapphire.

"No. It's not possible," Eosh whispered as he hurried to the gate.

"What happened to the gate?" Nicolas asked quietly.

"It closed. But it's not possible until the Crystal Shade twilights," came the soft dismay as he crouched down and touched the pulsating gate's sapphire surface.

Angeni opened her mind but no false crystal chime, no sad bassoon music, only intense silence ruled. The Sacred Mother didn't call her anymore. Only Eosh's words came through, whose hand was still on the gate, *Why don't you tell me what happened?* Disappointed, the old Aserian stood up and looked around. *So many things are different. So many. It makes no sense.*

Eosh snapped his attention to the bridge. Taking his breaths softly, his old eyes reflected the misty darkness that yawned, threatening all of them; Angeni felt it, too. In her mind, dozens of whirling evil thoughts came from all around them at once; she couldn't make out a single word, but they were so cruel. The young guardian quickly shaded her mind to not hear these whispers, but to focus instead.

"The shadows are moving," she whispered, seeing a tiny distortion in the fog. Eosh nodded.

"What is it?" Nicolas question came on a whisper while he detached his grip from his belt.

The old Aserian studied the bridge in tense silence. Under her feet, Angeni felt the ground rumble, it betrayed those who approached from afar. Something or someone was coming toward them from the bridge. And it wasn't alone.

"The trouble that we attract," Eosh grated with hatred, facing the arch that opened onto the bridge while a sapphire blade and a shield came alive from his separated grips ready to defend. Angeni and Nicolas looked to the dark distance, their blades opened in their hands as the cold breeze carried the sound of heavy footfalls that approached with frightening speed. The three souls waited. Within the swirling mist, shadows moved and red eyes shone. Growling, hateful barking echoed from the darkness.

Like a veil, the mist slowly revealed the grotesque creatures that raced out of the darkness. Angeni recognized what they were, Lhachae, the most faithful of human friends. Now they snarled from demented, scarred faces and the mist whirled around their fleece-like fur, which was gone in patches. With skin scraped and raw, their once kind canine features were distorted with evil; their souls demented, these creatures were something else. Their normally intelligent eyes now glowed dark red with unparalleled evil hatred.

Behind the hellhounds, other dark silhouettes escaped the mist to run toward them; sinister crystal blades whispered of evil souls when they opened blood red in the darkness.

"Stay on safe ground and fight!" Eosh ordered. His steps carried him faster and faster toward the dark silhouettes. Determined, their blades ready, Angeni and Nicolas raced after him.

The first hellhound bounded through the archway into the sanctuary and sprang at Eosh, who stabbed his blade deep into the creature's chest in mid-air. The crystallization barely began to spread from the hound's wound when Eosh's momentum dropped the dying evil from his blade right into the chasm. The second barking hellhound quickly followed the first as Eosh struck again, but the third one jumped at the young guardian.

Angeni spun as she ran; her wings flared and batted the lhachae with the strength of her disgust while it was still in the air. A small yowl echoed as the hellhound disappeared in the darkness of the chasm. As she came out of the spin, her sapphire blade struck into the closest hellhound before it had a chance to reach Nicolas, who was a few steps behind her. Pulling the blade out of the crystallizing howling beast, the voice of death rang as the other hound's body just hit the deep bottom of the chasm with an echo of shattering bones.

Icy sapphire eyes flashed as Angeni looked up to face the next beast. The last of the lhachaes fell before her eyes as Eosh and Nicolas finished them fast. Right before the demons with dark crystal blades and dozens of demented human souls brandishing metallic scythes and hatchets, reached them with a harsh battle cry. The old Aserian met the demons first, stabbed two with relentless precision. Demonic death cries echoed

315

as the deadly blades left their bodies; ruby and onyx started to spread from their wounds. The two demented souls hadn't even fallen to their knees, and Eosh's old sapphire aura blades swung around to end the life of the next beast.

A heavy clink echoed as the determined young guardian spun her blades to deflect a quick, burning dark blade, she then stabbed the demon through who had left his chest undefended. Black tourmaline spread from the beast's wound as the sapphire blades pulled back fast from his body. Then Angeni majestically spun to shatter and silence her half crystallized victim.

From the corner of her eye, she saw the demented humans with their archaic weapons focused on Nicolas; they never had a chance against Aserians, they were well aware of that, but their weapons could take his life. Yet, the Prince was fast, well trained, and lethal. The scythes, hatchets, and other deadly tools turned to dust by the sapphire blade before they had a chance to hit. The crystal blade in his hand quickly changed its deadly shapes to both strike mercilessly and defend.

Demons and demented humans alike fell to the sapphire blades of the three heroic defenders. These demons were not as well trained as Matriarch Lilis. Not even close. Begging evil death cries echoed in painful. Their song of fallen souls; ruby, garnet, tourmaline, black quartz and other sinister splinters shattered, evil souls left this mortal world.

A loud battle cry came from behind. Surprised, Angeni snapped her attention to the arches around the crystal gate. In the darkness, demons scampered up the walls; their sinister blades came alive as they dove into the battle. The Aserians were surrounded.

The battle in the small sanctuary became a flurry of intensity. Demons and demented fell one after another, yet more demons arrived from the deep chasm and scores of the demented rushed down the bridge toward them. While Eosh and Nicolas took the lives of two evil souls, Angeni ran toward the closest demon, which had just clawed his way out of the chasm, opened his blade and boldly faced her.

The burning red menace struck at the fragile woman, who immediately spun aside and her hand already pushed her blade toward the beast. A sultry breeze stroked her wings as the enemy's blade passed under her raised wings, which she tucked behind her back before she came out of the spin. The sapphire blade sliced only the air; the demon was faster. The beast suddenly grabbed the young woman's neck from behind and slammed the guardian against the closest column. She wanted to scream in pain, but no voice left her throat as the hit pushed all air out of her lungs. Her golden hilt fell from her hand, clinked among the shattered crystals as it hit the ground and the sapphire blade went silent.

Dark red eyes glared into her desperate eyes. Angeni tried to liberate herself, her hands grabbed the strong arm, but the Shaina didn't release her. Pressing her with one hand to the column, preparing his blade with another, he raised the red burning menace to strike her down.

Closing the gate won't stop us, Aserian! she heard the thoughts of the furious evil beast. Angeni didn't understand why the demon believed they had closed the gate but she didn't have time to dwell on it. A choking fearful scream left her shaking lips, seeing the deadly red blade arcing down at her.

A sapphire crystal arrow embedded itself in the demon's hand, and the striking blade jerked back from her. The beast dropped his blade, howled in pain as he released the choking woman. The beast fell away while dark red emerald spider-webbed up from his wounded hand. Angeni quickly grabbed a breath; the damp air filled her lungs while she ducked away and snatched her blade from the ground. Sapphire blades shot to life once again when she separated the grip.

Nicolas loomed up majestically behind the screaming demon and shattered it into silence. Angeni gave him a thankful nod, and yet another demon struck toward her from the front. The crystal shield opened in her left and reverberated as it stopped the deadly red blade. No time to think, no time to rest, the sapphire blade sliced past her solid defence to slam deep into the demon's chest.

A raucous battle cry echoed from the mist that swirled above the bridge. Angeni spun toward the bridge to behold dancing silhouettes in the fog as another wave of demented humans rushed toward them.

The old Aserian evaded a demon by stabbing his blade into him with a flurry of movement that landed him under the bridge archway. Rushing up to the bridge, he jabbed his two sapphire blades into the solid bricks. The mossy stone in front of him crystallized while his large wings flapped once to push him back. Eosh dove back into the immediate battle as his feet touched solid ground.

The young guardian's sapphire blade had just silenced a demonic beast forever when the crystallized part of the bridge turned to dust and the ageless, once regal stone bridge shifted and dropped stone blocks away from the sanctuary. With fear-shot eyes, the demented humans on the bride desperately tried to run from a fate they could not avoid; the fate that even put Angeni's soul in so much fear. So quick, the whole bridge fell into the dark chasm, followed by desperate echoing screams.

Dust plumes and loud rumbling marked their end as they hit the chasm floor far below.

A demonized human landed on Nicolas. His blade skittered away as he fell back, forced to the mossy stone, Nicolas stared up. A rusty chipped blade rose high in the air above him. In protective fury, Angeni's weapons changed to single blades as she ran in to help Nicolas, who desperately tried to reach his blade hilt. Two demented humans with raised weapons blocked her as they rushed in between the guardian and her charge.

Angeni didn't let them stop her. A majestic spin between them and her blades turned their weapons to dust and stabbed deep into their chests. The two humans screeched as the dark plague started to embrace them while the guardian came out of her spin behind them. At the same moment, Nicolas realized he could not reach his blade, suddenly drew in all his strength and slammed his free fist into the evil's crowing face; his wrist armour sliced open its face. The painful bellow reverberated around the sanctuary as the human stepped back. The prince was loose.

Still too far to reach the bellowing human, Angeni watched him strike at the Prince, but then the human rolled away, its sharp metal blade sparked across the stones. Nicolas grabbed his grip and twisted back with it pointed at the demented one coming in for another chop. The sapphire blade opened right into his chest. Blood topaz rushed outward from the wound while the Prince's vengeful fury pushed the bellowing demon touched human over the edge of the chasm.

Angeni was relieved no more demons or demented humans had arrived. She thought there might be a victory in this hopeless situation, until a dense red flame blew toward Nicolas. He leaned away from the flame and his heel tipped over the ledge. Hissing in pain as the flame shot past and burnt his cheek, he barely caught himself from falling into the deadly darkness below.

The young guardian united her grip fast; her will gave life to the full crystal shield, a protective shadow to stop the whirling flames reaching for Nicolas once again. Her silky skin sensed the fiery heat as the flame flowed toward the ceiling and her shield deflected the fiery death from Nicolas.

From the corner of her eye, she saw Eosh's swinging blade shatter the last two red crystallized demons, but her attention was drawn back as another flame flowed against her shield. Angeni's eyes flashed furious sapphire as she focused on the fire breather; his face blurred from behind the large crystal shield. Shattered crystal fragments pinged as the old

Aserian shattered another evil soul. Continuously, the dark skinned fire breather blew fire toward her large shield, which deflected the flames.

Eosh's weapon reverted to a crystal bow and after an arrow quickly manifested, he shot another demented woman who rushed out of the mist. Her desperate scream echoed as the force of the arrow pushed her over the edge of the chasm.

The young guardian was determined to protect Nicolas who stayed behind her protective shadow; she was ready to kill the one that threatened her human charge. She waited until the fire breather blew out the next flame and she immediately spun toward him. The majestic body evaded the licking flames, while the crystal shield closed in the golden grip which mirrored the flames as they flicked closer and closer to her. The deadly crystal blade came alive, firmed to a razor edge as her instincts led the weapon.

The guardian's eyes flashed sapphire as she came out of the spin and slammed the crystal blade through the fire breather's chest. The man screamed as the rhodolite garnet quickly spread out from the wound across his dark skin while his eyes flashed murderous red.

As he dropped to his knees, a so familiar soul glared back at Angeni. The young guardian just recognized him; the pleasant fire-breather that taught a little fire apprentice back in Odess'iana.

"No. Please, no," she whispered. The shocked guardian immediately pulled her blade out of Ashan and the deadly sapphire turned silent. But the crystallization did not stop. The fire sticks rolled from his cramped hand while rhodolite garnet quickly spread from the wound to overtake the body of the screaming man. The red brightness of his eyes slowly faded and became clear. His face smoothed as the madness disappeared leaving the kindness of the dying fire-breather looking at her in wonder.

"I'm sorry. I'm so sorry," desperate, Angeni whispered as she clasped the fire-breather's cold, spasming hand so tight, like she could hold him to life, so these last moments never happened. From the touch, Ashan's soul shared his entire life with the young guardian; a life which ends here. Her mind tried to push the memories away, but she couldn't. Everything the fire-breather ever saw and knew was burned into her memory.

A human life revealed itself within a touch; a life lived in a little natty house that was built with two hard-working hands on the endless green fields of Jizan. The great tall Arecaceae tree in the great garden when so shy, he first told his feelings to a beautiful Saira. Hijazian wild tasunkes galloped free across the fields with his happy little boy, Nasib who had inherited his mother's eyes and smile, but the strength of his father. The sweet smell of a tiny white Nivale flower that grew only up on the peaks extolled his love for Saira without words. He climbed the tallest Andrenian Mountains for the flower that his love cherished more than anything since and wore proudly. The citizens who always welcomed him, the towns that awaited his return as he discovered every little corner of Eecrys Aredia with an eagerness to see and learn everything overwhelmed him. She had been that little girl who tamed the wild fires of Hijaz so bravely at the Great Feast of Odess'iana, the young soul who now killed him to redeem him.

In his soul, Ashan had already forgiven her; the only regret felt was he would never see his family anymore. All his soul asked from Grace of Odess'iana reborn as the noble Ridwan of Jannah, the Guardian of the Heavenly Paradise, was to never forget what old Ashan taught her young soul. A Hijazian never dies if his teachings live on in the apprentices.

"I will never forget, Ashan. I promise," Angeni whispered, while a tear rolled down her cheek. "Now sleep. The Sacred Mother is calling your soul."

Ashan's smile was grim with pain. Holding his cramped hand, the young guardian felt dread of the unknown within him. Her angelic soft voice sang as her hand tenderly covered his eyes.

> Don't cry, don't fear, close your eyes,
> You will arise to be one with the stars.
> Brothers, sisters greet you at heaven's gates,
> Don't fear, eternal peace awaits.

The spreading rhodolite garnet slowly encased his trembling body. The soul, which was scared, was trapped inside; he wanted to follow that peaceful motherly crystal chime which called him home. Another tear moistened Angeni's eye while she stared down at the painful crystal statue of the once kind fire-breather.

"What happened to you, dear Fire Master?" she asked in her quiet desperation. "We were never enemies, but friends."

The young guardian gazed at the crystal statue. It begged to her in silence to release the soul so it may finally go home to rest in peace. Deadly sapphire glowed on the red garnet as the crystal blade came alive in her hand.

"All souls must go home," her quiet whisper assured as she raised the blade with both hands. She closed her eyes in silent prayer; a tear rolled down her cheek. "All of them."

And the blade struck down. The garnet statue cracked and exploded into thousands of pieces. The crystal fragments pinged across the shiny surface of the pulsating gate, and then silence fell all around. Embraced by grief, Angeni kept her tear-laden eyes closed while she looked away. The darkness that her soul tried to hide in couldn't dull her pain. Then the sapphire blade pulled back into the grip as her crushed soul desired.

Opening her eyes, the slowly pulsating sapphire surface of the crystal gate looked back at her. Yet, the mirror image that it reflected wasn't hers. A little girl watched her with open curiosity. She immediately recognized her. Young Grace Sessa Aredia who had looked into the magic fountain back at Odess'iana a lifetime ago, the little girl who dreamt to become the greatest guardian one day, but became a senseless killer instead.

What have I become? her desperate thought asked. She felt ruthless, cold as ice; her emotionless eyes didn't want to hide the guilt and the sadness. Everything she ever desired to be now looked with endless remorse in her soul at the little girl.

Then the illusive moment, when past, present and future met, had passed silent and only the killer Aserian looked back at Angeni from the mirror image. She looked up, she couldn't face herself with the all-encompassing shame she felt. Wherever she looked, her sad eyes reflected the colourful shattered crystals that looked back, sad and innocent from the pulsing gate's surface.

"What have we done?" she asked quietly.

"We needed to do this. There is no other way to save them," Eosh's content determination reached her.

"We didn't even try," she whispered.

"They or us, Angeni. It's that simple," Nicolas responded calm.

"Look around at what we've done! Look at them!" her angelic voice echoed. "We took the lives of these people! We destroyed their souls, their lives, all their knowledge, everything, because…" she sighed sadly and studied the silent tomb that embraced them. "Why?"

"Darkness corrupted their souls, my child. Our belief and judgment served us tonight to protect Eecrys Aredia," Eosh softly soothed with ancient wisdom.

"Don't hide behind belief to justify murder," Angeni hissed, her furious eyes flashed sapphire. "I believed all my life that Aserians are to protect life with wisdom, nobility and compassion. But I see everything that I believed is just an illusion. We're born to kill, we're trained to kill and we kill. Not to protect humans, but to protect some ideals, our own damned belief."

"We're fighting in the name of the Sacred Mother! Never forget that!" responded Eosh's determined, superior tone.

"Don't ever dare to say that we're fighting in her name!" her furious angelic voice echoed, stepping to Eosh, her eyes flashed in anger. "She never asked us to kill! She never asked us to slaughter these people, her very own children in her name! Our Sacred Mother never dared to ask her people, her children to take the life of the other! It's we, who cowardly label our actions with her name! It's a lie, and we know that!" Angeni paused as she realized that maybe she is the only one who believes in the truth of her words. "It's a lie. I know that," she whispered as she really believed it.

Eosh and Nicolas just watched her silent.

"Lilis was right. All souls are the same," she continued silent, turning away from them. "We're no different from them."

"She lied to break your belief! Look where her evil words have guided you!" Eosh's voice echoed his determination.

"Evil? From whose view? From ours!" shouted Angeni, snapping her eyes back at him. "We're the same evil as they are and she knew that."

"Please, don't ever say that, Angeni," Nicolas added with quiet horror.

"Even if I don't say it, it won't change the fact," she whispered. "You didn't see the desperation in her eyes, Nicolas. She feared for the humans, both of our people and our home, from the Angeni soul. From me," Angeni looked deep into the eyes of the Prince. "She didn't want to kill me; I couldn't defeat her and she knew that. But like a true guardian, she gave her life to protect all of us, to show me what I may become. She gave her life to give me a chance to live."

"You can never trust the empty words of a demon," Eosh's fury pushed his voice down to a hiss.

"Lilis knew that I would never listen to her. Instead, she sacrificed herself to open my eyes even without words." Angeni let out a sad sigh before she continued, "I don't need to fear any lie. I need to fear truth itself; that in my blind belief I might become the destroyer both of our people and our beloved home."

"You don't want to be a hero, Angeni. There are no heroes in the Crystal Shade," Eosh said desperate, stepping closer to her. "You can't save everyone. Because when you fail, and you will, it would crush your soul for the rest of your life."

"You can't save anyone if you never try," Angeni whispered, looking at the crystal fragments. "And I didn't even try. What kind of guardian am I?"

"Don't blame and feel sorry for yourself, my child."

"I'm not feeling sorry for myself." A tear appeared in her eyes, which mirrored the shattered souls. "I'm feeling sorry for these people and their families, for their lives and souls," Angeni whispered, and then looked at Eosh. "But I will defend them from our blind belief. I'm never going to take the life of another human. Never. I swear."

"You can't keep this promise in the Crystal Shade, Angeni. You don't even know what you're fighting for and against," said Eosh sadly. "Please, see what they did. Please, see what we'll all face if we fail," the old Aserian whispered as he touched Angeni's arm and looked into her eyes.

The surroundings blurred around Angeni; harsh sounds echoed in her mind as Eosh's memories came alive in her mind. As if she had stepped into the forgotten past, Mer Petraea slowly took the shape of its former glory around them. The city wasn't buried anymore. The cavern ceiling was gone, ominous clouds hung dark and menacing in the red sky. The giant red sun Naamare looked down at her like an evil flaming all seeing eye whose stifling beams scorched the hell-land. Death, cries echoed from all round and cruelty tactile in the air.

Hot air filled her lungs, heat burned her silky skin; her eyes mirrored the suffering that bent human backs and souls. Slavery, the impurity ruled this place. Ragged scraps of humans in cages desperately awaited the relief of death that would be granted slowly, through starvation and thirst. Evil barbarian souls sacrificed the weakest souls as humble offerings to the Sacred Mother. Then slowly thousands of demons moved in to surround. Shocked, she couldn't do anything, just watch. Every move of these beasts and look exuded hatred toward her, and they got closer and closer.

A flash blinded her for a moment. The brightness cleared and she wasn't alone anymore. Thousands of Aserians surrounded her in a fever pitched battle against thousands of Shaina. A battle so desperate and so cruel, Angeni wanted to look away to not see, but she couldn't close her eyes, or her mind. She felt the darkness and she had seen the infinite hate that ruled the demon souls. Sick joy beamed from their eyes as they sliced the angels in the heat of the battle. They killed everyone who turned against them, man, woman, and even children who tried to escape from the midst of the battle. They were killing because they revelled in it as they recklessly ploughed into battle to kill more, and more. They loved the taste of it, loved the feel of it. They lived to kill, to destroy. It was their way of life.

Eosh suddenly released Angeni's arm and she snapped out of the trance with a horrified shudder. She stared at him, silent while her body gradually calmed. Her skin still felt the heat, but it slowly faded away. Looking into the old Aserian's eyes, Angeni knew Eosh didn't show her all the cruelty, all the horrors he had ever seen to protect her soul. What she saw was already enough for her. The young guardian let out a grateful sigh as reality came clear.

"I understand your hatred toward them," Angeni whispered. "But whoever can't forgive, hate may swallow and encase the soul, turn it into one of them. Whoever lives in the past doesn't have a future."

"Who-so-ever forgets the past, can't determine the future," Eosh responded just as determined.

"Making me feel your guilt of the past, which I never lived does not make you right," said Angeni quietly. "Revenge will never bring back the lost ones."

"My intention is not to make you feel guilty, but to show what you must fight against," Eosh responded on a soft tone, overwhelming sorrow swept his eyes. The young guardian looked at him; begged with her desperate eyes.

"But, but we're good souls. Why can't we respect life and be good? Guardians should respect and protect life, not take away." Her words tried to fix her shattered illusionary dream world; her eyes begged for the peace that she had lived not long ago. "I don't want to fight. I don't want to kill. Why is that so hard to understand?"

Eosh slowly lowered his head in sadness.

"You believe your words are wise. And I admit you are right, my child," the old Aserian admitted heartbroken. "But just as I did, when I was young, on a slow and painful path you'll learn that our honourable and valorous ideals, what we believe to be right will not defend our home or our loved ones." He looked deep into Angeni's eyes. "Please, meditate on the words of this old Aserian before you make a decision you'll regret later, that's all I ask."

Angeni stayed silent for a moment; her soul didn't know what to believe anymore. Then she looked at Eosh.

"I will. I promise," she whispered, and then the crushed young guardian turned away from them and silently strolled away.

"Where are you going, Angeni?" Nicolas asked from behind her, his concern pushed him to follow.

"I'd like to be alone. At least for a short time," her sad whisper hurt Nicolas as she stopped looking back at him. Nicolas stopped and nodded grim confirmation of her wish.

"Give her time, Nicolas. Every soul must find its peace to heal," Angeni heard Eosh fading whisper while the thickened mist slowly embraced her protectively as she left them behind.

Nothing can heal the wounds of the soul, the young guardian thought as she strolled down the foggy stone stairs carved inside of the mountain, leading her to the unknown, the small measure of peace that her soul so desired. *No one can hide from a past that cannot be changed.*

* * *

"The belief, everything you believe is false. All of it," the crushed young guardian whispered desperately though her sorrow while she hugged her knees and stared numb at the water of the ancient fountain. Only a cold stone ledge gave refuge to the mourning angel. Her eyes beamed her soul's endless remorse and mirrored the multitude of tiny white Nymphaes. The water lilies listened in silence as they floated peacefully on the surface of their little world. Only they and Angeni's reflection heard her confession. Only her wings lent sympathy as they hugged and embraced her so protectively.

Soft breezes fanned her feathers and the silky hem of her sapphire gown. The silence that ruled the ruined ancient square was only broken by the quiet gurgles of the waterfall that had gradually worn through the wall to feed its own small lake, which it had created over thousands of cycles. The swirling mist thankfully hid the shattered red and black crystal fragments in the shadow of the crystal gate's rocky mountain.

"Blind burning religion. What good is belief if you kill people in its name? Is this good or just a mere illusion? Belief must give hope in the name of freedom and justice. Never this," she whispered. "Everyone must wake up from the crystal reality that blinds us. Every soul must grow up one day."

A tear formed in the corner of her eye to slowly slide down her cool cheek. A tiny ripple spread as her teardrop fell into the water.

"I want to be Grace Sessa Aredia. Why I can't be her? Was I a bad soul?" she asked her desperate reflection, no response came. "That's all I want to be. Grace Sessa Aredia, with her beloved family, young life, great dreams and drawings," her whisper begged for salvation, while another tear rolled down her cheek. "I want to live. That's all I want."

So strange, her tear did not appear on her mirror image. The mirror image smiled and unfolded its wings as it looked into the young guardian's surprised eyes. The Aserian woman's reflected lineament seemed mature, great wisdom emitted from the image's existence, she seemed so proud, loving, and kind. With a voice so angelic, she spoke to Angeni from within the rippling water's surface of the fountain.

"You're only at the beginning of your journey, and you already begin to understand what the Crystal Shade is about, my little girl," the mirror image said. "You can't hide from it; your nature will never let you. But you can understand it. And you will."

A smile graced the mirror image while the reflected background blurred beyond *her* to reveal the sacred crystal mother. Angeni just watched, breathless.

"Your proud young soul has just begun to reveal itself, Angeni. You were ignorant as a babe. Yet, you desired to learn. You believed blindly. Now you have doubts as you look back at your short life. You are crushed and disappointed, but you are on the right path," Angeni's own tender voice echoed from the mirror image.

"Who, who are you?" Angeni asked, but the mirror image just smiled pleasantly at her. "What do you mean; my enlightenment?"

"You make me proud, Angeni. You always have," was the soft echoing answer. "You can see what others will not. Willing to know what others fear. Enlightenment will be yours when you face and end the Crystal Shade," her own mirror image's kind motherly advice continued. "Sooner or later you'll have to choose. Don't fear the paths that others dare not walk. Don't fear thinking and acting on what others fear. Ask the questions others never dared. Don't feel alone, because you never will be. I'm always watching over you." The voice slowly changed into the soft crystal chiming, so pleasant to the young angel's ears like the clearest flute, "Always."

"Please don't leave me, mother," Angeni reached out desperate to touch the mirror image, but the water's surface distorted in waves. As the surface calmed, her true mirror image surprised, sadness-tinged face looked back. "Please don't leave me alone," she whispered and started to cry in loneliness. Only her quiet weeping and the waterfall's gurgle broke the deep silence.

Then, the white mist carried soft growling whispers to her. Angeni sniffed as she looked around, her hand already felt the cold surface of the golden crystal blade grip. The growling gradually turned into discernible words. By the tone, the young guardian wasn't sure if it was a man or a woman's voice.

"Children must sleep," the air carried the calm echo to her ears. Angeni looked toward the source while her crystal battle armour shaped itself all around her body, ready to protect her. The strange, distorted voice came from a dark corridor. It merged with the humming of a woman that was so familiar; a pleasant hum she last heard when she was a child. It called her.

The soft white mist swirled in the dim darkness. Like a warm blanket, it gently embraced her as wary, she edged down the ruined stone corridor carved into the rock. Vigilant, her fingers gently embraced the closed crystal grip on her belt.

"Sleep, sleep my daring," a woman's whisper came louder and louder as she moved through the dancing mist.

A small orange-red kimama flew out of the fog and happily circled around her. Angeni followed the delicate quickly flapping tiny insect with her eyes. The aura glowed up around her hand in sapphire as she reached out to show a safe landing spot for the curious creature. After a few circles, it landed on her palm.

"You're far from your home, alone, like me," she whispered and smiled tenderly. "Where are you going? Where are your friends?"

So sudden, her palm's aura enveloped the insect, encasing the small insect in solid sapphire crystal. Angeni felt the pain of the little life, and it didn't last long. It faded quickly as the kimama died.

"No," she gasped in horror, her hand let the crystallized kimama fall. Tiny fragments tinkled as the tiny crystal statue, which was alive not long ago shattered on the mossy stone. Angeni closed her eyes and tried to hide from the pain that shot through her soul.

"I'm sorry. I'm so sorry. I never meant to hurt you," she grieved, crouching down to the fragments. Then, the tiny crystals turned to dust and the soft wind carried it away from her. Her soul whispered that something was not right; she couldn't kill with a single touch. Everything was so surreal as she looked around the misty corridor. Yet, everything was real.

"Sleep my darling," the motherly voice came once again as far ahead in the mist, a baby's soft mewing cry echoed.

"Children must sleep," echoed the slightly distorted voice up the corridor. "Little, little, little child. You will be beautiful. Yes. Beautiful."

Angeni hurried along the misty corridor, searching until a clear female's song reverberated in the distance and pulled at her heart.

Sleep, my darling, I will be here,
Sleep, my little angel until morn's near.
Sleep deep, sleep well, my little child of light,
Sleep well my angel, sleep well tonight.

"Mother," Angeni whispered. Desperate footsteps reverberated as she hurried toward the voice to hear more of the lullaby her earthly mother had always sung at bedtime.

"She will come to you as God promised," a calm echoing male voice intruded. "She will come."

The mist slowly dissipated to uncover an ancient dark vine-choked ceremonial hall at the end of the corridor. Large scuffed mirrors and weathered columns watched the young guardian as they stood guard along the cracked old walls. Small pools caught the crystal-clear runoff of the two broken fountains.

A lone cradle drew her attention to the far end of the long hall. Carenia Seli's pale blue moonlight sifted through the broken ceiling right above it. A heartbroken feeble cry, coming from the cradle suddenly broke the fountains' monotonous calm gurgle.

Angeni looked around; no one was here. Her hand rested on her grip as she cautiously made her way deeper into the hall toward the cradle. Her eyes mapped the place; she felt the cold breeze stream gently from the two side entrances. Wary, she stopped. Someone watched from behind the column near the cradle, she felt it. A soft hushing soothed the unseen baby and the cry slowly faded.

The crystal blade's grip clicked quietly from her belt, the guardian separated the hilts in her hands. Her large white wings flexed before she lowered them behind her back.

"No. Please don't be afraid. We never intended to harm you," her earthly mother whispered as she looked out from the shadow of the column along with her father.

"We've been waiting for you," her father said.

Angeni's soul leapt as her long deceased parents stepped out from behind the columns.

"See? Our lost, little daughter has returned to us," her mother's joyful eyes shone.

"As the almighty has foretold us," her father's awe was so great that he grabbed his wife's hand as they stepped closer to Angeni.

"What damned trick of darkness is this?" Angeni hissed, her eyes flashed sapphire. Her instincts gave life to her blades as she crouched, her wings rose up to threaten. Frightened, her parents backed away and stopped. Her mother snuggled close to Eion in fear, and he held her defensively.

"Don't you recognize us?" asked her terrified father.

"You can't be real. You're dead," Angeni whispered bewildered, she was sure of that.

"The Aserians abandoned us for their belief," her mother whispered with a trembling voice. "But God was with us and helped us. God saved us."

Angeni just watched them. Her heartbroken mother lowered her head.

"What did we expect from those hypocrite Aserians?" she asked her husband with a small measure of hatred, and then she looked back at Angeni. "They didn't tell you, Grace, did they?"

"Tell me what?" Angeni asked while she held her blades in readiness.

"They created you to fulfill their belief," her mother said sadly. "They took our little girls from us to fulfill their blind belief. They killed both of you."

"Liar," Angeni retorted; this venomous woman could never have been her mother. "The Aserians do not kill humans! They do not kill without reason!" her furious angelic voice echoed around the hall. Her mother cautiously backed to the cradle as the baby cried.

"Sssshhh," she tried to calm the baby in the cradle that Angeni still had not seen, and then she looked back at the young guardian with begging eyes. "Please, don't scare her. Please, my little girl."

"All of you kill for your belief," her father added with sad determination. "You've killed humans already, haven't you?

The cruel words hit Angeni, but she said nothing. She knew her words would be empty; they wouldn't change the truth and wouldn't bring redemption. Her blades and wings lowered, and then the shining sapphire blades suddenly closed in her hands.

"They created you for a reason, my daughter," said her father. "To fulfill the long awaited arrival of their legendary Angeni soul, the Sapphire Guardian. You."

"God knows what the Crystal Shade is. It's not about fighting and preparing for wars, as the Aserians believe. It's not about living for the empty words of a belief, blindly awaiting the end of the world." Angeni remembered her mother's peremptory voice all too well.

"You don't know what the Crystal Shade is. You don't know what my role in it is," the guardian tried to debate. Her furious determination resounded from the rafters, but deep in her soul her cracked crystal reality slowly shattered. She did not know what to believe in anymore.

The baby cried again. Her mother hurried to the cradle and soothed the baby inside.

"No, little lady. It is you who doesn't know what it really is," her father's imperative tone continued. "Please, do not believe what you hear or what you read. Do not give your life for a false belief, my daughter. Please."

"The Aserians planned to kill five of us for their belief," her sorrowful mother added while she comforted the baby inside that Angeni still had not seen.

"Five of us?" the guardian asked almost silently.

"Come near to me, my little princess," her mother invited. Angeni reunited her golden grip and clipped it onto her belt. She cautiously approached her parents, her hand still rested on the crystal blade.

"On that day not four, but five of us traveled to and left Odess'iana," her mother's love filled eyes watched the cradle. As the guardian stepped closer, the cradle slowly revealed a little baby girl. The tiny curious eyes watched the angel woman.

"I... who is she?" asked Angeni curiously.

"The innocent little one is your blood," her father said. "She is beautiful, isn't she?"

Angeni nodded, her eyes mirrored the little baby.

"What is her name?"

"She has no name yet," answered her mother. "We waited for you to choose a name for her."

The little human baby charmed the young guardian; she seemed so familiar to her. The guardian carefully stroked the small baby's face to feel her soul. The baby smiled happy and babbled in her very own baby language enjoying the touch. Only innocence was inside of her; she was a little angel.

"Angeni," the young guardian whispered. "Her name should be Angeni."

"But, but that's your name, my daughter," her mother said.

"I'm Grace Sessa Aredia, a young soul who dreamt to live in a nightmare," the young guardian whispered. "I'm not an Angeni soul. I never was. I never will be. Unlike me, she has a clear soul. She is innocent as an Angeni soul should be."

Her mother smiled and gently touched Angeni's hand. The young guardian felt the great person in the woman, who seemed to be her mother. Her instincts cried that she was not her mother, regardless how she looked or how similar her soul was.

"No. You're not real. You cannot be real," Angeni backed up a few steps as her instincts dictated to her. Her parents looked at her. "You're not my beloved parents," she whispered and stopped few steps away from the cradle.

"Why are you afraid of us?" asked her mother before she sadly bowed her head. "That's what the Aserians have made of you. A puppet of their belief, seeing what they want you to see."

"You seem to be my mother and my father. But, but they're dead," the guardian blurted in confusion.

"See?" her mother showed her pearl necklace. "The daughters and sons of Yuraqilla, as you called them. I've never taken this off since you gave it to me at the Great Feast in Odess'iana. A treasure you gave to me with all your crystal-clear soul. So, a tiny bit of you was always with me."

Careful, her mother stepped to her and caressed her face. Angeni closed her eyes as she felt the love that emanated from her mother.

"Mother," Angeni's eyes filled with tears as she quickly hugged her human mother with all her heart.

"My beautiful, little girl. How much I missed you," her mother whispered into Angeni's ear.

"Father," Angeni's love shone as she looked at him. Eion smiled just like she always remembered. "I missed both of you. I thought of you every day." Her spirit filled with endless love, hope, and happiness.

"How beautiful and mature a woman you have become," he said holding his eldest daughter. Angeni looked up as her mother took off her necklace.

"The daughters and sons of Yuraqilla protected me to this very moment, my beloved daughter," she caressed Angeni's face stepping to her. "I'd like for it to protect you from now on."

But so sudden her father grimaced in terror as her mother's face reflected horror. A soft growl came from behind Angeni. She immediately pushed her father away and spun around, the sapphire crystal blades came alive in her hands.

Soul frozen in fear, Angeni turned to a shadow beast; the Daharra! The misty creature studied them, growled, and then barked sharply from the end of the hall. Angeni felt she had faced this creature somewhere, she couldn't remember. She knew she couldn't stop it.

"Please. Please, save us!" begged her mother behind her as the beast bolted toward them.

"No, please don't." Angeni spread her wings to cover her parents and desperately prepared her blades. She knew, they were useless, and the whirling misty creature ran closer and closer.

The Daharra jumped right at Angeni, but before it reached her, its shadowy body spread in the air and like two whirling snakes reaching and wrapping around her parents. The young guardian quickly turned as her parent's screams rang out. Horrified, she had seen the horrid pain of her parents as they quickly began to crystallize within the whirling black mist. Then the mist tightened, and they went silent, crushed in the embrace of the beast.

Angeni's grief filled her eyes with tears as her mother's pearl necklace bounced with the black crystal pieces of her parents on the stone floor.

"No," soft denial wrenched from her throat in a pain that wounds forever. The twisting shadows slowly tweaked toward Angeni. Like a mingan stepping out of a whirling mist, it regained its Daharra form. It growled as it slowly stepped toward her, just then, the baby cried in the cradle.

"Angeni. Sister," gasped the guardian, her eyes snapped to the cradle, as did the creature's eyes, it stopped. Her little sister was in mortal danger, but she couldn't do anything as the Daharra stood between her and the baby. "Get away from her. Please," she begged in desperation. The creature looked back at her and growled, it barked so hatefully. "Please, don't hurt her. I won't hurt you," whispered Angeni. The crystal blades went dark as she reunited the golden hilts.

Screaming, a large whirling cloud rammed in through the broken ceiling above the cradle behind the Daharra. Like a raging river, a blanket of orange and red silk raced toward the guardian while its eerie scream echoed and the baby cried in the cradle.

Angeni jerked a step back; the little girl in her soul afraid of the cloud. She didn't want to see it. She knew it would hurt her. She knew she had to run. Run fast.

The Daharra bolted after the young guardian, quickly followed by the shouting cloud; columns shattered, the fountains exploded in its destructive path.

The white mist rushed in to protect the guardian as she reached the corridor she had come from. She just ran and ran, and didn't look back. Soon, she saw nothing in front of her, just the steaming haze. Dead silence ruled. Angeni slowly stopped and looked around desperate to find the way out. Where to go, where to run? Trying to find the right way she faltered, her terrified soul believed the Daharra and the cloud would reach her soon to kill her. But it never happened. She didn't hear the eerie screaming anymore. She hadn't heard it for a long time, only the wailing of a young woman that echoed from so close; as it was hers.

"I'm sorry, I couldn't save you," her emotions overwhelmed over. She cried harder than ever before. The crystal blade clinked on the stone floor as it fell from her hand, the heavy feathery wings dejected as she sunk to her knees. "I'm sorry. I'm so sorry," she curled up on the cobblestones and held herself in desperation. Only the soft wind that held her so protectively and stroked her cheek heard the echoing cry of the young guardian.

* * *

Heaven's captivating frozen touch lighted on her skin as cold snowflakes drifted down from the encompassing white mist. Pure timeless flakes swirled to meet her icy cheek.

"Mommy. Daddy. Sister," her spent throat rasped as she lay on the bleak cobblestones. Angeni gradually stifled her tears and wiped her eyes. Another's soft sniffles told her she wasn't alone. The fog became softer and started to thin all around to reveal many shadowy silhouettes staring at her. She held her breath; her scared eyes mirrored the tall frightening faceless figures veiled behind the mist. Deathly motionless, they watched her.

Angeni's hand slowly reached for her lifeless blade grip on the ground close by. Still, the figures silently watched. Vengeful sapphire blades flared to life as she jumped to her feet to face the murky shapes.

"What did they ever do to you? Why did you kill them?" echoed her angelic fury. Her hands prepared the deadly blades, but the motionless silhouettes veiled by the slowly dissipating haze remained silent. "What are you? Who are you?" Angeni hissed as she watched them, waiting to see their faces. The misty mask slowly pulled back to reveal grotesque lifeless angel and demon statues stuck in their painful stance for all eternity.

Wary, the young guardian lowered her weapons, the sapphire blades dissolved to silence. She slowly calmed herself, sniffled once while the fog whirled and pulled back further to reveal an ancient statue garden around her. Further beyond the embracing weather beaten wrought iron fence, sprawled a large ruined city. So ancient it could be even older than Mer Petraea. Strange colourful clouds, orange-red satiny waves of light flickered and swam across the dark horizon to hide Carenia Seli behind a misty laced veil. Snow and ice softened the jagged edges of the ruins. Snowflakes swirled in an attempt to escape the invisible wind that haunted the dark city.

"What is this place?" she wondered while cautiously strolling between the grotesque statues. Soft dejected whimpers came from close by.

"They left me alone. No one cared about me," echoed a soft boy's voice ahead of her. "Only you. Only you." The vigilant guardian slowly rounded a large shattered and silent fountain, while the whispering continued, "I stopped seeing things that other people can see. Their beauty, their joy is meaningless to me. They left me. I'm alone, yet not alone."

Sapphire, amber, and ruby petals drifted silently in the air as if they welcomed the guardian. Her surprised eyes reflected the dancing petals while she cautiously stepped closer to the broken fountain's ledge. A few more steps and a vibrantly alive garden peeked out from behind the ruin.

Green grass gently leaned under her feet, the silky petals fluttered against her cheek before they peeled to the ground. Stricken and cautious, she approached a large, blooming sakura tree that cast its giant shadow at her. Life spread from its roots in a small radius; life embraced by silent ancient death, which ruled the rest of the place. The colourful petals fell from the twigs; as one flower fell, another grew in its place quick and silent. A sad little boy sat on his knees, silently weeping beneath the frozen shadow of the living tree.

"What happened, little boy?" Angeni asked quietly, approaching him vigilant as her instincts demanded. The little boy looked back innocent and sniffed once. "Where is everyone?" she asked, looking around the frozen garden. "Where are your parents?" she crouched down in front of him in the silent petal-fall.

"No one wanted to play with me," said the boy softly. "No one."

Angeni slowly rested her hand on the boy's shoulder. A relieved sigh left her lips as she felt the innocence and great fear in him. Protective and caring, she slowly encircled the little boy with her hand and her wings.

"I will be here with you," Angeni whispered in the boy's ear. "You're not alone. I will not leave you. I promise."

From the touch, she felt the boy calm a little. The large wings slowly pulled back as she released the boy. Angeni clicked her grip onto her belt and looked into his tearful eyes.

"Who are you?" she asked quietly.

Colourful kimamas fluttered out from behind the boy that Angeni swore weren't there before. The tiny beautiful insects circled around them. The boy looked up and smiled at how quickly their wings flapped.

"They are my friends, see," he whispered, his eyes full of happiness. "They understand me. They played with me when I was alone. Their life is similar to mine; I live free like they do," he glanced up. "Look." He pointed to a tree limb.

A small kimama cocoon hung from the limb above them, wiggled and twisted until a bright colourful kimama slowly fought its way out.

"We are all like them; false like a kimama," he continued. "Every soul is born so innocent and fragile. And every soul hides in a chrysalis to turn into something greater and stronger, to be something else for the rest of their life." The kimama slowly opened its magnificent wings. "Beautiful, isn't it?" the boy asked.

A reassuring cheery smile and a pleasant nod was the guardian's answer, and then she looked around. Death, silence and ruin looked back all around the tiny paradise. Snow, like a cold blanket silently covered the grievous and despaired angel and demon statues, but not the frozen fear etched into their faces.

"What happened here? What is this place?" she asked. The little boy looked at her, his face wasn't terrified anymore.

"It's my home. It can be your home too," he whispered. His eyes flitted from statue to statue. "To me, they are beautiful. Finally, all of them remain silent and will listen to me. None of them deserved to live. None of them," he whispered. Angeni just noticed that the gazing eyes of all the grotesque and cramped statues – wherever they stood, distant or close – they all looked at the boy, scared and terrified. The wind slowly whisked thick dirt from the statues to reveal their true crystallized surface; all of them were living souls before.

The boy looked back at the guardian. "But you're different," he said calm.

"You did this," Angeni whispered, her fingers slowly curled around her blade grip.

"They created me, just as they created you for their blind belief," he smiled, and then so sudden his face distorted as chaotic craziness replaced the sad innocence. "Don't ever look into my dreams! Don't defy me again!" screamed his demented, crazy voice.

Desperate, Angeni tried to pull her blade, but something held her arms motionless. She snapped a look at her hands to see dark shadows twisted around them, holding them away from her grip. A rumbling growl built as the boy's entire form melted and morphed into a whirling shadow creature. Dark red eyes glared from the shadows at the Sapphire Guardian.

"Your soul will be the next!" thundered the chaotic, scraggy voice.

The trees, and statues, the entire city suddenly exploded into whirling ashes and the solid mist quickly circled to entomb the young guardian. Angeni tried to escape, but the shadow arms that held her were too strong. An undulating scream of a woman, so terrified, full of pain reverberated in her ears. She dimly realized it was hers. The embracing touch was so hot and grievous, and then the shadows let her go. The painfully screaming angel fell to her knees; torturous pain wracked her entire body.

"You again? Get out of my head!" cried the shadow entity. "GET OUT! GET OUT! GET OUT!"

A strong hand reached out of the mist and snatched Angeni into the dense whirling fog. From the touch she felt safe. She heard the echoing thoughts of the one who grabbed her, but she was not capable of understanding the words of this soul.

The painful screams slowly faded. In the whirling white haze, Angeni quickly took deep breaths while the pain eased in her body like it never existed.

"You must leave. Now," the old, so familiar male voice of the one who always came in her dreams insisted. The guardian's eyes snapped to him. The mysterious stranger stood in front of her. The white haze swirled in front of him, leaving him in the dark. The hood covered his face, shadows covered his eyes; Angeni couldn't see into his soul. His cloak and old wings ruffled by the quiet breeze were majestic, mysterious, and scary to look at.

"Why, why should I listen to you, Demon?" Angeni hissed hatred while she slowly gathered her strength. Her fingers already weaved around her blade grip. "You brought darkness to Eecrys Aredia! You brought evil to this sacred land!" the furious angel accused and the vengeful sapphire blade came alive, but the stranger remained cold calm.

"I warned you. Nothing and no one is what they appear to be," his determined voice said. "You must ask questions like you always have to see the truth. Use and trust your instincts before you use your weapon. That's the only thing you can ever trust."

Silent, Angeni watched him, tried to read the eyes hidden in the shadows, but there was no trace of emotion, nothing she could pick up from them.

"As I protect you I am in its way. Eosh and you saw what the chaotic one intended. It knows visions never betray any soul by a glance, not even Its own chaotic soul," he continued softly. "I cannot open the gate to hell. No Aserian can," his voice was full of honesty.

"But no demon was here. Then..." Angeni paused as she slowly realized. Her blade closed in her hand. "Only one who was born from light and darkness, from both of us, can."

The stranger nodded silently.

"False like a kimama, living in a chrysalis," Angeni whispered, silently meditating, and then looked back at the stranger. "Is he, the little boy is the one who hides between us?"

"Yes, but it is far from being a fragile little boy. Everything plays in your mind in a chaotic world It created. Everything was an illusion, as were your parents and your never born sister."

"Weren't they real?" Angeni barely dared ask as a great weight slid off her soul, but so sudden a thought struck into her mind. She looked at the stranger curiously. "What do you mean my never born sister?" The stranger remained silent. "Please tell me it's not true. Please." Her begging eyes filled with tears. "No," her sorrow bowed her head.

"You must remain strong. It's playing with your mind to crush and confuse you again."

"What do you mean again?" the flashing sapphire eyes snapped at the stranger and her angelic voice echoed in celestial fury. "What are you hiding from me?" She was unable to stop the tears of loss for what would never be. "What!"

"Everything that I must to protect you!" the celestial fatherly voice ordered her silence. He took a step closer to her, and then his old ragged wings snapped wide open, threatened; even the white mist pulled back scared.

Angeni scurried backward few steps and remained silent; sniffing and feeling like the little human girl she once was back in Odess'iana. That's what she was; a so young soul trapped in a mature body.

"Please, please don't hurt me," she whispered crushed and so innocent. The stranger lowered his wings and the haze curiously drifted closer to him once again, but kept its distance. Silence ruled for a long moment.

"I would never hurt you, Angeni," a small measure of guilt echoed in his soft tone. "But I will do anything to guard and guide you as in the end, you'll be on your own."

The crushed woman looked at him sadly.

"I don't know what I should believe anymore," she whispered.

"Yes, you do. You just don't know it yet," the stranger was certain.

"Why didn't you stop it if you knew its existence?" she asked quietly.

"I've tried so many times. But no one can change what is beyond our reach," guilt-ridden, he whispered, and then looked around the whirling mist. "You must leave this place. Here, I can't protect you any longer. In its sick dream world it can do anything it wishes," he added as he stepped back. The frightened mist quickly whirled out of his way. His silhouette slowly disappeared in the darkness, but his voice still echoed. "Always do what you know to be right. Destiny will take you where you are needed the most," his voice faded while the haze slowly covered the darkness.

Alone, Angeni looked around as the fog whirled all around her.

"It's just a dream," she whispered, closing her eyes. "Nightmares are just a mirror of my fears." Her breath quickened as her ears picked out a strange eerie wind that approached from afar. Opening her eyes, her own terrified image looked back from a large mirror, which stood in front of her. The surface of the polished mirror gave a tingling feeling in her fingers as she touched it, and then it started to crack.

"Every nightmare can be shattered by facing them," came calm and quiet. The strange eerie screaming came closer, began to throb in her ears and her existence began to fear. "My dreams are my own," her determination whispered as she stepped into the cracking mirror, shattering it further with a harsh scream as she passed through the solid surface. A tingling caress went through her entire body. In the broken mirror, she saw the whirling colourful crazy cloud break out of the mist behind her. But then the shredded mist dissolved around her and the cloud disappeared into safe embracing darkness. Silence ruled.

"Angeni," Nicolas' soft voice called. "Angeni?"

Her eyes slowly opened. Confused as if her soul and spirit had just snapped back into her body after a terrible nightmare, she found herself sprawled on the fountain's cold ledge in the main square.

"Are you all right?" Concerned, Nicolas faced her along with Eosh.

"I, I don't know," her soul still confused, she sat up slowly in her sapphire gown. She barely remembered her dream. But even without remembering, fear clutched at her.

"You fell asleep, my child," said Eosh. Angeni shook her head softly in denial, trying to force herself to remember.

"No. Something is not right," she whispered as she stood up. Danger; a threat was present yet she couldn't know what it was. "Something else is here that is neither darkness, nor light."

"What do you mean?" curiously piqued, Eosh's eyebrow rose.

"I..." confused, she started. For a moment the mist, the little boy, and the kimamas flashed into her mind in small fragments. Determined, her eyes looked at Eosh as she continued, "Chaotic thoughts in an upside down world, a place of cruelty and love, hate and joy. A soul of an angelic demon, living between light and darkness."

"I lived for long, and I can tell you I've seen everything," said the old guardian with a determined kindness. "There is only light and darkness with nothing in between."

I see you, came the demented voice into Angeni's mind. The chaotic face of the boy flashed in front of her eyes. *I see all of you,* the voice screeched with over enthusiastic, childish joy. Then the vision dissolved in her mind and the voice faded.

"It's here," she whispered with a step back while her eyes desperately searched the square. "We must leave now."

"I agree," his tenseness added that was as great as hers, Eosh's eyes also searched for something. It was clear he had also heard the voice.

Tiny cracks appeared, split, and raced along the wall accompanied by great rumbling. The ground began to shake harder and harder and the nearby ancient buildings started to collapse. Boulders broke loose to fall from the rocky mountain high above them. Eosh snapped his attention to the corridor carved into the closest rock escarpment.

"This way!" he ordered running. Ancient ruins collapsed and shattered, heavy dust churned, large debris crashed from the sky and smashed all around them. The ground shook and opened behind them as they sprinted for the corridor entrance. Destruction rippled after them, just them and approached fast.

The three souls slammed into the dark carved corridor and the entrance collapsed right behind them. The loud rumble echoed as the falling debris cut the last measure of light away. The shaking suddenly stopped. Everything went eerily silent; only soft quick breathing and coughs echoed in the entombed darkness as the dust drifted away. They were still alive.

A sapphire aura lit up around Eosh' hand to show the once ancient grandness of the now collapsed corridor. Angeni took a quick glance at Nicolas who still sucked in fast breaths, but seemed unharmed. Resigned she turned to the debris, which completely blocked the way out.

"I hope that wasn't the only way out," Nicolas whispered, and then he coughed once again while the dust slowly settled around them.

"This corridor leads to an ancient ceremonial hall," Eosh said looking toward the other end of the corridor. "From there a long walk will take us back to the gates of Mer Petraea," he continued, and led the way.

"You feel its presence too. What could this being be?" Angeni asked. Along with Nicolas, she followed Eosh down the corridor.

"Something that I haven't seen before, something that can't exist, yet it does," Eosh admitted softly. "And now it's shepherding us. The question is why and where," he added quietly, looking around suspicious.

A short walk brought them into the large ceremonial hall, ruled by a dim light. The shining aura faded from around the old Aserian's hand.

Large mirrors and weathered columns stood guard along the cracked old walls. The water trickled almost silently from two broken fountains. The place seemed so familiar to the young Aserian. She had been here before, but when?

"A cradle?" looking at the far end of the hall, Nicolas asked in surprise. Shining in, the pale moonlight sifted in bands through the broken ceiling. "What was this place used for?" Nicolas raised his eyebrow curiously to Eosh. The bewildered old Aserian slowly shook his head.

"I know every corner of Mer Petraea, but I've never seen this cradle before in my home," he pondered as they stalked to the middle of the hall. Vigilant, their eyes scanned the long hall, but the crystal blades in their hands remained silent. The old dusty mirrors reflected them sickly. Then, the pale moonlight glimmered on something on the stones close to the cradle. It glinted right into Angeni's eyes.

It all flashed back into her mind, her parents, and the cradle, the Daharra. Everything.

"No. Please, no," Angeni whispered shocked, she stared at shattered crystals. "Mommy. Daddy. Sister." Tears filled her eyes as she hurried to the fragments. "Everything was real. I trusted him and he lied to me! Why?" The crushed guardian fell to her knees; all she could see through tear filled eyes was her mother's pearl necklace among the crystals. "Everything is a lie. Everything. It's all my fault. I failed them. I failed to protect them."

The wailing angel woman bowed to the marble floor in torment. There was only pain, endless pain.

"What are you talking about, Angeni?" thoroughly rattled Nicolas asked as he crouched beside her.

"What was your fault, my child? Who did you believe?" asked Eosh's caring voice almost silently. A baby's loud cry shattered the silence. Angeni looked up to the cradle; tears ran down her cheeks.

"She, she is alive. Little Angeni is alive," she whispered in awe, wiping her eyes. Hope filled her soul.

"What are you talking about, Angeni?" Nicolas stared at her, while Eosh set cautious steps toward the cradle. The sapphire blade came alive in his hand.

"No! Wait!" Angeni cried desperate. "What, what are you doing?"

"I must do this, Angeni. You know that," Eosh replied on an emotionless tone.

"He is right. No demented soul may leave Mer Petraea. Not a single one," the Prince agreed.

"No! She is just a little baby! She can't hurt anyone!" her shouting begged. Anger boiled within her listening to the baby's cries from the cradle.

"Darkness embraces this child. You feel it too," Eosh intoned while he approached the cradle, raising his blade.

Don't hurt her! Please! begged a strange distorted voice in Angeni's mind; anger boiled into her mind like she had never felt before. She felt her wings spread wide.

"No human will be sacrificed for a blind belief," she hissed with vile hatred, approaching the old Aserian faster and faster. "I will not let you harm my blood."

Almost at the cradle, Eosh snapped his look back at her. Sapphire blades came alive as they crackled in the air like lightning and struck toward him. The old Aserian crossed Angeni's blade at the very last moment. But the young guardian didn't stop. She spun around and struck once more, but the defensive blades stopped her again. The old Aserian's sapphire eyes flashed at the disobedient young guardian. Right at that moment, the world around Angeni began to spin, as if Eosh had drawn the strength out of her somehow. The surrounding voices echo in her mind. But no, it wasn't the old Aserian who did this to her. Something else drew her strength; she felt it.

"Something is not right," Angeni whispered, her eyes begged Eosh in despair while everything started to blur and whirl around her. She shook her head to clear it, but it had no effect. She had seen the wall behind the cradle explode and a whirling orange-red cloud like satiny waves rammed into the hall, then darkness fell over her eyes.

"DON'T HURT MY CHILD! GET AWAY FROM HER!" shouted a scraggy crazy voice.

Harsh crackling assaulted her ears, which echoed from all over the hall. Every mirror exploded inward all around. Sharp mirror fragments hit. It felt as if a thousand pins ripped through her delicate skin and silky-feathered wings like her body would rip apart to the tinkling pings of glass fragments. A loud scream left her shaking lips at the feel of burning cuts.

Angeni heard the shields come alive to protect Eosh and Nicolas; the sharp menacing fragments pinged as they crashed on the shields. Nicolas bellowed painfully as one of the fragments sliced past his shield. Angeni wanted to look up, open her eyes to see Nicolas, but she couldn't. Darkness encompassed her mind.

"LEAVE MY CHILD ALONE!" cried the crazy voice.

So weak, held by exquisite pain Angeni forced her eyes open, trying to look around, but her tears blurred everything all around. For a moment she had seen a bright red-orange blade slice in the darkness toward Eosh, but then once again, she was cut off by complete, spinning darkness, and couldn't see a thing.

"PERISH ASERIAN!" echoed the crying crazy, yet strangely familiar voice. Angeni heard a crystal blade rip into flesh, and the old Aserian's bellow of pain.

She felt the overwhelming fear that descended upon Nicolas. Surrounded by debilitating darkness, Angeni felt herself fall to her injured knees onto a large pile of sharp mirror fragments. A solid metallic clink hit her ears as her cramped fingers let her crystal blade fall to bounce on the stone floor. An abrupt splash of exploding cries as a crystal blade shattered a large crystal statue to silence Eosh for eternity. The crystal pieces sang sadly as they bounced on the stone floor.

"No. It can't be true," the dusty air carried Nicolas' shock. "No one can kill him. No one."

"DON'T TOUCH MY CHILD!" cried the crazy voice and Angeni feared she would be next. She was helpless, her weapon on the ground and her assaulted mind awhirl in chaotic darkness.

Embraced by the darkness, Angeni tried to regain her balance knowing her crystal blade to be temptingly close. She wanted to act, face and stop an enemy that she couldn't see. But she was too weak, her every move so painful.

So much pain, the young guardian slowly opened her eyes. Shattered sapphire crystals and broken glass sparkled back from all around the floor.

"No," the prince whispered, staring at Angeni shocked. "Please no!" terror rippled over his face as he took a step back while the sapphire blade closed in his hand. Angeni felt the instinct of survival, the urge to escape, and the all-consuming fear that embraced Nicolas. But what terrified him so much? What had he seen?

Dazed and weak, Angeni knew she had to face this dreaded enemy to protect him. Taking her breaths fast, she gazed ahead of her at the ground. Large wings, so strange and terrific rose majestically to cover her pale shadow that sat right in front of her. The mirror fragments all around reflected the preying shadow back into her eyes.

Her injured hand desperately tried to reach her blade grip among the sharp glass, and then she finally felt the cold grip between her fingers. She snapped her attention back to see what Nicolas saw, while the crystal blade in her hand came alive.

342

Chaotic red eyes glowed. A blurry, demented face, its skin like grey ash stared back at her. Large red membranous wings flicked, threatened, and spread wide. A deadly red-orange crystal blade glowed in the darkness.

"NO MERCY!" cried a scraggy, eerie voice so loud. The young guardian screamed as debilitating pain hit her. She heard her crystal blade bounce among the mirror fragments while she fell to the floor. Then everything faded to darkness all around her. Only the endless fear and trembling that ruled her defeated existence told her she was still alive.

The face was so familiar to her soul. She had seen it somewhere before, but her dulled mind failed her. On the other hand, was it just an illusion, a play of her mind?

I know you. I saw you before. I think, she thought desperately around the endless pain that gnawed deeper. *Who are you?*

Footsteps echoed and slowly faded away in the distance; her soul smiled victorious, as she knew Nicolas had gotten out. She had protected him while she was able. He might be safe now. Maybe.

The torturous pain slowly faded; at least she didn't feel it anymore. She didn't feel anything at all.

"My child," the demented voice in her mind sang peacefully.

"They hurt my soul," came a young, purring voice scared and crushed, it sniffed and cried in despair. "They're killers! Senseless killers! All of them want to kill me! All of them!" the young voice cried. "What did I do to them? Nothing. Nothing. I just want to give life back that they take away."

"Hush, my beautiful child," echoed the demented voice. "See how beautiful you are. Look."

"Beautiful," the young voice purred in awe. "Yes. Beautiful."

The blunt mind of the young guardian heard the crazed awe that reminded her of a little child. The voice was so familiar, but she couldn't decide if it was male or female as it distorted in the echoes as the purring voice changed tone. Her mind was confused; everything was so chaotic and scattered. All her thoughts faded as her consciousness slowly ebbed away.

"You're safe now," the older voice echoed with great adoration. "Sleep and dream, my darling. Your world awaits you."

Then everything went silent.

* * *

343

"On that cold night she faced the deadliest and cruellest being who ever opened its wings to exist," the old man shook his head with dismay. "No one knew for a long time what the mysterious being was. And no one knew how she survived that night, why the It did not kill her," he looked sternly at the boy and girl at his feet. "Maybe it was her destiny to survive. Maybe the It gave mercy to the one who protected its demented child. But a long time was spent before the young guardian learned the truth." He paused for a moment as he gathered his thoughts.

"As she said, truth is like a crystal. Clear, faultless, able to blind those who gaze too long upon its shiny surface. Many have fought for truth blindly. Crusaders believing in a fragile crystal reality, an unbreakable truth; glory, justice, honour shone right into their eyes. But sometimes, truth might have a pale shade that is able to change everything; break the crusaders' courage, honour and valour to banish their created crystal reality forever." He sighed to cover bafflement.

"The world that she always cared for and loved wasn't the same anymore. Nothing and no one was what they appeared to be and the young guardian had to question everything that she ever believed to learn the truth. But to do that, she had to dare to ask once more," he looked deep into the eyes of the children.

"What the illusionary Crystal Shade really is?"

TO BE CONTINUED IN
CRYSTAL SHADE: ANGENI
VOLUME 2

TABLE OF CONTENTS

ABOUT THE AUTHORS

István Szabó, Ifj.
"Creator, Writer and Illustrator"
Based out of Budapest, Hungary, István began his writing and art career at a young age. His strengths include science fiction, fantasy, thrillers, as well as spiritual, romantic, and political works. At the beginning of his career, two companies entrusted István to create and write the stories of two of their video games. Since 2007, working parallel on several different projects, István mostly developed and worked on the Crystal Shade franchise and wrote Crystal Shade: Angeni. As an artist for hire, he has created illustrations, character art, short CGI animations and marketing materials for various projects as well as for his own works, Crystal Shade: Angeni, 7 Post Meridiem, Nightfall and other unannounced projects. In 2007, István produced his first short movie "15 Minutes of Fame", in which István was the screenwriter, director and storyboard artist. "15 Minutes of Fame" won 3rd Place at the UPC-AXN Film Festival 2007.

Homepage: www.crystalshadeangeni.com
Email: istvanszabo@crystalshadeangeni.com

Orlanda Szabo
"Crystal Shade: Angeni, Volume 1 Co-writer and Editor"
Orlanda Szabo screenwriter/author lives in the middle of Canada. Her writing skills include edits, rewrites and consultations in a wide variety of genres. She is adept at adapting book to screenplay and screenplay to book. She is currently under contract to script Lisa R. Taylor's Welcome To: I Don't Know, Idaho. She has written numerous features, shorts and TV series pilots, some of which she will be adapting to book. She truly loves to work in science fiction, fantasy, supernatural and thrillers.

Homepage: www.orlandaszabo.com
Blog: www.orlandaszabo.wordpress.com
Email: orlanda@orlandaszabo.com

CRYSTAL SHADE: ANGENI

www.crystalshadeangeni.com
www.facebook.com/crystalshadeangeni
www.twitter.com/csangeni

Lightning Source UK Ltd.
Milton Keynes UK
UKOW03n0521120214

226314UK00002B/25/P